The Strange Michael Folmer Affair

by

John Rigbey

Bloomington, IN      Milton Keynes, UK

authorHOUSE®

AuthorHouse™ UK Ltd.
500 Avebury Boulevard
Central Milton Keynes, MK9 2BE
www.authorhouse.co.uk
Phone: 08001974150

First published by AuthorHouse 5/17/2007

ISBN: 978-1-4343-0298-4 (sc)

Printed in the United States of America
Bloomington, Indiana

This book is printed on acid-free paper.

For Genevieve

London. Saturday 30 August 2003.

Kings Cross in the heavy, stormy rain of late summer. Just after 10.00pm and the massive, baroque railway station complex was quiet with just the few stragglers either sheltering from the rain or trying to locate platforms for late trains to points north of Watford. Thunder, barely heard over the traffic noise, rumbled and grumbled away to the west and the accompanying lightning was lost in the garish brightness of fluorescence and neon. A light wind blew discarded fish-and-chip papers under the wheels of passing buses and cars and the sour smell of stale and over-stewed onions hung in the air. The place had the air of bus and train stations all over the world: an atmosphere created by people who are transient, on their way to or from somewhere else and who do not, under any circumstances, want to be there. Within the twin stations of St. Pancreas and Kings Cross the bars and restaurants were in the process of clearing up prior to closing, and the drunks and vagrants had one eye on the benches and draught-free corners and the other on the duty railway police officers.

To the traveller arriving and leaving by taxi, bus, train or underground, the stations are bleak, featureless places only visited when the occasion arises and instantly and thankfully forgotten the moment the whistle blows and the train starts to move. To Londoners, however, particularly those in the lower strata of society, there is more to Kings Cross than stations. Situated between the West End and the East End, since the late 1800's "the Cross" has maintained a tradition of being a place where one can have one's pocket picked, lose a week's wages playing "Find the Lady" and find the services of the lowest type of street woman available in the city. Once ruled by the Italian race-course gangs of the early twenties, today the local underworld is largely slanted towards prostitution and is now mainly controlled by a criminal element emanating from Glasgow. To refer to the girls who work this area as being the dregs of humanity is accurate and at the same time unkind: they are more to be pitied than pilloried. Ranging in age from twelve to seventy, they line the back streets around the stations, competing for the custom of hundreds of kerb-crawling men from all walks of life and with varying tastes who nightly inspect what is on offer. The meat rack. A price agreed, there will be a five-minute fumble either in the back of the man's car or in some dimly lit lane or alley and within fifteen minutes from the time of pick-up the girl will be back in situ wearing fresh lipstick and chewing the inevitable gum. Her pimp, who will have watched the whole process from the start, will take the money and any objection from the girl will be resolved with violence ranging from a slapped face to broken bones.

The Canterbury Pilgrim was situated in a depressing street between Kings Cross Road and Grays Inn Road. The vast pub, dating from the middle of the nineteenth century, had seen better days. Now long forgotten, there were lunchtime gentleman with oysters and steak and kidney, pints of stout and glasses of port and nights of rowdy but controlled singing to an old upright piano, the landlord with a yellow-checked waistcoat and an Albert chain stretched taut across his over-indulged middle, nightly at eleven bellowing "Time, gentleman – please" and asking his customers if they "ain't got no bleedin' 'omes to go to." These were days of a century past, a time when the Old Queen was hiding and grieving on the Isle of Wight, when horses could still be seen in the city streets and policemen were big men with belted tunics buttoned to the neck.

In recent years the Pilgrim has not opened at lunchtime at all: converted into one huge room with a stage and a bar tended by over a dozen young men and women, the first customer is served at one minute past 8.00pm and the last promptly at 2.00am the following morning. Shaven-headed, dinner-jacketed doormen with several heavy gold or silver rings on all fingers, control admission and ensure that the behaviour both inside and outside of the premises remains at all times acceptable; there is an admission charge which varies according to the popularity of the entertainment being offered, the noise from which can invariably be heard a fair distance up the Caledonian Road, and the whole place has more the atmosphere of a down-market night-club than an English public house. Preferred beverages are lager consumed straight from the bottle for the gentlemen and any one of dozens of sugary, fizzy alcoholic preparations for the ladies; other than crisps and nuts there is no food available which has lead to the owner of a coffee stall on the street corner opposite being able to purchase a BMW motor car and to take bi-annual holidays of the sort requiring long-haul flights.

Saturday night is drag night. Upwards of a dozen female impersonators of ages varying between teens and pensionable present an assortment of acts ranging in entertainment value from fair to atrocious. There are no live musicians: each act is required to provide its own accompaniment by way of pre-recorded audio tape or compact disc and between acts the clientele sways and dances to selections of hip-hop and garage, so loud that dust raises from corners of the ancient ceiling and hangs in the multi-coloured light of an enormous, revolving glass globe suspended high above the crowd. There is nothing serious about drag acts generally and especially those at the Canterbury Pilgrim: comedians – the later the hour the more obscene - impersonators, strippers and those who mime to the hits of stars such as Shirley Bassey and Dusty Springfield. The show, which seemingly has no end with acts following each other in a form of organised confusion, is compéred by an elderly man with a risible and exaggerated lisp; it is high camp, sometimes hilarious - often not.

That night the place was packed, bar staff working flat out. With two friends, the girl stood at the end of the bar furthest from the stage. Her face, once pretty, evidenced hard, streetwise features and her ultra-short skirt, five-inch high heels and a vast display of cleavage and a bare midriff left little doubt as to her chosen way of life. Aged perhaps twenty-five, in less than ten years she would look fifty. If she lived. One of the wiser of her kind, she had steadfastly evaded and resisted the attentions of pimps and the Scottish gangs. Over the years she had developed a dislike for all men seeing them all as untrustworthy and largely dishonest. In recent years she had realised that she was developing certain lesbian tendencies but she lived alone and the only short and relatively unfulfilling foray she had experienced in this field was some months earlier whilst she was on remand in Holloway prison for offences of fraud relative to state benefits. She worked alone and had been engaged in prostitution for several years, having started in a back street behind St. Pancras Station. More recently, and in what she considered to be an upward career move, she had abandoned the streets and had taken to plying her trade in the countless pubs and bars in the area, thereby reducing the risk of arrest for soliciting and, she felt, allowing for a better class of client who would be prepared to pay more.

The management of all of the local public houses had strict instructions from the owners that under no circumstances were prostitutes of either sex to be allowed on their premises and in the larger establishments such as the Pilgrim it was the business of the doormen to ensure that this rule was enforced. Doorman, though, could be bought. It had cost her a twenty pound note backhander to get her in to the Pilgrim and no matter how long she made her Bacardi Breezer last she knew she had to get some business. If she left the pub, no matter for what purpose, only another twenty quid would get her back in. The larger part of the crowd consisted of young men and women, couples and groups, out to enjoy themselves and to take in some mildly titillating entertainment. People of all classes, the only requirement being that they had money to spend. She sipped her drink carefully and her practiced eyes strained to pierce the semi-darkness of the smoke filled bar.

On the brightly illuminated stage three aging black men, ludicrous in satin sheaths with vast behinds and bulging stomachs, gyrated to a sixties motown hit, their ill-fitting and worn wigs and the lack of synchronisation both with each other and with the music causing hilarity with those interested enough to listen.

She scanned the room, narrowed eyes squinting through the haze, searching. She knew the age group to look for, who would want business and who wouldn't, and she knew the time wasters and those who seemed to be able to get a cheap thrill merely by talking to street women. Probing every corner for a regular, a face she knew, she strained her mascara-rimmed eyes until they ached. Ever watching, she talked briefly with her friends smiling at some comment, some joke, half-heard above the noise. Nicotine-stained fingers with nails bitten to the quick raked through her dyed blonde hair, wet from the rain, and catching sight of her reflection in one of the vast mirrors behind the bar, she applied fresh lipstick.

A barman, short, dyed yellow hair with dark roots, approached and placed a Breezer beside her existing, half-empty bottle. Realising that she could not hear his effeminately-spoken words over the noise, he indicated towards the far end of the bar.

As she made eye contact with her benefactor she moved further along the bar away from her friends. She smiled, nodding her thanks. Without expression he stared back through cold, empty, eyes. Eyes with nothing behind them, dead, like a doll's, and suddenly she felt coldness, an icy chill which seemed to freeze the beads of sweat on her shoulders and caused an involuntary shudder she could not explain. With the slightest, almost imperceptible, movement he inclined his head towards the door.

Sod him. Let the bastard wait. She finished her first drink and picking up the second bottle she gulped the cold fizz. She winked at the barman and then, straining to see through the smoky, ill-lit haze, she looked for her punter.

Gone.

She swore and stubbed out the cigarette. She finished her bottle in one swallow and turned to her companions.

"Pulled one there, didn't I, and now the bastard's got away. Just my bloody luck." She pushed through the swaying crowd toward the door, her over- high heels causing her to take short, staccato steps.

The rain had turned to a foggy drizzle, yellow in the street lighting and cool on her face after the humid interior of the bar, thick with tobacco and cannabis smoke and the sweat and other body smells of several hundred people. She looked around, searching as before, and realising that the bird had flown she cursed again and kicked the pub wall causing the thin leather skin of her cheap shoe to tear, exposing compressed fibrous material beneath. The doorman, a hulking man in an ill-fitting dinner suit, scowled mockingly at her tantrum. Eating chips from a cardboard envelope, he shook his head in response to her enquiry. Fucking pig, she thought; he must have seen her business leave. She knew that he would demand another twenty pounds to let her go back inside, money which she did not have, and she cursed herself for her stupidity and the doorman for his greed and arrogance.

He ignored her as she took shelter in the pub doorway but she knew he would not allow her to be there long. She lived in Kentish Town, too far to walk especially in the rain, and without the money for cab fare she depended on a punter for the money to get her home. She peered, blinking, at the black sky hoping for a respite in the downpour and seeing none she lit another cigarette. The doorman finished his chips and threw the empty packet in the gutter. He turned towards her, no words but a look which said all she needed to know.

He knew her profession and he knew the arrangement he had with her, but he was also aware that his job would be lost if his employers became aware that prostitutes were allowed to enter the pub or to loiter outside. Sensing the man's attention and unwilling to spoil future visits to the Pilgrim she moved away from the pub and crossing the street she took shelter beneath the canvas awning of the coffee stall opposite.

She ordered coffee. It arrived, watery in a polystyrene beaker, no handle and too hot to pick up. Sugar was provided in a green plastic container, the spoon drilled at the handle and attached to some invisible mooring point by a length of greasy, ragged string. A pound. She glared at the man: "A fucking pound – for that?"

The man shrugged. He was not paid to engage in pleasantries with customers. "Don't have it, then."

He reached for the coffee but she threw the coin on the stained and cracked formica counter. She turned her back on the stall and then, through the drizzle, she saw him again.

2.

Sunday 31 August 2003.

Durward Street, off Commercial Road in London's East End.

The rain had stopped but the streets were still wet and the approaching dawn was grey and misty and with an autumnal chill in the air. In his late seventies, Wally Stander still worked every Sunday morning. Out of bed and washed and shaved before 4.00am he walked from his terraced house off Cambridge Heath Road to the small café in Brick Lane where, as he had done for the past forty-odd years, he would serve teas and bacon sandwiches to the traders and the thousands of Londoners and tourists who flocked to the East End Sunday street markets. Turning from Brady Street into Durward Street he shivered and cursing the damp and the rheumatism he knew it would bring, he pulled his thin raincoat tight round him, hoping that the belted closeness would generate some warmth.

Stopping on the corner of Fulbourne Street, with an ancient lighter capped in his two hands he lit a cigarette. He inhaled deeply and watched the tobacco smoke as it hung in the still mist coming off London's river. At first, curious, he thought it was a shop window tailors' dummy, thrown out by some clothes shop and now the basis of countless jokes by local kids. The white legs and bare, twisted arms lay at right angles to a wall, partially propped into a position of half-sitting and half lying and although he could not see the head he imagined it would be pink plastic, bald and without eyes or ears. A few yards nearer and he saw hair. Nearer and he knew that what he had taken to be a rain puddle was blood. Not spots or spatters nor even splashes, but a pool, still liquid, viscous, which surrounded the horror, running across the pavement and dripping lazily of the kerb. He bent, peering through short-sighted eyes minus the customary spectacles.

"Oh, Gawd! Oh, Jesus Christ!"

He took a pace back and turned his back on the sight which he would later describe as the worst he had ever seen in a long life. "Seen nuffink like it in the blitz, I didn't. Nor in the bleedin'army." He fumbled in his pocket for the seldom-used mobile telephone his daughter had given him for his birthday and after three failed attempts due to his shaking fingers he reached the emergency services.

The first policeman on the scene, a probationer, shone his torch on the grisly pile and was promptly sick in the gutter. Named John Wayne by unthinking parents and already tagged with the inevitable, he would be known for the rest of his police career as "Duke the Puke."

Within an hour the street was blocked off and the blue and white 'crime scene' tape was everywhere. Scenes of crime staff in hooded white polythene overalls, masks and galoshes commenced the microscopic examination of the scene and a bad tempered pathologist, caught leaving home for Wentworth and exotic in green checked golfing trousers, was about his business. Due to the unavailability of a more senior officer, Detective Inspector David Mott, roused from his marital bed, stood opposite eating a bacon sandwich fetched from a nearly café by an obliging PC. Mott was near retirement, unenthusiastic and, like the medico, thoroughly ill-humoured. The flash of the cameras as the SOCOs made a permanent record of one more incident of violent death and misery unnerved him and his stomach was loose, due both to the alcohol intake of the previous evening and the several hours he knew he would be spending in the mortuary. Known as "Dig 'em up Dave" due to a past involvement in a case involving an exhumation, Mott was past his best – which many of his colleagues felt had never been up to much, even at its peak.

The body was that of a female aged between twenty and thirty, the pathologist told his audio recorder. The cause of death, quite evidently, was a laceration to the throat so wide and so deep that the head was almost detached from the torso. The windpipe, the main arteries and the oesophagus were severed and death, pretty much, was instantaneous. There were two parallel slashes to the throat and a bruise on the left side of the head below and to the side of the eye; torn and muddy knickers had been pulled to a point below the knees and the body temperature and absence of rigor indicated death only an hour or so earlier. The girl's eyes were wide and staring, her mouth open, bubbles of bloody spittle taking the place of her scream.

The pathologist, resigned to a golf-less day got to his feet. Mott stuffed his half-eaten sandwich into its paper bag and putting it into his raincoat pocket he crossed street. Mott did not like pathologists. Nor did he like mortuary technicians. In his opinion, anyone who spent his day up to the elbows in death and misery must be strange and to be avoided at all costs. The pathologist that day seemed nice enough, though; a man in his early forties, thin-faced and with pleasant, almost kind, eyes and a slight Irish accent of the sort which, unaccountably, he associated with Dublin's Trinity College. Mott, though, had an ever-lasting memory of a man of many years earlier who mid-examination of the body of a young woman, raped and strangled on Wimbledon Common, had asked her occupation. On being told that she had been an actress, and at a point when the skin of the skull had been pulled over her face and the cap of the skull was being removed, the pathologist remarked: "Well, if she's acting now she deserves an Oscar." Mott understood that so-called black humour was essential in some occupations, but he had wondered long and hard what the girl's family would have felt had they known of the insensitivity.

The Irish pathologist (his name was Sean Findlater) did not know Mott. Accustomed to dealing with more senior officers he called him 'superintendent' which caused Mott to chuckle.

"Afraid not, sir. Just Inspector. But I expect there'll be someone else along later."

Findlater was not fazed by Mott's lack of importance: "Well, you're here now, so we'll make the best of it, eh? Now. Our young lady there: I wouldn't say she's been dead more than a couple of hours and judging by the mess, she was killed where she is, poor little cow." Making sure there were no press near, he went on: "I've never seen anything like those lacerations to the throat. Damn nearly took her head off. And —" he looked round, doubly ensuring they were not overheard — "I can't be sure until we get her in the mortuary, but I'm pretty sure there's more hacking in the abdomen area."

As the East End woke so the crowds gathered. The press arrived, television cameras set up at the end of the street and the bolder journalists, ducking under the blue and white tape, approached. Having bribed access to houses opposite, photographers appeared in upstairs windows, bulbs flashing and calls for information. Mott was uncommunicative. For the time being.

But he was a shrewd man, this David Mott: years of dealing with the scum of London's sewers does not leave one lacking in a certain cunning and resourcefulness. He had not paid for his bacon sandwich and he would not pay for his lunch. He felt sympathy for the wretched girl a few yards away; compassion but no real interest other than that her death had spoiled his Sunday. He knew better than to take the tragedy to heart, to become personally effected by it, and he knew that even if he was to be involved in the enquiry, it would be as second-in-command to a senior officer. Dispassionately, he watched as the SOCOs pursued their various tasks, well knowing that at this stage they and the medics were the only real detectives and that their findings may in all probability be crucial. By 11.30am the rubber-necking crowds had dwindled to a handful and there was barely a ripple of muted comment as a black undertaker's van was allowed through the tape.

Finding the remains of his breakfast in his pocket, Mott handed it to a passing uniform PC. "Ditch that, son, will you" he said, barely looking at the policeman and, his eye ever on the main chance, he walked to the tape at one end of the crime scene. He knew the journalist by sight but not by newspaper, but at that stage that was unimportant. "I don't know about you" he said quietly, "but I'm having a pie and a pint. In the Frying Pan."

Some fifteen years previously, Mott had stood trial for corruption. As a detective sergeant on the Flying Squad he had been accused of accepting a bribe of £500 in exchange for bail from a man he had charged with robbery. The evidence was thin and mainly circumstantial and at the conclusion of the Crown's case the judge stopped the trial. Following an internal discipline enquiry, Mott was moved to Tottenham in north London. Disillusioned and believing that his career was at an end he went into some sort of a decline: arriving at the station never earlier than 9.30am, he would wrap his overcoat around himself red-Indian style and with his feet on his desk and with one eye on the clock he would scan the racing papers. And every morning as the hands on the clock touched 10.00am his feet would hit the floor with a resounding crash and, jumping to his feet, he would announce: "They've drawed the bolts" and in less than five minutes he was at the bar of the Beehive, the first of the day's countless half-pints of bitter in front of him.

One morning a young probationer constable on CID attachment for a week and in awe of Mott – who he saw as being everything he had ever imagined a seasoned detective should be – approached him and asked: "Hey, Sarge, do you ever get up the Old Bailey?"

Mott eyed the boy, peering at him through red-rimmed and rheumy eyes. He licked his lips as if savouring the moment and replied: "How do you mean, son? As a participant or a fucking contestant?"

Like wildfire, word of this wit went round the village which is the CID of the Metropolitan Police and David Mott became a legend.

Poplar mortuary early afternoon.

Like most places of business enjoying the Sunday lull.

Instead of the usual complement of a half-dozen cadavers in various stages of autopsy and the bustle of two pathologists, several mortuary technicians and an assortment of hangers-on, there was just the one pathetic corpse, surrounded by those who will attend to the final indignity of post-mortem. Amongst the living, the body seemed isolated, an exhibit and far removed from the warm, vibrant creature it had been hours earlier.

White rubber boots squeaked on the tiled floor and bright green plastic overalls, head covers and matching aprons seemed strangely out of place. Beneath the intense lighting, bright, shining scales, steel bowls and dishes were ready and the pathologist's tray of instruments, some delicate as an entomologists' tiniest tweezers, others of awful dimension, were ready aligned on a table.

Mott arrived. Struggling into an ill-fitting overall he reeked of his lunchtime excesses at the expense of the third estate but he was far from drunk. With over twenty-five years heavy drinking, literally under his belt, he was one of the old guard, a dinosaur in a modern police service. Half a bottle of scotch at lunchtime was no problem – and if called upon mid-session he had the strange ability of being able to shrug off whatever degree of intoxication he had attained and to carry out his duties efficiently and in a normal manner.

He approached the steel post-mortem table. A SOCO was taking photographs and a second, a young woman, was taking a set of fingerprints from the body, now naked and grey/white from the immense blood loss, and strangely firm due to the process of rigor. Her thick dyed hair was stiff with dried blood and the bruise on the left side of her face had gone to a vivid purple. The terrible lacerations to the throat, one ear to ear, the other below and not so long, exposed the severed blood vessels and windpipe and as a technician cleaned the wounds, irrigating with hosed water followed by suction, the vertebrae could be seen.

Mott was no stranger to violent death but the sight of the wounds to the body of this girl, now doll-like and strangely fragile in death, appalled him. Horizontally across the abdomen, below the navel and at a point level with the hip joints were three lacerations, each an inch deep and exposing yellow subcutaneous fat. Two of these extended from one side of the body to the other and the third, the lowest, was a jagged, shorter slash confined to the left side. From the right side of the body, extending down from the base of the rib-cage were three further cuts, these less deep, and extending to a point almost level with the navel. Lower still, there was evidence of an assault on the pudenda, almost as though some sharp instrument had been inserted into the vaginal cavity and then turned, the sharp edge scraping on bone and reminiscent of the manner in which one would core an apple.

Findlater noted Mott's scrutiny.

"If I'm right, the throat wounds have been caused by a knife with a blade no less than nine inches in length and by a right-handed assailant, I imagine. Assuming it was the same implement used throughout, some restraint seems to have been used inflicting the lower wounds." Rubber-gloved, he probed the horizontal slashes to the abdomen. "It is almost as though he held the knife at the end of the blade so as to avoid cutting to any great depth." From his implements he selected a large post-mortem knife and, holding it between thumb and finger at the end of the blade with just an inch or so of the tip exposed: "Something like this, you see. Alternatively, of course, he may have had a second weapon, one with a shorter blade – a Stanley knife for example."

Mott nodded. "And the genitals?"

"Very much the same. Restraint, almost care." He moved to the head of the table and lifting the chin: "Not like this – no restraint here: frenzied butchering and probably from the back, holding the hair, pulling back the head and drawing the knife across the throat."

Mott left the table and joined one of the SOCOs who was listing the victim's clothes and possessions. Less than a pound in cash, cigarettes and a lighter and four contraceptives. Nothing in the way of identification but he knew that the fingerprints would clear that up: poor little cow, he thought, she's bound to have form. Clothes safe in sealed and labelled exhibit bags and ready for the laboratory examination, Mott returned to the body. He watched the examination, making notes and feeling nauseous but unwilling to show it. From time to time he checked that the senior SOCO was listing the swabs and tissue removed for laboratory examination. There was no evidence of recent sexual activity, he was told by the pathologist, but Mott knew only too well that this absence does not preclude the attack having a sexual motive.

3.

Monday 1 September 2003.

New Scotland Yard, fourth floor. 8.30am.

The offices were quiet but Michael Gregory had been at his desk for two hours. In his mid-forties, Gregory had over twenty-five year's police service, most of it in the criminal investigation department. A Detective Chief Inspector, he was vastly experienced in the investigation of serious crime and was known never to have left a murder unsolved. Like many senior detectives, he was something of a drinker and he had a reputation for intolerance of those who hold rank but do not have experience and ability. A grammar school boy, he left school at 16 with poor GCEs and joined the Metropolitan Police after three years in the Royal Marines. He was married and it was his first day back from two weeks annual leave spent in a lack-lustre hotel in Tossa del Mar, the greater part of each day having been devoted to arguing with his wife about the long hours his job required of him. The strain of marital disharmony had caused a more-or-less permanent frown on his forehead and of late he had noticed that he was suffering from almost permanent heart-burn and, always a hypochondriac, he feared an ulcer.

He stretched at his desk and looked at his sun-burned hands through heavy-rimmed glasses. In his shirt-sleeves with wide, brightly-coloured braces depicting characters from "The Flintstones" and a loosely-knotted silk tie he looked more like a successful businessman than a senior police officer. A handsome man, if a little worn and with a hint of an expanding waistline, there was a charm about him; he had a style, a way of talking to people that hinted at equal confidence with either costers or countesses; he had what some would refer to as "charisma" and what his parents would call "middle-class gentility." A Londoner, he had a "home counties" accent and was proud that since joining the police he had managed to educate himself and was able to hold his own and give acceptable opinions on most subjects. He had a fear and lack of understanding of most things rural and although he would rather die than acknowledge it, he disliked the dark in areas other than city streets. He was an easy-going man, always ready to smile and, he liked to think, of an understanding and compassionate nature. Gregory liked flat-racing, best bitter and scotch, the company of male friends or ladies who smile and flirt a little and, above all things, his job. He did not like "over the sticks" racing, doctors and dentists, people who pried into his private life and junior officers who grovel.

Shortly after 11.00am. The door of his office opened. Ira Strathearn, Assistant Commissioner (Crime) and the most senior detective in London. Gregory stood up and reached for his jacket on the back of his chair. He was waved down by Strathearn who was carrying a file.

"Do you know about this murder in Whitechapel, Michael?" He sat down heavily in front of the desk. Nearing the end of his service, Strathearn was overweight, a problem not helped by his fondness for steak and kidney pies and whisky.

Gregory nodded. Referring to one of the piles of papers on his desk, he said: "I read it in the messages and there was something in the paper. Who's been lumbered with that?"

Strathearn, universally known as The Old Man, smiled. "Well, Dave Mott is minding it for the time being but you're taking it over as from now."

Gregory sat back in his chair. Although not something he would wish to show, he was pleased and elated with the news. His mind raced over the practicalities, the shorter daily travelling from home in Waltham Abbey to the East End and on the black side his wife's face when she learned he was once more to work in the field and that the hours of his already lengthy working day may well be doubled. The Old Man was talking and Gregory refocused.

"There's a problem out there, Michael – well, not yet perhaps, but I think there's going to be and that's why you're going over there."

He opened the file he was carrying and passed a sheet of paper to Gregory. It was a photo-copy of a letter. "This arrived this morning."

> *Dear Old Boss,*
>
> *Well, here I am again and I bet your not too pleased to see me! First time I had my fill and never did get buckled – but times was different then. Second time – oh, I forgot! that's a secret and I'll leave you to find out - and now I'm back for another go. You won't see no JUWES letters and no KIDNYS either – that were never me, see – but you'll find a few pointers from time to time. I just hope you give me a worthy adversary, dear old boss, not one of your modern college coppers, all political correct, university degrees and no common - but that's up to you I suppose. I'm still down on whores and I loves my work and this time I won't be stopping until I'm dead or nailed.*
>
> *From Hell, yours,*
> *Jack.*

Gregory read the letter, apparently printed on a word processor. Seeing his apparent lack of understanding, Strathearn said: "You're not a Ripperologist, then?"

"A what, Guv?"

"Jack the Ripper, Mike." He looked at Gregory, his brow furrowed like an autumn field. He pointed to the file. "This poor girl was a hooker. She was cut to pieces in Durward Street between Saturday night and Sunday morning – thirtieth and thirty-first of August." He paused, and then: "The first Ripper murder was over that same night in 1888 and it was in Bucks Row – which is now Durward Street." He nodded towards the letter: "Now read it again."

He did so and looked at Strathearn: "Perhaps some nutter wrote the letter. One of these Ripperologists: sussed the similarity in the date and place and is pissing about."

The Old Man shook his head slowly: "I don't think so. It was in this morning's post and that means it was posted yesterday. The body was found yesterday morning, there were no evening papers because it was a Sunday and not much on the tele about it either." He thought, rubbing his nose and gazing at Gregory's blank computer screen. "You could be right but I don't think so. The "dear old boss", the whole style and some of the words and phrases used – they're almost a replica of the letters the Ripper was said to have written, even the misspellings, the "kidnys" and the "juwes." No, Michael, I think we've got a maniac of some sort and I think he's going to cause us some trouble."

Gregory read the letter a third time. "But I thought the Ripper – the original I mean – never got caught and that was the end of it."

"That's right."

"But this chap's talking about a second time: 'Second time – oh, I forgot! that's a secret and I'll leave you to find out' – what's he mean by that?"

"I wish I knew." Strathearn handed the file to Gregory. "You'd better read this and then get over to Leman Street. Dig 'em up Dave knows you're coming." He got up and walked to the door and then, almost as an afterthought: "By the way, the letter is covered in dabs – almost like they were left on purpose, just for us. I'll let you know what the fingerprint people say as soon as I hear."

19

The door closed and almost immediately re-opened: "Oh, and you'd better read up on the first Ripper. If I'm right, and I'm praying to God I'm not, he'll be having another go next Monday night - his second was on the eighth of September."

Gregory opened the file and then, hearing the rattle of the tea-trolley in the corridor, he got a coffee and two doughnuts from the ever-smiling black lady and closing his office door he started to read.

The dead girl was named Kelly Goggin. She was aged 25 years. Precisely as Mott had surmised, she had thirty-seven previous convictions for soliciting prostitution and minor crime and she had been quickly identified by her fingerprints which were on record. To assist Gregory her criminal record and such background as was available was in the file. From this he learned that she had been born in Stoke Newington in east London to a single mother, and there was no record of school attendance after the age of fourteen. Within two years of that she had drifted into prostitution, favouring the so-called "meat rack" in the Kings Cross area. Her last known address was a room at 45, Glenconnor Road in Kentish Town and judging by the frequency of her attendance at magistrates' court she was soliciting in the Kings Cross on a nightly basis.

The telephone rang: it was Mott. He had visited the dead girl's room and from correspondence and enquiries he had located her mother who would attend the mortuary that afternoon for the purpose of identifying the body. The SOCOs were in the process of taking the room apart, he said, but there was no indication she ever used it for entertaining her clients and little was likely to be gained. Gregory agreed to meet Mott at the mortuary and returned to his reading.

There was no suggestion that the girl had any connections in East London; she had no convictions in that area nor had she ever been known to solicit there. Gregory knew that girls at the bottom of the prostitution market – and Kelly Goggin was certainly in that bracket - favour the back seats of cars or secluded back alleys and although from what he had read it seemed evident that she was killed where she was found he saw that the probability was that she had been taken there in some vehicle. Having read the sad file he stood in his window, gazing out across Westminster and wondering if Strathearn was right and yet another serial killer was about to make a mark.

The phone again: this time Strathearn warning him that taking books about the original Ripper from a library may go towards generating some sort of panic should it be known that they are for the purposes of the murder investigation. He had several of his own, he said, and he had arranged for his driver to collect them from his home and to deliver them to Leman Street police station from where Gregory would carry out his enquiries.

Kelly Goggin's mother, aggressive in a pink trouser suit and accompanied by a toddler in a push chair arrived twenty minutes late. A short, plump, pugnacious woman in her forties she gave every impression of being, or having been, closely associated with the profession of her late daughter. With neither tears nor, seemingly, a great deal of interest, she stated that she had not seen her daughter for almost five years and that, although she knew that she was engaged in prostitution, she had no knowledge of her activities. On reaching the mortuary viewing room and with the curtains drawn closed, suddenly she lost her swagger and became quietly subdued as the dread of what she might shortly be forced to see dawned on her. In the moments before the purple curtains were drawn she scolded the chattering child, shaking it by the shoulder in an effort to bring the quiet she evidently felt the occasion warranted. On being shown the small, pale body, sheeted up to the neck and with a deal of cotton wadding and mortuary technician's skill to conceal the injuries, there was a trembling intake of breath and she nodded. She wiped her eyes causing mascara to run and make-up to smudge.

"Poor little mare" she muttered, "she never deserved nuffink like that." She turned to Gregory and taking him by the arm, her fingernails making him wince: "Will you get him? The bastard what done that to 'er - will you get him?"

Later, at Leman Street, there were visitors. Alerted by the evening papers, the dead girl's two friends and the doorman from the Pilgrim, anxious to help. In statements taken independently the women agreed that the dead girl left the pub with a punter but alcohol and amphetamines and a lack of interest at the time lead to no description worthy of any note at all; the doorman, occupied with his work, never saw her after she walked to the coffee stall.

Gregory read the statements: "Well, if they're right and she went off with some feller she's pulled in the pub and if he's the one we want and if the quack is right that she's only been dead an hour or so, where the hell was she all night?"

Mott nodded. "Wherever it was I'll lay it was a pretty uncomfortable few hours."

"What about her room?"

"The SOCOs say no. All clean and the bed made and the other people living there say she never came home all night and in any event she never took her punters back there."

That night at the coffee stall Mott and a sergeant drank watery coffee and ate saveloys and bread and margarine: yes, he recalled the girl because she was rude about the price of coffee, she left it on the counter, didn't she, and next thing she's gone, in a right hurry. There might have been a van, white – or was it blue? Big, like a transit sort of thing, over there on the corner. Did she get in it? Gawd, I don't know, do I? She walked towards it, but I never see her get in it.

Later, in a room above the Canterbury Pilgrim, they saw the barman.

"Well, she had this drink bought for her, a Breezer it was, and next thing I know she's gone and so has he - him that bought her the drink."

In his early twenties, he was effeminate and very nervous. Originally from Lancashire, he said he had been in London only for a few weeks and had worked and lived in at the Pilgrim since his arrival. His forehead and face bore both old and recent evidence of acne and Mott noticed what he took to be self-harm scarring on both of his arms.

"Did you know she was a tom?"

"We're not allowed to serve –"

Mott leaned forward, face inches from the boy's, his hand squeezing the thin fingers, causing a wince and an intake of breath. Slowly, and very precisely: "I asked you – did you know she was on the fucking game?"

"Yes – and that's my fucking job gone down the tubes."

Mott was not concerned with his employment prospects: "So the man who bought her the drink was a punter?"

"He must've been."

"Had you seen him before?"

"No, not that I know of."

He was about sixty with greying hair, the boy said. He did not know what he was wearing or what he had to drink or how long he had been in the bar. He did not know if he would be able to identify him; he smiled capriciously at the sergeant with Mott, causing the man to blush. But he supposed he could always try.

Alone at Leman Street, Gregory scanned the books left by Strathearn and other than the dates and details of five murders, evidently committed by the same psychopathic killer, he learned nothing of any great note. In 1888 the Metropolitan Police had been in existence barely fifty years and although there had been a deal of squabbling between the Commissioner and the head of the (separate) City of London police about boundaries and who was to investigate which crime, there was no real evidence of incompetence as such. After the second crime the whole of Whitechapel and around was effectively saturated with policemen but still the murderer managed to slaughter two more women in one night without apprehension and a few weeks later a fifth, but on that occasion in her room. The killings were random and without apparent motive and from experience Gregory knew that these are the hard ones to come to come to terms with. There were suspects, of course, dozens of them. One author promoted a conspiracy amongst Freemasons to protect a member of the royal family which was a fine story if one ignored the fact that the poor prince was bolted up tight and fireproof at royal functions at the times that two of the crimes took place. Another author had it that the poisoner Neil Cream was the Ripper and that he had confessed on the scaffold: this was unlikely as he favoured strychnine and not a knife and impossible since at them time of all of the murders he was in prison in the Unites States. Apparently merely because they were alive at the time and without a scintilla of actual evidence, the crimes were laid at the door of an eminent surgeon, a famous painter, a Jewish slaughterman and a poor insane barrister who, it seemed, was only fancied because he lived in the East End, had a brother who was a surgeon and had committed suicide shortly after the last murder. Overall, other than the details of the crimes, the only factual statement in any of the books he read was that on the Great Day of Judgement when all things shall be known to all men, when the name of Ripper is announced, the so-called Ripperologists will all look at one another and mutter "Who the hell is *he*?"

He got home at 3.00am and spent a worrying, troubled night in an unwelcoming bed.

4.

Thursday 30 August 1888.

In a Victorian London far removed from that we know today, the East End was a festering slough of misery and vice with drunkenness and prostitution the norm for many. It was estimated that some eighty thousand souls lived in Whitechapel, crowded into a maze of courts and alleys devoid of effective sewers and with the only water supply being a pump or tap at the end of the street and catering for all. In one of the worst slums in Europe, families crammed together in filthy, rat-infested hovels where public houses, pawn shops and brothels were always busy and an atmosphere of hopelessness was perpetually in the air. It was a place where infants starved so their parents could buy gin, where the prostitution of children was rife and where death and decay were ever present. It was the East End of Oscar Wilde's Dorian Gray and many like him, nightly leaving the affluence of Mayfair and Belgravia in search of the vicarious and unlimited pleasures which could be readily available for the price of a couple of fish suppers.

Families with four and more children lived in one or two tiny cramped and rat-infested rooms, often sharing the space with pigs or goats while cattle and sheep were herded through the narrow streets on their way to slaughter, their droppings being left to rot. Broken windows were stuffed with rags or newspaper; beds, consisting of heaps of straw and rags were infested with lice and vermin and cooking facilities often amounted to an open fire in a yard. The brimming chamber pots were often left for a week before being emptied in the yards or the street and in many of the dwellings the cellars were awash with liquid sewage. Rags, rubbish and food waste were left in piles in the streets and rats, having little fear of human-kind, were everywhere. The child mortality rate was such that undertakers offered a special "children's practice" rate but it was common for the dead, both children and adults, to be left for days or even weeks after death, no money being available to pay for the funeral. Neglect and decay were everywhere and sickness thrived. Smallpox and tuberculosis were much in evidence and venereal infections, particularly the then fatal syphilis, were common and largely left untreated. In winter, unable to afford coal, banisters, doors and even floorboards were used as firewood and in the heat of summer the temperature in the huddled dwellings rose, as did the stench, to such a degree that sleeping outside was not uncommon. The men worked where they could, often for a pittance, and wives were forced to do what they could to supplement the income by shelling peas, matchbox making or sweatshop tailoring. Children, if they went to school at all, would go hungry and it was not uncommon for a half a pig's or sheep's head, boiled with the off-cuts from vegetables found in the street near Spitalfields market, to last a family of four for a week.

The countless homeless resorted to the dozens of common lodging houses where patrons were required to sleep two or even three to a bed and the price was fourpence per person per night. The proprietors of such establishments were quick to exclude drunks and lunatics and those without the price had no chance at all, no matter their age or state of health. Fights and disturbances in these places were common and as well as having the unenviable task of carrying out sanitary and health inspections, the police were regularly called to maintain order.

Hundreds of prostitutes would compete for business, coupling generally taking place in a back yard, lane or some other convenient place. Contraception consisted of a form of douching, the insertion of a wad of wet newspaper or cotton waste or by simple interuptus. For the greater part the women were of the worst, lowest sort of prostitute, alcoholics, homeless and the world's unwanted. The price was whatever they could get - and they gave as little as possible in return.

For a little over two weeks Mary Ann Nicholls had been staying at a lodging house at 18 Thrawl Street, Spitalfields and where she was known as "Polly." The owner of the premises had harboured serious misgivings due to her persistent drunkenness but the final straw was when she arrived late at night without the means to pay, drunk and boasting to all and sundry that she had spent her earnings from prostitution on a new hat. Refused entry, she made her way to Brick Lane where she met another street woman, an equally drab and unhappy creature named Martha Reynolds. Martha, perhaps unwisely, admitted she had a shilling or two and together they found their way to the Frying Pan, a public house at the top of Brick Lane near Whitechapel Road. There, Martha bought gins and Polly, well known to a large number of the clientele, laughed and joked with a group of costers.

Aged 42 she was an amateur prostitute, a compulsive thief and a chronic alcoholic. Her husband, William Nichols, was a hard-working and honest man employed in the print industry in Fleet Street and he had long since given up on his errant spouse. With their five children they had lived in Blackfriars Road but Polly had left the family and wandered off some three years earlier. There then followed a series of filthy work houses and common lodging houses and a slow but sure descent into the quicksand of degradation. Two months earlier, she had found work as a domestic servant with a family in Wandsworth but she had been dismissed for stealing and, once more crossing the Thames, she had drifted into Whitechapel where she had become an habituée of the lowest public houses where she would sell herself for pennies; a pathetic, caricature of a woman, five front teeth missing, filthy dress and underclothes, a creature worthy of pity in a place where such a sentiment did not exist.

The more gin she consumed the merrier she became. She laughed at the top of her voice and when prompted she sang.

Since our father joined the army
Ours ain't been a very 'appy 'ome:

'E wakes us up in the middle of the night –
Tells us we've all got to get up and fight.
'E puts our muvver in the dustbin,
A-goin' of the sentry-guard,
And there's me and bruvver John
Wiv our little nighties on,
A-marching rahnd the old back yard,
Gawd blimey......

Twenty minutes later with Martha and two of the costers in tow, Polly arrived at "Brighton's Penny Gaff" – a small, thoroughly disreputable although immensely popular theatre in Whitechapel Road. One of the gentlemen paid the fourpence entry and with a bottle of gin concealed beneath Polly's skirts, they made their way into the crowded auditorium. In a pit in front of the brightly lit stage were three musicians – a pianist, a violinist and a man who played a selection of drums. Above there was a gallery for the more well-to-do and no matter what was taking place on the stage, non-stop cat-calls and insults were shouted back and forth between these two sections of the social scale. There were no seats and no programme or notice of the evening's entertainment but approbation – or disapproval - of the acts was readily demonstrated. After a pretty girl had sung of love and a home in the country and two inept jugglers who left the stage after less than a minute in a shower of carrots and onions, there was a one act play, a parody of Romeo and Juliet, and Polly and Martha laughed until the tears rolled at the antics of the two elderly men playing the principal roles and the even older man playing the nurse who could not remember his lines.

They left the penny gaff just after midnight. There was a deal of kissing and fumbling on the pavement but the costers left the ladies and Martha, who now had no money but a ticket to doss in a lodging house in Mile End, left Polly on the corner of Brick Lane.

Friday 31 August, just before 4.00am. Chilly, damp, and with the scent of autumn in the air. The day the horror began.

28

Charlie Cross, on his way to work, discovered her in Buck's Row, Whitechapel.

Skirts round her waist, eyes staring sightlessly and her throat slashed from ear to ear with such violence that her head was almost severed from the torso. Later, in what passed for a public mortuary, it was seen that her stomach bore both vertical and horizontal lacerations and that there was also evidence of stabbing on her vagina.

Doctors, whose knowledge was in its infancy, gave opinions: left-handed or right-handed assailant, killed where she had been found or elsewhere, dead when the injuries were inflicted or alive. It went on for ever but the truth was there were no witnesses, there was no apparent motive, and there were no suspects and no clues.

5.

Several of the dailies had picked up the "Jack the Ripper" angle, connecting Durward Street with Bucks Row and noting the significant dates. The inevitable "police spokesman" – who Gregory suspected as being Mott – had revealed that although no clues have been found, certain leads were being followed. Secretly, Gregory wished he knew what they were. Late afternoon and Strathearn phoned: the "Dear Boss" letter was found to have eight fingerprints on it, all different and almost certainly left on the paper on purpose. None of these related to any individual in the Yard's main fingerprint index.

Over egg and chips in the canteen Mott was thoughtful: "So he's got no form then, the creepy bastard." He chewed, swallowed, and then: "I suppose if this is some clown trying to emulate Jack to the Ripper it would explain why he picked her up in Kings Cross and dumped her in Durward Street, but I'm not convinced, not by any means."

Gregory, with tea and a Kit Kat biscuit, and in an effort to be more constructive: "He's never going to able to replicate the original Ripper killings, you know. First, there are no toms working the streets in this neck of the woods nowadays and there hasn't been for years, so that means he's got to pick up a girl elsewhere, kill her here or somewhere else and then dump the body in the place where the original murder took place." He stirred his tea and licked chocolate off his fingers. "If he's going to go according to 1888, then the next one's the night of September the seventh and eighth and we know it's going to be – " he referred to the notes he has made from Strathearn's books – "in Hanbury Street, off Brick Lane."

"And we'll be waiting – he must know that."

"Of course he does, and I think that's all part of his game." Then, shaking his head: "No, I'm sure this man's no fool. If he's going to have a go at doing all five he won't be able to keep to the original pattern - he'll be varying it and I bet he'll let us know more or less what he's up to, just like the first one did. We've also got to consider that when he's done the five if he's really got the taste he'll just keep on going."

"Mind you Guv, it could be that the dates and street are a coincidence and it's just a one-off."

Gregory shook his head again. He bit the inside of his cheek and muttered: "Yes, but what about the mutilations – identical to the first Ripper job? I wish to Christ I knew, Dave, I really do, but I'm sure of one thing: we'll all know for certain after Sunday."

The days that followed were tense. Gregory and Mott shared a feeling of anticipation and expectation. They were restless. The "Dear Boss" letter had been released to neither the press nor the rank and file of the enquiry staff for fear that some sort of panic would ensue. The usual door-to-door enquiries and detailed search of the scene for God-knows-what had been done and the laboratory had found no evidence of sexual interference on the body. There were no clues, just the usual mass of information and advice from the public and, seemingly, little hope. By Friday evening the plans for the operation in Hanbury Street the following Sunday night had been formulated and finalised and leaving Mott in charge Gregory took the Saturday off.

He lived with his wife Sally and their 18 year old daughter Emma in a four bedroomed, detached house in Waltham Abbey, Essex. Never having been fans of modern furniture, they had managed to accumulate a number of antiques, many from each side of their respective families, and also by means of careful purchasing, and over the years they had managed to establish a comfortable and well-appointed home.

Gregory spent the day gardening and teasing his daughter about her forthcoming "A" levels and that evening he and his wife went to dinner with friends. Over the meal he acknowledged that he was in charge of the "Whitechapel murder" but would not be pressed and showed little inclination to discuss it. Drinking too much, his wife steered the conversation round to his long hours, her dissatisfaction with his career and their way of life all of which caused Gregory to telephone for a taxi and they were in separate beds before eleven.

Sunday 7 September 2003.

Gregory was at Leman Street just after 11.00am. In jeans, a tartan shirt and a worn sweater he was the focus of attention of junior officers, both CID and uniform, but he matched whispered comment about his choice of clothes with good-natured sarcasm and endured the ribbing, knowing that he must get the best from the men, many of whom would be on duty until the following morning. Mott had drawn a street plan on a blackboard and together they agreed the best positions for uniform and CID staff to be posted over the forthcoming night. Two vans, one sign-written as pertaining to a Halal butchery and parked near such a business, and the other appearing to be a mobile hot dog wagon were both to be positioned in Hanbury Street and at such points as most of the length of the narrow thoroughfare could be seen by the officers concealed in each. Keys to any vacant premises had been obtained and police would be concealed therein, and these measures, together with other men covertly positioned in lanes and yards adjacent and all in contact with each other and the police station by radio were felt to be ample coverage.

"Well, he's not going to kill anyone in Hanbury Street tonight, I'm bloody sure of that", said Mott looking at his blackboard plan. "There are more bloody coppers down there tonight than there is filling in forms at the Yard."

Untrusting of his relationship with the press and his fondness for free beer and meals, Gregory was unwilling to allow Mott to go for lunch on his own and together they went to a pub in Commercial Street. Their reticence to talk much about the murder was respected by most of the journalists but any impressions that Gregory may have had as to their lack of serious association with the 1888 crimes rapidly faded when one of them made direct reference to the forthcoming night being the anniversary of the second Ripper murder.

"Big night tonight, then", said the man, winking largely. He was a fat man in his forties, bearded and wearing a leather jacket several sizes to small for him. He had a cast in one eye making it impossible to know if he was directing the comment at Mott or Gregory. It was Gregory, though, who took the initiative. Wrestling with stringy meat in a beef sandwich he looked over his glasses and said: "Oh, yeah. Why's that, then?"

The man moved his head slightly, apparently focussing on Gregory.

"Eighth of September tomorrow isn't it. The anniversary of the second Ripper murder in 1888 isn't it? In Hanbury Street?"

Gregory swallowed his tough beef and washed it down with bitter. He stared the man coldly and said nothing. The man brandished a twenty pound note: "Have another?"

Mott, finding himself in a sensitive situation as to possible future benefits from Fleet Street, decided he should take a firm hand. "Not now, Jerry, thanks. We just want a pint and a bit of peace."

Jerry, though, was not about to let go. "Can you just confirm you'll be covering Hanbury Street tonight?"

Gregory took of his glasses and blinked at the man. He finished his beer and left the pub followed by Mott.

Thirty minutes later a man named Sterling Grant received a telephone call halfway through his Sunday lunch. The former editor of several minor provincial newspapers and a hack of thirty years experience, Grant was in overall charge of New Scotland Yard's press bureau. Still chewing roast lamb, he was told by Ira Strathearn that he was to get into the yard immediately and notify all newspapers that the Yard would not take kindly to references to past murders in connection with the current Whitechapel enquiry and although nothing could be done to prevent such comment, editors who disregarded the request would find future co-operation from the Yard seriously restricted.

Grant, ever conscious of free speech and the freedom of the press, swallowed his lamb and said he would do his best. Thirty seconds later, and following a terse comment from Strathearn to the effect that whatever his best was it may not be good enough and did he think that it would be difficult for aging and not over-successful hacks to find jobs, Grant's wife heard the front door of their Chingford home slam and she did not see him for the rest of the day.

Allowing Mott to go home until the evening, Gregory settled in his office with Strathearn's books.

6.

Saturday 8 September 1888.

Spitalfields 4.30am.

A week after the first killing and although the story was on everybody's lips, day to day existence continued as normal; life was cheap and violent death was not uncommon.

Other than Covent Garden, Spitalfields market was the main wholesale centre for fruit, flowers and vegetables and both buyers and sellers would travel overnight to be there well before first light. All of the local pubs catered for the vast market crowd and to many of the prostitutes it was an irresistible draw.

The streets around the market halls were busy with traders and their clientele and the public houses were full, serving breakfast as well as beer and gin. The one large bar of the Port of Calais, was full to capacity with a good-natured crowd, many having business in the market and others there for unconnected reasons. The bar boasted a dozen or so wooden tables of varying size and colour, all ringed by a myriad stains from both glasses and bottles and bearing the scars of decades of fallen hot tobacco. Cooking and food preparation were carried out in a room at the back of the bar and in such conditions and under such circumstances which may have been disconcerting for the even the most tolerant customer and at busy times dirty plates and cutlery were left to accumulate on the tables. Although saw-dusted, the floor often became sticky with spilled beer and spirits and the landlord's two cats and the occasional dog from the street would forage for titbits. The walls and ceilings were stained nicotine-tan and the air was always thick with tobacco smoke. In one corner a table was set aside for the playing of whist "for moderate stakes" but the only game which had ever been played there in living memory was the semi-fraudulent "find the lady", this being operated by three gentleman from Shoreditch who travelled daily to the Port of Calais for that purpose.

A pianist was seated at the old upright piano and the landlord, perspiring and red-faced was entertaining:

> I'll be up your flue next week, Mary Ann,
> I'll be up your flue next week;
> I've bin busy wiv the widder next door –
> I've only one brush and I can't do more.
> Nah, I'm in the sweeping bizness,
> And doing such a roarin' trade –
> When I comes around
> It'll cost abaht a pound
> But I'll be up your flue next week.

The crowd joined in for the last three lines, many arm-in-arm with glasses raised and drink spilling; the smells of sausages, hot ham bones and pease-pudding did their best to compete with the body odours of a largely unwashed mass. There was a constant traffic of customers and with good food, cheap drink and the odd chance of an encounter with an obliging lady, the Calais was a magnet. Staff, though, particularly at unsociable hours, could prove a to be a problem and when the landlord was offered a couple of hours serving in the bar in exchange for a few pence and some small beer, he would jump at it.

Nearly fifty, and although she did not know it, riddled with tuberculosis, Annie Chapman, known as "Dark Annie", was a homeless alcoholic suffering from depression; formerly married to a coachman she had borne three children of whom one was dead of meningitis and another crippled. Following the death of her husband she left the two remaining children and drifted to the East End where she did what she could to survive. Remuneration from flower selling and the odd needlework did not go far and *seeing little alternative she took to selling her body. Short of stature, plump to a point of near obesity with her front teeth missing and her short, curly hair invariably dirty, one would think that she presented a daunting prospect for any would-be suitor. Oddly, this was not the case: of an easy-going, jolly, disposition and the ability to be caring and understanding if her clients wished to discuss their problems, she was, to one not too fussy about looks and hygiene, an attraction.*

That night she had been thrown out of her doss-house lodging due to lack of funds. She was hungry, homeless and in need of a drink and when the offer to help behind the bar in the Calais for a few hours was made she saw it as a life-line. From some time after 3.00am she served beer, washed pots and handed the steaming plates of food across the bar. She laughed and joked with the customers and when she knew the words she would join in with the singing. As well as her "in kind" wages there was the odd ha'penny from a half-drunk patron and the odd penny or so from those more under the influence and who did not check their change. She was bought an occasional half-pint and she would steal a drop more and by 5.00am she was pleasantly drunk and happy to talk to anyone who had the time or inclination, her eye always on the possibility that she could earn enough for a doss house kip in exchange for a five minute fumble in some nearby alley.

The landlord, always ready to please and entertain, offered the crowd the latest satire directed at the perceived decadence of the Prince of Wales:

> *"Prince Bertie said: "You are a proper marvel –*
> *At conjuring you've really got the knack."*
> *And from his coat he plucked a diamond stick-pin:*
> *He smiled at me - (long pause for effect) – and then he put it back."*

The crowd bellowed laughter and howled appreciation. She laughed, nodding and winking at the clientele and then: "He's a card, your landlord. A right character, I'd say."

The speaker was standing at the end of the bar. She had served him earlier with a pint of porter and a plate of belly pork and eggs. In his forties, she guessed, and not bad looking in a common sort of way. He wore no hat and unlike most of the locals, he favoured a collar and tie as opposed to a choker. A soft voice, London accent but not pronounced Cockney, and a pleasing smile which flickered more about his grey eyes than his mouth. Greying hair and matching sideburns, no moustache but white, even teeth and a slight dimple in the chin. She laughed: "Oh, yes dear, he's a card alright – and you oughter hear him when he gets going and the missus ain't around: proper makes you blush, he does."

He laughed. "Take a lot to make you blush, I shouldn't wonder." He finished his drink and nodded to her for a refill. "You going to have one with me?"

With British Summer Time still decades away the sun rose that morning shortly before 5.30am. They had wandered through the narrow back streets, occasionally stopping for a kiss, and having crossed Brick Lane they stood in a doorway, embracing and discussing price. After some haggling and a fee agreed, she led him down a narrow alley to the rear of a common lodging house at 29, Hanbury Street.

In a dark corner not yet reached by the dawn light, he stood behind her, his left arm across her chest, holding her close, kissing her neck and whispering quietly. Then, seemingly in one movement his left hand grabbed a handful of the short curly hair and, her head pulled back against his shoulder, for a brief and fully comprehending instant she saw the knife.

She died as the blade severed her main arteries and before the fountain of blood had splashed the fence. Any cry was instantly silenced as the two slashes, the first followed immediately by a second slightly below, cut through her vocal cords. Still holding her off the ground, blood pumping and body jerking with the spasm of violent death, he remained motionless for two, may be three minutes.

Listening.

Then, replacing the knife in the gaping throat, he cut and worried at the neck muscles, the razor-sharp blade dulling as it scraped the vertebrae, intent on decapitation. This failing, he lowered the corpse to the ground and then, raising her skirts to her waist and drawing her legs up, with a practiced sweep of the knife he laid open the abdomen.

The body was found just after 6.00am., face and tongue now swollen, the tongue protruding, and extensive bruising to the face and chest. The small intestines had been completely severed, lifted from the body and laid on the right shoulder whilst the uterus, the upper section of the vagina and two thirds of the bladder were missing. As reported in The Lancet, the police surgeon – a man of 23 years experience - was of the opinion that the perpetrator of the horror was someone with medical experience and knowledge of some sort, medical or post mortem, and that the manner of the opening of the cadaver, apparently with one sweep of the knife and the evidently practised excision of the organs clearly indicated this to be the case.

Oddly, the brass rings the woman had worn had been torn from her fingers and these, with what was apparently the contents of her pockets, two combs, a few coins and a paper case were found laid in front of the body possibly, it was felt, in some sort of symbolic gesture. To remove these, the assailant had cut through the small pocket beneath the woman's skirts.

Again there was a great deal of talk and the press coverage intensified. A "Vigilance Committee" was formed. A man named John Pizer was arrested, probably because he looked the part and was not over-popular in the area: he was freed when it was found that at the time of this crime he was staying with relatives, countless of whom swearing to this, and at the time of the first murder he was asleep in a lodging house, his presence there being corroborated by the owner. The police made no progress, there were no clues of any substance, there was no motive and there were no suspects.

7.

Gregory woke with a start. Rubbing his eyes he looked round the office and was pleased to see Mott with tea on a tray.

"Must've dozed off for a moment."

Mott, who ten minutes earlier had put his head round the door and seen his napping boss, said nothing. They sipped the scalding tea, each in his own way dreading the next ten hours or so. Gregory, tense and nervous, knew that if some maniac was loose his future could depend on his ability as a detective. He had no illusions: as the man in charge it was he who would be left to field the disapprobation and derision of the media and that, in the modern police force, failure in such a major matter would almost certainly mean that he would be side-lined, transferred into the uniform department and in put charge of abandoned bicycles or police women's uniforms on a rarely-visited floor of the Yard tower. For his part, Mott understood Gregory's position. Not usually one to empathise with the tribulations of senior officers and often heard to comment "he shouldn't've joined if he can't take a bleedin' joke" for once he found himself drawn towards his boss. Suddenly a fund of tasteless Ripper jokes, he tried to lighten the atmosphere, but Gregory remained in-drawn and morose.

****

The Spaniards Road, Hampstead. Between the Whitestone Pond and the Spaniards Inn.

Shortly after 8.00pm and almost night. A chill in the air and the breeze coming off the heath was cold and promising low degrees in the small hours.

The man Mott called Creepy drove his white Transit van towards the Spaniards, his eyes constantly on his offside pavement, that bordering the Heath. Watching. Looking. He passed the old pub and turning into Winnington Road he made a 'U' turn and headed back towards Hampstead. In his sixties, Creepy was thin of both frame and face; he wore no hat and his grey/white hair was short and well groomed. Like someone's grandpa. Brown overalls, buttoned at the neck and sleeves gave the appearance of blue-collar employment. His eyes, bright and clear blue but edged with deep crows-feet, scanned the nearside pavement in front as he drove, now towards the Whitestone Pond, and his hands, devoid of rings and with close-cut, clean fingernails, gripped the steering wheel in the recommended ten-to-three position. The radio, or perhaps a tape or CD played Dvorak. Softly. He was hungry but he knew that food must wait – if he was to maintain The Game Plan. Looking across the heath he saw low mist, rising from the ponds he imagined, and then, suddenly he saw her, at first a distant shape, almost a shadow, but as the van approached he knew she was the one.

She was not there earlier, he was sure – but no matter. As he approached her she smiled. A whore's smile. She was black and no more than eighteen, tight jeans and training shoes, a yellow T shirt and short, spiky, ribboned pig-tails sticking out from her head which strangely reminded him of the Millennium Dome.

He slowed the van and opened the passenger door. Her voice was soft and with an accent he did not immediately place. He caught the word "business" and it was only when she got into the van that he knew she had a stammer. "Th-th-th-thirty quid in the c-c-car, it is" she said, her head jerking at each missed syllable. "Th-th-there's a p-p-place at the back of J-J-Jack Straw's C-C-Castle."

He smelt body odour and petuli oil. Driving along the Spaniards Road he looked at her: painfully thin, almost angular, but with a strangely beautiful face, almost handsome in a boyish way but very female for all that. She talked non-stop, about her friends, about her lodgings in Finchley and about her dog and all the time with the painful stammer. He followed her directions and in the dark, far corner of a pub car-park backing on to the open heath he gave her a fifty pound note and they both climbed into the back of the van.

She started to remark on the plastic-covered mattress and blankets but managed to get no further than the first few pitiable broken syllables. A rubber-gloved fist smashed into her left temple and as she sprawled across the plastic he was on her, ejaculation without erection, manual strangulation and death within a minute. He smelt urine and cursed her as he felt the wet warmth seep into his overalls. Then, retrieving his money from her jeans pocket, he wrapped the broken and traumatised little body in the blankets, pushed the bundle into a far corner of the van and climbed back into the driving seat. He drove from the car park, only switching on the lights of the vehicle as he was negotiating the Whitestone Pond.

Monday 8 September 2003.

1.20am. The Transit parked four hundred yards away, Creepy took a room in a seedy hotel in an empty, featureless street between Albany Street and Regents Park. He paid fifty pounds for one night, telling the disinterested receptionist that he would be leaving early the following morning and would not require breakfast.

2.00am and Gregory and Mott were alone in the main CID office. Dirty cups and sandwich wrappers on the desks.

Waiting. Dozing.

Shortly before midnight they had driven along Hanbury Street, checking that all was as it should be and that there was no sign of what was a very large police presence in a small area. Then, back in the quiet of the small CID office they talked.

Mott was no expert on what had taken place over a hundred years earlier but he agreed with Gregory that, given the facilities available to them, the nineteenth century constabulary had done a pretty fair job and that, even today, without any apparent motive a serial of five random killings would be hard to pick up on unless clues were left. They disagreed on the original Ripper letters: for his part Gregory was sure that at least two were penned by the killer but Mott was having none of that and was adamant that they were all hoaxes – written by journalists with a view to bringing interest to a fever pitch, thereby increasing sales of newspapers. He was still unconvinced of the Ripper copy-cat theory but said little knowing that the forthcoming night would be the deciding factor.

At about 5.30am and at a time when Gregory was dozing, feet on a desk and snoring rhythmically and Mott was trying to find fresh-made tea, the man he called Creepy left his room and exited the grubby hotel. Walking back to the van he could hear the beasts in the nearby zoo, lions he imagined, as they roared at the coming dawn. Grimacing, he opened the front windows of the van in an effort to dispel the stench of blood and urine and within a few minutes he was in the Euston Road. Stopping at traffic lights at the Angel he turned in his seat making sure that his precious cargo is still intact and seeing the black, spiky head and the whites of staring eyes he said: "G-g-g-good m-m-m-morning, d-d-d-darling." City Road and into Shoreditch High Street. Cheerful, he sung to himself: "When I grow rich, say the bells of Shore-ditch."

6.45am and daylight: Gregory stretched and grinned at Mott. "That's it then, Dave; it looks like it's going to be just the one this time."

"I knew it Guvnor. No one would be mad enough to try to replicate the first bastard." He laughed and: "One up the arse for old wonk-eye and his Fleet Street mates, anyway."

By 7.10am the Halal van and the hot-dog wagon were gone and policemen, stiff and cold and with stubble itching on their chins were drinking mugs of tea in the canteen. As the watery and unenthusiastic sun started to show itself on the Thames estuary horizon, Gregory was driving up the Bow Road. He was happier, almost light-hearted and with the radio louder than he would normal have it, he hummed to the music and chuckled at the Wogan banalities.

At Whipps Cross his mobile telephone rang.

The eviscerated body of the girl lay partially concealed in a doorway at the Brick Lane end of Hanbury Street. Discovered by a kitchen porter on his way to work, it was cold, stiff; the right arm was raised, pointing strangely towards the sky, a phenomenon due to rigor mortis and the position in which it had had lain all night. The settling of the blood had caused blue post mortem staining at the lowest levels of the body. A yellow T shirt and training shoes, no skirt, trousers nor underwear. The throat was cut ear to ear but there was no great pool of blood, no evidence of any pressurised fountain or intense spurting, just seepage from the wounds, which enabled the pathologist to say with confidence that the girl was not murdered and mutilated where she was found but elsewhere and hours before. Gregory arrived at the scene; he supervised the photography and the forensic examinations of both the scene and the body and directing Mott to accompany the undertakers to the mortuary for the autopsy, with Hanbury Street closed off and the SOCOS and uniform police carrying a microscopic examination of the scene, he returned to Leman Street to await the phone call he knew would be coming from Strathearn.

Gregory was the arch-cynic and in many respects a sad man. The greater part of his adult life had been spent grubbing through the slime and detritus of London's sub-culture and dealing with the worst the city had to offer and he had become sceptical and distrustful. During his time in the Royal Marines and on his annual holidays he had seen and marvelled at the vast beauty and unparalleled wonder of the planet and he had become totally convinced that since Eve ate the apple the human race had become a cancerous growth on the surface of the earth. Hours of thought and soul-searching had left him with no religious belief and although, like most people, the idea of after-life had an appeal for him, he could not honestly bring himself to believe it. What he had seen earlier had sickened him and he questioned how any supreme being could sanction such horror and the destruction of the life of a girl little more than a child.

By 12.30pm Strathearn had not called. Gregory issued a statement for the press and busied himself organising the office space, telephones and computers for what he knew would be a protracted enquiry. The accommodation allotted for the enquiry occupied the whole of the top floor at Leman Street police station. One large room was to serve as the main, general office. This had twelve double desks, computers, printers and all of the general office equipment required plus a large white board showing the names of the various officers working in the field and the actions designated to each. The HOLMES (Home Office Large Major Enquiry System) computer was set up in another smaller office and an equally small office at the end of the corridor was allocated to Gregory. Thirty staff were engaged on the enquiry, these including CID and uniform officers and civilians, with SOCOs being available if required. Assisting Mott was Detective Sergeant Archie McGibbon, a 36 years old divorcee rumoured to live alone in the most appalling squalor in a flat in Hackney. Detective Constable Christos Iannou (known as Barney) was in charge of the HOLMES unit and Woman Detective Constable Jackie Daniel filled in as statement reader and assisted wherever she was required. On introducing himself to the staff, Gregory asked about Iannou's nickname. "Well, Guvnor", said the dark young man with an east London accent but with obvious Hellenic origins, "before we were dubbed as being institutionally racist I was "Bubble" – Bubble and Squeak – Greek, right? After McPherson though, they thought I might be offended so it changed, like Bubble to Rubble – Barney Rubble in the Flintstones and there you are – Barney."

The first call on one of the new office phones. Mott said that the post mortem confirmed that the girl had been dead about ten hours and that the cause of death was manual strangulation. Her throat had been cut and the terrible mutilations inflicted after death, almost certainly not where she had been found, and Mott confirmed that the uterus and a large part of the vagina and bladder had been removed. The pathologist was firmly of the opinion that some degree of medical knowledge would be required to remove the organs so precisely and this would have required more time than the assailant had available to him between when the police presence had left and the body had been discovered. There was no news on the identification and, as in the case of the Durward Street murder, the initial hopes in that direction hung on fingerprints. Mott was breathless and Gregory sensed, correctly, there was more to come.

"Guv, there's something else: the bastard has stuffed a bleedin' railway ticket in her mouth, poor little kid. What the hell does that mean?"

"A what?"

"A railway ticket, Guv. A return ticket from London Bridge to Blackheath."

Strathearn rang just before 2.00pm. Gregory was to present himself at the Yard at 3.00pm.

At 2.20pm he heard from the fingerprint department. The dead girl was named Cicelyn Jean Percy. She was known as "Toothpick" due to her lack of girth and she was an absconder from a care hostel in Liverpool. "Toothpick" was sixteen years of age. Her mother, a heroin addict, had already left for London and it was arranged that Barney would meet her at the station later that evening.

Gregory drove to Victoria Street and for the first time he was feeling the effects of the small amount of sleep he had during the previous night. Certain that a maniac was lose and bent on emulating another lunatic of a hundred-plus years before, he had a feeling of dread and trepidation. In the past, he had never had any doubt about his ability and his capabilities as a detective and although he would be the first to admit that lady luck had often played a part, he was proud of his reputation. Suddenly, though, he had become aware that this enquiry was unlike any other he or anyone else had handled. This time, the quarry was almost telling him where the next crime will take place – or where the next victim would be found; he had left fingerprints, written a letter and more correspondence was likely to follow. The previous night he had correctly assessed the situation and by arriving at his chosen location after the police presence - which he had certainly anticipated - had been dispersed, he had succeeded in making a fool of Gregory. Suddenly, the London Gregory loved had lost its appeal and as he drove down Whitehall past the Cenotaph he was very conscious of his fallibility and also of his matrimonial unhappiness. He thought of his wife, remembering the happy times before she came to see his job as a mistress and the jealousy which he was certain would drive them apart festered in her mind.

Arriving in Strathearn's offices on the fifth floor he was told to wait. The ACC's secretary was in her late twenties, a pretty girl but with blonde hair cropped short and in such a manner that Gregory laughingly wondered to himself if a left-handed blind butcher's boy armed with blunt shears may have been the culprit. In a short blue skirt and white blouse, she had a pleasant, relaxing manner about her and Gregory found his depression lifting and that he had become more focused. She offered him tea which he refused and seemed embarrassed when she realised that he was watching her as she typed. Reading the Yard directory on the waiting room table he saw that her name was Rosie Lewis and from her left hand he saw that she was evidently neither married nor attached. After ten minutes waiting, he winked at her and nodded towards the door of The Old Man's office.

"He's with someone" she said, almost a whisper: "Jim Bassett, is it? Head of fingerprints?"

Before Gregory could reply Strathearn's door opened and Gregory scented the unmistakable smell of whisky in the air. Detective Chief Superintendent James Bassett, in overall charge of the fingerprint department since anyone can remember, was known to him and they shook hands. He saw the two glasses on the desk and knew that he would be able to judge both his current standing and the esteem in which he was held by whether a third glass was produced.

Strathearn questioned him about Hanbury Street. His tone was terse, urgent and Gregory sensed worry and concern, sentiments he would not normally have associated with The Old Man. "We had the whole area saturated all night, sir. There were two plain vans in Hanbury Street and men concealed everywhere. We could never know the bastard was going to turn up in daylight and dump a dead girl there after the troops had left."

The Old Man nodded but said nothing. Gregory was unsure and wondered if Strathearn would understand his problem and also if he had seemed to be trying to over-justify his position. He watched as the ACC stared into space, his brow furrowed, lips pursed.

"And you're sure that she was killed elsewhere and hours before?"

Gregory sensed a certain acquiescence: "According to the quack there is no doubt about that." He thought and then: "Do you know about the train ticket?"

"The what?"

"The bastard put a return train ticket in her mouth. London Bridge to Blackheath."

Strathearn smiled: "He knows his stuff, this bastard. I told you we'd be having some fun with him – and I was right."

Gregory looked at him, shaking his head in an indication of lack of understanding.

"You haven't read the Ripper books, have you? Montague Druitt – one of the main suspects. He was a barrister and part time school master in Blackheath. He lived with his cousin in the Minories, near Mitre Square, and he used to travel on that rail line. He committed suicide after the last murder and a first class rail ticket London to Blackheath was in his pocket when they fished him out of the Thames. The journalist Dan Farson who used to keep a pub on the Isle of Dogs wrote a book years ago saying it was all down to Druitt but he couldn't come up with any real evidence. There was some bullshit about a letter from someone in Australia who could prove it was Druitt but Farson said it had been nicked from his office in the BBC or somewhere. It was all a lot of crap: Farson was an incorrigible drunk and all he did was blacken the name of a perfectly innocent man who couldn't defend himself."

There was a silence. Strathearn produced a third glass from his desk and poured whisky for three. Inwardly, Gregory sighed relief.

The Old man sipped his scotch and then: "Mike, we've asked you to come over because there's been a development." He looked at Bassett and: "I'll get Mr. Bassett to put you in the picture."

Bassett, a tall, thin man with the reputation of being something of a worrier, smiled nervously. A heavy smoker, he was known as "Fagash and Confusion": "Well, the fact is – and it is fact – we have identified the fingerprints on the Ripper letter." He looked at Gregory through thick glasses and: "And Mr. Strathearn and I have agreed that at this time the details of what you are about to hear must not go outside of this room."

Gregory looked at Strathearn. "But I understood that the dabs weren't in the system – that he'd not got any form."

"They're not, Mike." Strathearn looked towards Bassett to continue.

"The fingerprints on the letter sent by this so-called Ripper are those of a man named Michael Folmer. And Michael Folmer was hanged for the murder of a prostitute in 1957."

There was a silence and then: "That's not possible."

Bassett opened a large briefcase and placed a number of files on the desk. He took out what Gregory assumed was a copy of the Ripper letter with a series of fingerprints on both front and rear of the paper made visible by the application of black powder on the surface. He handed Gregory a table magnifier: "Look at these prints on the letter. You will see that on each print a number of points are picked out as indicated by the arrowed pointers."

Gregory studied the prints and then Bassett handed him several large sheets of paper each bearing the greatly enlarged copy of each print with the arrows clearly shown. Gregory studied these for a moment comparing them with the prints on the letter and nodded. Bassett then produced a set of fingerprints, both hands, all fingers, thumbs and palms: "These are the prints of Michael Folmer, taken after his arrest in 1957 and –" he handed Gregory a number of sheets of paper each with one print with points marked by arrows – "if you will be so good as to compare them with these on the so-called Ripper letter you will see that there is no possible room for doubt."

Gregory examined both sets of the enlarged prints, from time to time turning to the smaller, actual size sets. He compared the arrow marked points on each, gazing through the magnifier until his eyes burned.

Bassett continued: "And before you ask, the prints on the letter are not old prints - in fact they are very fresh – and there is no evidence that they have been lifted from some other source and planted on the letter. They are new and they are genuine and I will stake my reputation on it."

"It's still not possible."

Bassett shuffled the papers on the desk: "You agree they are matching sets?"

"As far as I can tell, yes. But there must a mistake somewhere."

Bassett shrugged, a gesture not of arrogance but of resignation. "What can't speak can't lie and they're a perfect match and that's all there is to it – the dabs on the so-called Ripper letter are a perfect match for this man Folmer. They are identical."

Strathearn got up from his desk and walked to the door. Leaning on the thick wood as if to guard against eavesdroppers he said: "Well, possible or not, the fact remains. Let us be quite clear on this: if word of this gets out there will be the most fearful repercussions. Every toe-rag who has ever been convicted on fingerprint evidence – not only here but all over the bloody world – will be appealing and screaming for damages and the effect on policing and methods of detection as we know them today will be disastrous."

Bassett pushed the files into his briefcase and Gregory sensed that he was almost in tears: "I agree that it is not possible. Science has dictated and proved time and time again that no two persons – alive or dead – have ever, ever, had the same fingerprints; even in the case of identical twins there are no similarities in the fingerprints. But here it is - and if I was asked in court, as the most experienced and foremost expert in the field, if the fingerprints on this so-called Ripper letter were identical with those of a man who most certainly has been dead for over forty-five years, I would have to say that not only is that the case but that there are seventeen identical points – seventeen, mark you – on each print which proves it beyond any conceivable doubt whatsoever."

Strathearn returned to his desk and poured more whisky. He was sanguine, more focused than Bassett: "The truth is, of course, as Mike says: there is something wrong here somewhere. Two people cannot have the same fingerprints, that is a fact, it is an irrefutable presumption, and it is going to be up to you to sort it out, Michael." He pursed his lips, pouting like a child: "Mike, when we see the magician make the lady in cabinet disappear and then pop up at the rear of the auditorium seconds later we know there are only two explanations: magic or illusion. Being sane and sensible adults we know there is no such thing as magic and so we must seek to uncover the illusion. I know you've got this Ripper nonsense to sort out, but the two things are connected and each one is relative to the other."

Gregory opened his mouth to speak, but the Old Man held up his hand: he took three large files from his desk drawer and pushed them across to Gregory.

"These are the papers on Folmer. If you need anything – anything at all – come to me or Mr. Bassett but whatever you do, for Christ's sake don't let a word of this get out. If the press gets wind of it – it doesn't bear thinking about."

"What about Dave Mott? He'll have to know."

Bassett looked up: "Dave Mott? Is he with you on this?"

Gregory nodded.

"Christ, he'd tell the papers about his mother's adultery for a free lunch. You can't tell him."

"I can't not tell him, can I? He's with me on the job, Guv – he's got to know."

"I'll speak to David Mott" muttered Strathearn, almost to himself. "Leave that side of it to me. Just you don't forget that if this Ripper bastard is going to keep to the plan – and I'm betting he will – his next go'll be on thirtieth September – " he looked at is calendar "-that's a Tuesday. The original did two that night: the so-called Double Event."

It was after 6.00pm when Gregory left Strathearn's office. Rosie Lewis had gone for the evening, her desk was tidy and there was a smell of perfume in the air. He telephoned Leman Street and spoke to Mott who told him that the black girl's mother had identified the body and left. The tragic little victim had several convictions for prostitution and drug-related offences; she had been in and out of care since she was a baby and had never had a chance since the day she was born.

Suddenly, Gregory's depression was back: he was tired and hungry but the prospect of the drive to Waltham Abbey and unwelcoming company did not appeal. Leaving the Yard he took the short walk through the back streets to the Two Chairmen. The old pub was full of Yard staff relaxing, avoiding the rush hour traffic - or any one of a hundred excuses they may have for an early evening drink. He exchanged small talk with colleagues and falsely indicating that he was meeting someone he settled in a corner with a pint of bitter. His mind was racing, full of the afternoon's developments: in his heart he was quite, quite sure that Strathearn was right and that the killer had found some way of planting a dead man's fingerprints, but for the life of him he had to admit that he could not see how. And eight prints? It was just not possible.

The Old Man was also right in his assessment of the reaction if such a revelation ever became public. The effect on police methodology and the subsequent appeals and civil claims would be such that in many places law and order could be reduced to a state of collapse. He sipped his beer and giggled to himself as he watched two Americans as they sniffed and tasted the two half pints of bitter they had ordered, before leaving them on the counter and re-ordering cold lager. Then, looking past them, he saw the blonde, spiky hair and suddenly Rosie Lewis was looking straight at him. And smiling.

****

Sally Ann Gregory was aged 41 and did not look it. A pretty, dark haired woman, she had been married to Gregory for 21 years and had given him one daughter, Emma, now aged 18 and looking towards going up to university. When they had married, Sally had known that her husband was a career policeman and that his goal was high rank in the CID but, and she was the first to admit this, she would not have married him had she known his career would always come before everything else. For years, through his employment as a junior CID officer she had sat at home alone as he worked fifteen hour days and her boredom and the lack of the attention she had experienced had left her sour and miserable. Although she had shared in her husband's pride and pleasure as he progressed to higher rank and responsibility, she harboured a loathing for the police service and for the harm it had done to her marriage.

He arrived home just before 9.00pm to find the house in darkness. He poured a large glass of whisky and settled in front of the television. Emma, he knew, was staying with a friend for the week but before he could focus his mind on his wife's absence, his long period without sleep caught up with him and, dropping his glass and contents on the carpet, he feel asleep.

What seemed like seconds later he was awoken.

"You're back, then", she said. It was a statement, not a question.

"You've been out."

She sat on the settee tucking her legs beneath her and picked up a newspaper. "I have that right. Especially with you not being here."

Gregory found his fallen glass and managed to pull a magazine over the damp carpet. "I had to go to the Yard, Sal. To see Strathearn. You know there's been another murder and on top of that there's a complication." He poured more scotch and was about to continue but:

"It's almost thirty-six hours since you left here, Mike. Do you think that's fair?"

"Sal" he pleaded, "I have a job to do and a responsibility to the public –"

"Hah! A responsibility to the public? What about a responsibility to your wife and daughter? Normal people don't live like this, Mike and I don't see why we have to." Getting up from the settee she threw the newspaper she was holding into

Gregory's lap and walked out of the lounge. Glancing at the headlines he saw it was a London evening. "JACK'S BACK!! MODERN DAY JACK THE RIPPER RUNS RINGS ROUND YARD'S FINEST: IS A REIGN OF TERROR ABOUT TO BEGIN?"

Beneath the half page scrawl was a photograph of Gregory.

An hour later he found the bedroom door locked.

8.

Tuesday 9 September 2003.

Mott had never been an early riser and since his son had joined the navy and his daughter had gone to live with her long-time boyfriend in Sidcup things had not improved. Mrs. Mott (Big Shirl) had his breakfast on the table never later than 8.00am which with a three quarter of an hour drive from their bungalow in Walthamstow to Leman Street invariably meant a 9.30am arrival.

At 7.40am and with Mott still in the bathroom the door bell rang. Moments later and in response to Big Shirl's urgent tapping he opened the bathroom door and, wide eyed and half-shaven, he learned that Ira Strathearn was downstairs. Mott had known The Old Man since he joined the Met; they had served together with Mott always two or three ranks lower, but the early morning visit to his home terrified him. Minutes later and struggling into a tie and buttoning his shirt collar he found the ACC in the small lounge. Strathearn, furnished with a cup of tea by Big Shirl, got to his feet.

"Dave! A long time, eh? Hope you don't mind my early call, but I was just passing – on way to the Yard."

Mott, who knew that The Old Man lived in Wembley which could never have involved Walthamstow in a route to Victoria Street, didn't believe a word of it: he felt cold inside and his bowels suddenly loose, and he feared loss of control.

"No, Guvnor. Not at all. Um, always very nice to see you."

Strathearn resumed his position in the armchair and sipped his tea. "You're doing these Whitechapel murders with Mr. Gregory, right?"

"Yes sir."

"Yes, well I just want to make sure that you look after him, Dave. He's a good man, Michael Gregory, and I know if you work together you'll get a good result."

Mott's mind was in turmoil: something was wrong but for the life of him he could not fathom what it was. Strathearn put his briefcase on his knees, the locks clicking as he unfastened it.

"Dave, something's come up on this job which is quite unusual. Mr. Gregory knows about it and he'll be discussing it with you later today. Now, this is something which it is totally essential is known to as few people as possible and, well Dave, you know, you and the press have always had a close relationship, haven't you?"

"No, Guv, I'd never –"

"Dave, a few quid here or there or free lunch and a few pints – no one's ever bothered before – ." He broke off and looking at the door he lowered his voice: "Do you still have your little friend in Caunter Close over at Canning Town?"

Mott paled visibly and was frantically trying to assess his position. Before he could speak, Strathearn opened his briefcase and took out a plain brown foolscap envelope and laid it on the leather surface of the case. "It was the funniest thing, Dave: sometime in 1998 or 1999 I believe it was, CIB[1] were doing some sort of surveillance in that same street and, bugger me, quite by accident they end up getting you on film. Two or three times a week, what do you think of that? Now, they knew you were nothing to do with what they were looking at, but shagging a water board worker's old woman, Dave? When the poor bugger's at work? It's not the thing is it?"

Mott said nothing, trying to collect his thoughts. The Old Man got to his feet leaving the envelope on the coffee table.

---

[1] Complaints Investigation Branch: the Metropolitan Police department responsible for internal discipline and the investigation of complaints.

"Now I know I can rely on your complete and unreserved discretion, Dave. Can't I?"

"Yes Guv. Absolutely."

And Strathearn was gone.

Later, on his way to Leman Street, Mott pulled into a lay-by. Sixteen black and white photos of him either leaving or entering the water board gentlemen's house, some with the lady admitting him, kissing him as he left and, all in all, leaving little room for any matrimonial wriggling on his part.

Shortly after 9.00am and with coffee organised, Gregory called Mott into his office. He skated around the accommodation and the staff he had been given and then, deciding to take the bull by the horns:

"Sit down, Dave. We need to talk."

Mott, who had been unsure until then, decided not to mention Strathearn's visit.

"As you know there were a number of dabs on Creepy's letter and, well, they have been identified."

"I thought he had no form."

"Yes, well, he hasn't as far as we know. The dabs are identical with those of a man named Michael Folmer. And he was hanged for murder almost fifty years ago."

There was a silence during which Mott stared at Gregory, a half-smile on his face. "Let me get this straight, Guvnor: you're saying that the dabs on the so-called Ripper letter match those of a man who was hanged for murder half a century ago?"

"In Pentonville. He murdered a tom in the West End."

"It's not possible."

"I know that and you know that. But the fact remains."

Mott was unsure if Gregory knew of Strathearn's call at his home and if he had any doubts as to whether it was connected with this most recent development, what followed left him convinced.

"The Old Man and Jim Bassett at fingerprints are paranoid, Dave. Like us, they know that it's all bollocks and that someone's pissing us about although God knows how, but the fact is that if the press get hold of it the repercussions don't even bear thinking about."

And suddenly all was clear to Mott. His mind worked overtime, the end-focus being on life for him outside of the police. What he had at Leman Street was something of a sinecure and the thirteen hour days he worked several times a week were, for the greater part, excuses to stay away from the varying demands of Big Shirl. Resignation or the sack would mean endless days at home, gardening, daytime TV and – he shuddered inwardly – what she referred to as "family matters." A job was out of the question of course: security officers for big companies and solicitor's managing clerks were expected to earn their salaries. He paled inwardly.

Gregory was staring at him across the desk, squinting over the top of his glasses. "It cannot go out of this office, Dave. Just you and I, and The Old Man. And Bassett of course. Is that clear?"

Mott nodded: "I know I've been a bit too familiar, say, with some of the press boys over the years but this, Guv, Jesus, this is a nightmare."

Again he was tempted to mention Strathearn's earlier call but saw no point and went on: "You've got my word, Guv: nothing'll come from me."

Gregory nodded and Mott thought he may not have been convinced. Still peering over his glasses, Gregory said: "The train ticket in that poor kid's mouth: that's not to be disclosed to the press either. Make sure that the SOCOs know that we're keeping it under wraps for the time being."

Anxious to be seen as contributing, Mott said: "Well, if this is a Ripper reproduction, and I have to say now it's beginning to look like it, there's about three weeks to the next one which is (he referred to his notebook) Tuesday the thirtieth of September and I'll tell you this, Guv, he's going to have his bleedin' work cut out."

Gregory looked up: "Go on."

"Well, that night he did two: one in Mitre Square and the other in Berners Street. Well, Berners Street's not there any more, it's called something else and has been for years.

"So if he's going to try and do them it could be anywhere – but there'll be a pointer of some sort, you can bet. That's his game and he wants to see if we can learn to play it." He drank his coffee and then: "I can't see what has made him start now, Creepy that is. Why not ten years ago or in ten years time – or next year? Something's kicked him off, some catalyst."

"What made the first bastard start? And stop, come to that?"

"The shrinks say that the only reason they stop, this type of killer that is, is when they're either dead or banged up. That's why there's a school of thought that puts the original down to poor old Montague Druitt – because the murders stopped after he killed himself."

"Shrinks! Like bleedin' pathologists they are: all guess work before they've got a body and then they know it all - but only when it's too late." There was a silence and then: "You'll be telling me next they're going to do one of those psychological profile things to tell us who we should be looking for."

"They are. The Old Man has commissioned it. It's general practice nowadays with anything contentious."

Laughing, Mott took at his notebook and a pen. He wrote for a minute and then, tearing the page out of the book he handed it to Gregory.

Aged 30-50 - single – loner - probably abused as a child - previous convictions - high intelligence - low self-esteem - abandoned by mother – unemployed – broken home - only child – social misfit.

Gregory read and it and grinned at Mott: "You've seen one before, then?"

"There are twelve points there. I'll lay you a pound to a pinch of shit that nine of then come up on the so-called profile and I'll go double or quits that when we get the bastard there's no resemblance."

A knock and Archie McGibbon put his head round the door. "Guv, that idiot at the Kings Cross coffee stall: he talked about a van, a Transit type, maybe white or blue."

Mott nodded: "Go on."

"Well, about ten to six Monday morning we've got a white Transit van on CCTV cameras, first in Shoreditch High Street and about five minutes later down on the corner of Bethnal Green Road."

"Have we got the films?"

"Yes, sir, but the problem is we can't bring up a number. We would have been able to but the bastard's got the plates covered up with what looks like pieces of rag. Front and back."

Much to the relief of traders, Hanbury Street had been re-opened. The SOCOs had concluded their microscopic examination of the scene and the dead girl's clothes which had been sent to the laboratory for examination. "Toothpick" had been living with another girl and a small dog in two basement rooms in a dingy street off the Swiss Cottage end of the Finchley Road. Her flat mate, another pathetic teenager little more than a child named Em-Lee Tobias, also an absconder from a Liverpool care home, was detained and the dog moved into kennels. In a statement Em-Lee said that she had known "Toothpick" was engaged in prostitution, as she herself was. They both solicited in Spaniards Road, Hampstead but never, under any circumstances, would they have brought a punter back to their flat. Later in the day, evidently shocked and terrified, she fell tearfully into the arms of social workers who had come from Liverpool to collect her and Gregory's feeling was that that she could not have got back there quick enough. The SOCOs spent the day in the two wretched rooms but found nothing they considered to be of any great significance.

During the afternoon Gregory took the bulky files relating to the Folmer murder from the locked drawer in his desk.

He removed his jacket he hung it on the back of the office door. At his desk he tried to picture the West End of almost half a century before. The officer in charge of the case had been a Detective Superintendent Herbert Castle assisted by Detective Sergeant Stanley Cutler. Earlier that day, and for the purposes of security going through Strathearn, he ascertained that Castle had been dead for some twelve years but that Cutler was not and was still drawing his pension.

As he read Castle's report and scanned through the statements Gregory started to have a feel for the West End of the fifties and at times in the small and claustrophobic office he felt he could almost sense the atmosphere of a different era.

The organised criminal activity of the West End in the mid-fifties was largely under the control of the Jewish Jack ("Spot") Comer and Billy Hill, a man from an established criminal family originating from Seven Dials, the "rookeries" and home of Dickens' Fagin. That said, this iniquitous pair seemed quite happy to have but a fringe involvement in prostitution, allowing that aspect of business to be retained by the Messina brothers of Maltese origin and who had been active in the field since before the war. Pimping (or poncing as the London criminal world would have it) was not for Englishmen: it was the territory of foreigners and the Messinas were suited to it. There seemed, however, to have been a steady "contra" arrangement between the Maltese and Hill and Spot and no real trouble or antagonism seems to have existed.

The Messinas were adept at organised vice and were actively importing women from France, Belgium and elsewhere on the continent, seemingly with scant regard for the law. There was every indication that regular payments were being made to the police at West End Central and over the years they had been able to build up an empire of prostitution encompassing the whole of Westminster and beyond. Soho, the area bounded by Regent Street with Oxford Street to the north and Tottenham Court Road and Leicester Square to the east and south was the epicentre of their activities. It is accurate to say that there was no thoroughfare within the maze of streets, alleys, courts and lanes in which the Messinas did not own at least two properties, each house divided into numerous small rooms each catering for one street woman and her maid. Outside of each address postcards would inform the interested party that a "French Model", "Swedish School Mistress", "Latino Lady" or similar was available within to cater for their various and often bizarre requirements. The fee was £2.00 for a basic "short time" but this could escalate dramatically depending on the needs of the patron. Nothing, though, is ever quite what it seems and it was very rare that the client got what he was lead to believe was on offer and very often the unsuspecting punter, 80% of whom were tourists, would find that the trek up two or three flights of rickety stairs, the hesitant and furtive knock on the door bearing a reproduction of the downstairs advert and the wait in a seedy passageway while an existing customer concluded his business, was worth neither the money nor the effort. "Heidi from Hamburg" would invariably turn out to an aging housewife from Deptford or Stoke Newington, "young" would cover anything up to fifty or even above that and "exotic" and "exciting" were epithets which simply did not apply. Clients were always pressured to pay an additional five shillings to the maid – invariably a retired prostitute herself – and in each house there would be at least one Messina thug available to sort out any problems caused by difficult or recalcitrant punters who may have felt they had cause to complain having found that they were in and out in less than fifteen minutes and far from satisfied on any count.

Monday 17 June 1957.

Had the man called Michael Folmer been kept under surveillance during the afternoon and early evening of this day it would have been noted that his interest was solely relative to the activities of prostitutes. From Soho Square he walked the length of Dean Street, crossing from side to side and carefully scrutinizing the advertisement cards outside of the various addresses occupied by the street women. On the corner of Dean Street and Old Compton Street he stood in a shop doorway for forty-five minutes watching the soliciting girls, each with her long-handled umbrella, the fashion of the day, and each with the insignia of her trade, the rattled bunch of keys. On two or three occasions he followed one of the girls with her newly-acquired client, watching as they entered the building where her room was situated and waiting the fifteen minutes or so until they came back on to the street. Later, crossing Shaftesbury Avenue, he walked the length of Lisle Street and returned to Cambridge Circus by way of Monmouth Street, all the time carefully examining the postcard advertisements. Stopping only for a salt-beef sandwich and a cup of lemon tea in Rabins in Great Windmill Street, he maintained his erotically-obsessed patrol until just before dusk and when the great whirling, swooping flocks of starlings were screaming and twittering their clamorous good-night to London above Leicester Square.

Thérése Bougon was aged 41 years and a native of Bordeaux, France, where she had worked as a prostitute since her late teens. In 1947 she had married Gian-Franco Zammit, a Maltese, and by early in 1950 this pair had moved to London. Zammit, a cousin of the Messinas, had never made any bones about what was required of his bride and, wholly without reservation of any sort, she was a willing partner. Daily at noon Gian-Franco drove his wife from their small semi in Mitcham into the West End where she carried on business from two rooms in Berwick Street. During this time, and until she took her last client near midnight, Gian-Franco would play cards in a room above a barber's shop in Wardour Street either losing from or adding to, his wife's receipts of the previous day.

Therése had the services of a maid, another, older French woman named Bérthe Petit. Herself an ex-West End whore, her proud boast was that during the war years she had entertained no less than eleven members of the coalition cabinet. Their second floor rooms were reached by a narrow, uncarpeted stairway and the red door bore a card informing callers that "Miss Lamour" was entertaining (Therése advertised herself as "Gigi Lamour – Modéle Parisienne). Once across the threshold, the would-be client was met by Bérthe and ushered into a small living room/kitchen where he was asked to wait until "Mam'zelle" was able to see him. The inner sanctum, he would later discover, was a cupboard-sized room with cracked and crumbling lathe-and-plaster walls, a double bed and (strictly for winter usage only) a two bar electric fire. Therése, in a peignoir which she insisted on keeping on throughout, would receive payment (plus five shillings for Bérthe), the client would be advised to remove as little clothing as possible and entertainment would be concluded in less time than it would take to boil a fairly firm egg.

The man called Michael Folmer arrived *chez* Therése a little after 9.00pm. He was admitted by Bérthe who settled him on a wooden chair in the ante-room. "Mam'zelle" she said offhandedly "will be a few minutes." As he sat and looked around the room, at the two armchairs, the heavily curtained window, the small table and the lamp with its tasselled, maroon lampshade, he became aware of a strong smell of garlic, not that associated with the raw, chopped garlic of salads but the stronger, pungent, almost acrid scent of the fried or roasted cloves.

The door to what he assumed was the bedroom opened and an elderly man was framed in the doorway. Seeing Folmer, awkwardly he put his hand to his face and muttering what Folmer took to be words of thanks, he left hurriedly. Therése, clad in her peignoir and green towelling mules, smiled at Folmer, indicating for him to join her.

Bérthe attended to dinner. Going to a small gas oven, she took out a baking tray containing a half-leg of lamb, liberally stuffed with sliced garlic cloves. Tilting the tray, she basted boiling fat and meat juices on to the joint, watching as the liquid seeped into the garlic-filled crevices. Her mind on French beans and apple compôte, she stirred the meat residue and fat in the bottom of the tin, hoping that the all-essential gravy would form, but in an instant she was jarred back to reality by the sound of Mam'zelle's emergency bell.

The sound was brief, barely a split second but there was no mistaking: someone had pressed the button on the wall above Mam'zelle's bed and with a client on the premises Bérthe knew what was required of her. Dropping her basting spoon, she burst through the bedroom door, almost instantly recoiling with horror and fear.

The client was on the bed fully clothed, his legs either side of Therése. In his right hand he held a knife, short and of the type used by butchers for "boning out" carcasses. Mam'zelle's gown had been slashed from neck to knee and what Bérthe took to be intestines had spilled out on to the bed cover and were reaching towards the floor. The bed was soaked in blood and there was a splash on the wall behind the bed, so recent that it had not finished its downward flow towards the linoleum. Bérthe ran back into the living room and opening the door leading to the stairs she screamed a mixture of French and English: "Murder, oh, Mon Dieu, Mam'zelle is dead, oh, *aidez-moi, aidez-moi.*" From the corner of her eye, seeing the man leaving the bedroom she turned and, severely burning both her hands but oblivious to the pain, she picked up the tin of roast meat with its hot fat and flung it straight at the head of her mistress's assailant.

Police Cadet 8718 Roger Desborough had left Hendon Training School three weeks earlier. Posted to Bow Street police station, he had been allocated a room in the single man's quarters at Trenchard House in nearby Broadwick

Street. A religious man who had been ridiculed in the Hendon dormitory for kneeling to pray before going to bed, he had never left his birth place in rural Gloucestershire before joining the police and he found that the vibrancy and excitement of London was an adventure to be explored, something strange to him, something with which he had to come to terms if he was perform effectively as a police officer. That evening he was on his way back to Trenchard House having been wandering the West End streets, looking and trying to become accustomed to what would for at least the next quarter century be his home city, and as he passed the open door in Berwick Street and heard Bérthe's scream for help his heart leapt into his mouth. There was no time to remember what he had been taught at Hendon: he turned into the short passage at the foot of the stairs where, he would later recall, he smelt garlic.

On the first landing he saw a woman screaming in a foreign language and as he climbed the first few stairs he realised that she had been joined by a man who was also screaming and frantically rubbing at his eyes and face which seemed to covered in some sort of grease. As he watched, the man slipped and fell down the entire flight landing at Desborough's feet.

"Ees 'im" screamed the women: "ees 'im. 'E 'as killed *la pauvre* Therése."

Once at West End Central police station Folmer had said, in effect, nothing at all. He had given his name as Michael Folmer but had declined to make any further statement. Although his guilt was quite evident, Castle would have preferred a statement of admission but this was not forthcoming. He was questioned for a considerable period by both Castle and Cutler but remained silent, declining to give any home address or any details of any employment, family or general antecedent history. His fingerprints were not on record at the Yard, the inference being that he had no previous convictions of any sort.

As he read this, to his surprise Gregory felt the hairs rise on the back of his neck as he realised that the fingerprints of this man, certainly dead for many years, were identical with those on the Ripper letter, almost as though they had climbed out of the pit beneath the scaffold.

On his third appearance at Bow Street Magistrates (and on the occasion he was committed for trial at the Old Bailey) Folmer was represented by a Counsel who had been briefed by Lassiter Varcoe a West End firm of solicitors. In his report Castle had noted that this was a not a matter of free legal aid but that discreet enquiries on his part had failed to get any significant information as to who was funding the defence. Folmer had been kept in custody at Brixton Prison since his arrest and he appeared at the Old Bailey seven months later. He was represented by a leading QC and a junior counsel and pleaded not guilty to the charge of murder. His defence that he had been engaged in robbing Thérése Bougon and that he had panicked when she screamed and pressed her alarm button was, of course, ludicrous and this, coupled with his disinclination to give any evidence on his own behalf and his inability to call any witnesses, lead to the inevitable: the jury retired for fifteen minutes and quite rightly convicted him and he was sentenced to death. Still he said nothing: there was no home address and no antecedent history; medical examinations in Brixton both before and after the trial revealed no suggestion of any mental disturbance and despite further detailed enquiries by Castle and Cutler nothing further was ascertained relative to his background. An appeal of the verdict on the grounds that the judge had misdirected the jury on various points was dismissed, the Home Secretary saw no reason why justice should not take it's course and Michael Folmer was hanged at Pentonville prison on 12 January 1958 by the public hangman.

****

After curries in Brick Lane Gregory and Mott got back to Leman Street well after 11.00pm. Gregory, by then absorbed and keyed up with the enquiry, did not fancy the idea of aggravation with his wife: he needed to relax, to unwind, and above all he need conversation. In his office he produced scotch and two glasses and for an hour he went through what he knew of the Folmer aspect, putting Mott fully in the picture.

"So this geezer who's got no form chops up a tom in Berwick Street and to all intents and purposes gets caught on the job" said Mott. "Then he's straight off to Savile Row, charged, backwards and forwards to Bow Street and Brixton – up to the Bailey, convicted, sentenced, sent to Pentonville and topped a couple of months later. That's it isn't it?"

"In a nutshell, yes."

"He gives no address, no job, nothing. So the name could be wrong as well?"

"Bert Castle's report details the efforts they made to find out who he was: the tax people, unemployment, all of that and nothing – nothing at all."

"It's a strange name, Folmer."

"Yes it is. Strathearn's done a bit of digging and says there's no record of anyone in the country with that name."

"Could be foreign, I suppose."

"That's what I thought."

"And they said he wasn't a nutter?"

Gregory nodded. "That's what they said. No motive, no explanations, total silence – but not a nutter."

There was a silence. Gregory poured whisky and wished he hadn't given up smoking.

Mott fiddled with his tie and then: "This is what Creepy means when he talks about the "second time" whatever it was, in that letter. He's talking about Folmer, isn't he?"

Gregory looked at him, frowning and biting his upper lip. Suddenly he was angry, very angry with himself. He pulled a file from, the dozen or so on his desk, leafed through and read: '…first time I had my fill and never did get buckled – but times was different then. Second time – oh, I forgot! that's a secret…' "Oh, Jesus Christ, Dave, of course it is. What a bloody idiot I am not to see it."

They sat then, each engrossed in thoughts and trying to make sense out of what was a nonsense: Jack the Ripper, back from the grave in 1957, nicked and topped and now back yet again? Strathearn, of course was right: magic or illusion – and magic does not exist.

Mott left the station after 2.00am getting the night-duty CID to drive him home. The following morning found Gregory at his desk shaved, breakfasted and as bright as he had ever been. No-one on the team knew, although Mott suspected, that he had slept in his office and that shave and shower came by way of York Hall Baths at Bethnal Green and breakfast had been taken in a café in Aldgate.

For Gregory and Mott it was a time of frustration and a time for waiting. Gregory felt totally constrained by what was going on around him and saw that anything seen as inactivity on his part, no matter how enforced by the surrounding circumstances, would be construed as incompetence and failure by those above him. Much as he had expected, the laboratory had identified a wealth of clues by way of fibres, hairs and other material on the clothes of both of the victims. Cross matching had revealed fibre traces from Kelly Goggin on "Toothpick"'s cheap clothes and vice versa and both sets of garments bore traces of a foreign fibre, not associated with either sets of clothes. Considering that Goggin had been murdered and found days prior to "Toothpick", the clear indication was that both bodies had, at some time, been in the same place and that both had come into contact with the same material which had yielded the foreign fibre. Invaluable as such evidence was, it would only go to assist the enquiry at such times as a suspect was in view – which at that time there was not. Policemen generally agree that murder is the easiest of crimes in the calendar to solve, mainly because most are unplanned, spur of the moment killings, the assailant is nearly always known to the victim and by reason of motive, opportunity and the clues that are left. The "Agatha Christie country house" type of crime with house-guests and butlers is pure fiction and most crimes committed *en famille* were generally cleared up within a matter of days. However, the man who travels from, say, London to Portsmouth where he kills for no apparent reason and then returns to London leaving no clues will, more often than not, never be apprehended and Gregory knew that both the 1888 and current Ripper crimes lay in that area.

That Strathearn was right in his assessment that the two murders and the Folmer matter went hand-in-glove could not be disputed but Gregory wondered how he would be able to handle what were two very serious investigations, one of which needed treating with the greatest secrecy. After an hour's discussion it was agreed that for the time being Mott would run the main enquiry into the two murders and although it would appear that Gregory was in overall charge he would, in fact, be trying to come to terms with the Folmer aspect.

9.

Thursday 11 September 2003.

Stanley Baines Cutler joined the Metropolitan Police in 1945 just after the war and retired in 1975 with the rank of Detective Superintendent. For several years he had lived in a village named Fishbourne on the Isle of Wight and, said Strathearn, his lady companion - who would not be drawn as to a precise relationship - said that Stan would be pleased to see Gregory and suggested he should come early so they could have a full day. Fearing that his ancient Mondeo may not be up to the job, Gregory arranged for a Rover 75 to be available from the Yard pool and by 6.00am with two bulging briefcases he was on his way down the M3 heading towards Southampton and catching a ferry to the Isle of Wight he was in Cowes before 10.00am.

Situated in the north-east of the island, Fishbourne was a pretty, boating-orientated village situated between Ryde and Wootton Bridge. It was peaceful, genteel place, off the beaten-track, mainly inhabited by a middle-aged and retired section of middle-class England, liberal-democrats to a man, reasonable golf handicaps and for most a love of all things maritime.

Cutler's house was named "Toppings" and Gregory chuckled as he recalled Folmer's fate and also that he had noted from Cutler's record that he had been involved in enquiries into seven other capital murders, all bar one having ended on the scaffold. The property was detached and, Gregory estimated, with four bedrooms. Constructed of red brick with a pantiled roof, it had a small garden at the front and at the rear, behind an ornate and spacious conservatory, large lawned and well-maintained grounds extended to a small, shingle beach.

And suddenly there was Glad, a no-nonsense lady in her eighties who turned out to be Cutler's sister and favouring green canvas trousers, a red, ill-fitting, hand-knitted jumper which was full of holes, and worn plimsolls. "You must be thingummy from the Yard" she said, swiping at an elderly spaniel which was looking up adoringly at Gregory and at the same time rubbing itself against his trousers. She smiled behind pink-framed glasses and lowering her voice she said: "Do the old bugger the world of good, this will. Gets in a bit of a rut from time to time, he does, and this is just what he needs."

Taking one of the heavy briefcases from Gregory she said: "You've come equipped then", and walking up the path: "Stan's in the kitchen – we're just having coffee."

Like his sister, Stanley Cutler was in fine form for his age. Just over six feet tall, he had a slight stoop and deep-set lines around his eyes and mouth but his lean frame and tanned face gave fair indication of good health. His eyes were a piercing, bright and clear blue and seemed to combine with his lips in an ever-present smile – not amused or condescending but the sort of look an elderly man has when everything pleases him and he has reached an age where he sees little wrong and that he understands and is able to tolerate faults in others.

When he left "the job" Cutler said, he had worked a security consultant for a bank until he was sixty-five and when he and his wife moved to Fishbourne. He was ex- Royal Navy and both always having had a fondness for the sea, they had bought a small yacht. All was well for a few years but his wife died of cancer in 1992 and having had no children Stan suddenly found himself alone and isolated. Glad – his twin sister – who had never married, sold her home in Clacton and moved to Fishbourne "to look after the old sod."

After coffee and alone, Cutler and Gregory settled in the conservatory at the rear of the house. Cutler, eyeing the bulging briefcases said: "Looks like a big job, Mike – I can call you Mike, can I?" Gregory nodded and smiled assent and Cutler went on: "Especially to bring you all the way down here."

"Take you back a few years, Stan. Can you remember Michael Folmer?"

"Folmer? Fol – oh, yes, wasn't that the chap who killed the tom? One of the Messina girls - ?" and before Gregory could answer he went on: "They're not trying to get him pardoned as well, are they? He was guilty as hell, Mike, you take my word."

Gregory shook his head, grinning at Cutler's comment. He opened both briefcases and put the contents on the floor. "No, nothing like that." He looked at Cutler closely and: "Stan, I've been told to tell you that that what I am about to say must not go out of this room and to remind you – not that you need reminding – that the Official Secrets Act still applies, even after retirement." The need to tell Cutler this embarrassed him but Strathearn had insisted.

Cutlet nodded. "You intrigue me."

"Well, the truth is that Michael Folmer's fingerprints have turned up. On a letter written by a very current serial killer."

Silence, and Gregory could hear the chatter as the keen wind rattled the rigging of the moored yachts against their masts. He watched Glad as she patrolled the rose bushes, snipping off the dead flowers.

"Say that again."

Gregory did. "That's not possible. He's dead: I ought to know – I was there when they topped him."

Gregory nodded: "We know and we know it's not possible, but the fact remains and that's why I'm here – to try and make some sense of it."

"There is an explanation, there must be." The old man thought for a full minute and then, looking towards Glad and in a whisper: "The job's in a load of bloody bother if there's not."

They never really knew who Folmer was, Cutler said, although they always felt that he was a foreigner. "He spoke perfect English when he spoke at all, but just a few years after the war and Europe full of displaced persons whatever they called them – well, it was a possibility but we were never sure."

He explained that he had been in overall charge of the aspect of the enquiry dealing with the true identity of Michael Folmer and he was quite sure that everything possible had been done to establish an identity. As well as in-depth and detailed enquiries in the United Kingdom, through Interpol contact had been made with police forces throughout the world but all with a totally negative result – no one had any knowledge of Michael Folmer.

"Are you sure C4 haven't made a cock-up?" He used the old departmental name for the fingerprint section.

"Not a chance", said Gregory. "Believe me, they're more worried than anyone else, as you can imagine."

Cutler shook his head, smiling, and Gregory felt that he may have seen the predicament in which the notoriously stuffy fingerprint department found itself was somewhat amusing. "Who took his dabs after he was nicked, Mike?" He nodded towards Gregory's files: "Have you got that there?"

Gregory sorted through papers and produced a photo-copy of the prints taken at the time of Folmer's arrest. Looking at the back he said: "PC614C A. Sellick. An aide to CID, I suppose. Do you remember him?"

Cutler shook his head slowly: "No, Mike, it's gone I'm afraid."

The door of the conservatory opened and Glad, all gardening gloves and a blue and white polka-dotted headscarf said: "Lunch in half an hour you two." She looked at Gregory and: "Pork pie, salad and new spuds. That okay?" and before he could reply: "Me and the old fart'll have a G and T. Are you up for a small one? Driving and all that?"

After she had gone Cutler said: "He was a weird bastard, Mike, he really was. He just cut that old tom to bits for no apparent reason and then he says nothing – not a sodding word. He was creepy, Mike, really bloody strange."

Creepy, thought Gregory. Where had he heard that before, he wondered. And then he remembered and felt cold inside and uncomfortable about the back of his neck. He asked: "Did you ever find out who paid for the defence?"

Cutler laughed. "The Solicitors were….." he paused, thinking. Gregory helped: "Lassiter Varcoe."

"That's them! Well, they were a big criminal practice somewhere in the West End. They had a managing clerk, an ex DI called Percy someone. Anyway, when it was all over Bert Castle told me he ran into this Percy, at a lodge meeting I think it was, and he told Bert that there was a family hidden away somewhere and they'd paid. He said they'd coughed up because they felt they had to, if you see what I mean, but they were all hoping that he'd get topped and no one'd find out who he really was and the family name would stay intact. I think they knew he was a bad bastard and the best thing was if he got what was coming to him and it would all be forgotten in time."

"And nobody ever knew – who they were, I mean?"

Cutler shook his head: "Not as far as I knew. My recollection is that Percy told Bert that only the partners knew and it was something they were going to guard with their lives."

After lunch and back in the conservatory with coffee Gregory said: "Tell me about the hanging."

"In Pentonville. Not much to tell, really. Bert told me to go, cunning old bastard. He didn't like anything like that. Anyway, it's everyone walk down the passage just before nine, the prisoner governor, the quack, the executioner and his mate and the deputy Lord Lieutenant of the county. They put a carpet down so chummy can't hear anyone coming. Everyone's outside the condemned cell and they open the door and at the same time they open another door right opposite. In goes the hangman and his mate, literally seconds later and he's out with his hands strapped, across the passage, a few seconds more and Bang! – he's gone."

"Quick as that?"

"Quick as that."

"And he never said anything?"

Cutler blinked behind his glasses, his blue eyes clouding over and a frown on his face. Gregory knew he had hit a nerve.

The silence seemed never-ending and then: "He did, you know, he bloody did." The eighty-one year old brains – Gregory wished his were half as sharp – were working and the old man chewed his lip. Then: "He walked across that passage and he must've seen me in the crowd. He laughed and he said to tell Bert that it wasn't all over and that he should watch out for him, something like that. It was so quick, Mike, like I said – seconds: he was still talking when he was on the drop and I think he was laughing when he went."

Back at Cowes Gregory found he had an hour to wait for the ferry. Putting the Rover in the line of waiting cars he bought a Daily Telegraph and a cup of tea in the buffet. When he had time, Gregory liked the crossword although he would admit he rarely finished it.

One across: "Riding to Somerset town on Oaks winner" (15 letters). Clever bastard, he thought and pencilled in "Weston-super-Mare."

Twenty-six across: "Despite shiny trousers?" (15 letters). He'd seen that before and in went "Notwithstanding."

Seven down was an anagram. He hated anagrams. He wrote the thirteen letters in a disorganised jumble on the side of the paper and stared at them for what seemed to be like half an hour without an idea. His mind drifted off to Stan and Glad Cutler, to Lassiter Varcoe and to "Creepy" and along the bottom of his paper he wrote: "MICHAEL FOLMER."

He stared at the two words, pinching and rubbing the bridge of his nose behind his glasses and then, one by one, he crossed letters out and beneath them he wrote four words: "I CAME FROM HELL."

Back in the car and with his hand shaking he phoned Mott. "I think we've got a bigger problem than we ever thought, Dave."

Later, on the boat and with the butterflies still in his stomach and with Cowes receding in the distance he went back to his crossword.

Seven down: "Take positive action: never assess it" (13 letters).

Without hesitation he wrote in: "Assertiveness."

10.

The letter from his wife was simple enough. Sealed in a pink envelope he found it on the kitchen table, a few lines in girlish writing. She was unhappy, she said: she was contemplating a divorce and it would be better if he moved out immediately if only on a temporary basis. She pointed out that his continued presence in the marital home would, in her opinion, only go to exacerbate the situation and that should he not leave she would have no option but to seek legal advice. As he packed a suitcase, Gregory felt guilty as he sensed relief: as much as he loved his daughter, his home life had been miserable for some years but it was only in recent months that he had come even to consider that things may have come to a head. Now though, as he threw clothes into the old case and a Nike sports bag, he felt sad but at the same time elated, almost as though a new segment of his life was about to commence and that he was off on another adventure.

Through Mott, who he had felt obliged to tell, the whole of the investigation team soon became aware of his plight. There was an embarrassing moment when Archie McGibbon came into his office: "Guvnor", he said hesitantly, "I heard you've got a bit of trouble and I thought I'd mention that I've got this big flat in Hackney, three bedrooms there are, and you'd be very welcome to stay there until you get fixed up."

Gregory, touched by the offer, was about to accept when he saw Mott and Iannou framed in the doorway behind McGibbon and out of his view. Both were frantically making signs – shaking heads, hands waved in a negative manner in front of the face, a hand drawn sharply across the throat – clearly indicating that acceptance on Gregory's part of this offer, no matter how kind and thoughtful, would be a grave error. He coughed, uncomfortable and feeing guilty, and explained that he had a flat lined up and that in the meantime he would be staying with his mother. Later he learned the true meaning of "a fate worse than death" when he heard stories of a large and unsanitary cat, washing up left until the maggots crawled and McGibbon's bed which was rumoured not to have had a change of sheets since, as Mott put it, "the old king died."

Two days later (during which time he did not stay with his mother but with his younger brother) he had done a deal on a one-bedroom flat in Fulham. Situated in an unfashionable turning off Filmer Road the terraced house had been converted into three flats, Gregory's being on the first floor. There was a small lounge/dining room a large bedroom with a double bed, a well fitted kitchen and a small but adequate bathroom with both bath and shower. The furnishings were of the type purchased by landlords at Lotts Road auctions especially for flat-letting but although he did not feel "at home" he knew he would be comfortable and that the flat would serve until circumstances changed.

****

The arrival of the second letter, this one sent direct to Gregory, provoked a change of policy.

> **Dear Old Boss,**
>
> *I am really surprised at you! Calling all the coppers off so early – you're never going to buckle me like that. What did you think of my handiwork, old Boss? Better than I used to be, eh. Did you like the train ticket? Poor old Druitt – it were never him you know. It is all getting so difficult, what with Berners Street gone and no whores on the manor any more but I'll be about my work just the same. Two next time, Old Boss. Catch me if you can – but where will I be I wonder.*
>
> *From Hell,*
> *Jack.*

With Mott, Gregory took the letter to the Yard. This time no fingerprints could be traced and with the document copied and sealed in an evidence bag they met with Strathearn.

The Old Man was adamant: "Well, it's quite clear now what we've got to do: we've got no option but to put the press fully in the picture and the public, especially the toms and street girls, have to be told in no uncertain terms that there's some sort of maniac loose."

There was a knock on the door and he paused as the tea lady requested his order and three coffees were set on the desk. Then:

"The Folmer aspect, of course, must be kept under wraps until Mike here has some answers."

"The press'll have a field day" said Gregory, remembering the headlines in the paper his wife had thrown at him. He felt sick as he thought about Christians and lions and sacrificial lambs. He had no reservations whatsoever as to how he would be seen in the event of failure and he knew very well that Strathearn, nice man that he was, would be ensuring that no criticism could be levelled in his direction.

"There's nothing we can do about the press, Mike, nothing at all. If we don't go public and another girl dies they'll have our guts for garters you can be sure of that."

He looked at his calendar: "Just over two weeks to the Double Event, then - and he could do it just about anywhere, the bastard. And we haven't got any ideas at all."

"Just the white van", said Gregory, the frustration he felt showing in his tone. "And there's a few of those about."

The Old Man gulped half a cup of the lukewarm coffee and: "There's nothing more that we can do. Let the press know the situation - go on that Crime Watch thing, Mike, that might be a good idea – but above all let the public know that (a) there's a nutter on the loose and (b) that we're doing everything humanly possible to catch the sod. We know he's the letter writer because of his reference to the train ticket which he couldn't have known about unless he did it –"

"What about the van?"

"No, don't release that. Don't let him know we know about that or he'll go and change it and that's the last thing we need right now."

"And what about the so-called Michael Folmer? What do we do about that side of it?"

Strathearn shook his head: "There's a connection, there's got to be, but for the life of me I can't see it. This bastard with the van: what do you call him – Creepy, is it? Well, as I see it, Creepy's got some way of leaving Folmer's dabs all over the place and now we know, due to Michael here's detective ability, that Michael Folmer is an anagram of I Came From Hell, and we also know that the original Ripper signed himself From Hell just the same as Creepy is doing now –"

"And we know that there's no such thing as magic," said Gregory, sensing sarcasm in the reference to his "detective ability" and looking at The Old Man with a half smile on his face, "nor ghosts –"

Suddenly, seeing that he was being mocked, albeit very gently, Strathearn was angry, or gave that impression: "I wouldn't take the piss, if I was you, Michael. As I see it, you're not in the best position to do that. If you believe in ghosts and ghoulies, that's fine – but I'd keep it to myself if I was you."

"Guv, that's not fair" said Gregory, "no one's talking about magic or returning from the grave or even bloody ghosts –"

Strathearn, smiling now, broke in: "You are – you distinctly said two minutes ago those very words –"

"Be fair, Guv. I said that we know that those things don't apply and I was going to say that we're looking at some jiggery-pokery somewhere." He looked at Mott for support, grinning: "isn't that what I said, Dave?"

"I have to say, Guvnor –"

The Old Man laughed. "You're a right pair of bastards, you are." He got up from his desk and walked to the window and gazed out across the city. "Tell me about these solicitors, Lassimans whatever they're called, they must have case papers in their archive – they'll tell us what they know about Folmer – and if they won't, then get a Court order."

"Lassiter Varcoe", said Gregory. "They're long gone I'm afraid. They were involved in some sort of trouble with the Law Society in the early seventies. Lassiter was struck off and committed suicide the next year and Varcoe was also struck off and went to South Africa and died there in 1982. When they got into bother the Law Society put another firm in to caretake Lassiter Varcoe and they took on most of the existing clients when it was all finally wound up. They're called Gunnell Grimes and Dodd and they're still going strong in St. Albans."

"Can they – or will they – help?"

Gregory shook his head: "They only took on existing clients and Folmer was not current by any stretch of the imagination. I have spoken to the senior partner and he says they have no idea what happened to the Lassiter archive. Guvnor, this is thirty years ago, no one wants to know now. It's a needle in a haystack and we're not going to get anywhere down that path, I'm sure of it."

"What about the Law Society?"

"Well, they're as helpful as they can be, but the bottom line is that they don't know what to say other than try an advert in the Law Society Gazette or whatever it is - and they are very quick to point out that the dreaded "client confidentiality" will still exist.

Strathearn switched his attention from the skyline and deep in thought he studied a jet as it progressed through the clouds above London, heading, he imagined, somewhere warm, exotic and problem-free. He knew that in the event of Gregory's failure it was odds-on that at some stage he would be called upon to report to the Home Office illustrating that everything possible that could be done had been covered and that if flaws in the enquiry were perceived early retirement would almost certainly be strongly suggested. Minutes passed as he pondered, figuring what would be the best move.

"Right. We'll dig the bastard up. Get an exhumation order or whatever it takes, Michael, and we'll see if there's any fingerprints on what's left –"

"Not a hope, Guv."

"No, probably not, but we'll get some DNA –" and holding up a finger to Gregory who was about to interrupt: "I don't know what that'll give us either - but we're better off with it than without it. I'll speak to the Coroner at St. Pancras and you get over to the Home Office – but for Christ's sake keep this under wraps."

Mott, who had kept silent until then, said: "Stan Cutler was there when they topped Folmer, right? And he says he laughed and made some comment about telling Bert Castle that it's not all over and he should watch out for him."

Gregory nodded. "Along those lines."

"Right. Well, taking into account there's no ghosts coming back to haunt us all, then it's clear to me that when he said that on the drop, Folmer knew there was something dodgy somewhere about the dabs and that they were likely to surface again –"

Strathearn made to interrupt but Mott continued: " – and taking into account he had no form and his dabs had never been taken before, then whatever it was that caused him to make that comment happened between when he was nicked by that cadet and when he got topped."

****

The young man at the Home Office (Department of Prisons) in Page Street, Westminster was very helpful. Until the word exhumation was mentioned. In a dark blue, pinstripe three-piece suit with a deal too much yellow silk handkerchief flopping out of the breast pocket, he looked momentarily flustered.

"Oh", he said , "exhumation: that's diggin' 'em up, isn't it? Well! That's new: I've never done one of them before." He smiled at Gregory and fingering the gigantic knot in his wide, silk tie and evidently regaining confidence and composure, he said: "You just wait here a moment and I'll get some advice."

Gregory waited while assistance was sought from those better qualified and after a few minutes the young man was back. "Yes, well, there's precedent for it, diggin' 'em up, that is – but not for putting 'em back in again, if you see what I mean. Ruth Ellis was uplifted – that's the word they use, uplifted; and that 'Anratty, so was he, and lots of others."

He shot his cuffs, fiddling with gold cuff-links set with red stones and then: "See, when they uplifted them, they took them off to be interred somewhere else: they can do that, relatives can, after a few years. What you want, though, that's not at all the same is it? I mean what you want is to dig one up, snip off a few bits here and there and put him back again. No precedent for that there's not, I'm afraid."

Gregory smiled patiently. He knew that any perceived irritation or impatience on his part would be counter-productive. "There must be a procedure, surely?"

The young man smiled happily and disappeared again. Gregory looked out of the window at the traffic queuing to get through to Millbank and wished that he had sent Mott. After five minutes the young man was back.

"Well, it seems we'll have to create a precedent, won't we? Best thing is for you to send in a report detailing what you want and why and it'll all be sorted out I'm sure. Copy it to the St. Pancras Coroner – he covers Pentonville see – and I can't see there'll be too many problems, especially if it is to further a current investigation into serious crime. I mean, we'd have to notify the relatives – if there are any after all these years - but I don't suppose there's a great deal anyone can do to stop it."

He thought for a moment and then: "But look, best thing, before you get into all that, let me have his name again and I'll make sure we're looking in all the right places."

"Michael Folmer. Hanged in Pentonville in January 1958."

"Just a minute, then" and again the young man disappeared, returning after two minutes with a large leather bound book. Placing this on the counter he leafed through and then: "Well! There you are! Someone's only got there before you, haven't they?"

Gregory looked at him quizzically. The young man referred to the book, placing it on the counter diagonally so they both could see examine it. Leaning nearer, Gregory smelt expensive after-shave. "There, see. Michael Folmer – Pentonville 16 January 1958 – just like you said. But.......ten years later in 1968, permission sought to uplift – granted by Home Office and HM Coroner 23 August 1968 and body uplifted by Nodes undertakers 28 August 1968." The young man looked at Gregory proudly, evidently pleased he could help.

Gregory felt his pulse rate accelerate and his blood pressure surge. "Who made the application?"

The young man pointed to the book: "There look: solicitors called Lassiter Varcoe - acting for the family", and seeing Gregory's change of expression: "Not what you wanted to hear?"

"No, I'm afraid not."

"Oh, I am sorry." He smoothed the pages in his ledger and said: "That's all, I'm afraid. Other than he was taken off down to Devon. Re-interred in the parish of Nether Sampford, Church of St. Paul's."

Gregory could have kissed him but knew that such rashness could be misconstrued.

***

Tuesday 16 September 2003.

The village of Nether Sampford was situated in the Exe Valley and surrounded by the green and yellow hills between Exeter and Tiverton. Turning off the main road Gregory crossed the river and within a few minutes found himself in the village. Seemingly built around the intersection of four or five narrow country roads, the settlement was said to date back to Saxon times; there were a number of thatched cottages, three pubs and a small shop which doubled as the post office. One of the pubs, The Ring of Bells, was situated directly facing the church and Gregory took a room for the night, with the proviso that there may be more. He had a pint and a sandwich in the small bar and having locked his room he walked across to the small church.

St. Paul's, said the flaking notice board, dated back to 1540., the present incumbent being The Reverend Charles Savage. The grey-stoned building was in Norman style and typical of English country churches: a bell tower with a chiming clock, lych gate, cool porch and a vast, nail-studded oak door with iron hinges, lock and hoop-shaped latch handle. Inside, Gregory estimated the oak pews would seat about 150 worshippers; the floor was stone flagged and the walls bore a number of memorials to the dead of what he assumed were the parishes most prestigious families, the great and the good of Nether Sampford. The churchyard, he found, retained graves and stones dating back to the seventeenth century and earlier; it was well-kept, the grass was short and recently cut and every effort seemed to be being made to maintain it as a peaceful and sacred corner of the village.

Behind the church the cemetery sloped up towards a lane at the rear and as Gregory walked up the yew-lined path he realised that there was an extension to the grave-yard to the right, this containing the graves of the most recently deceased. In this section he found stones dating back to 1936, but as he walked along the lines of memorials he realised that none related to Michael Folmer, although he knew that the body may well lie in an unmarked plot. He walked back across the grass to the path and turning towards the church he almost bumped into a little man whose dress left him in little doubt that that he was the Reverend Savage. In his early seventies and barely 5'2" tall he was portly or rotund (Gregory could not decide which was the kinder) and the clearness of his grey eyes broke up what was an otherwise very florid countenance. Wearing a dog-collar and a cassock, the latter belted and stretched across his middle to such an extent that the button-holes evidenced signs of stretch-enlargement, he was smoking a small cigar.

"Ah! I saw you from the pub. Are you just passing through – or is there anything I can help you with?" He held out his hand: "Charlie Savage – the vicar here – for my sins. Or rather lack of them!" He spoke with a slight West Country accent, tinged with Oxford and the ward-room or officer's mess and, if it is possible to laugh as one speaks, Charlie Savage had the knack.

A man for all seasons, Gregory thought, and shook his hand. "Michael Gregory. Yes, I'm trying to sort out a branch of my family tree" he lied, "but I think I may have been mislead somewhere along the line."

"Mmnn, Gregory – I don't think we've got a Gregory, but we can always see what the church records say."

"No, it's not Gregory. It's on my grandmother's side." He wondered if lying to a priest was any worse than to anyone else. "The name I'm researching is Folmer."

As Gregory looked into the little man's face he knew that whatever said next would be a lie. As he had spoken the name he saw the slight change of expression, the drop of eye-focus and the almost imperceptible movement of lip which has cost poker players millions.

"Folmer? No, I can't say I've heard that one – I can certainly say that –"

"Can we look at the records?"

Savage half-turned towards the door of the church. "Not today, I'm afraid. Too busy today, old chap – and I'm in Exeter all day tomorrow at the cathedral."

Gregory knew when he was being side-lined. He nodded his thanks and leaving Savage to go about his devotions or whatever he needed to do in the church, he walked to the village square and dialled his office from his mobile telephone.

"Dave I'm being pissed about down here and I need some help. I want you to get on to the Exeter council or whatever covers the burials in St. Paul's Church, Nether Sampford. I need to know the names of all of the people buried in the churchyard after 28 August 1968, say for a year. Can you do that now and get back to me?"

He wandered round the village fascinated by the immaculately-kept white cottages some with their thatched roofs. The stillness of the air and the peace of the countryside compared to the crash and clatter of the city seemed to bring out in him a sense of lethargy and relief of pressure which he could not understand. At the end of one narrow street the cottages came to an abrupt end and the tarmac road changed to a wide bridle-path, red clay with grass growing between the tracks of farm vehicles. He picked blackberries, staining his fingers and licking the juice, something he had not done since boyhood. Suddenly the peace was shattered and he cursed mobile telephones.

Of the seven people buried in St. Paul's churchyard between 28 August 1968 and 28 August 1969, four were women, Mott told him. Of the remaining three one was a man aged 86 and another a boy of 14 who had drowned in the Exe. "That leaves one", said Gregory suspecting that Mott was keeping the best until last.

"Have you got a pen, Guv?" A pause and then: "John Hawker Marriott born 1923 and buried there in St. Paul's 30 August 1968."

"Two days after they dug up Folmer."

The headstone, a plain and unostentatious marble slab read:

To the Memory of John Houseman Marriott,
Born 5 May 1890 and departed this life 12
June 1973.

**And to his wife, Victoria Jane Marriott, born
23 September 1892 and called to join him 7
May 1975.**

**And to their beloved son John Hawker Marriott
Born 16 June 1923 and laid to rest here 30
August 1968.**

Forgive us our Trespasses.

Gregory, squatting and writing in his notebook.

"I thought you told me you were looking for someone called Folmer."

Gregory stood up and looked across the grave at Savage. "And I thought you told me you'd never heard the name."

He took out his warrant card and handed it to the priest "It's a criminal offence to mislead police carrying out an investigation."

Savage smiled: "I wouldn't have mislead you Michael, not if I had known who you were, would I now?"

Tea at the vicarage. It reminded him of the title of a repertory theatre play or the start of a short story in a women's magazine. The tea was strong, though, and Savage's study was comfortable and conducive to conversation.

"What is it that you want to know about John Marriott – if that is who you are interested in?"

"As much as you can tell me – if he is the man I am interested in."

Savage smiled and lit one of his small cigars. "Well, there's not much point beating about the bush, is there? You've obviously done your homework and you know that poor John and the so-called Michael Folmer are one and the same, so where do we go from here?"

"You can tell me what you know."

Savage poured more tea: "First, can you tell me what it's about, this enquiry of yours?"

It had been well anticipated that this question would come from one source or another and total honesty being out of the question a half-truth had been agreed with Strathearn. "Well", said Gregory, "I am authorised to say that as a result of two anonymous letters we have reason to suppose that there is a possibility that there is more to the conviction for murder of a man named Michael Folmer than had previously been thought and that his conviction and subsequent events may have a bearing on a current investigation into serious crime."

Savage sipped his tea and grinned. Gregory did not think for one minute that he had fooled him.

"Police-speak if ever I heard it."

Gregory nodded: "That's all you're getting. Now it's your turn."

"Well, John Marriott was born in Nether Sampford and his sister still lives here. The Marriotts were, and still are, a family of some substance and what happened all those years ago had a devastating effect."

"What is your understanding of what took place?"

"That the lad went mad; that he murdered a street woman in London, refused to allow his true identity to be known in an effort to preserve the honour of his family and to save his parents from the disgrace and that he was hanged."

"The doctors of the day said he was sane enough but, well, who knows?"

Savage stubbed out his cigar and wiped his fingers on a large red handkerchief. "I came to Nether Sampford three years after John was buried here. Suzanne, that is his sister, had told everyone that he had died in Australia in 1968 - in some sort of accident she said it was – and that she'd him brought back here for burial." He looked at Gregory: "No one queried it then, Michael: but now?"

"I'll have to see her, you know that don't you?"

"Yes."

Back in his room in the Ring of Bells Gregory phoned Strathearn and updated him and then he dozed, a fitful nap, full of dreams of hangmen and condemned cells and Mott and train tickets, the cooing and squawking of pigeons in the fir trees outside his room being the only thing preventing him from drifting into deeper and far more welcome sleep. Suddenly, just before 6.00pm he was jerked into reality by a violent knocking on his bedroom door. "Charlie Savage 'as bin on the phone, sir. 'Er says you'm having dinner up to Suzanne Marriott's and 'e'll pick 'ee up seven sharp."

***

Half an hour later and while Gregory was shaving in his oak-beamed bathroom, the window open and the sound of the evening birds arguing and twittering over roosting places for the forthcoming night, in another, far less pleasant pub two hundred miles north, the goal posts were being moved.

Following an extensive press release, the London evening papers had been prolific in their coverage of the murders. Photographs of both victims (extracted from criminal record files) were published, as were pictures of the Canterbury Pilgrim, Hanbury Street and Durward Street. Much was made of the "Ripper" angle with copies of news items of that era and, inevitably, parallels being drawn between the competency of Inspector Abberline (who investigated the original killings) and Gregory.

Unlike the Ring of Bells in Nether Sampford, the Row Barge in Lower Clapton, East London was neither ideal nor was it idyllic. Situated in a bleak turning off Lea Bridge Road there were no pigeons or oak beams, there were no cosy bars with log fires and there was little in the way of cheer or comfort. On its own, with brick and rubble-strewn sites on either side, the Row Barge was awaiting demolition and the current licensees, Mickey and Kath Warne, were due to move to a larger and better pub in Croydon. Since the redevelopment of the area had commenced, the pub had opened rarely: never at lunchtimes and evenings only when Mickey or Kath felt like it. Apart, that is, from Saturdays, when they both felt obliged to entertain such locals as were still living in the area.

But that night was not a Saturday. Coming home from Tescos, Kath found Mickey asleep in front of the television. She shook him awake and thrust the evening paper under his nose: "Look at that, Mickey: that's the tart who was in the bar that night that Connie Farmer was took bad and went off home. I remember her coming in just as the Farmer tribe was leaving – with that weird geezer, she was. I remember saying to you she looked like a hooker." She shook him again and pinched his arm: "Lazy bastard! Look at this, will you. I'm going to phone Old Bill."

Later that evening Kath Warne explained that the Farmer's were the only regulars that the Row Barge had. The family had used the pub for years and, she said, their regular attendance on a Saturday night was the only real reason they bothered to open. The Saturday night in question – she was sure it was 30 August – the entire family had turned out *en bloc* to celebrate the silver wedding anniversary of George and Connie Farmer, the heads of what was a large local family.

Seated in the dingy bar, sour with the smells of stale beer and tobacco of thousands upon thousands of hours of boozing and conviviality, Barney Iannou and Jackie Daniel listened and wrote.

"Well, they all got here about half six – must've been Farmers from all over bleedin' London. Mickey said there was more Farmers here that night than what they gets at the Smithfield Show." She laughed at her joke and nudged her husband, poking him in the ribs with her elbow: "Didn't you, Mickey?" She was a plump woman, in her forties and with pleasant features beneath a fringe of dyed blonde hair.

"We'd laid on the usual sausage rolls and all that and Connie and George had stuck four hundred notes behind the bar as a starter. Anyway, by about nine they was well away, singing and going on, no trouble nothing like that – just a good old knees up." She grinned at her husband who was equally stout, and indicating the battered and bottle-stained upright piano in the corner of the bar: "They had Mickey on the bleedin' joanner non-stop, they did – a right old go they had."

Iannou, anxious to get to the point, asked: "When did she come in, Mrs. Warne? The woman in the paper?"

Kath was not to be outdone: they would have all or nothing. "Well, about half nine I suppose it was, Connie says she's feeling a bit dickey and she goes out to the lady's and pukes up. I never thought nothing of it, I mean after all what she'd had, God knows how many gin and limes and then they're making her have 'Arvey bleedin' Wallbangers – one after the other, they were. Well, about half ten, twenty to eleven she's out cold, Connie is: I took her in the lady's and tried wet hankies and all that, but a waste of time, weren't it?"

Seeing that Jackie Daniel had stopped writing and that Barney Iannou's interest may have been waning, Mickey Warne took over: "Anyway, about then they all decides to get the old woman home: I suppose they carried on back at their place, but anyway, as Kath says, about twenty to eleven they're gone." He went behind the bar and poured a pint of bitter and looked enquiring at Iannou and Jackie, both of whom shook their heads.

"Well, just as the last of them's gone out the door and I'm thinking I'll shut up and go to bed, in comes this couple. Pissing down with rain it was, the tart looked like a drowned rat, she really did." He sipped his beer and looked at Iannou: "Are you sure you won't have one?"

Barney looked at Jackie who grinned: "Go on, then. I'll drive."

Warne poured another pint and put an orange juice on the bar for the WDC but before he could continue his wife took over: "They sat at the bar, they did, right on the corner there. He had a half of bitter and she had a Breezer."

Jackie Daniel asked: "And you're sure it was the same woman?"

"Oh, I'll swear to that. No bleedin' doubt at all, is there Mick?"

Warne shook his head: "No. It was her alright – million per cent."

"And at this time they were the only ones in the pub?"

"That's right." She took a sip of her husband's beer and: "I was washing glasses and tidying up and that but I could hear them talking, clear as that, I could. He's trying to get her to stay the night with him and I heard him talking about two hundred quid and telling her it was only up the road. Next thing is, I'm standing over there, right, by the till, and I see him in the mirror, plain as that: he takes out a wad of money you could choke a bleedin' donkey with: he gives her a handful of notes and next thing is he's ordered two more drinks and they went and sat over there."

She pointed to a small table and four chairs. "Laughing, they was; she had a couple of fags and used the lady's and that was it, really. They went about a quarter past eleven and Mickey saw them getting in this van, didn't you?"

"I went out the back to make sure the cellar was locked and I see them go to this white Transit parked on the demolition site next door. They had a quick kiss and then they jumps in the van and off."

Iannou, knowing the answer before he asked, said: "I don't suppose you got the number?"

Warne shook his head: "I had no reason, did I?"

Iannou got up and walked to the table and four chairs: "Who does the cleaning."

"We both do", said Kathy Warne. "Mind you, no-one's been in here since then and it'll have to be given a going over again before next Saturday."

"And you're sure he said he only lived up the road?"

"Quite sure."

"Tell me what he looked like."

"Much older that her, he was: must have been over sixty, grey hair, very thin geezer, very smart. Not much more than that, really."

***

Suzanne Marriott lived on the outskirts of Nether Sampford in what Savage said was known as a 'Devon long house'. Within red-brick garden walls, the thatched, white-rendered property was on two stories, long and narrow and surrounded by immaculately-kept gardens with lawns at front and rear. The sash windows were free of double-glazing, the thatch was plain and without the fussy and over-stated embellishments of reed peacocks or squirrels, there was an ancient boot-scraper on the front porch and the whole vista was of taste and refinement.

A jangling bell was answered by a single, loud and resounding "whough" and seconds later the door was opened by a tiny woman, tweed skirt, cardigan and glasses, bent double evidently by age or ailment, and an enormous St. Bernard dog. The little woman smiled and looking up said: "Evenin' Charlie: missus says you'm to sit in the drawin' room an' have a drink an' she won't be a moment or two." She pushed the dog out of the way, muttering what to Gregory sounded very much like: "Gertcha, stupid big bugger" and showed them into the flagstone- floored hall.

The drawing room was long and low. The yellow-brown tan of the polished wooden floor boards of several centuries was broken by occasional rugs, the walls were white and bore paintings, both portrait and landscape, and the ceiling was beamed and unoriginal only where electric light fittings had been fitted. The furniture consisted of several armchairs and settees, all unmatched but with carefully selected linen loose-

96

covers; there was a grand piano, closed and with numerous silver-framed photographs on the polished black wood; several occasional and coffee tables were strategically placed and, at the far end of the room, a log fire burning in a stone fireplace which bore the smoke discolouration of centuries.

"This is Mags Doidge, Mr. Gregory", said Savage: "She's been Suzanne's housekeeper for more years than any of us like to remember – and her husband's responsible for the gardens." They sat in armchairs and the dog occupied a large rug. Mags Doidge poured pink gins – no selection was offered – and they were alone.

"I think you'll find she's quite a character, Suzanne Marriott" said Savage. "She's an institution in Nether Sam – nearest thing to a squire we've got, I suppose." He sipped his gin and pulling a face and in a low voice: "Filthy stuff – that's all she'll let you drink before dinner – says it doesn't deaden the palate, if you please." He looked round, apparently fearful of being overheard: "And you can't smoke in the house – she makes me go into the bloody garden!"

Stifling laughter, Gregory asked: "She never married?"

Savage shook his head: "No, never", and again in a low voice: "Mind you, she was never short of male company in her younger days, so I'm told, but I don't think there was ever anybody permanent."

As he spoke, the dog, apparently sensing the arrival of his mistress, struggled to his feet and with a line of silver spittle inching floorwards from his jaws, gazed at the door, tail swaying like some feathery punkah.

Gregory estimated that Suzanne Marriott was in her late seventies. She was tall, slim and her white hair was carefully, although not fussily, arranged. Wearing woollen trousers and a sleeveless jacket over a plum-coloured blouse, she favoured a single string of tiny pearls, a small and evidently ancient gold watch and a ring with a stone he imagined to be onyx on the little finger of her left hand. Behind rimless glasses her face was free of makeup; her hazel-green eyes were clear and although she bore the wrinkles and lines of age, it was plain that she had been a not inconsiderable beauty. There was a hint, the merest insinuation, of a discreet and expensive perfume, and overall there was the air of confidence and assuredness of a woman who understood the problems that life had to offer and had dealt with them as best she could.

The men stood up: "Suzanne", said Savage, "this is Chief Inspector Michael Gregory from Scotland Yard. And Michael, may I present Miss Suzanne Marriott."

She went to the drinks table and Gregory watched as she put drops of Angostura into a cut glass, immediately wiping it out with a napkin so that only the barest trace remained and half filling the glass with gin. She sat on a settee, pushing away the great dog as it sought to climb up beside her. She smiled at Gregory and said: "Well, Michael Gregory from Scotland Yard, I am not going to say that I am pleased to see you – because, honestly, I am not. And I am not going to say that I always knew this would happen, because I did not: I believed that what was dead would stay buried – but as so often happens, things have a funny way of catching up with one."

Dinner, she said, would be at 9.00pm which left ninety minutes for them to talk, meals not being meant for serious conversation. Seeing what she felt may have been embarrassed reticence on Gregory's part, she broke the ice: "I do hope that this isn't some misplaced effort to say that Johnnie was innocent: he wasn't you know, he was as guilty as hell and, well, to be very honest, he got just what he deserved."

Gregory sipped his gin: "No, it's nothing like that, Miss Marriott. As I explained to the Reverend Savage, we have received some anonymous letters relative to another case we are investigating and we feel that your brother's case may have some bearing."

Like Savage, she was not to be fooled: "After all these years?" She paused and then looking at Gregory, her eyes hinting amusement: "What can I tell you?"

Gregory smiled. Guiltily, he wondered what she had looked like forty years before and how she had stayed single, but hiding his fascination he said: "Everything, really. Right from the start."

She poured more drinks and placed a small dish of olives on the coffee table in front of them. Back on the sofa, she tucked her legs beneath her and brushed dog's hairs off her trousers.

Johnnie, she said, was born in 1923 which made him two years older than her. He had been born in Nether Sampford and after a preparatory school in Exeter he went off to a public school in nearby Tiverton. He went as a day-boy, she explained, the nearness of the school obviating the need for boarding. Their father was a solicitor, the senior partner of a thriving practice in Exeter with branches in Plymouth and Truro and it had always been understood that the boy would be articled into his father's office and, in time, follow him into a career in the law. "Mind you", she said, smiling sadly: "Ma and Pa understood that, but I don't honestly think Johnnie ever did. I never saw him as a lawyer and I don't think he saw himself as one either."

All he ever wanted to do, she explained, was to enjoy himself and from the time he was a small boy he was always in trouble of some sort. Not serious trouble or police trouble, but the scrumping apples and tying tin cans to cats' tails type of trouble. Clearly enjoying the memory, she said: "Once, some of the local lads had been sea fishing and they came back with an enormous conger eel one of them had caught. Anyway, Johnnie got hold of this thing and in the middle of the night he went up the Exe and put it in the best salmon pool for miles. Not right in, but just lying there, in some stones in the shallow water with a salmon head in its mouth. The next morning, the water bailiff found it and had a fit: he told the owner of the water – an awful, mean old bugger named Aaron Crask – and he got the river board people out, had the pool netted and

God knows what else." She smiled, the sad, wistful smile of those who have enjoyed good times with friends and relatives no longer here but sorely missed. "Pa walloped poor Johnnie" she said, "I can hear him now, howling in his bedroom."

She looked at Gregory and Savage and the policeman thought he detected the hint of tears. "He was such a practical joker. There was always something going on with Johnnie. Anonymous telegrams to people telling them to ignore the previous telegram - which didn't exist, of course; stealing garden gnomes and having post cards sent by them from all around the world to their owners – you name it, Johnnie did it." She sipped gin and ate an olive and then, looking closely at Gregory: "You know it was an anagram, don't you – Folmer?"

Gregory smiled and nodded: "Yes, I worked it out."

"What?" asked Savage: "Am I missing something?"

"Michael Folmer", said Gregory. It's an anagram of 'I came from Hell'."

"Oh, God, is it. I never knew."

By the time he was sixteen Johnnie Marriott had discovered both girls and alcohol and it was hard to discern which of these he saw as the most important. Unsmiling now, Suzanne described several years of telephone calls from local landlords, warnings of varying severity from the local constabulary and regular appearances at the front door of the parents of local young ladies. By that time, and knowing that the legal profession was not for his son but noting an interest in farms and farming, Pa Marriott agreed to the boy leaving school and found him a place as a trainee farm manager on a local estate.

"That was the year the war started" said Suzanne, "and it was the year he had the accident."

To get to the estate, she explained, Johnnie Marriott had to have transport. There were no buses and not being of an age to drive a car, his father bought him an old motorbike, a move the old man regretted for the rest of his life. Farm cider and motor-cycles do not mix and late one summer evening in 1939., whilst riding home from harvesting he was involved in an accident which put him in hospital for five months. "There was no one else involved which was a blessing. He just lost control and hit a tree, the fool, and got a fractured skull and broken leg for his pains. The farmer who found him ten minutes later said he was so drunk he could hardly speak. That was Johnnie all over."

She stared at Gregory a moment, and taking off her glasses and wiping them on a small silk handkerchief she said: "No breathalysers in those days, Chief Inspector, and Pa was always there to square things up. Not so much for Johnnie though: more for the family name."

Seeing their glasses were empty she made more pink gins and when seated she said: "Poor Johnnie was never right after that. He came home and never went back to work again. It wasn't that he couldn't work, his leg was right as rain, it was that he wouldn't. It was awful: he'd lie in bed until the afternoon and then he'd wander up into the woods with a shotgun and shoot pigeons and wander back just after dark. He was eating in his room, barely speaking to anyone and I knew he was never right."

Once home, he refused to see the doctor, she said. "He said he was alright, and I suppose Pa was happy to go along with that, but Ma and I knew he was far from well. Then he had some sort of fit, I always thought it was epileptic; that was on Boxing Day of 1940. Not a date I will forget."

Gregory was intrigued and fascinated, not only by what she was saying, but by Suzanne Marriott. With his drink on the table at his side, he sat in his armchair, relaxed, legs crossed and both hands behind his head and watched her; Savage, he suspected, knew only part of the story and was equally as enthralled.

"Well, Johnnie was born on the sixteenth of June 1923 and on that day in 1941 when he was eighteen years old he joined the army. There was no announcement, no discussions, nothing. That morning he opened his presents and his cards and I remember that at half past five when Pa came home he told us he'd joined up."

She looked into the fire, blinking at the heat and light and Gregory thought he saw moisture in the clear eyes. "Nothing was said, really. Ma was her usual worried and neurotic self and Pa – well, I always felt that he was pleased. Pleased and proud."

The next few years seemed a blur to her, she said. She remembered her brother coming home in uniform and she knew that he was in North Africa for a long period. She recalled that their parents waited for the short and rare letters with impatience and that her mother became frozen with fear if she saw a telegram boy within a mile of house.

"June 1944 he landed in Normandy on D Day and about a week or two later we heard that he had been wounded and that he was in hospital in Portsmouth. He came home here a month later, on some sort of sick leave and he stayed for several weeks as I recall."

"Tell me about his injuries", said Gregory, reaching for his gin.

"I never knew", she said. "All I know is that he was dug out of some bombed building where he had been buried for two or three days and that the injury was more shock and trauma than blood and broken bones. He stayed in his room for days at a time; I can remember hearing Ma say that she had heard him crying in the night a few times and there were a lot of whispered chats with the local doctor but not much more."

After a few weeks, she said, he went back to the Army and very shortly after the German capitulation he was posted to Berlin.

She breathed in deeply through her nose several times: "And then we were informed that he had been arrested for murder."

Confused, Gregory said: "You heard nothing from 1945 until the mid-fifties?"

She shook her head. "He was charged with murdering a woman in Berlin. In 1946."

Gregory said nothing. He saw that she was in control of the narrative and knew it was best she tell it her way and with as little interruption as possible. She breathed deeply again, the stress of bad memories showing. "They said that Johnnie had killed a street woman."

Savage looked at Gregory and back at Suzanne: "I never knew this."

"There is no reason why you should. At the time there was newspaper publicity of course and they reported the Court Martial in detail. Pa got the best possible solicitors and barristers for him and went over for the hearings himself; it was a nightmare at the time, Pa on the phone from Germany every evening – and phones in those days weren't like they are today – and Ma weeping and hiding herself away from the neighbours: you can imagine. Anyway, come the end, Johnnie got off: they never let me know too much, you know, but from what I remember Pa's barristers were able to convince the court or whatever it was, that the case against him was far from proved and that was the end of it. There was a bit more in the papers and then it was old news and forgotten."

She looked at Savage and: "I suppose by the time you got here –"

"Early seventies", he interjected.

"Yes, well by that time it had been long forgotten I suppose, and those that did remember would probably say nothing out of respect for Ma and Pa."

There was a silence, only broken by the soft snoring of the vast dog and the soft scratching of wisteria as the wind rattled it against the window panes. Gregory moved in his chair, not wanting to ask what he knew he must: "So, the business in London in 1957 –"

"– was the second time." She finished the sentence for him, sensing his awkwardness. "Yes, Mr. Gregory, Johnnie'd done it before."

This time the silence was prolonged, broken finally by Savage: "Perhaps I'm a bit dim, but when he was arrested again, what, only ten or eleven years later, why was it that the police didn't work out that Folmer was Johnnie Marriott? What about fingerprints, records – all that sort of thing?"

Gregory shook his head. "After he was acquitted at the Court Martial his fingerprints would have been destroyed and so they would not be on file at the Yard and could not be identified. Again, so long as he kept silent – as we know he did – the chances of identifying him today would be remote and in the fifties even more unlikely."

"But if he kept so quiet in 1957" persisted Savage, "how did the family find out about it?"

"I never knew that" said Suzanne Marriott, "but I always assumed that those Solicitors –"

"Lassiter Varcoe" said Gregory.

"- yes, that was them – I always assumed that they told Pa."

Gregory nodded agreement: "I think that's about right. One of the officers who was involved in the enquiry felt that your father may have instructed them, but it's more likely that Johnnie went to them in the first place and told them to get in touch with your parents and they took over from there."

"Well, Johnnie certainly knew all about Lassiter-thingy because Pa had used them when he had the problems in Germany but whatever happened, I can tell you that my parents were totally devastated. I remember that Pa went to London and saw Lassiters and when he came back he locked himself in his study and no one saw him for days. Later he told Ma and me that Johnnie was guilty as hell and that he was going to be hanged and we all had to pray that no one would ever know who Michael Folmer really was." Taking off her glasses she wiped her eyes and then: "There were to be no letters to him and no visits and I know it sounds awful but all we wanted – me included – was to get it over as soon as possible and hope that everyone would forget it and that no-one would ever know."

"But what had happened to him between then and Berlin? How did he live?" Savage asked.

"I only found out after my mother died that they had looked after him. They were sending money, some sort of allowance I suppose, every month. It went to Lassiter-whatever and I imagine he collected it from them. I don't know where he lived or if he did any work and I don't think anyone else did either."

Gregory looked at his blackberry-stained fingers, hoping that they would not be noticed over dinner: "But your parents evidently cared enough to have him moved down here to be buried in the local cemetery."

"Yes, they did."

"You know that later on Lassiter Varcoe were investigated by the Law Society and taken over by another firm?"

She nodded grimly. "That was awful. Poor old Pa must have been well over eighty when that happened. One morning he got a phone call out of the blue saying that they were in trouble and that afternoon I drove him to London. We stayed at the Savoy over night and at nine o'clock the next morning we were at their offices, very close to the Palladium they were. Pa was in with one of the partners for about an hour and then a mass of boxes of files, oh, must have been close on half a ton of paper, were put in the boot of the car and all over the back seat."

"The case papers?"

"Everything that related to Johnnie Marriott. The Court Martial in Berlin, all the payments they had made to him, the London trial, the appeal, moving his body down here – everything. My father was not going to take a chance on anyone seeing those files so he collected them and later he told me it took him three days to shred them in his office."

Gregory smiled and nodded. Glancing at the clock he saw it was a few minutes before nine and he knew, spoiled dinner or not, he had no option but to state the main purpose of his visit to Devon.

"Miss Marriott", he said, looking straight at her and as assuredly as he could, "I have to tell you that there is a possibility that we may apply to the Coroner to have Johnnie's body exhumed."

"Why ever would you want to do that?"

"To obtain a sample of his DNA. It would be done very discreetly, I promise and –"

He stopped mid-sentence, suddenly aware that she was laughing. "Can you get DNA from ashes, Mr. Gregory?"

"I'm sorry?"

"He was cremated, I'm afraid. The London undertakers took him to a firm in Exeter and Pa had it cleared with the Coroner. All there is in there is a metal box of ashes."

She got up and walked to the piano. Returning, she handed Gregory a silver-framed photograph of a boy in his late teens proudly sitting astride a motor-cycle, fair hair falling over his broadly-smiling face, a cigarette between the fingers of his left hand.

"That was Johnnie", she said. "Before he went mad."

II.

Thursday 18 September 2003.

After the rural peace of Nether Sampford, no matter how brief, Gregory had known that his return to Leman Street would be something of a culture shock and at 7.20am in a traffic jam in the Strand his fears were confirmed. The move to Fulham had created what Mott had referred to as being "a sod of a drive" across central London to the East End and although he saw the hour or so alone in his car as time for thought and deliberation, privately he was beginning to wonder how long the cooling system of his ancient Mondeo would cope with the daily overheating of the engine. He had been informed of the development at the Row Barge and that a set of four fingerprints matching those of Folmer/Johnnie Marriott had been found on the underside of one of the pub chairs but unlike Mott he was sceptical. He had gone along with instructing all police stations within a two mile radius of the Row Barge to report and sightings of a white Transit van but his personal opinion was that Creepy was far too astute to let himself be identified unless he wanted to and that wherever he lived it would not be "only up the road" as he had been heard to say. Who leaves four complete fingerprints on the underside of a chair, he asked himself; and why take the immediately-recognisable Kelly Goggin into an empty pub? Inching past the Strand Palace Hotel he watched a group of Japanese tourists as they stood on the pavement outside the building taking photographs of each other, collars up in the early morning drizzle, and he wished he could join them for breakfast and a leisurely stroll around London's historic monuments and palaces, lunchtime burgers, a lavish dinner and a warm bed ten floors above the sewers through which his job required him to trawl.

By the time he was in Aldwych he was sure: Creepy was playing games – and Creepy was winning. At Leman Street he put Mott in the picture regarding the revelations turned up in Devonshire and the absence of remains from which DNA could be obtained.

"Still", said Mott, "if push comes to shove we can always get a sample from the sister, I suppose."

"Yes, but I don't think it's ever going to come to that. Marriott or Folmer, doesn't matter what you call him, he's brown bread, Dave, and that's all there is to it. This Creepy bastard's having a game with us – and that's all it is, a bloody game."

There was a silence and then Mott said: "Yes, I'm sure of that, Guv, but for the life of me I cannot see how he is splashing a dead man's dabs about all over the bloody place. It's all very well for Ira Strathearn to scoff about ghosts and bloody ghoulies or whatever he calls them, but you must admit the whole thing's as spooky as hell."

"There's no talk, is there?" asked Gregory. "In the main office?"

"No", said Mott shaking his head. "Not a whisper, Guvnor. As far as they are concerned when you were away you were tied up with Strathearn over at the Yard."

"The press?"

Mott shook his head: "No, Guvnor, I promise." And then, laughing: "If they were on to anything I think we would've heard by now."

Later, with all of his team present, Gregory expressed his doubts about the Row Barge aspect.

"This bastard's far too clever, I'm sure of it. Never in a million years is he ever going to take a tart he's made up his mind to kill into some deserted pub, leave dabs all over a chair and show his face to anyone who's interested unless he wants to let us know what he's about. He's playing a game with us – and he knows he's miles in front."

Iannou, disappointed at what he had taken to be a significant breakthrough, said: "So you don't think he lives just up the road like he said he did?"

"No, I don't, Barney. My bet is that he lives this side of the river, but I'm not even sure of that. I'll go along with getting the local beat blokes to report sightings of any white Transits and who knows, we might get lucky, but it's bloody long odds – nearly every Transit you see is white." Turning to Mott, he asked: "What's happening about the E Fit, Dave?"

"They're going to the Row Barge his afternoon, Guv. We should get it tomorrow, but to be honest from what I can see of it both of the Warnes are a bit short on description other than general age and build. They were spot on with Kelly Goggin but I'm not so sure about Creepy. From what they say I get the impression that he didn't give them too much of a chance to see his face, but I imagine we'll get some sort of image and once it's on the front pages of the papers, who knows."

"That's what I can't understand, Guv; by showing his face, he's playing into our hands. Why would he do that?" asked Iannou.

Gregory nodded and smiled: "That's true. He's going to get caught sooner or later and he knows it and I don't think he's bothered; he's a nutter, Barney, you can sure of that, a raving flake. The problem is how long it's going to take to nail him and how many toms he can carve up in the mean time."

Partially hidden behind Archie McGibbon, Jackie Daniel got to her feet: "Guv, this chap seems to know an awful lot about the original Jack the Ripper – he must've been reading up on him, so I was wondering if he'd get the books from a library."

Aged 26, Jackie Daniel was one of those woman coppers that everyone fell in love with. She had straight, shoulder-length dark hair, pretty brown eyes and a slim and head-turning figure. Her hands were brown and small and with a tiny, gold signet ring on the little finger of the left; she never wore trousers, favoured minimal makeup and had managed to stay single. She lived in a small house in Stepney Green and the truth was that there was not one London policeman who could honestly say he had ever seen the inside of it – although many liked to boast otherwise.

"What's your point, Jackie?"

"Well, let's have enquiries made at all the major libraries, say north of the river, and see if anyone's been taking out Ripper books in any noticeable fashion? You never know, we might come up with someone taking out masses of Ripper stuff, someone with some sort of fixation and, well –"

"Good one, Jackie!" He glared mock frustration over his glasses at the rest of the team: "Useless bloody crowd." He turned and spoke briefly to Mott and then: "You and Archie get on to that, will you Jackie? Start with every major library north of the river, okay? Send a message to all of the relevant nicks, they're to get a CID officer to call and make the necessary enquiries - and I want the answers back yesterday, tell them."

During the mid-morning he phoned Strathearn, updating him as to what had taken place in Devonshire and what was already a bad day was further tainted by news that a press conference has been scheduled for 5.00pm that afternoon at the Yard. Gregory felt sick.

***

Wonkeye Jerry was not about to allow his treatment at Gregory's hands to go unpunished: "Are you aware of the identity of Detective Inspector Frederick Abberline?" he asked, one eye on the line of policemen, the other not.

Tight-lipped and loose-bowelled, Gregory agreed that he knew that Abberline had investigated the 1888 Ripper crimes. "A man very much like yourself, "wouldn't you say" sneered

Wonkeye, "inasmuch as he had a great many ideas but was short on definitive action?"

Gregory felt himself blushing at the ripple of amusement. Angry, he felt he needed to answer the man but at the same time he was fearful of his temper. In the event, Strathearn saved the day: "Let me make it clear, to all of you, that as the head of the Yard's CID I am perfectly happy that this enquiry is in the best possible hands. I am confident that Chief Inspector Gregory is doing everything within his power to resolve the situation as soon as possible and, further, that he is the best man for the job."

Wonkeye, evidently unwilling to let go, started to speak but Strathearn ignored him. He pointed to an elderly hack from one of the dailies and unknowingly lurched from the frying pan into a very, very hot fire.

"Will you confirm that for some unexplained reasons an aspect of this enquiry seems to be centred on the murder of a prostitute almost half a century ago, that the perpetrator of that crime was hanged and, therefore, cannot possibly be involved in current matters?"

Gregory felt sicker than ever and hoped that the assembled press would not notice that nerves had caused one of his legs to start shaking. He caught a glimpse of Wonkeye, both wide eyed at the revelation and smirking at his enemy's discomfort, and The Old Man's flat refusal to discuss the details of the investigation seemed to him to be lost to him in a mist of both anger and apprehension. From the corner of an eye he saw Mott at the back of the room and although distance and the lighting impaired his view, he knew his assistant had turned white and that, like his own, Mott's bowels had turned to jelly.

Arriving in Stathearn's outer office immediately after the press conference he was told by Rosie Lewis to wait in The Old Man's room. Barely smiling at the girl and finding it hard to contain his fury, he stood at the window watching the rush hour traffic edging along Victoria Street and wishing that he was anything other than what he was and anywhere other than the Yard. Hearing the door, he turned to see Strathearn entering the office, a distinctly pale Mott behind him.

"You bastard" he said to Mott, his eyes flashing his rage "I just knew you would never be able to keep your fucking mouth shut."

Strathearn, by then seated at his desk, raised his hand and glared at Gregory. "That's enough of that."

He rang Rosie and having ordered teas, he said: "It was nothing to do with Dave, Michael. That reporter's from *"The Sun"*: I'm owed a few favours from that direction and I've called in the lot. They got it from some kid who works in the prisons department of the Home Office…" As he spoke, Gregory suddenly smelt expensive cologne and thought of yellow silk handkerchiefs. He looked at Mott and sensed resentment and hurt in the return gaze. There was nothing to be done, Strathearn said, and no blame to be apportioned. The Home Office clerk had been sacked on the spot and he had been able to convince the paper's editor that the Folmer aspect was of no great importance to the main investigation and that, in return for no further reference to it, favours would be returned as the enquiry progressed.

"Dave", said Gregory, "Dave, I'm sorry, I really am. I was shitting bricks in that conference and when that came out I nearly died –"

"And put two and two together", said Mott, regaining colour and a degree of arrogance.

"If you like, yes. And I am truly sorry."

The tea came and with Rosie gone Strathearn said: "Yes, well, we all over react sometimes, I suppose and, well, Dave, you have got a bit of form in that area so let's just forget about it and get on with the bloody job, okay?"

He wanted to know the details of what had taken place in the Row Barge and seemed inclined to agree with Gregory's view that the fingerprints had been left on purpose. He produced the newly-arrived E fit pictures showing a thin, grey sixty year old man with no especially peculiar points at all and it was agreed that it would be given to the press and, Strathearn said with a large wink: "*"The Sun"* a day before everyone else." They all scoffed at the so-called "psychological profile" which had arrived on Strathearn's desk that morning and Gregory was relieved when Mott, grinning at him, claimed that most of the points he had written days before were in the description, that he had won the bet - although he could not recall what his prize was to be.

Turning to Gregory's visit to Devonshire, Strathearn said: "It's hard to believe that Castle couldn't have connected Folmer or Marriott whatever he was called to the Berlin business, but I suppose what with the war and him getting away with it, well, I suppose it was possible."

"Stan Cutler said they did all they could, Guvnor, and if they could've ID'd him I'm sure they would have done – they had no reason not to, did they?"

Strathearn nodded agreement, and then: "Would the sister go along with a DNA sample if we needed it?"

"I imagine so."

"Good. Because we've got a trace. Off the stamp on the first letter."

"But it won't match will it? No ghosts and ghoulies, remember?"

The Old Man smiled and nodded: "Aye, but it would be nice to be sure, wouldn't it?"

Later, in the Two Chairmen, Gregory bought bitter for himself and a double whisky for Mott. "Dave, I'm so sorry, I really am."

"Guv, if you don't trust me, best say so now and I'll get myself taken off the enquiry –" Gregory made to speak, but Mott continued: "I know there's been problems in the past and I know that, well, let's say I've got a weakness for the odd Fleet Street steak, but I'd never shaft you – you've got my word."

Gregory said nothing. Through the smoky crowd of noisy one-for-the-roaders, he glimpsed fair, spiky hair and covered a grin with his hand as he thought of blind butchers boys. Apparently sensing he was extraneous to requirements, Mott said he had things to do back at Leman Street and again, assuring Gregory of his close-mouthed loyalty, he left.

Rosie Lewis was with two friends, Gregory guessed from the typing pool or somewhere else within the Yard. Evidently aware of his presence, she looked at him across the bar and smiled and nodded as he signalled an offer to refresh her glass; suddenly she was by his side and minutes later they had found a small corner table and for the first time that day Gregory felt relaxed. She was 27., she told him, divorced and without any children and living alone in what she referred to as her "rabbit hutch" in Ealing. He sensed that she felt he would be averse to talking about his work, although later he realised that her position with Strathearn meant that she knew as much – or more – about the enquiries as he did himself. Going to the bar he ordered more drinks – a whisky for himself this time and her usual orange juice – and as the evening progressed he felt at ease with the girl with the funny hair and started to wonder where it would end. Suddenly, though, and quite unaccountably, he felt uncomfortable, uneasy in a manner which he would have been unable to explain. In the hot, crowded pub he experienced a glacial chill down his back and as he felt the long hairs on the back of his neck rise he shuddered inwardly. "You okay?" she asked seeing his uneasiness and taking his hand. And then, "Mike, you've gone white as a sheet."

"Yeah, I'm okay" he said, smiling at her, at the same time trying to disguise the feeling of dread and unease he was experiencing. He sipped his scotch, hoping that the alcohol would restore him, but he found his eyes wandering round the room, scanning the crowd of drinkers, searching for the face of a grey haired sixty year old and knowing, beyond any doubt, that someone had been watching him.

He woke up in a room he did not recognise and with the taste of stale scotch and curry in his mouth and the smell of frying bacon in his uncomprehending nostrils. He was alone in a double bed: his watch registered 6.40 and he knew from the sound of a radio playing in an adjacent room that it was morning and not later in the day. He stretched, his back arched and his clenched fists pushing into the wall behind the bed, and then crushing his hands into his face to clear his eyes and to bring some awareness back into his being, he recalled an Indian Restaurant in Notting Hill, Tiger beer, too much scotch and Rosie Lewis.

12.

The papers the following day were kind to Gregory. Editorials in one broadsheet and two tabloids sympathised with the difficulties he was facing and drew attention to the apparent mental state, and therefore the unpredictability, of the man responsible for the crimes. Open reference was made to the anticipated "double event" and conjecture as to any probable location for the crimes and, overall, it was accepted the police were doing everything possible and that Gregory was the best man for the job. Mercifully, not one paper mentioned the Folmer matter, but during the day Gregory gave much thought to his role in the whole scenario and the fact that, in reality, he was spending more time on the Folmer aspect than he was on the current spate of murders. He was sensitive of the implications behind the hanged man's fingerprints being associated with the current crimes and although like Strathearn he did not subscribe in any manner to a "ghouls and ghosties" theory he was concerned as to what was happening and to how what was most certainly some sort of trickery was being carried out. A further matter which was causing him much unease was that he was certain that he had been the subject of some sort of malevolent scrutiny the evening before in the Two Chairmen.

That evening he and Mott were due at the BBC in Portland Place for the Crime Watch programme and compared with the recent press conference he found this a simple exercise, mainly because all the questions directed at him were from friendly sources, they had been rehearsed and everyone there was on his side. It had been agreed with Strathearn that the white Transit van would not be mentioned so prompting Creepy to change vehicles, and the programme started with photographs of both of the dead girls, the Canterbury Pilgrim and the locations where the bodies had been found. It was decided that the similarity to the original Ripper killings would be mentioned but not dwelt on, and the forensic evidence linking the two crimes would not be made public. The E fit reconstruction was shown at length as was the Canterbury Pilgrim, Hanbury Street and Durward Street and photographs of Kelly Goggin and "Toothpick" and viewers were requested to make contact with even the slightest information they may feel could be useful. Gregory realised that the picture was so general and vague that a large number of calls could be expected and he had arranged for a team of thirty officers be available to receive and deal with incoming calls throughout the evening and late into the night. After the programme he went to a nearby pub with Mott and two of the BBC staff finally arriving at his unhappy flat in Fulham shortly after 11.00pm. Relaxing in an armchair with a large whisky his mobile telephone rang: the screen told him, "Rosie" was calling. He turned the phone off and went to bed.

The Saturday and Sunday were chaos with the whole team sifting the hundreds of telephone calls which had resulted from the Crime Watch programme. Three officers were deputed to deal with what were referred to as "the nutters" and returned calls to people who believed the original Ripper had been reincarnated, that Peter Sutcliffe (the so-called Yorkshire Ripper) was getting out of prison when he felt like it and that the killer was an eighty-six year old disbarred solicitor from Bromsgrove. There was a lady from Stockton-on-Tees who said that one morning she had seen "spirit writing" in the condensation on her bathroom window, this being to the effect that the killer was the mayor of Pontefract and an elderly man from Brighton who had regular dreams of the 1888 Ripper and believed that he had never died and was alive and well in an old people's home in Stamford-le-Hope.

Seventy-six persons from locations from the north of Scotland to the south coast recognised the E fit picture as someone they knew; twelve people had single male neighbours who entertained prostitutes at their homes and a large amount of information came in from friends and acquaintances (and the odd former client) of both Kelly Goggin and "Toothpick". To Gregory, watching the activity from his office, it seemed that his staff was weighed under with information from well-meaning people but that most of it was worthless and resulting in massive time wasting. He also knew, as did Barney Iannou who was running the HOLMES computer, that there was a very real chance that some small and insignificant fragment of information passed on by a member of the public could lead to a break-through. And so it went on: a lady from Worthing who knew another lady who had told her that her friend's grandson visited prostitutes and had a tendency towards violent sex; a man from Barkingside whose neighbour was a match for the E fit and who he had seen in Kings Cross the night of the Goggin murder – or it may have been the night before – or even after, and the man who worked in a hotel in Camden Town who thought that a man who matched the E Fit may have stayed in the hotel the night of the second murder.......

Monday 22 September 2003

The librarian, Jane Calloway, was a spinster in her late fifties, thin of both lip and frame and with the air of a primary school teacher who firmly believed in even the most extreme forms of corporal punishment. She favoured tweed suits over unfussy blouses, no jewellery whatsoever and small, unfashionable glasses suspended around her neck by way of a thin gold coloured chain. She had never worn trousers in her life (she called them slacks) and some years previously she had threatened resignation if her female staff be allowed to wear them. In the event, the Council (her employers) called her bluff: trousers arrived and Jane Calloway capitulated. Neither tramp nor loafer in for a scan of the racing pages and a warm kip got past Miss Calloway; conversation raised above a whisper was silenced by way of an angry, narrow-eyed glare and she saw to it that the usage of the microfiche viewers was strictly by appointment with no queue-jumping tolerated. Soft shoes and matching conversation were *de rigeur* for the staff and an unfortunate trainee who spilt coffee on the photocopier and had giggled biscuit crumbs over Jane Calloway when taken to task had been summarily dismissed.

Jane Calloway did not like what was going on in what she considered to be "her library." When she had been asked for information as to the habits of the various regular users, she had primly informed the Council that the police request was a clear contravention of data protection legislation and that it would be unlawful to comply with it in any way. Within an hour, her branch received a lengthy e-mail reply pointing out that since the request was relative to the prevention and/or detection of crime it was clearly outside of the Act and that she would render all possible assistance to the Police. Before it came to her attention the mail had been read by most of her staff, causing laughter-stifling handkerchiefs to be stuffed into numerous teenage mouths, and when the reply, which was little more than a snub, finally reached her office it caused her to burst into tears of both anger and humiliation and to spend the next hour locked in the ladies' lavatory.

Early in the afternoon, and beside herself with fury, she learned that wholly without authority a young man working in the lending department had telephoned the local police and informed them that one of the borrowers, a man in his late sixties, had withdrawn every book they had on Jack the Ripper at least five times over the previous six months. It seemed that more recently he had gravitated to the reference section where he was engaged in avidly scanning relevant copies of the London Gazette and similar publications of that period and that he had been requesting that searches be made for obscure books and periodicals germane to the 1888 murders.

Later that day, and compounding Jane Calloway's anger and frustration, the library was visited by a detective sergeant from the local station who spoke to her briefly, interviewed the young assistant at length and having flirted outrageously for the best part of an hour, arranged a date later that evening with one of her trainees.

Worse, though, was to come.

Leonard Marjoribanks, his library card stated, was a retired British Rail employee who resided at 54, Glendower Road, Wood Green, London N22., a small turning off Lordship Lane bordering on the Noel Park Estate. Within ten minutes of his return to the station the amorous CID officer had established that that this data was incorrect and that the property was, in fact, occupied by persons named Paul and Felicity Shackleton who had lived there for some sixteen years.

Jackie Daniel looked excited. "Guv, it looks as though the library enquiries have come good."

Gregory looked up from the statement he was reading: "What's happened?"

"Well, a library in North London has been on: they've got an old boy who comes in two or three times a week who's obsessed with the 1888 Ripper killings. Apparently he's had out every book they've got on the subject about six times in recent months and now he's going through all the old newspapers of the period and asking the library staff to dig out all sorts of out of print books and God-knows what else about them."

"Maybe he's a fan – or writing a book."

"He joined the library in July this year and he's put a false address on the registration card."

Gregory thought a moment and then: "Don't they have to prove who they are when they sign on at a library? They must do, surely, otherwise anyone could just register and nick all the bloody books."

Jackie Daniel shook her head: "I don't know, Guv. I just took the call and –"

"You better get out there. Now. And take Barney with you."

At 4.45pm and an hour before she was due to leave for home, Jane Calloway received a telephone call to the effect that she was not to leave the library and that officers from New Scotland Yard would visit her there as soon as was practicable. On their arrival she took Iannou and Jackie Daniel into her small office. Although still very prim and resentful at the intrusion, she knew she had no option but to assist the police and she had made up her mind to do it with as much dignity as she could maintain. She said she knew nothing personally of the man in question but she understood from staff that he appeared obsessed by the Ripper crimes and that he was in attendance at the reference section of the library, more or less on a daily basis. She produced his registration card and handed it to Iannou.

"Did you know that the address given here is false?"

"What?" She felt her control ebbing.

"The address on the card – 54, Glendower Road, Wood Green – it is a false address."

"How do you know that?"

"We have made enquiries and spoken to the people who live there, Miss Calloway."

"Well, you've probably made a mistake." Her tone had a trace of a sneer: she knew it, had not been able to resist it, and instantly regretted it.

"The addresses are checked aren't they?" asked Jackie Daniel. "Against a utility bill or something similar?"

"Of course."

"And the manner of the check – gas bill, electric or whatever – is noted on the card."

"Yes."

Jackie handed her the card: "Not on this one, though."

Jane Calloway took the card, almost snatching it, and paled visibly having looked at it. "I don't understand – it must have slipped through somehow."

121

"You are the head librarian?" asked Iannou, anxious not to let her previous rudeness pass. "And as such you are responsible?"

She nodded, tight-lipped as ever but with fear starting to replace her anger.

Tuesday 23 September 2003.

The man named Marjoribanks arrived in the library just before noon and was immediately pointed out to Jackie Daniel. On entering the reference library he stopped at the reception and having spoken to an assistant he collected a pile of what Jackie took to be old magazines and moved to the rear of the room near Iannou who was seated at a table with a pile of books. He was a tall man, Iannou saw, and aged in his late sixties. He was wearing a double-breasted fawn raincoat, belted at the waist and a grey cloth cap, both of which he removed and hung on the provided hooks. There was no jacket but a heavy, long-sleeved woollen cardigan, buttoned down the front and which Iannou felt was probably home-made. The brown trousers, apparently part of a suit, were several inches too short at the ankles exposing grey, woollen socks over clean, brown laced shoes and although he could not be sure Iannou thought that the shirt behind the plain green tie was of the old-fashioned loose-collar variety, used with collar studs. He placed a black, plastic briefcase on the table and having fiddled with the two combination locks he took out several books and a large pad of writing paper, closed the briefcase and having reset the locks he sat at the table. Iannou, who could clearly see Marjoribanks, noted that Jackie Daniel had taken up a position on the other side of the room and he guessed that although she was largely concealed behind a pile of books and writing materials, she would have a clear view of their target. In accordance with the library regulations their mobile telephones were turned off and both were well aware that a combination of instinct and luck may well come to play a part in what was to follow.

Marjoribanks read minutely and carefully through his recently-acquired pile of magazines which Iannou thought were mainly copies of the Illustrated London News, presumably of the period surrounding the 1888 murders. He wore small, rimless spectacles and from time to time he used a large magnifying glass, apparently to examine some small print or picture in the publications. Using a fountain pen he made copious notes on his pad, from time to time he seemed to be cross-referencing from the periodicals to his books and, Iannou noticed, there were long periods of gazing into space, apparently deep in thought, a large hand stroking his thick, white hair. Catching his eye shortly before 5.00pm., Jackie showed Iannou her mobile telephone, carefully pushing it out from behind her pile of books, and by glancing towards the exit she let him know that she was going to leave to make contact with Gregory or Mott. She returned after ten minutes and Iannou almost laughed out loud at her face when, on looking across the room, she saw that Marjoribanks was missing only to realise, on catching Iannou's eye, that he had taken a pile of magazines to the photocopier and was busy copying.

They left the library shortly before 7.00pm. Marjoribanks had paid no attention to either officer, not even glancing in their direction at any stage, and they were totally confident that he was unaware that he was being observed. Outside the library and directly opposite the tube station he went into a fried chicken restaurant and takeaway and while Barney Iannou watched from across the road as he sat in a window seat and ate fried chicken and chips, Jackie phoned Mott.

"He says to stay on him", she told Iannou, joining him in a shop doorway. "No matter what."

He left the restaurant at 7.40pm and carrying his briefcase he walked to the tube station where, with Jackie directly behind him, he purchased a ticket to Finsbury Park. Having told

Barney the intended destination, she followed Marjoribanks down the escalator and on to the train. In a different carriage, she watched as he read an evening paper and arriving at Finsbury Park she lagged behind as he exited into Seven Sisters Road and having walked in the general direction of the West End for a hundred yards or so turned right into Fonthill Road. She phoned Iannou who joined her moments later and they watched as Marjoribanks entered the Devon Arms, a scruffy pub on the corner of Fonthill Road and Gladstone Terrace.

"We've been with this bastard all day, Jack", said Iannou. "We daren't go in there – he's bound to suss us, don't you think?"

Jackie agreed, phone calls were made and Mott and Archie McGibbon arrived an hour later, both moaning. They parked their car in a side street and sitting in Iannou's vehicle they heard what had happened during the day and noted the detailed description of Marjoribanks.

The Devon Arms, like most of the area in which it was situated, had seen better days. Like the Canterbury Pilgrim at Kings Cross, it had once boasted three or four bars but in recent years the requirement for entertainment in pubs had forced the owners to convert the whole ground floor into one enormous public area with a central servery catering for all sides. At one end of what had evidently been the "club room" or function room was a stage but, unlike the Canterbury Pilgrim, the Devon Arms provided live music to a middle-aged, even elderly, clientele. Mott and McGibbon ordered pints of bitter and stood at the bar playing "spot the Marjoribanks" and listening to the strains of "The Lea River Seven", a traditional jazz-cum-swing-cum-twenties ragtime band, all dressed in white Oxford bags, striped blazers and a variety of hats ranging from straw boaters to a "vicar" in dog collar and a round, black affair of the sort favoured by French *curés* . The bar was moderately full and the five or six girls working behind the oval bar were kept busy serving pints of bitter and lager and any one of dozens of choices for the distaff side. The lengths of the walls were taken up by bench seating and tables in booth format with the larger part of the crowd either standing at the bar or in the main room front of the stage and watching the performers, who Mott realised, were seriously inclined towards comedy. McGibbon spotted Marjoribanks almost immediately: he was seated in an alcove and Mott's blood pressure rose dramatically when he saw he was in company with two women who gave every impression of being ladies of the night.

As Mott and McGibbon watched, the little threesome became more animated and intimate every half hour – which was about the time between the rounds of two large gins and a large whisky being purchased by Marjoribanks. With his raincoat on a ledge at the back of his seat and his briefcase by his side, he had one arm around the shoulders of each whore, occasionally kissing the mouth of whichever took his particular fancy, at the same time singing and taking part in the entertainment.

And who done put that Spanish Fly
In Maggie Thatcher's apple pie?
Well, I declare, it must be Doctor Jazz.

Mott, half in to his beer and half to McGibbon: "Jesus H. Christ, Arch, I reckon it's him."

"So do I." McGibbon muttered. "What the hell are we going to do if he pulls one of those hookers out? Just the two of us?"

"I don't think he'll do that. He's got no transport, remember."

"He's not too far from, Kings Cross, is he?" said McGibbon. "That's where he pulled number one, Guv." He sipped beer and tipped the remains of a packet of salt and vinegar crisps from the bag into his open mouth. "What if he's got the Transit tucked out of the way somewhere?"

Long John on a chain-gang swingin' that pick,
Boss-man say take a piss and be quick.
But he run so fine
Right across the state line
Now no-one knows where Long John gwine.
Loooong gone - from Kentucky,
Loooong gone - ain't he lucky,
Long gone, what I mean,
Long Gone John from Bowlin' Green.

Mott looked his watch and saw it was 10.10pm.

Long Gone got a pair of shoes of his own,
Finest pair of shoes that ever was born:
Heels at the front
Heels behind,
No one knows which way Long John's gwine.
Loooong gone - from Kentucky,
Loooong Gone - ain't he lucky,
Long gone, what I mean,
Long Gone John from Bowlin' Green.

Leaving McGibbon he left the pub and in a quiet street he phoned the Leman Street office on his mobile telephone. No reply. He swore beneath his breath and phoning the Yard switchboard he asked for Holloway CID. Breathless, he waited: Mott knew that McGibbon was right and that if Marjoribanks was Creepy and if he had the Transit somewhere nearby…. There were a lot of "ifs", he knew, but the fact was that the two of them would never be able to handle the situation on their own and if there was another murder, under their noses and with the killer having been in their sights all evening, Mott knew the future did not bear thinking about. As he waited it started to rain and then, mercifully, there was a reply.

Once back with McGibbon in the bar Mott studied the face of the man they thought may be a homicidal lunatic. The grey hair had become a little sweat-dampened and unkempt but his dark eyes were lively and he was far from drunk. The mouth was small and seemed to be formed in a constant grin with laughter lines at each side and crows feet around the constantly smiling eyes. The two woman, both in the twenties, he took to be amateur hookers both from the manner of their dress and the way in which they behaved. There was no finesse about these two: when a drink was required an empty glass was waved in his face and there was no shortage of intimate touching and stroking.

Just before 11.00pm, and by which time Mott hoped that back-up was in position, the band left the stage and there seemed to be a lull in the proceedings during which, unaccountably to Mott and McGibbon, several members of the pub staff circulated the clientele handing out large paper napkins, the purpose of which seemed to be accepted and welcomed by the regulars. Suddenly the house lights went dim to the point of darkness, prompting McGibbon to move from the bar and to stand next to the booth occupied by Marjoribanks and the hookers. Then, suddenly, the stage lights came back on revealing The Lea River Seven in an assortment of turn-of-the-century military uniforms. They were greeted by an enormous cheer from the crowd and with a roll of drums, soft background clarinet and tuba with muted martial trumpet:

> *It's the soldiers of the queen, my lad*
> *Who've seen, my lad, who've been my lad*
> *In the fight for England's glory lad*
> *Of its worldwide glory let us sing*

The entire crowd joined in the chorus, and all waving their handkerchiefs at the stage:

And when we say we've always won
And when they ask us how it's done
We'll proudly point to every one
Of England's soldiers of the queen.

There was one more verse and with the last chorus, in the midst of the waving napkins, there were simulated smoke bombs and explosions going on all over the stage. Mott and McGibbon were convulsed with laughter at the same time trying to keep an eye on Marjoribanks, and suddenly he was off.

They followed him out into the street where it was still drizzling and with a cold wind whipping up ripples in the pavement puddles. Mott saw what he took to be the Holloway assistance parked in a car across the road and in an effort to let them know his identity he nodded towards them. Marjoribanks, who was probably more intoxicated that Mott had thought, put one arm around each of his ladies and the little trio wandered into Seven Sisters Road turning left towards the underground station. In the shelter of the station, quite unconscious that he was being watched, Marjoribanks kissed and cuddled his whores at some length and then, looking at his watch, he took money from his pocket and handing an indeterminate amount of cash to each woman, he walked into the station.

Mott heaved a sigh of relief. He gave a thumbs-up signal to the Holloway back-up and as he followed Marjoribanks down the station hallway with McGibbon behind him he laughed inwardly, imagining the faces of the two hookers if they were to know how lucky they had been. With Marjoribanks some distance in front of him, Mott did not hear the destination he asked for at the ticket desk: the end of the line was Cockfosters and Mott bought two, hoping that the target was going north as opposed to towards the West End. He had no need to worry.

Manor House, Turnpike Lane and Wood Green came and went. At Arnos Grove Mott noticed that Archie McGibbon was asleep and it took a kick to wake him as Marjoribanks exited the train at Oakwood. Lagging some way behind him and walking separately, they followed him along the platform and watched as he climbed the deserted stairs. Less than thirty seconds after him, they arrived in the empty station hall and found that there was no trace of him outside the station and that he seemed to have disappeared. Mott cursed his luck and McGibbon, coatless in what had turned to driving rain, ran into the road and round to the side of station. Moments later he was back in the station: "Bastard had a car in the car park. There's a car drove off down the main road towards Enfield then turned right: I'm bloody sure it was him – there's no one else about."

Without a car number they were thwarted; wet and miserable they waited for a train back to London, Mott telephoning Gregory with the news and leaving it to him to arrange surveillance on the library for the following day.

Gregory was in his office at 7.00am. He had decided that Jackie Daniel should run the surveillance at the library and that Iannou, Mott and McGibbon were to stay away. From what he had been told, Marjoribanks had no inkling that he had been under observation but it would have been foolish to take a chance on someone being recognised, although by the same token it was essential that someone who could identify the target was there, and Gregory thought that Jackie was the most suitable. Mott arrived shortly before nine, elated but complaining of "the flu" and at 10.00am Gregory called the team into his office and went over the most recent developments.

There was no evidence, he told them, that Marjoribanks was the killer but at that stage he was certainly a suspect. He seemed to fit the description of the man seen in both the Canterbury Pilgrim and the Row Barge, he had an obsession with all things Ripper circa 1888 and he was, apparently, an habitué of public houses where prostitutes could be found and he seemed to have a fondness for that type of woman. He had given a false address on his library card; the various databases and indices to which they had access had located no-one by the name of Leonard Marjoribanks in the Oakwood area of north London indicating that the name he had given to the library was also probably false and all things considered Leonard Marjoribanks certainly seemed to be well in the frame. Jackie was running the show at the library, Gregory told the team, and she was assisted by four Flying Squad officers in Wood Green and another pair in the Oakwood area to meet the target as he left the tube with a view to following him and to finding his home address.

The waiting seemed interminable. Barney Iannou went into Gregory's office every now and then with a fresh bundle of files relative to the Crime Watch programme and Mott and McGibbon were in the process of sifting through data on the 39 men named Leonard Marjoribanks that they had identified as being in the United Kingdom. By 3.00pm it was apparent that there would be no-show at the library and two hours later Gregory left for the evening, leaving Mott in overall charge.

He met Rosie in a pub in Hammersmith and after his second drink he realised that he was not the best of company. He was tired, more tired than he had thought, and although he dreaded the solitude of his flat in Fulham he knew that he was not too keen on the prospect of an evening with a pretty girl some twenty years his junior and a restaurant meal which he was not likely to enjoy. Rosie, though, had different ideas and half an hour later he found himself in a comfortable armchair in her small house, a glass of whisky in his hand and the smell of steaks emanating from the kitchen. The terraced house, in a narrow road facing Ealing Common, was paid for and had been all she had come out with after a miserable marriage to a homosexual cabinet maker from Sidcup – although, she said, neither of them knew he was so inclined until two years into the union. In recent years she had added a small conservatory to the rear of the house covering what had been a yard and with a downstairs conversion of what had been three small rooms into a larger area, the kitchen being integral but separated by a breakfast bar, she had achieved a deal of both taste and comfort.

He dozed before dinner, drank Tesco's plonk with his steak and enjoyed her company. Later they watched television, totally refraining from the slightest mention of the job he was doing; he was aware that her situation with Strathearn meant that she would have a fair insight into the manner in which the enquiry was seen to be going by his superiors but he was unwilling to embarrass her by even the subtlest of hints or enquiries and was pleased that nothing was said.

At breakfast they both sensed a feeling of awkwardness, the embarrassment perhaps of two people aware of an age difference and each hoping it would make no difference to the other. Gregory realised he liked the girl and that he wanted to see her more often; he was not over-concerned about any reaction from Strathearn but he was sure that should he get to know of the association, The Old Man would find a way of turning it to his own ends.

That day Marjoribanks arrived at the library at noon and books and magazines read, notes made and photo-copying complete he left at 6.30pm followed by Jackie Daniel who pointed him out to the waiting Yard officers and promptly left the area. He took his meal in the same fried chicken restaurant as before and with a detective sergeant and woman detective constable behind him in the queue and expecting to be on their way to Finsbury Park and an evening of entertainment, he purchased a ticket for Oakwood. Later, Mott would discover that The Lea River Seven were only in evidence at the Devon Arms on Tuesdays and Saturdays and that rock music and a totally different type of clientele were there every other evening of the week.

On the platform, the detective sergeant telephoned the Oakwood officers and having ensured that everything was in place, he followed Marjoribanks on to the train and held hands with his rather manly woman detective constable companion as they made their way into the outer suburbs. At Oakwood, the waiting mobile team watched as he got into a blue Ford Ka motor car and followed him without any problems to Greenbank Road, a turning adjacent to Chase Side, Southgate where he was seen to enter number 18.

An hour later Mott found Gregory in shirt sleeves in his office going over the Crime Watch results which Iannou had completed. Since hearing from the surveillance team Mott had not stopped and senior DHSS and Inland Revenue staff had had their evenings disturbed. "We've got him Guv! They followed him off from the library and housed him in Oakwood!"

Gregory took off his glasses and rubbed his eyes. He cleaned the glass with the end of his tie and: "Brilliant, bloody brilliant." He though a moment and: "They've not left him alone, have they?"

"No Guv. There two Squad blokes up there at the moment and I'm arranging round the clock surveillance right now." He grinned at Gregory, pleased they may be coming out of the woods. He referred to his pad: "Victor Malcolm Peace aged 69., widowed 9 years ago. He's lived at 18, Greenbank Road, Oakwood for years and he's got no form that we can find."

Gregory nodded: "Well done, Dave, bloody well done. Is Jackie in the office?"

"No Guv, she had the evening off."

"Get someone to ring her at home and tell her – she'll be over the moon with this."

Mott chewed the inside of his mouth, unhappy to spoil a rare good moment: "Do you want the bad news now – or will you wait for the morning?"

Gregory sighed: "Go on."

"He's an ex copper."

"Who is?"

"Victor Malcolm Peace." He referred to his pad and went on: "Born in Bournemouth in 1934. He joined the job in 1955 after National Service. He served at West End Central until 1960 by which time he'd married and he bought a house in Hornsey and got posted to the old "Y" division. In 1977 they bought the house in Oakwood and he got posted to Southgate a year later. He did his thirty years, retired in 1986., and his wife died of cancer in 1995."

Gregory looked bleak. Catching murderers is one thing, he thought, but it gets a bloody sight more difficult when the bastard's an ex copper and knows his way round. "When he left the job – did he work?"

Mott looked at his pad: "He worked as a security officer in a West End hotel, sir, and packed up when his wife died. Since then he's done nothing."

"What sort of a hotel? One of the big ones?"

Mott shook his head. "No, Guv, nothing like that. A small tourist place at the back of Tottenham Court Road. It was called the Royal Glencross; it's gone now, apparently: been knocked into flats." He looked at Gregory, reading his thoughts and knowing that investigating ex-colleagues of no matter what rank was never easy and always distasteful. "I've sent for his personnel file and we'll have it in the morning."

Getting up from his desk Gregory unlocked a large steel cupboard and took out a thick file which Mott knew contained the Folmer papers. Urgently, he thumbed through and finding what he wanted he adjusted his glasses and read for a minute. "Folmer – Marriott whatever he was called was topped in fifty-seven. He was taken in to West End Central –"

"And Victor Peace was a uniform PC there at the time."

There was a silence. Gregory's mind was spinning and the butterflies of excitement and tension were as active as a hive of angry bees. "Was he an aide to CID?"

"The file wouldn't say that, Guv. Aides were only on secondment to the department, weren't they, so it won't show. I had to get to get a civvy out from home to dig out the file and from what he read to me over the phone there was no record that he'd ever been in the department."

Gregory knew that day and night surveillance on Peace was essential and that not to do so was a risk he was not prepared to take. He also knew that the next killings, the so-called double event, were scheduled to take place over the night of the following Monday and Tuesday and whatever happened he had to ensure that Peace was out of circulation over the crucial period. Mott went off to arrange the surveillances which were to follow and swivelling his chair he faced away from the door, leaning back with his hands behind his head. The answer was there, and he knew it: it was far too coincidental that PC Peace should have been at the same station at the same time that Folmer/Marriott was charged with the West End murder and now emerge as a prime suspect for the current spate of crimes. Somehow – God above knew how – Peace had been able to replicate the hanged man's fingerprints and if he was that clever, Gregory knew, he was going to have his work cut out.

The surveillance at Oakwood was carried out by officers of NCIS - the National Criminal Intelligence Service. Three shifts each of eight hours using an assortment of vans, cars and a motor cycle watched Peace's house from both the front and the rear and wherever possible his every move was subject to surveillance. His telephone was intercepted and had Gregory had the time, some form of internal listening device would have been introduced into the house. The first day, the Friday, Peace was seen digging, tidying and similar in both the front and rear gardens of the house. He neither received nor did he make any telephone calls and appeared to spend the evening until almost 2.00am in what the surveillance team took to be a back bedroom where, through powerful viewing equipment, he was seen to be working on a computer or word processor.

The following day, Saturday 27 September Peace left home in the mid-morning and drove to Enfield Town where he was seen to visit a supermarket, several other shops and the George public house, returning to Greenbank Road in the early afternoon. No further movement was seen until he left home at 6.00pm and drove to Oakwood Tube station where he parked the car. The surveillance team had been apprised of his previous activities and the entertainment schedule of the Devon Arms and they were, therefore, anticipating his exit from the train at Finsbury Park. Crossing the Seven Sisters Road, he was seen to go into a small Indian restaurant in Blackstock Road where he remained until shortly after 8.00pm when he walked slowly along Fonthill Road and was followed into the Devon Arms. Like McGibbon and Mott, the NCIS men thoroughly enjoyed the programme laid on by the Lea River Seven and watched as Peace entertained two women who they were sure were prostitutes, giving each money as he kissed them both goodbye before getting his train back to Oakwood.

During the course of the evening the telephone intercept had picked up a message left for Peace. This was from a woman, apparently his daughter, and confirming that she and her husband and young son would be coming for lunch the following day, that he should remember to get a leg of lamb from the freezer and she would do the cooking for them all.

Monday 29 September 2003.

They were on the doorstep at 7.00am. Gregory was anxious to cause minimal fuss and to avoid press attention at the address if at all possible. The surveillance team had been allowed to leave and as Gregory and Mott knocked on the door 18, Greenbank Road the only other police personnel in the area were the forensic staff who had strict instructions from Gregory that they were to enter the house only when instructed, that a low profile was to be maintained with protective clothing being put on and worn only when they were in the house and with as little attention as possible being drawn to themselves. Waiting with them in a side road was Jackie Daniel.

Peace, in dressing gown and pyjamas blinked at his early visitors. Still half-asleep, he listened as Gregory told him who they were that they had a warrant to search his house and, seemingly unfazed, he showed them into the lounge.

"Warrant or no warrant, I'll make some tea", he said, rubbing his eyes. "You'll have a cup of tea, won't you?"

Tea made and settled in armchairs, Peace adopted the high ground; he was not aggressive and did not give the impression of being angry, but they were in his house, on his territory, and he would remain in charge as long as possible. "What's this about then? You know I was in then job, don't you?"

"Yes", said Gregory "we know that." He sipped strong tea. Copper's tea, he thought. "Vic – may I call you Vic - ?" Peace nodded, and he went on: "We understand that you have got, well, let's say a great interest in the Jack the Ripper crimes. Is that so?"

Peace nodded and smiled. It was a smile, Gregory thought, of a man who not only knew the rules of the game but also of one who thought he had the winning hand. "You spend a deal of time at the Wood Green library." It was a statement, not a question.

Peace nodded again, his grey hair falling on to his forehead: "And I gave false name and address, I suppose you know that, too."

"Why did you do that?"

"It's not an offence, is it?"

Gregory finished his tea. The man was getting to him: his super-confident air and the smiling, almost mocking eyes, were needling him.

"No, I don't suppose it is. But why would you do it?"

"Suppose you tell me why you're here."

"You've read about the two murders in the East End – the papers are saying that it's someone copying the 1888 Ripper –"

"And you think it's me?" He got up from his armchair and put his empty mug on the table. "Then you better nick me, hadn't you?"

Gregory stood up. "We were hoping that –"

"You can hope off, Chief Inspector whatever-you're-called and (glancing at Mott) take your poodle with you." Again, there was no anger, just animosity. "Now, I'm going to get dressed and you can do what you like but I hope for your sake you've got some evidence to come barging in here."

He started to leave the room but Mott moved between him and the door. "I'll come with you" he said smoothly. "And then you'll come with us."

An hour later at Enfield Police Station, Peace was in a different frame of mind. He knew that the forensic staff were in his house and he understood that Gregory was doing everything he could to maintain a low-key operation, for which, he admitted, he was grateful. He was less abrasive but still very calm and, Gregory felt, superbly confident of his situation. No, he said, he did not need a solicitor – he hadn't done anything, had he, so why waste money? While Mott arranged for an interview room and recording equipment Gregory phoned Strathearn and told him the position.

"Do you think it's him?" asked The Old Man

Gregory was guarded, careful. "It's too early, sir. He's very calm, doesn't want a brief and I'm pretty sure he knows that we haven't got all that much." He saw no point in mentioning that Peace was too composed and unruffled and that something inside him somewhere was telling him they were on a loser. "Let's see what the boffins turn up."

Mindful of the forthcoming and anticipated "double event" Gregory imagined, Strathearn asked: "He'll be in overnight, I imagine?"

"Oh yes."

The interview commenced at 10.00am. Initially, Gregory skated over Peace's police career, his home background and his family circumstances. He had one daughter, he said, married to a self employed printer and living in Watford. They had become very close since his wife died and she often visited on a Sunday to cook him lunch. They were careful not to let him know that he had been under surveillance too early, feeling it better to watch his reaction as he worked it out for himself. It was obvious that he thought that the cause of his problems was the library and that someone from there, having noted his interest in the 1888 Ripper, had contacted the police and Gregory was keen not to alter to this.

"Why a false name and address at the library?"

Peace laughed and shook his head. "Silly, really. I just didn't want them to know who I was. I had a feeling that digging out all that Ripper stuff may cause a fuss and I just didn't want them knowing who I was and what I was doing. You have to put your occupation down and if I had put "police officer –"

"But you weren't a policeman when you took out the library card, were you? Why couldn't you have put "retired"."

He looked blank and shook his head. "I'm telling you the truth."

A knock on the door and Mott left to speak with Jackie Daniel phoning from the house. "He's writing a book, Guv. About a chap called Frederick Abberline from what I can make of it. There's piles of research stuff in a spare bedroom where his PC is and from what I can see on the computer that's what he's doing."

"Thanks, Jackie." Mott thought a moment, and: "Anything else?"

"No, not really. The boffins are hard at it but there's no liver in bottles or anything like that I'm afraid."

Back in the interview room Mott said: "Fred Abberline, eh? So that's your library interest, is it? He was the copper who chased the Ripper, right?"

Peace nodded agreement: "Chased and never caught."

"Why him?" asked Gregory making a note on his file. "Where's the interest?"

"More personal than anything else. I was born in Bournemouth - 192, Holdenhurst Road to be precise. Fred Abberline lived at 195 after he retired, my parents knew him and that's it really. Just something to do, really."

"When were you last at the library?" asked Gregory.

"Oh, about a week ago I suppose."

"You drive down there, do you?"

"Always. There's no problem parking and it's cheap."

"What's the matter with the Enfield library?" asked Mott. "It's much nearer."

"They didn't have much of a selection to be honest. And when I asked them if they could get some unusual stuff for me they hummed and hawed so much I thought sod 'em, I'll go somewhere else." He looked at Gregory, the same mocking gaze and: "I think –"

"I'll tell you what *I* think", said Mott. "I think that you're a liar. I think that you were at the library last Tuesday and again on Thursday. You don't drive you go on the rattler and you go to Wood Green because it's on the way to Finsbury Park on the tube and you go to Finsbury Park every now and again for a bit of relaxation."

Peace stared and Gregory knew he was trying to maintain his composure but the slightest, most minute twitch in the corner of his mouth betrayed him. Mott, unable to resist it any longer, took out his handkerchief and, waving it towards the wall: "*It's soldiers of the Queen, my lads, who've been my lads …*"

Gregory smiled. "I think this calls for some tea", he said. "Dave, see if you can chase someone up, will you?" He curtailed the taped interview and with the recorder off and Mott out of the room he leaned towards Peace and said: "Let me tell you this, Victor: you're here overnight, like it or not, and if I think it warrants it, I'll go to court and get another couple of days. Now that seems to me like a bit of a strain on a man your age, especially if you haven't done anything."

Peace made to interrupt, but Gregory raised his hand and went on: "Now I suggest you stop being the hard man and tell us the truth – all of it okay? The scientists are taking your drum to pieces right now but they're doing it very quietly and with no fuss, but one word from me and there'll be more press sat in your road than there are in Brighton for the labour party conference. You know the game, Victor, as well as I do and you know that I'm holding all the cards."

Mott came back and sat down. "The tea's on its way."

"I was just telling Vic a few home truths, Dave", said Gregory. "Hopefully we understand each other a bit better now."

"Do we need that thing?" asked Peace, indicating the recorder.

"Not for the minute, perhaps. Let's see how we get on."

The tea arrived and with the door shut once more Peace asked: "You've been watching me then?"

Gregory nodded. "For a few days." He sipped tea, grimacing at the taste and: "Have you got a van, Vic? A Transit sort of thing?"

"No. Just the little car." He thought for a moment and: "The book – that's true. You can check with the bloke at the Black Museum in the Yard – they've been helping me out with it – quite a lot, really."

"It's a good old night in the Devon Arms isn't it? You seem to enjoy yourself," said Mott.

"I don't shag them, you know, the toms. It's just a bit of fun." He looked at the table and then straight at Mott: "Look, I'm getting on for seventy, I've been on me own since the missus died – for fuck's sake, I'm not doing anything wrong, am I?" He looked at the desk again and then: "From what I've read, there's been a couple of toms done – on the same days and in the same streets as the first Ripper. Is that right?"

"That's about it", Gregory agreed and then: "The first one was pulled out of a pub in Kings Cross on – (he referred to his notes) – thirtieth of August – it was a Saturday night. Where were you that night?"

Peace thought. He sipped tea and, pulling a face similar to Gregory's of earlier he glared at the cup: "Christ – that don't change much, does it?" He thought, gazing at the wall and then a grin and: "I was in Paris. Went on the twenty-seventh and back third of September." Apparently forgetting the quality of the tea, he emptied the cup. "Whew! Thank God for that – I was starting to get worried."

He had travelled alone, he explained, flying from Heathrow, but in France he had stayed with another retired policeman and his wife They'd served together years ago and been mates ever since, he said.

Gregory's heart sank and felt slightly sick. He was on a loser, and he knew it, but he went on: "But you were back on Saturday 8 September?"

Peace nodded, and Gregory sensed his mood had changed and that he knew he had the upper hand: "Is that when the second one was?" The tone, once more, was arrogant.

"That's right. Where were you that night?"

"How the fuck do you expect me to know that? Look, you're saying it was the same man did both toms: I'm bolted up tight for the first one so it wasn't me done the second one, was it? Now you charge me or let me go, okay? Put up or fucking shut-up, okay?"

Gregory and Mott had lunch in the canteen leaving Peace eating cod and chips in the care of a PC in the interview room. He had declined to furnish details of his ex-colleague in Paris at that stage saying that the travel agent and airline should be able should be able to give them what they want and make his alibi stand up. Unsurprisingly, he was not keen to have friends know that he was a suspect serial killer and said that he would only disclose the identities if all else failed.

"If he was in Paris – and I think he was – he's out", said Gregory, toying with corned beef and salad. "How long are they going to be, the airline and the travel people?"

"Sometime this afternoon, they said", said Mott. He frowned and chewed at some imaginary ulcer inside his mouth. "Guv, if that alibi stands up we're going to have a hell of a job keeping him in overnight."

"Just because the airline and travel people say someone by that name went to France, it doesn't mean it was him does it?" He pushed his plate away from him and leaning towards Mott: "Hell or high water, that bastard's not going out of here until the morning, I can promise you that, Dave." He looked round, and sure that he could not be overheard, he went on: "If he goes tonight and it is him after all, and if he does two more, you'll walk a beat in South Mimms for the rest of your life and they'll probably hang me so don't even think about it. He's staying, and that's that."

Mott nodded, although he was evidently concerned. They had the whole of the Whitechapel area, including the fringe of the City of London, flooded with police over the coming night and everything had been done and every precaution had been taken to ensure that a double murder in the streets would not be possible, but both he and Gregory were well aware that if the killer was on the loose he could strike anywhere – and had said as much in his second letter. Gregory, though, was sure there would be some close association with the 1888 murders and that should he perform again, the modern-day Jack would keep as close to the original script as he could.

"What's worrying me, Guv, is if he stays in all night and there are no murders. Then what do we do? I mean it's going to look like it may be Peace, isn't it?"

"What can we do? We've got no evidence: he'll walk."

He did not want to mention West End Central and the Folmer aspect at that time, Gregory said. To do so would mean that Peace would, by necessity, be made aware of the association of the two crimes – which Gregory was anxious to play down at all costs. "Best leave it", he said. "Don't give him opportunity of hitting back at us by going to the press with the Folmer story; we can always have him in again later if we think he was involved."

"He's got to be involved", said Mott. "Christ, Guv, he was in the same nick at the same time: that's more than a coincidence."

In the event, they heard from both the airline and the travel agent late in the afternoon. Both confirmed that a man named Victor Peace had travelled to Paris through Heathrow on 27 August returning on the 3 September but his passport, retrieved by Jackie Daniel from then house, bore no immigration stamps – normal for movement of EEC citizens between EEC countries. The scientists were finished shortly before midnight: a mass of material had been taken away, mainly samples of fibres, sweepings and most of Peace's clothing and these would be subjected to laboratory examination over the coming days and comparisons made with the traces found on the bodies.

Watching the clock, Gregory was gloomy. Allowing Mott to go home, he spent the night at the police station sleeping in an empty cell next to that occupied by Peace.

13.

In the autumn of every year, hundreds of impoverished Londoners, men, women and children, left the city, making their way to Kent for hop-picking. There they lived in sheds, tents and makeshift accommodations, often in the most appalling conditions, but with the chance to earn some money for their labour. There was a communal and family atmosphere with times of drunken conviviality around camp fires after the back-breaking labour of stripping the beer-fruit from the high poles and rope-covered frames. They lived like gypsies – in fact many of them were of that origin – but if the late summer weather was kind and the bosses had one blind eye, the annual trip into the Garden of England was a month-long holiday.

Catherine ("Kate") Eddowes had made the journey many times and she was well-known and well-liked by the pickers. Formerly married to Tom Conway, a violent wastrel by whom she had three children, she had lived with a man named John Kelly for some eight years, their most recent permanent place of residence being Cooney's Lodging House in Flower and Dean Street, Spitalfields, the superintendent there being a man named Fred Wilkinson. John Kelly was a good man, hardworking and although he was known to be of somewhat intemperate habits from time to time, he cared for Kate and had never been known to beat her. Kate, though, had a distinct problem with drink, this being mainly that she had a virtually nil tolerance for anything alcoholic and was prone to become drunk and unmanageable after only one or two small glasses of gin. It is not known if it was drink which caused Kate and John Kelly to leave the village of Hunton near Maidstone half way through the hop-picking, but they were certainly back in Whitechapel sometime during the morning of Friday 28 September and without a penny to their names. By early evening and true to his nature, Kelly had managed to earn sixpence and telling him to spend fourpence of it on a bed at Cooney's, Kate took twopence and found a bed in a casual ward in Shoe Lane where she was well known.

The following morning she caught Kelly as he was leaving Cooney's. "What's this, gel? You're aht bleedin' early!"

"They pushed me aht, John, said I was drunk and causin' trouble. Took me bleedin' money they did, then pushed me aht. I been dossin' in the rag pickers yard back of Fashion Street." She was pale and looked ill, her breath full of gin fumes and raw onion. "John, I'm froze right through, I am, and bleedin' starvin' as well."

Kelly took his best boots to the pawn shop and pledged them for half a crown and then, his arm tightly round Kate's waist, they walked to Commercial Street and bought tea, sugar and some fat bacon. By this time it was raining with a thick fog building up from the river and the sorry pair made their way to Cooney's where, against his better nature, Fred Wilkinson allowed them to cook and eat breakfast in the lodging house kitchen.

Again without money, they parted at 2.00pm in Hounsditch. "I'm going over to Bermondsey, John", she said, "to see my oldest. She'll give us a few shillings to see us over."

Kate Eddowes was not known to have been an habitual prostitute but the odds are very much in favour that if hard pushed she would sell herself. She did not see her daughter that day (in fact she had moved months before) and at 8.00pm she was totally drunk in Aldgate High Street, singing at the top of her voice and entertaining a large crowd with her impression of a fire engine. She was wearing a black straw bonnet trimmed with green and black velvet with black strings to tie beneath her chin, a black cloth coat with imitation fur collar and cuffs, a dark green chintz skirt patterned with daisies and lilies, a grey stuffed petticoat and several underskirts - although she did not run to underwear as such. She wore men's lace up boots and had a red gauze imitation silk scarf about her neck. Evidently she had acquired the wherewithal for the drink, and it would not be unjust to assume that some form of immorality had figured.

The arresting officer was PC Louis Robinson, a seasoned policeman who was prone only to apprehend drunks for their own safety or if they were causing trouble. By the time he arrived on the scene, Kate was lying on the pavement and intoxicated to a point of near unconsciousness. There was no one in the crowd who knew her and so, with the help of another policeman, George Simmonds, Robinson pulled her to her feet and having prevented her from slipping sideways and falling into shop widows, the two policemen managed to get her to Bishopsgate police station where she was too drunk to give a name and was locked in a wooden floored cell. Later she gave the name of Mary Ann Kelly and a false address in Fashion Street Spitalfields.

She left the station at 1.00am. On asking Sergeant Hutt the hour she was told it was too late for her to get any more to drink and, laughing she said: "I'll get a damn fine hiding when I get home."

"And serve you right! You had no business getting as drunk as that."

She laughed: "Good night, old cock." Later, Hutt recalled that instead of turning right outside of the police station which would have taken her to Fashion Street (the false address she had given) or to Cooney's in Flower and Dean Street, she turned left, completely in the opposite direction.

Almost at the same time as Kate was leaving Bishopsgate Police Station, a few hundred yards away, Louis Diemschutz, a Russian Jew, was driving his pony and cart along Berner Street. With his wife he lived above the International Working Men's Recreational Club. His principal employment was that of caretaker of the club, an establishment patronised primarily by eastern European Jewish socialists, but to supplement his income he sold costume jewellery at street markets around London and it was from one of these that he was returning late that night. As he turned into Duffield Yard and into the storage area at the rear of the club, his horse shied and refused to advance further. Getting down and taking the bridle to lead the animal he saw what he took to be a bundle of rags laying against the wall of the club. He lit a match and recoiled in shock as the dim light revealed the body of a woman. Rushing into the club, he called in Yiddish and a member left his card game and ran to assist.

The body, they found, was still warm. There was no sign of a struggle but a viscous slick of uncongealed blood oozed from a gaping slash across the woman's throat. Two policemen arrived, shortly followed by Dr. Frederick Blackwell. Later, Diemschutz was to say that he had seen no one as he had driven into the yard - but that both the street and the yard at the rear of the club were unlit and pitch black. Taking into account the unusual behaviour of the horse, he felt sure that the woman's assailant had been concealed in the yard and had escaped whilst he sought help in the club.

Unaware of what had taken place barely minutes earlier, singing softly to herself, Kate had wandered into Houndsditch going towards Aldgate High Street and it was at the corner of Duke Street and Church Passage that she became conscious that she was being followed. Nervous, she turned round.

Joseph Levy, Joseph Lawende and Henry Harris left the Imperial Club in Duke Street and at 1.35am all three saw her engaged in animated and loud conversation with the man. Slightly the worse for wear but by no means drunk and in full control of their senses, the men made ribald comments and laughed as to how much it would cost to couple with such a dishevelled and sorry drab. She paid no attention but her companion turned his back towards them and pressed her close to the wall.

He knew a place, he said, not far from there, and he'd give her a shilling for a bit of a kiss and a knee-trembler. He wasn't fifty, she reckoned, and she liked his soft and friendly voice and the smell of soap she sensed about him. She'd rather have half-a-crown, she said and laughed as he said the best he could do was two bob and for that it'd have to be a lying-down job. He had a soft voice, a Londoner he was, but not coarse like a coster or her John Kelly; she felt comfortable – and two bob'd see to breakfast for her and John and a few gins beside.

They walked through Church Passage and into Mitre Square and passing several empty houses they found seclusion and darkness in a corner by warehouses owned by Kearley and Tonge, wholesalers. He smelt stale urine, vomit and the stench of a long-unwashed body and as she lifted her skirts and several under-petticoats he experienced a barely controllable surge of nausea rising from his stomach and he felt faint and dizzy. He turned her from him, one arm tight round her waist with the hand reaching to her flaccid breast, whilst the other hand with it's curved, cold extension was by his side.

"Do you think I'd connect with you, you dirty slut? Do you think I'd soil myself on your foul, infected, stinking flesh?" His voice was choked, a hissing and breathless, guttural rasp brought about by anticipation and excitement.

And suddenly the knife was there, at her throat, and tears and terror stifled words and screams. In a moment her drink-sodden mind cleared and she knew she had met the man of whom the slum women were living in fear and she knew that those seconds would be her last. He forced the knife against her throat, breaking the skin and causing the blood to start.

"You're number two tonight, you are, you sad sack of filth. I near got buckled a while ago and had to leave her. Prettier than you, she was, and not half the stink, but you and me'll have some fun", he whispered, "you be sure of that."

She felt the knife go deeper and knew it was in her throat and touching the artery. As he cursed her, with words and expressions so foul and evil that even she, the lowest of street creatures, had never heard, she wept, the salt tears mixing and diluting the ooze of her blood. Then, as if in an awful dream, she saw herself die as the jugular fountain spurted in front of her dimming eyes and she felt the tearing of the blade as it severed her wind-pipe, working through muscle and blood vessels, worrying, slashing and hooking. Her legs were kicking in spasm as he lowered her to the ground and, still muttering the vilest obscenities, he slashed at her face severing the tip of her nose and causing deep lacerations to her cheeks, nose and eyelids.

Breathless from the exertion, he paused, kneeling over the still twitching body and then, sure that they were alone in their corner…..

Later, the doctors found that the abdomen had been laid open from the sternum to the groin. One deep slash ran the length of the torso to the navel and then branching first left and then right, exposed the larger part of the viscera. About two feet of the colon had been removed and more intestines had been detached. The left kidney and the womb were missing, the latter having been sliced through horizontally and removed leaving only a stump; the liver had been stabbed and there was evidence of stabbing in the left groin.

Soon after it was established that the first body of the night, that found in Duffield Yard, was that of Elizabeth Stride, a 45 year old part time prostitute who had been born in Sweden. Originally married to a man named John Stride, she had more recently taken up with a man named Michael Kidney and was well known and liked in the area. She lived in a lodging house at 32, Flower and Dean Street and during the afternoon of the day of her death she had managed to earn a pittance by way of cleaning rooms there. She was a drinker as well as an occasional whore and by the early evening she was enjoying a glass of gin in the Queens Head in Commercial Street. Some time after 8.00pm she had moved to The Bricklayers Arms in Settles Street where there was a blind pianist and on the occasional evening spoon-playing twin brothers from Bromley-by-Bow would add to the entertainment.

"My Gawd! It's Long Liz" shouted a chimney sweep, still soot-faced and with a leather cap and neck-guard on his head. "Where've you bin, gel? Ain't seen you for bleedin' ages."

Three Jewish men playing **clabioche** at a table in the corner looked up from their cards and smiled and nodded a greeting and the landlord, a man in his sixties, thin like a ferret, waistcoated with watch and Albert and with the look about him of an unsuccessful undertaker with a side-line as a music-hall comedian, allowed a thin, grudging grin. "'Ello, Lizzie, darling – we all fought you was brahn bread!" His voice was as thin as his frame and seemed to be forced out from his chest in an airy ravenlike croak.

"I'm 'ere and there and I certainly ain't dead", she said, winking at the card players. "Keepin' aht the way of the bleedin' bailiffs, I am." In the West End, the cross Scandinavian – Cockney accent would have drawn attention but in cosmopolitan Whitechapel where all religions and nationalities melded into one, Long Liz Stride was no different from thousands.

She ordered small beer and sucking the head from the top of the glass she crossed the sawdust-covered floor to the old upright piano. "Fought that was you, Liz", said the blind man, reaching out his hand for hers. "'Ow you bin goin', gel?"

She took his hand and bent to kiss his cheek. "Bleedin' Kidney's gone off again", she said, referring to her most recent man friend. "Seein' some tart from over by the Isle of Dogs they reckon, but 'e ain't the only man in the world – not by a long chalk, he ain't."

She drank sparingly, aware that punters steered clear of drunks. With Mickey Kidney gone case and taking his income with him, she had to make a living and the best payers, she knew, liked a bit of conversation first and wouldn't have anything to do with some falling-down drunken slut. By 10.00pm the Bricklayers was full to capacity, thick with smoke and with almost as much beer being spilled on the floor than down throats. The card players had long since dispersed and plates of hot eels and mashed potato and fat pork and boiled cabbage were being served. The pianist and the spoon-clicking twins were worked flat out with the most current Harry Champion music hall songs being requested time after time.

The man had bought her two glasses of port. He didn't look fifty, she reckoned, and as they shared a plate of boiled beef and peas pudding she caught the slight scent of soap and she relaxed in her chair, happy that her new friend seemed to be something of a gentleman.

Later, the landlord and several customers recalled that she had left the pub at 11.00pm and three quarters of an hour later she was seen in Berners Street, talking quietly to the same man, at the same time and kissing cuddling with him.

"I know Lizzie Stride well", said the occupant of a Berners Street dwelling. "I see her ahtside number 50 – not thirty feet away from where I was standin' mind – and so bleedin' close I 'ears him laughin' and he says to 'er: "You'd say anything, you would. Except your bleedin' prayers, that is."

At 12.30am they had moved up Berners Street and as PC Smith passed on his beat he saw the shadowy form of what he took to be a courting couple in the gloom as he passed by. The woman, he said later, was Lizzie Stride – who he knew well and had arrested for being drunk on several occasions.

She wanted two shillings, she said facing him in Duffield Yard, and she wanted it before she'd let him touch her. The man felt anger and hatred welling up inside of him, this combined with an inexplicable feeling of savage lust which he could not understand and which even he feared. He barely heard as she whined in her strange accent, his mind almost a half-century away and thinking of his dead sister and their mother with her peeled ash stick and the man's belt with the bright brass buckle she wore about her waist. Shuddering at his shoulders as he felt a terrible, sudden coldness, he closed his eyes and found the honed, curved blade in his right hand. In one movement he grabbed her by the hair, turned her from him and in one sweeping left-to-right he opened her throat, silencing her for ever.

She felt nothing. Wide-eyed she saw her blood as it splashed the fence and as her senses and sight diminished a second before she died she wondered why she smelt horses.

The man cursed. From a corner of the yard and covering his face with his sleeve, he watched the horse as it shied, smelling the fresh blood. As the carter got down he moved nearer to the side of the cart facing away from his victim and as the match expired and the man ran shouting into the club, he left unseen.

But far from satisfied.

14.

At 5.00am and having ascertained that no murders had been reported in the East End or anywhere else, Gregory knew that he had no option but to allow Peace to leave. Although instinct and his judgement told him that Peace was not the Ripper, he was well aware that the non-occurrence of the "double event" with Peace in custody may well indicate the total opposite. He saw that whatever he did he could be damned and, watching the early morning rain as it formed oily puddles in the station yard, he imagined that such was the privilege of rank.

At 11.00am and with still no murders reported Peace was allowed to leave. He was handed a list of all of the material and items which had been removed from his house and was told that he may be interviewed again. He refused a lift home and as Gregory watched him run through the rain towards a bus stop, he wondered if he had made the right decision. For his part, Mott wondered if they would be sued.

**

Ishmael Ishmael, a recently arrived – and legal – 68 year old immigrant from Albania was short in both English and money. He lived alone in one room in Camden Town and existed on the pittance paid to him for cleaning the Knights of Erotica massage parlour a mile or so distant from his lodgings and on the fringe of the West End. He did not know that he was paid less than the minimum wage and although he knew that to attempt to claim state benefit whilst he was employed may put him in trouble with the authorities, he did not realise that some supplement may be possible. The brothel where he was employed – for that is what it was – did not open until early afternoon and every morning Ishmael would leave his home and walk to work. He had a key to the premises, a building on three floors, and having let himself in he would make himself strong, sweet Turkish coffee and sitting in the small kitchen he would smoke several cigarettes. Although he was well aware of the nature of the business carried on at the Knights of Erotica, he had little contact with the staff and collected his wages every Sunday morning, an envelope being left for him behind the waste pipe of a sink in one of the cubicles.

In a short, blue cotton coat which had come from Albania with him, he started by tidying the small reception area, polishing the counter and desk, hoovering the grimy carpet and emptying the filthy, overflowing ash trays. There were four cubicles on the ground floor and six on each of the two floors above, these being divided from each other by thin, plaster-board partitioning. At the end of each passage was a door letting on to two lavatories situated side by side each behind a flimsy door. The "massage" compartments were large enough just to contain a single divan, a wash hand basin, a chair and a waste bin. Starting downstairs and singing all the while, he vacuumed the worn carpet in each cubicle, then stripping the thin, single sheet from the bed he replaced it with a fresh one; he washed the hand basin, emptied the waste bin into a black dustbin bag and changed the greying threadbare towel supplied to each of the work spaces and then tidied the pile of pornographic magazines on the floor by the chair. Moving into the toilets, he washed the linoleum floors, wiped down the tiled walls with a wet cloth and ensured that the containers were full of toilet paper and that spare rolls were available.

By 12.30pm he had reached the top floor. Age and a great many Turkish cigarettes had effected his heart causing occasional breathlessness and angina, and going into one of the cubicles he sat on the bed to catch his breath. After several minutes and feeling better, he cleaned the six cubicles, dragging his black dustbin bag with him as he progressed down the passage towards the toilets. He opened the door from the passage and seeing that both of the cubicle doors were closed he pushed them open with his mop handle.

The girl was in front of the lavatory in a kneeling position, a mass of blonde hair spread across the seat, her face and head apparently in the basin. She was naked and although Ishmael's mind told him that something about what he saw was not normal, the shock of seeing her seemed to overlay everything else. He closed the door immediately.

"Escuse" he said. "I not know…."

His lack of English combined with his instinct caused him to stop, and as his mind became ordered he knew that the girl was dead. He opened the door again, this time seeing the grey white legs and body, and the stiffened, almost marble fingers of the left hand, extended towards the back wall of the cubicle, reaching for something that was not there. Hesitatingly, he reached out and touched the girl's shoulder and even though he felt the chill of death, human nature made him shake her, hoping for a sign of life.

The body slipped to the left and he saw that the lavatory bowl was full of blood and that the black, plastic seat was caked in one vast congealed mass. The girl had fallen between the toilet and the wall; she was laying half on her back and half on her side and as he looked, Ishmael saw that her throat had been cut from beneath the left ear to a point just above the right collar bone. Her eyes were wide open, blue and staring at a point above Ishmael's head.

***

Gregory looked up, phone in hand as Mott came into his office. Seeing the look on Mott's face he said: "I'll have to ring you back" into the receiver and looking at Mott: "What now?"

"It's look like we've got one, Guvnor. A tart in a massage parlour with her throat cut."

Gregory frowned. "How does that make it one for us."

"She's Swedish, Guv. And the massage parlour's in Berners Street –"

"I thought you said –"

"Berners Street West One, Guv. Off the Tottenham Court Road."

They were at the scene within the hour and pushing their way through the crowd of journalists and sensation-seekers they found themselves in the dreary little reception area of the massage parlour. In overall charge of the enquiry was Detective Chief Inspector Tony Carter, a man Gregory knew well. Aided by an interpreter, a detective sergeant was taking a statement from Ishmael and in response to Mott's enquiry he said: "This is the cleaner, Sir. He found the body."

Mott nodded. "What's his name?"

"Ishmael, sir."

"Ishmael what?"

"Ishmael, sir."

"I know that. What's his other bloody name?"

"That's it, Guv. His name's Ishmael Ishmael."

Mott blinked, looking from Ishmael to the sergeant. "I see", he said, and then apparently as an afterthought: "Born in Baden-Baden in 1919, was he?"

The sergeant and the interpreter both creased with laughter as Mott and Gregory went towards the stairs.

Gregory found that Carter was well aware of the possibility that the latest murder may be the latest in the Ripper sequence. The two senior detectives shook hands and, Gregory having seen the body, they went into one of the massage cubicles and closed the door. Gregory knew that he dare not disclose the Folmer aspect to Carter but at the same time he had no option but to put him in the picture to a large extent, In the event, he had no need.

"I know what you've got over there, Mike", said Carter. "We're all watching it and no one envies you, believe me. Now, if I've got this right the 1888 bloke did two the night of 29

– 30 September and you reckon this could be one of the copy cat bastard's efforts?"

Gregory nodded: "One of the women was done in Berners Street which was at the back of Houndsditch; that's no longer there, but you'll see the significance. She was a Swedish tom and so's this one, isn't she?"

Carter looked at his notebook: "Katarina Aaronson, aged 27, born in Stockholm, came to the UK a couple of years ago. She's got four previous for tomming and one for possessing an offensive weapon. She lives in a flat in Brixton with another tom – one of my lot's gone over to get her and bring her back here now. We've been in touch with the Swedish police and they're doing the necessary over there – family and all that."

Carter was a younger man than Gregory. He had a reputation as a determined and successful detective who did not mind standing on a few toes if it meant getting the required result. The older man smiled inwardly as he noted the silk tie and the unfastened top shirt button, the three-quarter length leather coat and the well-pressed khakis. Give it ten years, he thought, and they'll be giving evidence at the Bailey in jeans and bloody T shirts.

Turning to Carter, he said: "Who owns this hole, then?"

"You may well ask. The geezer downstairs, that Ishmael, he says he doesn't know other than it's a Turkish crowd. His wages are paid in cash every week he's got a key to come in and out and he's never met any of the management. The council say that the business rates are paid by a company called "Anatolaction" – we've looked at that and from what we can tell this early the directors don't exist."

"There must be some sort of manager, surely?"

"Smiley Smiley downstairs says there's a woman called Mrs. Caravan or something like that and we're waiting for her to turn up now."

The screen on Gregory's mobile telephone indicated that Strathearn was calling, and excusing himself he went to another room. Due to the absence of a second body, The Old Man said, Carter was to handle the murder but if a second was to turn up the whole situation would be passed over to Gregory. He returned to Carter who grinned slyly and said: "What was all that in the paper about some old job in the fifties – the murder of some tom in the West End?"

Prepared for this, Gregory said: "All crap, really. They got hold of the wrong end of the stick, as usual. I just went down to the Isle of Wight to see an ex DS and –"

He was saved further lies by a commotion from the end of the passage as raised voices and heated conversation came from the stairs and they were shortly joined by Carter's sergeant and an evidently very angry woman.

"I don't give two shits what it's about, you 'aven't got no bleedin' right comin' in here without a bleedin' search warrant and –"

She broke off, looking at Gregory and Carter and: "Ah, you're the Guvnors, I suppose. Now, we've been through all this before, Old Bill traipsin' in here whenever they bleedin' feel like it – just to have a look at the girls, I'm bloody sure it is –"

"And you are?" asked Carter.

"Me? I'm Mrs. Canavan, that's who I am. The manageress." Gregory estimated she was in her early fifties although make-up and wear and tear made a true opinion difficult. Her dyed blonde hair was shoulder-length, she was over-weight and over-dressed and reeked of cheap perfume and stale cigarette smoke.

"I see" said Carter coolly and, Gregory thought, with admirable restraint. "Well, Mrs. Canavan, you and I will be having quite a chat during the course of today and it would be better if we understood each other and –"

"Here! I'm not havin' any of this bullshit." Reaching into her coat pocket she pulled out a mobile telephone and: "I'm going to 'phone the brief and get 'im over here now. Fucking coppers walkin' in and out as they feel like it –"

Carter took the mobile telephone from her hand and put it in his pocket and then, taking the woman by the arm and to Gregory's horror and amazement, he pulled her into the toilet area at the same time saying softly: "Now, you sad brothel-keeping cow, you have a look at this before you call Slippery Sleaze and Shyster, okay?" The door letting on to the passage closed and immediately banged open as the woman and Carter came back into the passage, Carter still holding her arm.

Now the colour of cigarette ash and unsteady in her feet, she moved into the nearest cubicle and sat on the bed. Carter, pulling a chair to the bed, sat directly in front of her holding both her hands in his. "Right." he said. "If you want to phone your brief now – fine. As far as I'm concerned you can phone the Lord Chief bleeding Justice and you can tell him to come and see you at West End Central – which is where you'll be in about four minutes flat." Getting up from the chair he nodded at the sergeant. Mrs. Canavan, all fight gone, got up from the bed. "That's Katty – the Swedish girl", she said softly, almost reverentially. "Who'd ever want to do anything like that?"

By 5.00 pm, and with the second part of the "double event" not in evidence, the atmosphere at Leman Street was less tense. Gregory had been faxed a copy of the statement of Helen Canavan who said that she had been employed to run the massage parlour nine months earlier. She said that she knew her employer only as "Ergun", that he collected the cash receipts every afternoon and that she was responsible for paying the out-goings from the take. Each girl, and there was a maximum of sixteen at any one time, paid £200.00 daily for the usage of the premises and facilities offered, and everything over and above this that they managed to extract from clients was theirs. She was paid £750.00 per week in cash for her expertise and management abilities which, Gregory realised, were not inconsiderable taking into account that she had three convictions for brothel-keeping and living off the earnings of prostitution and was obviously something of an expert in the field. She had taken on the Swedish girl about three months earlier and other than that she seemed to have a number of regular clients and was a hard worker, she knew little about her.

Carter phoned. "I'm sure she's telling the truth, Mike," he said. "She's been in bloody tears here most of the afternoon and she's terrified she's going to be nicked again for brothel-keeping and poncing and going down for a stretch. I've told her that if there's one lie in her statement I'll do her up like a bleeding kipper but if she tells the truth she'll get a bit of help."

Needless to say, neither Ergun nor any other gentleman of Ottoman extraction had been near the massage parlour all day and Carter was of the opinion that the whole thing was a front. The names and addresses of the directors of Anatolaction Ltd were false and were the same as those supplied to both the landlord and the local council. "I don't have to tell you, Mike, do I? It's like the dirty book shops: the manager's some sort of front, he doesn't know anything so he can't tell anybody anything and when the shit hits the fan or if there's any bother everyone's done a runner and the whole set-up's a fantasy."

The forensic people were all over the massage parlour, Carter said, and the post mortem had been done that afternoon. He had not heard if the press had made the association with the double event, but Gregory knew that it was inevitable and just a matter of time. He asked Carter to ensure that any CCTV film which was available was examined for a white transit van and they agreed to meet later that evening to update each other and to discuss progress.

He called Mott into his office: "What to do think? Is that Creepy again?"

Mott nodded. "It's a helluva coincidence if it's not."

"But he's supposed to do two", said Gregory. "Where's the other one?"

Mott shook his head and pulled a face. "Well, if it is him, it lets old Peace of the hook. That's one good thing, I suppose. Until the bastard sues us."

Evading the ever-lurking press, Gregory slipped out of the back yard of Leman Street and took a taxi to the West End where he met Carter in a pub off Charing Cross Road.

"How long had she been dead, Tony?" asked Gregory.

"They reckon between twelve and fifteen hours, which makes it any time between nine and midnight the evening before."

"They couldn't've checked the place when it closed."

"No one ever did from what Helen Canavan says. See, Mike, there was no work schedule or anything like that. If a girl came in, she paid her two hundred quid, no matter how long she stayed. If she made her money by seven o'clock and wanted to go home, she'd go. Canavan could always phone round and get a replacement if she wanted to, but really she didn't have much of an idea about who was there and who wasn't and when she wanted to close for the night, she'd let the girls know and that was it."

"And nobody checked to see if they were all out?"

Carter shook his head. "No. She said that last night it was slow after about half eleven and one o'clock she shut the doors and they all went home."

"With that poor girl lying dead" said Gregory, shaking his head. He thought and then: "Has anyone got any idea what punters Katarina had yesterday?"

Carter drank beer and wiped his mouth with the back of his hand. "Well, Canavan hasn't, I can tell you that. She just sits behind the counter, cops a tenner admission off the punters and tells them where to go. She reckons yesterday they had as many as forty and she barely looks at them."

"No CCTV cameras?"

Carter laughed: "About the last thing you want in a place like that, isn't it? There's no one going to go there if they think they're going to be on candid bloody camera."

"What about the girls?"

"Well, eleven turned up for work yesterday and we collared all of them and got statements. The problem is that they spend most of their time in the little cubicles: if they've got a punter the engaged sign's on the door and if they're free it's not. They all say that Katarina had a following but no one's got the slightest idea who she saw, what they looked like or anything else."

Gregory gave a packet of the E Fit pictures of Creepy to Carter who said that they were doing all they could to trace as many girls who worked at the parlour as possible. "It's not as though they've got a membership list, is it? The people who use that sort of place are not about to advertise it, are they, and they're not going to come forward but we're going to keep the doors open for the next few days to see who and what turns up. Who knows?"

Later, at what he was obliged to call home, Gregory slumped in his uncomfortable armchair and drank whisky. Picking at a take-away curry, he watched Tony Carter on TV as he told the world that an arrest was imminent and was relieved to note that no association was made with the Ripper investigation. He dozed, too tired to move to the bedroom…..

His mobile bleeped at 6.20am.

***

Mannie Marks, the warehouse manager at Farmiloe and Hanks was allowed to park his ancient Escort in the yard at the rear of the premises in Mitre Square. This was a privilege not granted to many employees but Manny's length of service and his age – he was 67 – had earned it. He had been an institution with F & H for over fifty years; he knew everyone who worked in Mitre Square, and everyone knew Manny – he'd been there so long, they joked, that it was him who found the Ripper's victim in eighteen hundred and frozen to death! Manny wore his sand-coloured dust coat to and from home and no one at F & H could ever recall seeing him without his cap and a chewed pipe in the corner of his mouth. Every weekday morning he arrived at precisely 6.00am and opened the warehouse ready for the receiving and dispatching of the cheap perfumes and cosmetics in which his employer dealt. This morning, though, was an exception.

The evening before a late delivery had arrived at the warehouse. Mannie had his empty lunch tin ready on his tall desk and was jangling the keys in his pocket ready for the off when the case arrived, delivered by an elderly chap driving a white van. He had looked at his watch and muttering words his wife at home in Ilford would not allow him to use in the house, he helped unload the wooden case from the van and fork-lifted it into the warehouse. He signed the delivery note, was handed a copy for the file and within five minutes he had the premises locked, the alarms set and was on his way home to his sausages - with a mental note that he would need an early start the next morning to get the case unpacked.

Not long after 5.30am he arrived. Shivering in the autumn chill, he unlocked the steel roller shutters thereby opening up the loading bay and having deactivated the alarm system, he put the kettle on. The wooden case, of course, was where he had left it. He made the tea and covering the pot with a knitted woollen tea cosy his wife had given him when they made him warehouse manager in 1972, and muttering to himself about "flavour fluddin' out" he found his case-opener.

The wooden case was about four feet long by three feet tall and two feet across and was not the sort of container that Mannie was used to handling. The materials handled by F & H usually came in cardboard boxes, sealed with industrial size staples and thick packing tape: this was unusual, probably some special bleedin' order by one of the bosses, he thought. The lid off, he found the contents was wrapped in thick plastic and was so heavy that he was obliged to demolish one of the sides of the case and to roll it out on to the warehouse floor. It was doubled, like a carpet, and tied with thick string to keep the doubled-up shape, and when he cut the string with his old pocket-knife, the parcel partially straightened, lying there, returning to its original shape, moving of its own volition.

The plastic was secured by packing tape and once again the old knife came out......

***

In the mortuary, Gregory and Jackie Daniel watched as Sean Findlater set about exposing the cadaver. Assisted by two mortuary technicians and with one SOCO making a filmed record and a second collecting, listing and bagging possible exhibits and samples, he cut through the plastic sheeting which had been wound round the body several times. Mannie's initial cuts had exposed the feet but with the entire plastic wrapping removed and laid out on the floor it was possible to see the precise manner in which the cocooning of the body had taken place. "It's been laid on the sheeting and at one side, leaving the greater part of the material free and unused" said Findlater. "The ends have then been folded down, very neatly, one over the feet and the other over the head and the body has then been rolled over and over, the tucked-in ends sealing themselves and forming an air-tight, water-tight - everything tight -shell."

The body was that of a woman aged about thirty years. It was naked although the clothes were found at the feet end of the package. Findlater estimated that she had died no more than 36 hours before the time she had been discovered which made the time of death sometime in the evening of Monday 29 September. The dark hair was shoulder-length and both Jackie and Gregory detected the whiff of perfume; her eyes were blue, both fingernails and toenails were painted bright pink and an assortment of tattoos were evident on the arms, shoulders and in the small of the back extending to the buttocks. The clothes consisted of a green mini-skirt, a cotton crop-top type vest, torn tights, a brassiere and a thong and a blue cloth coat with imitation fur at the collar and cuffs.

There was large bruise to the left temple and the throat had been cut almost to the point of taking the head off. All of the carotid and jugular vessels had been severed as had the wind-pipe and there was evidence of scraping or worrying activity of a sharp implement, almost as though access to the upper vertebrae was being sought. There were extensive facial mutilations on the nose and both cheeks, the left eye had been cut through the lid and there were lacerations on lips, gums and nasal bone. Findlater was of the opinion that the cause of death was blood loss due to the slashing of the throat but that the bruise at the temple had probably been caused by a massive blow, probably rendering the victim unconscious before the lethal wounds were inflicted. One large zigzag laceration ran the length of the body from the sternum to the pubes, a jagged slashing cut which exposed the viscera and liver. The liver had been stabbed and slashed as had the vagina and pubic area, one slash running from the vagina to the rectum; the left kidney and part of the womb had been removed.

The excisions, Findlater was sure, could only have been carried out by someone with a degree of medical knowledge. The stomach contained traces of a recently consumed meal of chicken and potatoes and there was evidence and smell of recent and heavy ingestion of alcohol. The heart, lungs and the remaining kidney were healthy and overall there was no trace of any disease.

Halfway through the examination Gregory's mobile phone indicated a call from Strathearn and using Findlater's office he took the call.

"The double-event, then."

"Looks like it, Guvnor" said Gregory, wondering if the sickness he felt was due to the post mortem or the previous night's surfeit of scotch and lack of sleep.

"More than looks like it, Mike: the bastard left three dabs in the massage parlour – two in the cubicle he used and one on the lavatory seat and they all match Folmers."

"Does Tony Carter know?"

"He knows about the dabs but not about Folmer." There was silence and then: "What have you got there?"

Gregory looked out of the office window into the post mortem room and the sordid, ghastly chaos which marked the end of some woman's life. He looked at the SOCOS, busy in their white plastic coveralls and hats, and he looked at Findlater, blood covered apron and gloves, weighing organs and talking into his microphone hanging above the steel table. And he looked at Jackie Daniel, young, pale but doing her best, and feeling the sickness rise towards his throat he switched off his phone.

15.

Rosie had cooked lasagne and sensing Gregory's mood from his phone call she bought two bottles of wine and made sure that the whisky would last the night. He arrived at 7.00pm, wet from the rain, very depressed and full of apologies.

"I'm sorry, Rosie, lumbering you like this at such short notice. I just couldn't face that dump in Fulham and, well, to be honest, I wanted to be with you."

After dinner, deep in an armchair and armed with whisky, he said: "I'm not at all sure I can go on with this. In a way, Strathearn's taking the piss: I'm doing two murders at Leman Street and now there's two more, for Christ's sake. I know they're connected but then there's this fingerprint thing with the Folmer job –"

She cut in, anxious to ease his mind if she could: "Mike, I shouldn't tell you this, but I can tell you now that Carter's going to keep the Berners Street one. There was a heavy meeting yesterday afternoon and The Old Man was quite adamant that you were not to be saddled with that one as well."

Gregory laughed: "Oh, I see: but I've got Mitre Square, have I?"

She smiled. "Well, it is on your manor at Leman Street, isn't it?"

"Well, almost, I suppose." He drank some scotch and then: "But it's still too much. This Folmer thing's driving me mad, and what with that and the bloody press –"

"You've got a meeting tomorrow, Mike, with Strathearn. Tony Carter'll be there, Mott, that fingerprint bloke and probably some others. There's going to be decisions as to what is the best way forward and –"

"Carter's going to be put in the picture, is he? About Folmer?"

"I believe so."

There was silence for a while and then, with what Rosie thought was a catch in his throat, he said: "That PM today, Rosie; what that bastard had done to that girl." He breathed deeply and she felt he may have been near to tears. "It was like an animal, a jackal or a leopard, something like that..." Pushing his glasses up on to his forehead he put his head in his hands, hiding his eyes which, she suspected were tearful. She poured more scotch and pulling one palm from his face she pushed the glass into his hand. "Terrible, Rosie, terrible that anyone could do that and –" he gulped whisky and shook his head in a gesture of despair – "I can't help thinking all the time that he's doing them all to take the piss out of me, or perhaps not just me, the whole damned establishment in general."

Waking alone the next morning, she found him in front of the television, the sound low so as not to wake her. Shivering, she wrapped her dressing gown around herself and turned on the central heating. "Well?"

"Not good, Rosie, I'm afraid. They're not barmy in Fleet Street, are they? Four murders on the same days as Jack the sodding Ripper, Abberline who buggered it up then and Gregory who's going to do it now – especially seeing as he knows when they're going to happen, which is more than Fred Abberline did....I reckon I'll be in uniform Monday, teaching crowd control at training school."

The conference at the Yard was at 3.00pm. Arriving with Mott, Gregory noted the day's newspapers – most of which he had read - laid out on the conference table. Tony Carter and his deputy, a detective inspector named Ian Stokes arrived shortly after and within ten minutes or so they were joined by Strathearn and Bassett from fingerprints, the presence of the latter causing Carter to look at Stokes and raise his eyebrows, apparently wondering if there had been some sort of development. The Old Man started by saying that he assumed that everyone had read the papers and that his opinion and that of those on higher floors was that Gregory was doing a good job and that there was no question of replacement. A press release would be issued to that effect, he said, and as far as the Yard hierarchy was concerned the media could like it or lump it. As Rosie had said, Carter was to remain in charge of the Berners Street murder but with a proviso that as the killing was almost certainly linked with the matters being handled by Gregory, the two incident rooms would maintain a close contact. Strathearn went on to say that a telephone call had been received at the Yard by a woman who stated that she had important information relative to the massage parlour murder and that, for reasons best known to herself, she would only meet with Gregory alone. This prompted some leg-pulling from Carter and Stokes and brought a small degree of levity to a situation Gregory was finding far from stress free.

Turning to the Mitre Square crime, Gregory said that the girl had not been identified by fingerprints but that a full description, details of clothing and tattoos would be in the evening papers and the dailies of the following day. The facial injuries were such that a photograph could not be released to the public but he felt that identification would be established quickly. Mannie Marks' description of the white Transit-type van which had made the delivery was felt to be most important: films from all local street CCTV cameras were being examined but, he pointed out, the vehicle probably used in the Hanbury Street crime had been driven with covered plates and not much was expected from that aspect. Marks had not been shown the E Fit provided by Mickey and Kath Warne at the Row Barge. Although the description he gave of the man who had driven the van closely matched that given by the Warnes it was felt that exposure of the E Fit to another potential witness could jeopardise the validity of an identification parade at some later stage.

At that point Strathearn took over once again and emphasising that what was to be disclosed was not to go outside of that room, he put Carter and Stokes fully in the picture as to the Michael Folmer aspect. There was a silence and then Carter, running his hand through his long dark hair, said: "I think I've got this wrong, sir. I understood you to say that dabs found on a letter sent by the geezer who did the first two murders have been identified as those of a man who was hanged for a murder in 1957."

Strathearn nodded. "That's it."

Stokes, younger and smarter looking than Carter, took of his glasses and cleaned them on his handkerchief. "That's nonsense."

"I wish to Christ it was." Bassett opened his file and took out the various sets of fingerprints and forms with which Gregory was familiar. "It's all here if you want to see it for yourself, but you can take it from me: the dabs on the letter match those of Michael Folmer who was hanged in January 1958 for murdering a tom."

"And Michael Folmer is an anagram of "I came from Hell", said Gregory. "His real name was Johnnie Marriott."

"Guvnor", said Carter, addressing Strathearn, "this is all a load of bollocks: dead men's dabs, anagrams, Jack the bleeding Ripper –"

"Tony", said Gregory, "every one of us here knows that." His voice was tired and gave hint of impatience and even short temper. "But that doesn't alter the fact that it's happening. Let me nutshell it for you: to date four tarts have been chopped up in exactly the same manner and on the exact days and in the same places that the first four Jack the Ripper murders took place in 1888, okay? A letter arrives which is odds-on from the killer and that letter has got eight or nine fingerprints on it and those dabs, beyond any doubt, match those of man called Johnnie Marriott who was a nutter from Devon who chopped a tom up in 1957 and got topped for it, okay? When he got nicked he gave the name of Michael Folmer which is an anagram of "I came from Hell" and we have only just found out his true ID. Now, chummy – our killer – knows all about Folmer because in the letter he hints at a second time, meaning the first was in 1888, the second was Johnnie Marriott –"

"And the third is now," said Carter, nodding, at the same time frowning and biting his lip. "But it still doesn't mean it's not crap, does it? Dead man's dabs – Jack the Ripper back from the dead? Come on, Guvnor, we all know better than that."

Before The Old Man could speak, Gregory went on: "Like I said, we do know better than that, Tony. The trick is going to be to catch the bastard and to find out how he's done it. Hopefully before he does any more."

"There's one more thing that you should know, Tony", said Strathearn. "We had a chap in a couple of days ago: he's a retired PC from Southgate way somewhere called Victor Peace. Now, he looked a good bet at one time, mainly circumstantial mind, but we had him locked up over the period these two recent ones were done, so it looks like he's out of the frame. The odd thing, though, is that Marriott or Folmer whatever he was called was charged at West End Central in 1957., and this Peace was serving there at the time."

"Does he know about this, the dabs I mean?" asked Carter.

"No. No one outside of this room knows about that side of it."

"Was he on duty the day that the bloke was charged?"

"We don't know – all the records have been destroyed."

There was short silence during which Gregory reflected that everything seemed to be going against them and that if the devil was running the show he was making a pretty good job of it.

"What is the current situation in Mitre Square, Michael?" asked Strathearn.

Gregory looked at Mott who referred to his notebook: "No dabs on the delivery note - just a page torn out of one of those duplicate books you can buy anywhere. Mannie Marks remembers the delivery chap wore grey woollen gloves, like RAF issue ones, he reckons. The stuff the body was wrapped up in was plastic damp course sheeting, the rope it was tied up with was tatty old stuff, all frayed and like it had been used a dozen times before – everything's up at the laboratory, all her clothes, everything." He turned the pages in his book and went on: "Now. The Hanbury Street girl, that's Cicelyn Jean Percy, she had her womb and other bits removed and the pathologist who did the PM says that whoever did her must have had some sort of medical knowledge. Findlater – he did the PM on the girl yesterday – he says exactly the same thing."

The meeting over, The Old Man took Gregory and Carter along the corridor to his office.

"Now, I don't know whether this is any good or not – you'll just have to see. Mid morning today a woman phoned the Yard switchboard and she said she had some important information about the massage parlour job. She wouldn't give a name or say any more other than she would only deal with Mike Gregory and that she would meet him in Brighton."

Carter started laughing. "There you go, Mike: you've pulled. It's always the same, isn't it? You take a partner on a job and the minute there's any crumpet about, he shafts you!"

Laughing, Strathearn went on: "She says she'll meet you at half eleven Saturday morning on the corner of Charlotte Street and Marine Parade. She says you've to be on your own and any sign of any law she'll clear off and that'll be the end of it."

"How will I know her?"

"She says she will know you."

"Did they trace the phone?" asked Carter.

"Aye, they did: a pay-as-you-go mobile with no name and address for the user."

Later, when Carter had left, Strathearn said: "Michael, you've got about five weeks, son."

"Five weeks, Guv?"

"Aye. To the next one. Eighth and ninth of November it was. Mary Kelly. And if you think that what he did to that poor cow in Mitre Square was bad, have a look at the photos of what the first one did to Mary."

Friday 3 October 2003.

Mott was waiting for Gregory at 8.00am., and seeing him go into his office he collected two cups of tea from the canteen and joined him.

"Guv, I've been awake all night thinking about this: I know I'm right and I need you to see that I am."

Gregory could see that Mott was concerned. Recently he had come to have a regard for him, feeling that he may not be quite as black as he had been painted and at the same time he had come to see that the man had a sharp and incisive mind and a fair degree of detective ability. He took his jacket off and loosened his tie. *Á la* Carter, he thought; modern, trendy.

"Go on, Dave."

"Well, do you remember when you come back from, the Isle of Man –"

"Wight."

"Right. Well, I said this then and no one seems to have listened, Guv, and I honestly think it's important. When you come back you said that Stan Cutler was there when they topped Folmer. You said that Cutler said that just before he went Folmer laughed and said something about telling Bert Castle that it wasn't all over and he'd be back or something like that. Now, we know there's no ghosts, don't we, and we know dead men's dabs don't come again, so it's clear to me that when he said that on the drop, Folmer knew there was something dodgy somewhere about the dabs and he was taunting Castle and Cutler."

Gregory sipped lukewarm tea and cursed the Metropolitan Police Food Service.

"Now, Guv, Folmer or Marriott or whatever he was called had no form; he would know that the prints they took when he had the bother in Berlin had been destroyed – otherwise Castle and Cutler would have connected him with that – which we know they didn't do, so it must be that whatever it was that caused him to make that comment happened between when he was nicked by that cadet and when he got topped – and it was something to do with his bloody fingerprints."

"And he was only in West End Central, Brixton on remand and the condemned cell in Pentonville before they dropped him."

"Exactly! And I'll lay a pound to a pinch of shit it was in West End Central."

"Where Vic Peace was."

Barney Iannou and Jackie, it was agreed, would be detached from the main enquiry and devote all their attention to attempting to find out what had taken place at West End Central at the time that Johnnie Marriott had been there. The starting point would be the aide to CID who had taken the fingerprints, PC 614C Andrew Sellick. Gregory checked with The Old Man who after initial strong opposition came to see that for them to do their job effectively and to get the best possible result there was no alternative: Jackie Daniel and Barney had to know the full details of the Folmer/Marriott side of the matter.

The following morning Gregory drove to Brighton in his old Mondeo. He wore a pair of green cotton trousers, a sweat shirt over a red and white gingham shirt, a pair of worn trainers and a suede jacket and just before 11.30am he positioned himself in Marine Parade opposite Charlotte Street. He did not have to wait long and from the moment he saw the contact he could feel something was not quite right. She arrived shortly after him and evidently recognising him, she ran across the main Marine Parade, dodging between the traffic, low-heeled sandals bringing her perilously close to falling. She arrived at his side, breathless, and gasped: "It is Mr. Gregory, isn't it?"

He estimated she was in her late twenties with short, natural blonde hair, startlingly blue eyes and a clear, almost Scandinavian complexion. She was wearing dark blue trousers and matching jacket, a white and evidently expensive silk blouse and an embroidered silk scarf. The sandals were gold in colour and Gregory would have bet his life that the hosiery ended in stocking tops and suspenders as opposed to tights.

She was keen, he thought. Too bloody keen. She wouldn't say who she was, Strathearn had said, and here she is turning up on the dot and with him on the opposite side of a main dual carriage sea-front road, she doesn't even wait for a minute but hares across straight to him, almost as though she knows him. She could have recognised him from the papers or on TV, he mused, but, well, he would see. "You wanted to meet me?"

"Yes", she said, her breath back and speaking in a soft, well-spoken accent. "Shall we walk?"

They walked a hundred yards or so along the splendid esplanade and then she stopped and leaned on the rails, facing the sea. "I have to be so careful, Mr. Gregory; if my parents knew it would kill them." He said nothing, preferring to allow her to lead the conversation. "You see, I have been working in the Knights of Erotica for about three months and I knew Katty Aaronson. Quite well, actually."

Gregory watched some sort of container vessel ploughing through the grey, choppy sea and shuddered. She went on: "I live with my parents, in Hove, and they think I'm an actress; well, I was, for about two years and then I got into the massage. For the money, really."

Gregory looked at her and nodded. She went on: "I had a baby three years ago. The chap left me and I had nowhere to go except home and my parents are not really well to do you see...."

He moved away from the rail, facing back the way they had come. She took his arm, shielding herself from the sea wind. "What about Katty?" he asked.

"Well, it's this really. She told me that she had this regular, an old chap who was coming in to see her once or twice a week. She said he was strange, had funny eyes or something and all he wanted to do was talk to her for half and hour and then give her the same money. She said he talked about Jack the Ripper, you know, things like that, and that she was scared of him, but the money was too good to miss."

"What did she say he said about the Ripper?"

"About what he did to the women he killed, hooking out their bits and chopping them up – all that sort of thing."

"Which floor did you work on in the parlour?"

"The top floor. We never know which room we would have, but the newest girls were at the top and that was Katty and me, really."

"And you knew Helen Canavan of course?"

"Old bitch", she said. "She never gave a damn about who was in the place or who wasn't. All she cared about was getting her cash out of it."

"Did you ever see him – the chap Katty was worried about?"

"No, I never did, but I always knew when he'd been there – she always came and told me afterwards."

"Who owns it, Knights of Erotica? Do you know?"

"I always thought that Helen did, but now the papers are saying it was Turkish people or something. Is that right?"

They crossed the road at a pedestrian crossing. "Would you like a drink?" she asked Gregory and without waiting for a reply and holding his arm she steered him up the steps of a hotel and through the revolving doors. In the bar, him with a tonic water and her with white wine, he said: "I don't suppose you're going to tell me your name?"

She laughed and shook her head: "Sophie, if you like – but that's it. If you want to get in touch use the number I left when I phoned Scotland Yard."

They stayed in the busy bar for almost twenty minutes during which time she told him nothing he did not already know. She was not evasive, just non-committal and vague. Shortly before 1.00pm she excused herself to visit "the little girls' room" and did not return, which was of no great account to Gregory who was wondering if she was going to hit him for lunch.

He drove back through Newhaven and stopped for a pint and a sandwich in Lewes. For the life of him he could not understand why this Sophie had asked to see him. Certainly she had some knowledge of the Knights of Erotica and what went on in the place but the truth was she knew nothing of any use – or so it seemed. As he drove, his mind going over the meeting, a vague noise inconsistent with the worn engine of his Mondeo grated on his consciousness and he realised that his mobile phone, somewhere deep in a pocket, was summoning him back to sensibility.

"Guv", said Mott, "where are you, Guv?"

"Kent. Or Sussex. One of them."

"Guv, we've got an ID on the Mitre Square girl. Do you want to come in?"

***

An hour later at Leman Street and the heart-rending misery of a family who has experienced loss to violent, criminal death. In the office housing the HOLMES computer Gregory found Mott with the parents and husband of the dead girl. Introduced, he sat at the desk and was told by Mott that the victim's name was Tracy Gallop, that she lived in Camberwell and that although her husband, Terry, knew that she had been working for an escort agency for some months, her parents were not aware of this. Positive identification had been made at the mortuary by Terry Gallop who had suspected that the dead woman was his wife from the description of her clothes and tattoos given in the daily papers. Gregory sensed that feelings were running high and that great care was needed.

"She should never've been working at a bleedin' escort agency," said the dead girl's father, a small, thin man with sandy hair, his face grey and drawn through shock. "Whatever was you thinkin' of, letting her do that? It's no better than her being on the bleedin' game is it?" His voice was cracked and breaking, his face lined with tears.

Terry Gallop, a thin man with acne scars and a mop of iron grey hair shook his head. He wiped his face with a handkerchief and said: "You know what she was like, Stan; once she'd made up her mind that was it. Weren't nothing I could do."

"You should've told us – we'd've put a stop to all that, wouldn't we Marge?" He turned to his wife, a thin woman, like her husband grey with shock. She nodded and said nothing.

Gregory looked at Mott who, sensing what was coming said: "We've got all the details of the agency from Mr. Gallop, sir – everything's in hand."

***

Mayfair and Society Escorts of South Audley Street, Mayfair turned out to be run from a bedroom in a run-down and cheerless council flat in Kennington near the Oval Cricket Ground. The proprietors were two aging sisters, Annie and Elizabeth (Bessie) Abbot: both were spinsters and both had apparently devoted their entire adult lives to servicing the underbelly of the nation's society in one way or another. Mott's initial research had revealed that the prestigious Mayfair location was an accommodation address and that the central London telephone numbers rerouted to a worn telephone/ answering machine in seedy south London. Annie, Mott had ascertained, was aged 68 and had a matching number of convictions for soliciting prostitution as well as two for brothel-keeping for which she had been sent to prison. Bessie Abbot, three years younger, had qualified as an abortionist following a three year course with her mother; this career, mercifully, lasted only a short time, the repeal of the legislation forcing her to seek other fields of endeavour, but not before she had been convicted twice for procuring illegal abortions and sent to prison on each occasion. Since then she had been convicted on nine occasions for living off the immoral earnings of prostitution and had served several short sentences of imprisonment for her determination.

Bessie opened the door of the second-floor flat and in the no-nonsense manner which policemen have when they know they are on good ground, Mott and Gregory were in. Bessie was wearing woollen trousers and a jumper and her sister favoured a dirty dressing gown and filthy pink slippers on heavily veined and grimy feet. There was a tea-pot and a milk bottle on a tray on the table and Gregory saw two dirty cups and a tin of biscuits on the tiled fireplace. An enormous wide screen television was showing "Big Brother" and in a corner a vast black cat appeared to be addressing bowel evacuation in an overflowing cat-tray.

Gregory turned off the television. "You are running an escort agency from this flat. Is that common ground?"

"No, oh no, sir", said Annie, "there's not nothing like that here."

"Mayfair and Society Escorts of South Audley Street – does that ring a bell? The address there is a letter drop for which you pay the rent in cash every week, the two phones are rerouted through to this flat, the girls get calls from either "Annie" or "Bessie" and both of you have got more form than a Derby winner and most of it for tomming and running brothels. Now - do we understand each other?"

Bessie sat down in one of the grubby armchairs and started grizzling: "It's only a bit of pin money – we got to live, haven't we? What we get off the social and that don't come to a lot –"

"Do you know a girl named Tracey Gallop?"

The two women looked at each other and shook their heads. "No, no, sir. Not a Tracey Gallop."

"Girl about 30", said Mott, "dark hair, blue eyes, painted finger and toe nails and tattoos on her arm and down at the bottom of her back. Lives in Camberwell."

"Oh" said Bessie, "that's, um, er - what's she called Annie?"

She got up and went into a bedroom, emerging almost immediately with a large photograph album. She leafed through, turning pages quickly and then, holding the open pages out for Mott and Gregory to see: "That's Tanya – Tanya Shapiro."

Gregory blinked at the pretty, grinning face looking at him from the album. He found it hard to compare with the slashed and broken features he had seen in the mortuary and at the same time wondered how Terry Gallop had been able to handle such pain. He nodded: "That's her. Her real name's Tracey Gallop."

"What's happened" asked Annie Abbot. "She's alright, ain't she?"

"She's dead."

During the next hour they learned that Bessie and Annie inserted advertisements in such publications as they thought suitable and that they would make the arrangements for the "escort", the client first having chosen the girl with whom he wished to spend the evening from the assortment of pictures in the album which he would be shown by one of the sisters at a suitable West End location, generally a hotel. The client would pay the Abbots the fee - £200.00 for the night's escort service, half of which would be remitted to the girl by the Abbots. To protect themselves, the Abbots required that all of the girls signed a form to the effect that they were not prostitutes and that should any immoral behaviour be involved it was outside of the knowledge of the sisters and certainly not procured or condoned by them.

"I mean, human nature's human nature, ain't it?" said Bessie, picking some unidentified foreign body from the corner of her eye and examining it closely. "I mean, if some nice chap comes down here on business and he goes out with one of our ladies and after a nice dinner and a bit of theatre or something they decides to go back to his hotel and he gives her a few quid – well, s'human nature, ain't it – nuffink to do with us, is it?"

"Monday night, the twenty-ninth, he booked Tanya" said Annie. "He phoned up on the Saturday afternoon, I remember 'cos I was watchin' the racing and Bessie was over Safeways. He knew her name – Tanya he said he wanted, the tall girl, the one with the tattoo on her back – and he said he'd meet her in the bar at Liverpool Street station. He said he'd know her and she weren't to be no later than half seven."

"Had he booked her through you before?" asked Gregory.

"No, he's never been to us before, not that I know of."

"How did he pay you?"

"The money come in the post the Monday – cash. She wouldn't have gone else."

"Was there a letter?"

"No. Just ten twenties in an envelope."

"And you're sure you've never dealt with him before?"

"Sure."

She had thrown the envelope away, she said. When Tanya didn't come for her money the next day, she never gave it a thought: it was there when she wanted it – and anyway, you know what them girls are like!

They took away the photograph album and an assortment of magazines with the Mayfair and Society advertisement and told the sisters that they would be seen again for statements to be taken and that decisions would be made as to possible prosecutions. Going over London Bridge in the Saturday night traffic, Mott said: "He must have known her, then."

There was a silence. In a queue of traffic approaching the north side of the river, Gregory watched as a discarded fish-and-chip paper swirled in the yellow street light above the bridge, seemingly held in some strange thermal born of exhaust fumes and the river, and then: "He must've done, the bastard. But how, I wonder?"

He got to Ealing just after 11.00pm. Locking his car he suddenly sensed the same ice-cold feeling at his neck and down his spine. Suddenly, he was afraid, scared of God only knew what, but he knew as he had known that night weeks before in the Chairmen: some bastard was watching him. He crossed the street, peering into the misty darkness of the Common, venturing on to the wet grass and feeling the drips from the trees on his neck. There was no one there – no one that he could see. But there had been - he'd stake his life on that.

In the house with whisky comfort and Rosie's over-cooked, dried out but deliciously welcome shepherd's pie. He had barely settled when the phone rang. She answered it, and looking at Gregory, she said voicelessly, carefully enunciating each unsaid word: "It's The Old Man – for you."

He hesitated but knew he had no option.

"Mike Gregory."

"Michael." The voice was calm and smooth and without hint of irritation. "I thought I better let you know: you're all over one of the tabloids tomorrow morning. Press bureau have just been on to me; apparently the editor has just notified them – conveniently late so that we cannot get an injunction to stop it –"

"What's the story, Guv? What are they saying now?"

"More pictures than a story, Mike. You and a young lady arm in arm on the prom at Brighton, drinks in a hotel bar, all that sort of thing with the inevitable accompanying splash about lack of activity with what they call the "Ripper Hunt", senior officer in charge has time to enjoy himself - you get the picture?"

"It was that tart, Guv. The one that phoned and wanted to meet me –"

"Mike, we know that. The point is that it's too late to stop it now it and by the time we can get press releases out to the effect that we have been set up it will be too late and the damage will have been done. They're going to have a field day, Mike, and there's nothing we can do to stop them."

"The bastards. I knew there was something fishy about that tart." He thought a moment and then: "Can I – we – can we sue them, Guv? Saying I'm down in Brighton getting my end away when I'm chasing a possible witness – surely I can."

"Well, I expect you could if you wanted to, but I doubt the Commissioner'll get involved and if the job'll swallow it –"

Later, when they were in bed, he asked her: "How did he know I was here?"

Half asleep she muttered: "He's a detective, isn't he?"

16.

The house called "Southwold" was a large, semi-detached property in Churchley Avenue in the North London suburb of Palmers Green. It was so-named as the original owners had met whilst on holiday in the Suffolk seaside town in 1926., and the current owner, their son, had seen no need to change it. Change, in fact, was something which Martin Calder Sturge abhorred and avoided at all costs; to him any form of change, particularly modernisation, could never be for the good and must, therefore, be detrimental to society in general and his way of life in particular.   That said, Martin Calder Sturge was no fool: well aware that change to the outside world was inevitable and beyond his control, he had long chosen to ignore what he saw as the descent of civilization into the pit and had satisfied himself by ensuring that his corner of the world remained the calm and nuisance-free haven which it had always been.

Although the local estate agents described Churchley Avenue as being tree-lined, the truth was that the elms, beeches and ornamental cherry trees were few and far between. Age, and the wear and tear of weather, the ravages of both children and animals and a lack of attention from the local council had resulted in ill-kept and scruffy growths, bare and in need of pruning in winter and bearing diseased leaves in the spring. But situated adjacent to Broomfield Park, it was in a nice area – very London suburbia kippers-and-curtains, perhaps – but Martin Calder Sturge saw nothing wrong with a kipper from time to time and curtains were an absolute necessity. The residents at the far end of the avenue, that nearest to the park, were prone to tell interested parties they lived in Southgate, but N13 was a fair trot from N14 and Sturge thought they were opinionated fools with ideas above their financial capabilities.

"Southwold" was a double-fronted, semi-detached property; substantial and well-kept it was, quite evidently, the residence of persons of some class and significance. The fussily-maintained front garden consisted of a small lawn and surrounding flower beds with a paving-stone path leading to the front door. The threshold bore a sheet of hammered brass, polished and shining, the step before was of red tiles and the brass letter-box and door knocker were spotless, rain or shine. The front door, black-painted, contrasted with the white sash windows and guttering, the white enamel bell-push set in a brass housing bore the instruction "PUSH" and the rooms on either side of the door were heavily curtained with deep red velvet. To the right of the house, and accessed through a second street gate, there was a high, black-painted door which let on to the kitchen door, coal bunkers and a garden with a small shed. The rear garden was laid to lawns and borders of shrubs and annuals with a predominance of rose bushes; in one of the corners farthest from the house was a fish pond with a flagstone surround and a replica of Brussels' Mannekin Pis set on rocks in the centre. To the left of the back garden and behind a low hedge was a garage with a door leading to the garden and car access from a lane at the rear; this was home to Sturge's ancient but immaculately maintained Ford Fiesta and an old bicycle.

Martin Calder Sturge was born in "Southwold." Never having married he had lived there all his life, and since 1984 when his mother died he had lived there alone. In his early seventies, neighbours who knew him at all saw him as a solitary man, shy and distant and if there was rudeness the truth was that it was due to his introverted nature and not an intention to offend. He was polite when spoken to, as far as anyone knew he paid his bills on time and although he was unlikely to be invited to a neighbour's Boxing Day cocktail party (and even less likely to have attended) he was accepted and left alone.

Sunday morning. Sturge was up and dressed before five as he was every Sunday. The first job of the weekly routine was the polishing of the metal threshold plate, this followed by the dusting, polishing and hoovering of the hall, lounge, dining room and kitchen. Shortly before seven he made himself a cup of black coffee and sitting at the kitchen table he drank it slowly watching the start of the day through the tall window.

****

In Ealing, Rosie found Gregory in the small kitchen. Black coffee and a newspaper.

"Look at this."

Two thirds of the front page was devoted to a photograph of Gregory and "Sophie" enjoying drinks in a Brighton hotel below which, in the largest print possible for the size of the paper, the world was told: "TOP COP SWAPS MULTIPLE MURDER HUNT FOR COCKTAILS." There then followed several paragraphs as to how Gregory had been seen taking "A Romantic Stroll" along Brighton's Marine Parade with "An Attractive Friend" and that the public should note that whilst a wicked serial killer was roaming London's streets the officer in charge of the enquiry was enjoying himself at the coast. Inside there was more: several photographs of "Gregory's Girl" walking along the Brighton esplanade arm-in-arm with "Yard's Top Manhunter", one as they hurried up the steps of the hotel and alongside the generally critical blurb accompanying the photos there was an editorial comparing Gregory with Abberline and wondering if the result of the modern-day investigation would be similar to that in 1888.

Gregory fumed and Rosie cooked breakfast. By ten his mobile telephone had rung two dozen times and unable to stomach any more coarse mockery from colleagues – some anonymous and others not – he switched it off.

***

His coffee finished, Sturge washed the cup and saucer, carefully replacing them on the dresser, regardless that he would be using them again in an hour or so with his breakfast. The stairs vacuumed and the banisters polished he turned to the three unused bedrooms, hoovering and polishing and ensuring that no crease spoiled the made beds, each with it's own counterpane and quilt, and once satisfied he closed the doors and went to his own bedroom. He made the bed, changing both sheets and pillowcases and only when the room was to his liking and smelling of Mansion polish did he return to the kitchen. By 8.00am he had hand-washed the bed linen and hung it on the small line at the side of the house and his cup and saucer (the same as he had used for his coffee) was laid at the end of the kitchen table together with two plates, cutlery and a serviette in a silver napkin ring, all awaiting the bacon and eggs cooking on the gas stove.

Breakfast eaten and the crockery and cutlery washed and replaced in drawers and dresser, Sturge carefully locked the back door of the house and five minutes later, with cycle clips firmly in place and wearing a flat cap and a beige anorak, he rode his bicycle to the junction of the North Circular Road and Green Lanes, Palmers Green adjacent to the Cock public house. Turning left towards Edmonton and shortly after left again, he eventually arrived at the place he loved more than any in the world: his allotment.

Of the thirty sites on the few acres of land set aside for keen gardeners there was no dispute that Sturge's was the best. Two rows of cabbage, two of brussels sprouts and two of parsnips were immaculately hoed and the adjacent rows of runner beans, high on poles, were as straight as the guardsmen on parade at the trooping of the colour. In one corner were marrows and pumpkins, in another was a flower bed with chrysanthemums soon to be ready for autumn display. The garden shed was painted white with a black roof and even the green, plastic water-butt, full of rain water from the zinc guttering, was bright and evidently well maintained. Sturge parked his cycle by the shed and undoing the padlock he entered the shed, like everything else in his life, tidy and ordered and with everything in its place.

***

An hour or so before lunch and just ready to leave home for the pub, Terry Gallop had visit a from Mott and Archie McGibbon. Mott, who also had a fancy for a Sunday lunchtime pint, was not in the mood to tip-toe around: a widower Gallop certainly was – and Mott fancied him for a pimp as well. "The geezer who did your missus knew her. Does that surprise you?"

The Gallop residence was a small flat in a dingy turning off Camberwell New Road. Dirty dishes were piled high in the kitchen sink and on the twin draining boards and the greasy containers and remains of last night's take-away curry were on the table. Gallop sat down on a grubby settee. "He knew her? He can't have done."

Mott, chancing his freshly washed beige trousers and tan raincoat, sat down beside him. "Son, I'm telling you he knew her and I'll tell you something else as well, shall I? We're not leaving here until I know how he fucking knew her."

Terry Gallop looked at the floor and said nothing. McGibbon sat down on a dining chair, anxious to show solidarity with Mott but inwardly terrified that this treatment of a recently bereaved and grieving man may result in complaints and censure or worse. Mott put his hand on Gallop's knee: "This so-called escort agency that Tracey was tied up with, the Mayfair and whatsit – well the owners are these two old dragon sisters from Kennington and they say that last Saturday a geezer phoned for an escort for the Monday night and he asked particularly for your missus - particularly. And, before you start telling me more porkies – he asked for her by name - Tanya. That was what she was calling herself, right?"

Gallop looked at Mott and then at McGibbon. It was a look that begged that he be granted respite from the aggressive intrusiveness of Mott's questions, but at the same time it was a look of guilt and the most awful, searing remorse. Mott, seeing the man's weakness and his own advantage, pushed on.

"She told them over at Mayfair that she was called "Tanya", right?"

Gallop nodded: "Yeah, she liked that. She reckoned it sounded better than Tracey."

"The geezer who phoned asked for "Tanya", the tall girl with the tattoo on her back – there's only one of those, right – your missus. And he said he'd meet her in the bar at Liverpool Street station at half seven Monday night. So don't tell me he didn't know her."

Gallop was crying then, the tears running down his face and dropping on the thin carpet. "He must've done, but I don't know –"

"You don't know what? How he knew her?" said Mott, "I do." He got up from the settee and taking Gallop by the lapels of his coat he dragged him up and, his face inches from the crying man, he said: "He knew the bold Tanya because he'd met her before. He'd met her before she got tucked up with the bleeding dragon sisters over at Kennington because you had her on the bleeding game, you bastard." He shook the lapels, his knuckles pushing against the man's chest. "Didn't you?"

Gallop nodded, the tears running from his closed eyes. Mott let him go; his voice softening, he said: "Son, if you want us to catch the bastard who did this to your wife the best thing you can do is tell us the truth."

Gallop sat down again. He wiped his eyes and nose on the sleeve of his jumper. "I never got her on the game, Guv, and that's the truth. See, it was the money with her, not wanting to speak ill of the dead and all that, but it was."

He worked as kitchen porter in a West End restaurant, he told Mott and McGibbon. Awful hours and worse money. "There was always this and that she wanted and then, sort of before I knew it really, she's going out nights while I'm working and there was always a few quid there in the morning."

"Where was she going?"

"Anywhere took her fancy, really. Up West, over the Bayswater Road, anywhere."

"When did this all start?" asked Mott.

"About a year ago, and then she started with that agency thing about six weeks ago. Better people and better money she said it was." It was mainly business men, she had told him: a few drinks and a nice dinner with the punter and then back to his hotel and a taxi home. "She got a oner off the agency for every client she done for them and then there was whatever she could get off the punter for the other."

"What about last Monday night" asked Mott, turning up the pressure. "Did she tell you about that?"

"Yeah, I knew she was out that night because the agency phoned Saturday afternoon and I took the call. She rung them back that night and got all the details and that, and then she told me it was one she'd done before, before she went with the agency like, and that she was seeing him at Liverpool Street station. She said he was a nice old feller, that's why she told him when she went to the agency, so's he could get in touch with her if he wanted to."

"Did she know his name – or where he came from?"

"I don't know, Guv, I wish I did. All she told me was that the last time he give her a oner just for sitting in his motor and talking for half an hour. She said she didn't reckon he could do it."

"How long ago was that?"

"Gawd, must be two months ago – just before she signed up with that agency."

***

Sturge cycled home to Southwold , stopping only to buy a newspaper. Arriving before noon, he placed his basket of vegetables on the draining board in the kitchen ready for washing later in the day. He made a cheese sandwich and having poured a small bottle of brown ale into a glass he settled down at the kitchen table to read his paper.

17.

Monday morning and most of the dailies, referring to the Sunday tabloid's Gregory smear, printed the Yard's version of events, this being that the woman was a witness who had made contact with the Yard, but the seeming inability or disinclination to name the mysterious person went a long way to strengthening the scent of mendacity which seemed to pervade the whole issue. "That's all very well" said Mott "but that Sunday Smear'll be the one they remember, mainly because it's the one they want to believe." Inwardly, he was seething: he sensed that Wonkeye Jerry was involved somehow, but he dare not mention this to Gregory for fear of opening old sores which he hoped had healed for ever.

After what had seemed like an age Gregory found that the army records relative to Johnnie Marriott's court martial in Berlin had finally arrived on his desk. There were three dusty and dog-eared files, each several inches thick, with many of the pages hand-written in fading ink and a great use of both sellotape and rusting staples. In an envelope at the front of the top file was a photograph of Marriott and attached to this a hand-written memo, apparently from the Military Police, to the effect that in accordance with army regulations the fingerprints had been destroyed following acquittal.

The circumstances were that in 1946., the body of Helga Eva Schwimmer, a 24 year old German prostitute was found in a bombed building in central Berlin. The woman's throat had been cut, almost severing the head from the body, and a post mortem revealed that the body had been severely mutilated and the womb had been removed. The German police found a witness who had seen a man in uniform leaving the ruined building shortly before the body was found but other than that there were no clues. A week or so later, though, a Russian army officer came forward and made a statement. He said that he had had known the deceased woman well and that one of her most regular clients was a British soldier he knew as "Johnnie" and that on the night of the murder he had seen them together in a bar in the city. During the course of intense questioning he admitted that he was the dead woman's pimp and that he arranged for her to meet serviceman of all nationalities. He said that he had met "Johnnie" at a party in a hotel room and that in the months following their meeting he had bought a range of black-market goods from him and that he had engineered the meeting between him and the dead woman. At this juncture, realising that the murderer was probably a British serviceman, the German police handed the matter over to the British military police who promptly locked up the Russian soldier, seemingly without any justification whatsoever.

Johnnie Marriott was rapidly traced. He admitted knowing the dead woman and her Russian pimp but denied all knowledge of the murder. He was unable to account for his movements on then night of the killing saying that he was drunk and unable to recall where he had been, but on an identification parade he was picked out immediately by the witness who had seen the uniformed man leaving the scene of the murder.

At the court martial Marriott was represented by a leading KC. It was common ground that the trial hinged on the identification of Marriott by the witness and very quickly Marriott's defence was able to show that this was unreliable. The witness was a tram driver on his way home from work. He agreed that he had been some distance away from the person he had seen at the bombed building and although he remained adamant that it was British serviceman, he faltered and seemed unsure when it came to the precise identification.

Johnnie Marriott was acquitted of the murder but the other matters relative to his activities in the black-market were considered by the tribunal and he was sentenced to 12 months detention and dismissed from the service.

Mid morning and Strathearn telephoned. Doing as he was told, Gregory stood by the fax machine in the main office.

Dear Old Boss,

Well, how did you like my little outing on Monday? A little bit off on the first location I know, but the street names were the same. I thought it was quite original, all things considered. I took a few bits for my collection off the second one but like Old Jack – or was it Michael? – I left the Swedish one pretty much alone.

It's a bugger those fingerprints, Mr. Gregorie, isn't it? I bet your having a tussle with that little problem, aren't you? Still, it'll give you something to occupy your time till Old Jack comes around again in a month or so.

I had to have a laugh about what the damned paper said on Sunday. Good job I don't know who she is, this lady friend of yours, otherwise I might have to make it six instead of five this time.

From Hell, yours,

Jack.

"Cheeky bastard" said Mott on being shown the letter. He read it three times and then: "So, now he says the fingerprints are a problem, doesn't he? So if they are a problem, there is an answer, right?"

"What are you getting at?"

"Well, Guv, there's no more "second time around" or "Jack's back" nonsense now, is there? Now he's more or less saying that there has been some frigging about with the dabs somewhere along the line – it's almost like he's challenging us to sort it out."

Gregory concluded reading the army files which contained little more of any great interest and other than the details of the tribunal hearing were concerned with a civil claim made against the Government by the dead woman's family on behalf of her young son, and Johnnie Marriott's final severance from the military.

Sitting back in his tilted chair, his hands behind his head and his glasses high on his forehead, he pondered on the possibility that Marriott and "Creepy" had ever met: in some mental institution, perhaps? Or in prison? There was an association of sorts, there had to be, and he was sure that when he knew what that was he would have the answers. He had a month to when the next murder was due to take place, again in the East End; plenty of time, he thought, but should he not be able to prevent it, his career as he knew it would be over.

Just before lunch Tony Carter phoned with an update on the Berners Street crime. From the girls who had been collared as they arrived from work he had managed to get quite a picture of day-to-day activities in the Knights of Erotica but surprisingly little about the dead girl. It seemed that they all kept themselves very much to themselves, paying their daily dues to Helen Canavan and socialising very little. No one heard or saw anything likely to assist, no one knew much about anyone else's "regulars" and if any of the girls knew anything in the least important they were certainly keeping it to themselves. As Carter had rightly assumed, neither Ergun nor any of his associates put in an appearance and after the day following the killing when the girls had arrived for work unaware of what had happened, the place was deserted. The girl that Katty Aaronson lived with in Brixton said that her flatmate had never mentioned any special or particularly regular client. Helen Canavan had been seen again, this time with her Solicitor present due to her fears of possible charges being brought against her. She maintained her story of not knowing the owners of the massage parlour and Carter believed her when she said that if she would assist in any way with the murder of the Swedish girl, but that there was nothing that she could tell them.

Mid-afternoon and Barney and Jackie Daniel arrived, he frowning and looking worried, she as pretty as ever but less smiling than usual. As it had been suspected, there were no records of the comings and going of policemen at West End Central in 1957. After ten years everything had been archived and some years following that it had all been destroyed. Gregory knew that both of his officers would have been happier engaged on enquiries relative to the main thrust of the enquiry, either at Leman Street or with Tony Carter at Berners Street, but he was quite sure that the Folmer enquiries were pivotal and that once that element was understood, much more would fall into place.

He looked at his book. "So, 16 June 1957 which was the day that this chap Folmer was brought in, we have no idea who was on duty – is that right?"

Iannou nodded. "That's right. We don't even know who charged him because the charge sheet has gone – Guv, it's nearly half a century ago, it's a nightmare."

"So the truth is that the only police we know for sure who were in West End Central that day were this aide to CID Andrew Sellick, Vic Peace and the cadet who nicked Folmer."

"Well, not quite, Guv", said Jackie Daniel. "Peace was posted there but whether he was there that day is not clear."

"Right. Start with Sellick, Barney. I want him found: today if possible!"

They left the office and Gregory sat down. He gazed out of his window, watching three urchins demanding a "penny for the guy" from passers-by, the guy being a heap of rags and a cardboard face-mask totally unrepresentative of a human being, and he wondered if the same corner had been occupied by their forebears in the days when the original Ripper was about. Then, both amazed and annoyed by his own imperfection, he picked up the army papers, leafing through the files with such zeal that the yellowing pages were in danger of being torn from their fastenings and suddenly, in harsh confirmation of his self-believed ineptitude, there it was: the date of the murder of the Berlin prostitute was the eighth of September 1946 – the same day as the original Ripper's second outing. He sat down heavily, thanking God that no one else knew of his advancing senility. He picked up the phone.

Shortly before 5.00pm Mott came into his office with two cups of tea. "I thought you might need this", he said, gloomily. He put the tea on the desk in front of Gregory at the same time handing him a sheet of paper.

It was a fax from solicitors in Streatham notifying Gregory of their interest in the estate and affairs of Tracey Gallop, at the same time mentioning that Mott's Sunday lunchtime visit to Terry Gallop may result in "positive action with a view to a claim for damages" relative to an assault being alleged by their client.

"Lot of crap" said Gregory.

"Yes, said Mott." "That's not why I brought you tea."

"What now?"

"Andrew Sellick, Guv. Retired in 1975., and died three years later."

Gregory sighed. "They made a profit on that poor bastard's pension, then."

"That's what I thought."

Having told Mott the development regarding the date of the Berlin murder, Gregory told him to have Iannou and Daniel go out to Oakwood to see Vic Peace and having placed the army files in his desk drawer, he was about to leave when the phone rang.

In answer to his query there had been a murder in Berlin on 31 August 1946., an English speaking officer of the Berlin criminal investigation police told him. A prostitute had been found in an alley with the throat cut. No one had been arrested for the crime, he was told. And how did he know about it? And what was his interest?

Gregory arrived at Ealing before Rosie. He made tea and had not been in the arm chair more than five minutes when he heard the key in the lock. He got up from the chair and turning to greet her he saw she was out of breath and her face was the colour of ash and tears, which had been brimming her eyes as she entered the house, were running down her face. "For Christ's sake, Rosie – what's the matter?"

"There's someone out there, Mike, on the common. Watching me."

Gregory's mind went back to days earlier and his own feeling of being observed but he knew he dare not mention that. He held her close to him and: "Are you sure – how do you know?"

"It's not just tonight" she said, "it's been two or three days. I've had this feeling that there was someone over there looking at me and then tonight, as I walked up the road, I know there was someone over there who was walking parallel with me but in the dark, if you know what I mean."

He handed her a handkerchief and she wiped her eyes and blew her nose. "I was sure, Mike, and when I stopped the footsteps over there stopped, like in a stupid bloody Marx brothers film or something like that. Then when I got nearer the house I started running and I heard him laughing, Mike. Out there on the common in the dark – laughing."

"I'll go and look" said Gregory.

"No! Don't you dare leave me alone! Can't you get the local coppers to have a look?"

Within five minutes a police car arrived and having heard who Gregory was and that "the ACC's secretary" was a being stalked they called up another car and a search of the common was organised. Twenty minutes later a PC knocked and told him that the search had been negative but if there was re-occurrence Rosie should not hesitate to phone the emergency services.

Mid evening and the telephone rang. It was Strathearn for Gregeory. "I hear you've had a bit of a scare out there – with Miss Lewis."

"Yes, sir. A stalker she reckoned. I got the local car to go and have a look but they found nothing."

"You did the right thing. Can't have Miss Lewis getting upset, can we?" He coughed, an embarrassed, almost nervous cough and then: "Good job you're out there with her, Michael."

Looking at Rosie, Gregory laughed silently at The Old Man's discomfort. He shook his head in disbelief, amazed that Strathearn would allow himself to acknowledge the relationship. The Old Man went on: "Oh, while I'm on, Mike. We got some stuff back from the lab tonight: they've found fibres or something on the rope that was round the Mitre Square body and these match traces found on both of the first two – "Toothpick" and –"

"Kelly Goggin."

"Yes, Kelly Goggin. You'll get the report in the morning. What else? Oh, yes: Tony Carter's not getting anywhere with that mess in Berners Street, you know. The girl's family arrived from Sweden yesterday – her father's some sort of professor or something. Very nice, Carter said, but in a terrible state. They had no idea she was on the game – they thought she was a student, Mike. Can you imagine how they must feel?"

"Mmmn. And Carter's not having any luck?"

"Not so far." There was a silence and then: "Mike, I don't want you to take that newspaper crap too hard, you know. This is not an easy job by any means and you know what those bastards can be like when they need a story. I've got a feeling that we'll be able to put them in their place before very long. Just be patient – and don't let it stand in the way of you doing a good job."

***

The following morning Barney and Jackie Daniel were at Oakwood shortly after nine. Peace opened the front door, stared at them for a moment, and said: "WDC Daniel and friend, eh. What do you pair of bastards want?"

He turned in the hall, leaving them on the doorstep but with the front door open. A clear invitation to enter, thought Iannou, from someone who wants to talk and is not going to be antagonistic or confrontational.

They sat in the large kitchen while Peace made coffee. "I'm still not sure whether to sue that Gregory and Mott, you know. They took a dead liberty with me, locking me up and all that – to say nothing of little Miss Daniel here and her pals taking my house to pieces."

"You looked the part. Vic" said Iannou. "And if you hadn't told so many porkies they might not have kept you overnight."

Peace laughed: "No, it wouldn't've made any difference. They wanted me in over that night so they could see what happened, didn't they? And in the event there was two more killings and then they knew for sure it wasn't me."

"That's about it" said Iannou, well knowing what would follow.

"So why're you here now, then?"

"Just a chat really. Mr. Gregory thought you might be able to help on a couple of points." He looked towards Jackie Daniel who opened her brief case and took out a file.

"You joined the job in September 1955 and went to West End Central – is that right?"

"In the December: straight after training school."

"And you were at West End Central until you went out to Hornsey in 1960?"

"When we got married."

Iannou poured himself more coffee from the cafetiére: "Did you know an aide to CID called Sellick – Andy Sellick?"

"I never knew him like that – but I knew of him."

Taking a miniscule amount of tobacco from a plastic Golden Virginia pouch he expertly rolled it in to a thin cigarette the circumference of a thick match. He lit it with a battered Zippo lighter and then: "What's this got to do with these murders? This is all donkey's years ago."

"You know what the job's like Vic: I just do what I'm told."

"Did you know a cadet called Desborough? Roger Desborough?" asked Jackie.

Peace sucked at his extinct cigarette and relit it, the ancient Zippo making the trade mark 'clank' as it closed. At the other end of the table, Jackie could smell the lighter fuel. "Roger Desborough….." muttered Peace, "….that rings a – yeah, got him! He was the kid that nicked that nutter for murdering the tom, the geezer who fell down the stairs on top of him and he ended up getting a bleeding commendation for it." He laughed at the memory. Iannou sensed his readiness to talk and looked at Jackie, hoping to convey his thought.

"That's right" said Peace, "Roger Desborough. Christ, he was a funny lad. Religious nut of some sort, he was. I don't think he stayed in the job – I'm sure I heard years later he'd jacked it in and gone into a convent or something."

"Monastery perhaps?" asked Jackie, giggling.

"Something like that."

"Were you there when they brought the chap in for the murder?" asked Iannou.

"No – and I remember this well. I was nights; when I come on at ten everyone was talking about it, the Desborough kid nicking someone for a topping job, all that, the nick was full of it. Anyway, I went out, and half twelve I'm back with a drunk; got him charged, had me grub and then they had me sitting outside his cell for the rest of the night till I went off at six."

"Whose cell – the chap that Desborough – ?"

"That's right. They did that with topping jobs – to make sure he didn't do it himself before Albert Pierrepoint got round to it!" He laughed and stubbed out his cigarette in an ashtray.

"So by the time you saw him, he's been charged, his dabs have been done – everything."

"So the only time you ever saw him was when he was in the cell – alone?" asked Jackie.

"That's right." Peace got up from the table. Opening one of the kitchen cupboards he produced a bottle of whisky and removing the cap he waved it over Iannou's coffee mug, looking at him enquiringly. Barney grinned: "Too early for me, Vic – but thanks anyway."

"And you Miss Daniel? A livener?"

Smiling, Jackie shook her head.

"Pair of bastards." Peace grumbled. He splashed several double measures of scotch into his coffee. "I thought a few of those would have helped you tell me what this is all about!"

***

That evening Martin Calder Sturge finished his meal of a small tin of pilchards in tomato sauce with one cold boiled potato tomato followed by a third of a container of Tesco's custard. The plates and cutlery washed and put away, he switched off the light in the kitchen and made his way to the drawing room where he turned on the ancient radiogram and having placed a long playing record of The Pearl Fishers on the turntable and adjusted the volume to barely audible, he settled in a leather armchair. The room was in darkness, the only light being that from the street lighting in Churchley Avenue and the only noises were the yap-yapping of an irate dog being dragged home from Broomfield Park and the distant howl of a police car or ambulance, hurrying about its urgent business in distant Wood Green.

Sturge needed to think.

He sat upright in the armchair, his back supported by cushions and his head not touching the antimacassar, embroidered by his mother when he was at school. He looked round the shadowy room, at the old grand piano and the marble fireplace with its high mantelpiece and the polished leather chairs opposite him. All quality, he thought; all carefully chosen and made to last for years. Through the window he could see the leaves, torn by the autumn wind and swirling from one of the ragged beech trees, and as he watched a woman hurried by, clutching what he imagined to be the noisy dog of minutes earlier. He felt warm, he felt secure, and as his mind cleared he knew that no matter what Michael Gregory and his team of scientists had found, what the future held for him could not be changed.

The muted strains of Bizet's beautiful and unparalleled opera forced him to close his eyes and in a moment his white hair had touched the lacy covering at his head. Then, and as he knew it would, the fog crept in bringing the confusion and unordered chaos he had known for months and the thoughts and memories of what seemed like a thousand years ago came flooding into his already dysfunctional mind. His eyelids ceased to twitch and as his mouth sagged open and saliva filled the space between his bottom gum and lip, there was his mother, thirty-something and always smelling of perfume and cigarette smoke, silk petticoats, suspenders and prickly curler things in her hair. As in a film, moving from scene to scene, there was the private preparatory school in Southgate with Miss Carnoustie showing him sums and the intricacies of a copy-book; then, in another school and another age, blundering into the wooden-doored lavatories and finding boys and girls in a state of undress, all laughing and giggling, and on asking if he could join in of being buggered by three boys, all in early teens. Tearful and bleeding he had run home to tell his mother who bathed him and took him into her bed, into which he would creep every night after until the day she died.

His father, in his mind a shadowy wisp of a figure, had left about then and he could not recall mention of him ever being made again. There was bed-wetting and the associated whipping with a thin stick which he later came to enjoy and later there was the heat and anticipation of his mother's bed, a secret place which must never be divulged to others. There was no guilt, although later he came to know that there should have been, but by that time it was too late and in any event he knew of the wickedness of woman from both his mother and the Book. And he knew that the path he had chosen, twisted as it may be, was the way he wanted.

Sturge's mouth twitched as the wraith-like images hustled through the thick fog of his mind. He pushed himself deeper into the armchair, his thin hands clasped together, hoping for the warm and comforting memories to come. And come they did, crowding into his disordered and ailing brain and creating a feeling of well-being inside him, a feeling which he could not attain outside of sleep. But these dreams of contentment and happiness were not of family Christmases and holidays, neither were they of childhood games and the company of friends nor past and half-forgotten romances. Sturge's dreams were of the beatings whilst he lay on the kitchen floor in a pool of urine, the sublime ecstasy of being bound hand and foot and left in the stark, cold outside lavatory for hours on end and of the later arousal in his mother's bed – an awakening he had not known since her death. He dreamed of his sisters, dark-haired, pretty, for ever young and for ever in love with him and he knew that they were the only women other than his mother that he could have loved and trusted and that life with them would have been idyllic.

He woke suddenly. The record had ended and the silence in the room was broken only by the gusting wind and the spatter of rain on the window. He stretched, rubbed his eyes and walked to the kitchen where he set a saucepan of milk to heat for his Ovaltine. He went upstairs, carrying his mug carefully. He placed the drink on his bedside table beside the bed he had known since childhood and undressed. Then, in bare feet, he padded to each of the three spare bedrooms, opening each door in turn and ensuring that the beds were properly made and that the heating was on. There were to be no callers, no guests, no visitors, he knew that. He knew that the last person other than himself to be in the house since his mother died had been the pall-bearer at the back of her coffin as they carried her out. But his sisters might come, no matter what his mother had said. There was always time.

He drank his Ovaltine and got into bed. Warm and secure, he closed his eyes and sought his fog-free dreamland.

18.

Gregory spent the first half of the day reading the laboratory report. He already knew that identical fibres and dust traces had been found on both the bodies of Kelly Goggin and "Toothpick" and that this important forensic evidence tended to show that both had been in the same location at some time either prior to or after death. The most recent report, however, took this a stage further. Some of the minute traces, he read, matched the material from which the rope wrapped around the remains of Tracey Gallop delivered to Mitre Square had been made, thereby firmly linking the three murders. The trick, though, Mott and Gregory agreed, was to find the place where the three women had been prior to death.

Bringing him to date, Gregory told Mott of the most recent information received from Berlin and particularly the significance of the dates of the two murders.

"So Johnnie Marriott or Folmer whatever he's called started playing Jack the Ripper in Berlin in 1946." Mott put the Berlin papers back on Gregory's desk.

Gregory nodded. "And then he got nicked in London in 1956."

"But there's no relevance with the dates on that one is there? He did the old tom in the June and all of the Ripper jobs were in late summer through to November."

"Who knows?" Gregory muttered, almost to himself. He looked up at Mott, squinting through his glasses: "Johnnie Marriott knew our bastard, though, Dave; you can be sure of that and when we know how they met and when, we'll be a lot further down the road."

In the main office Barney Iannou and Jackie Daniel were not having much luck. Exactly as Vic Peace had remembered, Roger Desborough had left the force in November 1960. His last known address was single man's quarters in Broadwick Street in Soho and as far as the police were concerned he had never been heard of again and his personnel file had long since been destroyed. The Inland Revenue had no record of either PAYE or self-employment since he left the police and from the DHS Jackie ascertained that he had never drawn any unemployment or related state benefit and, oddly, he had paid no national insurance stamps since early in 1961. They had been able to trace no death certificate and no marriage certificate and to all intents and purposes Roger Desborough had disappeared off the face of the earth.

"Right", said Gregory. "Which magistrates' courts would they have gone to in those days? People nicked at from West End Central?"

"Bow Street or Marlborough Street, Guv", said Iannou.

"Hhmph. Marlborough Street's a Chinese bloody restaurant now and Bow Street's being pulled down." He thought a moment and then: "Okay: I want to know the details of everyone who went to those two Courts from West End Central on the day after Folmer was charged, that's the eighteenth of June 1957. Oh, and Barney: I want it yesterday, okay?"

Lunchtime halves of bitter and rare beef sandwiches in the Gun in Brushfield Street and Mott asked: "Have you thought about the eighth of November?"

"I haven't thought about anything else." said Gregory. He opened his sandwich and spread English mustard on the meat. "I have nightmares about it."

"He did her in her own room, didn't he? The 1888 chap?"

"13 Miller's Court. It's gone now, but we're almost sitting on it. Off Commercial Street towards Crispin Street – just round the corner from here."

"Have you thought, Guv – ?"

"Dave, I've told you: I have nightmares about it."

***

By the middle of the month, and two weeks since the double event, the hysteria was dying down. There had been no more murders and the attitude was one of relaxation and relief. The street women were back, soliciting in dark alleys and in the public houses and the miserable existence which passed for day to day living in the East End had more or less reverted to normal. That year it was unseasonably cold for the time of the year with bitter winds coming off the river and the sort of damp, shuddering chill never found in the country and which seems to come up from cold pavements and to be deep-seated in long-neglected buildings. Those who had slept rough through the summer were seeking the comparative warmth of the lodging houses, friends were sharing rooms and property owners and landlords had expectancies of fat profits.

John McCarthy was a man of worldly experience and some small fortune. Born in France in the Normandy town of Dieppe he had arrived in London in his youth and hard work and good luck had served him well. Married and with four children, he owned a chandler's shop at 27, Dorset Street as well as several neighbouring houses and on the other side of the alley, which lead to Miller's Court, he had an interest in a further six houses, all whitewashed up to the first floor windows, each split into individual lets and totalling about forty rooms. John McCarthy was a businessman and like all of his kind in that area at that time, if money came his way from prostitution, he was happy to turn a blind eye. He was not a brothel-keeper, nor was he a pimp, but each of his rooms (known as McCarthy's rents) were at one time or another all occupied by prostitutes and he was content to allow this state of affairs to continue so long as it did not interfere with his personal well-being.

Joe Barnett was a friendly, pleasant enough man. Thirty years old and London born but of Irish heritage, he worked in the Billingsgate Fish Market as a porter and when there was no work in the market he found casual employment as a stevedore at any of the hundreds of wharves along London's river. He had first laid eyes on Mary Jane Kelly on Good Friday 8 April 1887., when after his morning shift in Billingsgate he had gone for an Easter drink with his friends. Moving from pub to pub, in the early afternoon they had arrived at the Indian Queen in Commercial Street where Mary was drunk in the company of a number of prostitutes. She was 24 years of age, of medium height with blonde hair, blue eyes and although she was said by some to be somewhat over weight, she was attractive and unlike many of her female friends she was well-spoken, intelligent and well able to care for herself.

Barnett bought pints of beer and sent a gin to Mary Kelly who was at the other end of the bar leading the company in what he later found to be her favourite song:

"Only a violet I pluck'd when but a boy,
And oft'time when I'm sad at heart this flower has given me joy;
So while life does remain, in memoriam I'll retain,
This small violet I plucked from my mother's grave.
Scenes of my childhood arise before my gaze,
Bringing recollections of bygone happy days,
When down in the meadow in childhood I would roam,
No one's left to cheer me now within that good old home.
Father and mother – they have passed away;
Sister and brother now lay beneath the clay;
But while life does remain, in memoriam I'll retain,
This small violet I plucked from my mother's grave."

Finished, she joined him at the bar: "Gawd love us, gal: you'll 'ave us all in bleedin' tears in a minute", he said. "Can't you come up with somefink a bit more cheerful than that?"

She laughed and sipped her gin: "S'my favrit", she said and then, tears forming in her eyes: "Reminds me of 'ome."

Home, Barnett was soon to find out, could have been any one of several places and he soon realised that Mary Kelly was blessed with a most vivid imagination and that the more she had to drink the more lurid her stories became. During the course of that Good Friday and the following day he heard that she originated from Limerick, Ireland but had been brought up in Wales and that she spoke Welsh fluently. If she was to be believed there had been six or seven brothers and a sister, one of the brothers had been in the Scots Guards and the sister was on the London stage. She had been married and had a child by a Welsh collier named Davies who was later killed in a mine explosion, she had worked as a prostitute in Cardiff and on coming to London she had been engaged by a high-class brothel in the West End where regularly she had been driven around London in a carriage owned by one of her clients, a gentleman who had also taken her to Paris, a place she could not abide and from where she returned rapidly. Certainly she had something of a Welsh accent and whether it was that or something else which captivated Barnett is not clear but he became enamoured of her and together they took lodgings in George Street, off Commercial Street – on the condition that she did not return to the streets.

Not even Joe Barnett would have denied he and Mary Kelly were both seriously addicted to drink. They were a pleasant and friendly couple when sober but when either one were drunk all hell was let loose. They were evicted from George Street for drunkenness and failing to pay the rent; following a short spell in two rooms in Paternoster Row from where they were also required to leave due to their drunken behaviour they moved to Brick Lane and in the February or March of 1888., through his friendship with John McCarthy, Joe found them a small room at 13, Millers Court off Dorset Street. In reality this 12' X 12' room was the back parlour of 26, Dorset Street which the ever resourceful (and equally avaricious) McCarthy had partitioned off from the rest of the house with entrance from a door to the alley (Millers Court) at the side.

The room was square with a fireplace and two windows. One of these was boarded up and the other had several broken panes of glass stuffed with rags. There was minimal furniture, a single bed and a table. There were no cooking, washing or toilet facilities and overall the lodging was that of indescribable squalor and misery.

On a Friday afternoon in either the late August or early September of 1888., Barnett, who by this time had got the sack from Billingsgate, came home to find Mary and two other prostitutes drunk in the little room. There was a violent row and although Barnett stated his intention to leave, he remained with Mary, tacitly permitting her to work as a prostitute, but by late October he had had enough and left to live in lodgings in New Street, Bishopsgate.

"I can't stop her going on the game" he said to friends, "but she was letting other women use the room – even when we was there together, like. I mean, I don't mind them 'aving a doss when it's bleedin' freezin' aht, but to me it looked like they was movin' in permanent and I wasn't havin' that."

Evidently, though, Barnett was still fond of Mary Kelly as there were few days that he did not come to Millers Court to see her and to ensure that she was alright. On the nights of 5th and 6th., November a prostitute named Maria Harvey stayed with Mary in the Millers Court lodging but she found a room in New Court, another alley of Dorset Street, and moved out.

Thursday 8 November 1888.

Mary was busy. At 11.45pm, drunk and in good spirits, she was seen taking a man back to Miller Court. Her client, who was also drunk and carrying a pail of beer, was helping her stagger into the alley and cautioned her against singing too loud as she tried to open the door to her lodging. At 12.30am she was still singing at the top of her voice.

"Well I remember my dear old mother's smile,
As she used to greet me when I returned from toil.
Always knitting in the old armchair,
Father used to sit and read for us children there;
But now all is silent round the good old home,

They all have left me in sorrow here to roam,
So while life does remain, in memoriam I'll retain,
This small violet I plucked from my mother's grave."

Unable to sleep, a neighbour suggested that her husband should go down and tell her to be quiet, only to be told by him to "leave the poor woman alone." By 1.00am it was raining hard and an icy wind was whipping the puddles into wavelets as her neighbour Mary Cox came home. "Gawd a'mighty, Mair, give it a bleedin' rest" she muttered to her self on hearing the doleful strains coming from her neighbour's room.

Just before 2.00am Mary was out again, now in Commercial Street, bareheaded, drunk and soliciting. Standing unsteadily in a doorway, she spied an old acquaintance on the corner of Flower and Dean Street. "George", she called, "George, my darling: lend me sixpence for a bit of fish and a few potatoes."

"Mair, I can't. I spent all my money going to Romford" he lied, hurrying past her.

"I must get some money", she muttered incoherently, and glaring at George Hutchinson and cursing him for his lies she lurched towards Thrawl Street, wrapping her red shawl round her shoulders, shivering in the rain and cold.

A few yards further and he appeared from nowhere, smart, smiling and, she judged, not yet fifty.

"Lend me a tanner, Guvnor?" she asked, smiling her best smile and letting him see the curve of her bosom. She smelt soap and talcum as he manoeuvred her into a shop doorway out of the rain. She was sure that the astrakhan collar to the coat was imitation, but the leather gloves, the collar and tie and the general air of respectability impressed her. She liked his soft voice and the dimple in his chin: later, had she been able, she would have described him as "a bit of class – 'alf a toff.'"

"I'll give you ten tanners for a night's lodging", he said, white teeth smiling, his breath smelling of almonds. "So long as you're there with me."

*She reached up and kissed his cheek, the movement releasing
a body smell which caused his late dinner to surge upwards from
the stomach towards his throat. His instinct was to recoil but he
knew that he must not. "You'll be alright for that, Guv'nor – but
a bit of breakfast and a glass of something would be nice before
we goes 'ome."*

*They walked through the dark back streets, the thin drizzle
soaking into her cheap dress and through the cracked and open
seams of her boots. They did not speak, Mary being at a loss to
know what to say to such a well-to-do and evidently educated
gentleman, and he being so pent-up with the anticipation and
excitement of what was to follow that his breast was choking with
the imagined pleasures to come and rendering coherent speech
impossible. At the Port of Calais in Spiltalfields he bought her
fried fish and boiled potatoes and two glasses of gin and water.
He took a glass of small beer, impatient while she took her time,
speaking to acquaintances and laughing at the jokes and ribald
conversation.*

*They arrived at 13, Millers Court some time after 3.00am.
In her room, by the light of a single candle, she undressed down
to her cheap cotton chemise and smiling and coquettish she asked
him for her fee. He stroked her face and fair hair then turned her
round so she faced away from him; his hands caressed the white
shoulders and, trying to ignore the stench, his face nuzzled her
grimy neck. Above the fireplace was an old framed print entitled
"The Fisherman's Widow": it was the last thing she saw, and that
only through a spray of her carotid blood as it spurted across the
room. In an instant, she tried to scream but could not and in the
split second before she died she understood that her vocal chords
had been severed.*

*With his teeth grating and his mouth and eyes contorted in
fury and muttering the most appalling obscenities and blasphemy,
he grabbed a handful of the blonde hair. He pushed the twitching
body towards the bed, at the same time bending it forward from
the waist and with the razor sharp, curved blade working and*

sawing at the bone and tissue at the back of the throat, he allowed the massive haemorrhage to vent over the bed. Then, with the spouting blood reduced to minimal seepage from the terrible injury, he hoisted the dead women on to the bed and took of his coat. He secured the door and hanging his coat over the one window which allowed light to enter, he set about stoking the dying fire, even using a pile of old clothes which had been left the day before by Maria Harvey. It would be a long and cold night, he thought: and there's nothing worse than cold for nimble fingers.

John McCarthy was a man for whom breakfast was the most important meal of the day. Fried bacon or belly pork with a couple of eggs, sausages and maybe a chop, fried potatoes and tea with a drop of something in it. By ten he'd finished and the onslaught of violent indigestion and heartburn inflamed his normal ill-humour and, he knew, money would be far more likely to assuage his agonies than any bismuth. "Tom!" he bellowed into the yard. "Tom – get in 'ere you lazy bastard! It's pay day or bleedin' go day for 'er in thirteen. She's twenty-seven bob behind with the rent and if it ain't in by dinner- she's aht by tea-time, tell her."

Tom Bowyer took off his apron and walked to the corner of Dorset Street. He didn't know Mary Kelly well but she'd always been pleasant to him and the thought of having to put her on the street, whore or otherwise, irked him. He stood idling at the top of the alley and then seeing McCarthy eyeing him from an upstairs window he set about his master's bidding. It didn't surprise him that she didn't answer to his knocking and hammering: ladies of the night kept strange hours and she could have been asleep – or out at breakfast. He was about to give up and pass an exaggerated report of his efforts back to McCarthy but something prompted him to move to the partially boarded up window.

The scene was that of the most appalling carnage and butchery which would later cause case-hardened policemen to vomit and the doctors to remark that nothing they had ever seen could compare. The body lay on the flimsy bed, naked apart from the cotton chemise and with legs spread and one knee raised. The *flesh from the both inner thighs had been stripped revealing the bone and the removed slabs of tissue placed on the table beside the bed. A similar injury was evident on the right lower leg from the knee to the ankle. Both upper arms and forearms had sustained extensive slash wounds and the face had been lacerated to such an extent that the woman was unrecognizable. Both breasts had been hacked off, apparently by way of one circular, sweeping incision to each side of the thorax. The whole of the abdominal area had been stripped of flesh from the pubes to the sternum, the flaps of skin and flesh having been placed on the table beside the bed and the viscera had been removed. The kidneys, uterus and one breast had been laid, pillow-like, beneath the head; the intestines had been completely separated and draped beside the body to the right and the spleen and other breast to the left. The vast blood loss had caused the bed and its coverings to be soaked and a pool approximately two feet square had settled beneath. The heart was missing from the body and the doctors found Mary's last meal of fish and potatoes still undigested in her stomach. It was as though, one policeman said later, some demented, blood lusting animal – a wolverine or a similar creature – had tried to gain entry to the body by way of the natural orifices and, having failed to do so, had ripped and torn in a frenzy of uncontrolled and manic savagery.*

***

"On the eighteenth of June 1957 which was a Tuesday there were sixteen prisoners from West End Central at Bow Street" said Jackie Daniel referring to her notes, "and twenty-seven at Great Marlborough Street."

"Forty three all told, then" said Gregory. "How many women?"

"Seven at Bow Street – all toms, Guv and eleven at Marlborough Street, seven toms and the rest shoplifters. I take it you're discounting women?"

"For the time being, anyway."

"Well, that left nine at Bow Street and four of those were drunks or beggars which left five. Two of those were dips done

214

for sus by a pair of aides and you can pretty much discount them as they were both from Venezuela."

Gregory, who had been making notes, said: "That leaves three if I'm right – and one of those was Folmer?"

"Which reduces it to two" agreed Jackie. "But at Marlborough Street of the sixteen men, eight were drunks or beggars, four were shoplifters and I can't see –"

Gregory nodded: "Discount them, for the time-being anyway, and that leaves four, right?"

"Right. One of those was a chap nicked by the Sweeney for robbery – he died in 1983. A man of seventy-seven who was nicked for assaulting his wife – he must be dead now – there was an American nicked for having an offensive weapon: he was living in a hostel and got two months and was ordered to be deported and there was a Maltese done for immoral earnings: he was kept in custody until his trial, got eighteen months and was also deported."

Mott, who had also been making notes, said: "There's just the two left at Bow Street, then. Is that right?"

"That's what I make it" said Gregory.

"Well, one really", said Jackie smiling. She looked at Iannou, her partner in a job of research well done: "There was a chap nicked for malicious damage to three cars in Old Compton Street; but he was nicked at eight in the morning, hours before Folmer was taken in, and he was bailed before dinner time –"

"So that leaves one" said Gregory.

"Adrian Peter Short", said Iannou, taking a file from his brief case. "He was nicked for flashing in Walker Court at quarter to nine in the evening –"

"About half an hour before Folmer" said Mott.

"He was nicked by a pair of aides – Bernard Cleveley and Charlie Summerscales – he pleaded the next morning and he got fined fifteen quid. He had no form, he was aged 22 and gave his occupation as a clerk." He opened the file and handed it to Gregory. "He's never been in bother since, Guv, but the funny thing is there a note on the file: he gave his address as 13, Osbaldeston Road, Upper Clapton but it turned out to be false, so he stayed in overnight."

"So his name may not have been Adrian Whatever either, then", said Mott.

They all knew this was not in the least uncommon. If a man gave a false name at the time of the first arrest of an extensive criminal career, his criminal record file would bear that name, albeit erroneous, all his life – although when his correct name became known, note would be made on the docket. Also, as in this case, should a man without convictions be arrested and give a false name and address, the file would be formed in the name he had given, bail would be refused and should the offence with which he was charged be summary and dealt with by the court the next morning, the matter would be closed.

"What about his dabs?" asked Mott, sucking his pencil.

"They're digging them out, Guv." Said Iannou. "Hopefully we'll get them later in the day."

"I know it's a waste of time but you better get out to Upper Clapton, Barney, just to be absolutely sure", said Gregory, "then you better try and see those Aides that nicked this chap. See what they can tell you – you never know."

"It says here" said Mott reading the criminal record file "that this chap Short was seen by the Aides standing in a doorway in Walker Court and flashing at a tom who was working from a room opposite. It says he ran away when approached by the Aides but he was chased and caught in Trafalgar Square."

"What's your point?"

"In Trafalgar Square? Fair bloody way from Soho, Guv. He didn't want to get caught, did he?"

Although he would never admit it, the worry-factor was having an effect on Gregory. More recently, and probably due to the Brighton fiasco, the press had not been so harsh, but the fact remained that Gregory was saddled with four unsolved murders. He was well aware that in all but the first he had known of the likely location of the crime before it had taken place and this and the abundance of forensic evidence would certainly mean that in the event of failure his CID career would be over and that retirement would be expected as soon as practicable. He could live with the "Creepy" letters and the knowledge that the killer was mocking him but it greatly concerned him that his mind kept focussing on the two instances when he felt he was being watched and Rosie's insistence that she was being stalked. He was not a nervous man by nature but the idea that this insane murderer may be getting physically near to himself or those close to him, caused grave concern. The eighth of November was never out of his mind and, as he had told Mott, he was losing sleep. If "Creepy" continued to imitate the 1888 Ripper, then he would plan to murder a woman in her own home and with the most appalling savagery but, as Gregory knew, "Creepy" was not always predictable. In the cases of Hanbury Street, Berners Street and Mitre Square, contrary to what the press and public may feel, they had done their best and he was sure that any later enquiry would arrive at that conclusion but the next murder, if there was to be one, was a different proposition. Many so-called Ripperologists felt that the 1888 killer's degree of savagery had increased with each outing and having indulged himself in the blood-fest at 13 Miller Court his warped mind either cracked totally rendering him incapable of further rational action or he committed suicide. No one of course could say for sure, but the one certainty was that the first four murders had been carried out in the street and with all of the inherent risks, but in the case of Mary Kelly the killer had been able to take his dreadful time under the cover of a dwelling. If "Creepy" took that path, Gregory knew, the chances of capture became even more remote making identification and arrest before the eighth of November essential.

Short's fingerprints arrived the next morning. They had been taken by Charlie Summerscales, one of the arresting officers, who had signed the form, as had Short. There was no indication as to the time that the fingerprints had been taken but it was certain that both Short and Folmer were in West End Central police station on the same day and at the same time. Jackie Daniel, as usual, was on top of the situation: "The aide Cleveley's dead, sir", she told Gregory and Mott, "but Charlie Summerscales is drawing his pension and lives near Maidstone."

"And we still don't know who Short is or was?"

Barney Iannou took out his notebook: "Well, Guv, he gave his date of birth as the eighteenth of January 1957 and both the Revenue and the DSS say that there is no one in the UK called Adrian Peter Short born on that day: no national insurance number – nothing."

"What happened out at Clapton? Nothing I suppose?"

"Nearly fifty years ago, Guv" said Iannou, shaking his head. "Not a hope in hell."

Iannou and Jackie Daniel met Charlie Summerscales in his local pub. "The old woman's in a wheelchair nowadays" he explained. "She's not been too well for four of five years now, what with having a stroke and all that, and two coppers coming round - well, she's going to start wondering and asking. Best she don't know anything about it."

Barney bought two pints of bitter and a tonic for Jackie. "Got the plonk driving, then", said Summerscales, laughing. He winked at Jackie and: "You never mind, girl: they'd be lost without you." He looked round the bar, searching for 'no smoking' signs and seeing none he lit a large pipe. He was a big man, not shrunken by his 73 years, and evidently very fit. His fair hair was thinning but without a trace of grey, his thin hands bore a number of liver-spots but he walked with neither stoop nor evidence of rheumatic ache. His pipe well alight, he fixed Barney with clear, blue eyes: "Well? What's all this about then?"

Barney sipped his beer. "Can I take you back almost fifty years?"

"Well, you can try but the old grey cells are getting a bit dodgy nowadays."

"Nineteen fifty-seven. You nicked a flasher in Walker Court."

"I nicked a lot of flashers."

"You and Bernie Cleveley."

"That'd be right. We worked together for years."

"Adrian Peter Short he was called. He pleaded guilty and got fined."

Summerscales smiled and shook his head. "You're asking too much, son. Nearly fifty years ago – how can I remember one flasher – out of all of the hundreds I must have nicked?" He finished his beer and as Barney got up to get refills he said: "You know poor Bernie's dead I suppose? He was older than me, mind. He joined at the end of the war, died in about eight-one or two I suppose."

With Barney at the bar Jackie said: "They called you West End Charlie, didn't they?"

The old man laughed and said: "Well, they had to really, didn't they? I was posted to Savile Row from training school and I stayed there until I retired. Over thirty years."

Barney, back with the drinks, had no intention of allowing the meeting to degenerate into an afternoon of beer-fuelled nostalgia which, he suspected, Summerscales would have enjoyed. "Charlie, this flasher: you must remember this one: he did a runner and you and Bernie Cleveley chased him to Trafalgar Square. You can't have forgotten that."

Another half pint of beer gulped and after some deft scraping and rooting in the bowl of the vast pipe followed by several matches and some disagreeable liquid suction noises, he laughed and said: " That bastard. I didn't know his name when you said it, but God yes: I'll never forget that bastard."

He thought a moment, Iannou letting him hold the floor. Then: "He'd been doing it for about a week, flashing to this old tom who had a room in Walker Court. If I remember right, she complained, said he was standing in a doorway opposite and every time she looked out the window – bang – out it comes!" He laughed, enjoying the memory. "Me and Bernie sorted out an obbo site in a dirty book shop right opposite and we hadn't been there ten minutes on day one when he turned up and about five minutes after that he's flashed and we're out after him."

He knocked the pipe out causing a bundle of smoking tobacco and ash to fall into an ashtray. After further sucking and blowing he seemed to give up and put the pipe in his jacket pocket. "God, didn't he go, that bastard! He sees me and Bernie and he's off like a bleedin' greyhound out of a trap at Crystal Palace." They chased him out of Walkers Court, he said, into Windmill Street. In Piccadilly Circus he ran into the tube station and emerging the other side of Piccadilly Circus they pursued him down the Haymarket.

"The way he run, you'd think he done a bleedin' bank robbery. Anyway, in Trafalgar Square a uniform PC grabs hold of him: good job he did, mind, 'cos me and Bernie'd just about had it, I can tell you."

"How did you get him into the nick?" asked Jackie.

"The van, I suppose – I can't remember that."

"What happened in the nick?"

"He was charged I suppose. What else would happen?" He drank some beer and took his pipe out again, this time with a tin of tobacco. Then, looking at Jackie and Barney, one to the other, he asked: "Am I allowed to know what this is about?"

"You took his fingerprints" said Iannou.

"Did I? I can't remember that."

Jackie produced the fingerprint form, now contained in a plastic envelope and passed it to Summerscales who examined it. "So I did. But you still haven't told me what this is all about."

"Well, let's say that we think he might be mixed up in something a bit bigger than flashing." And then, choosing his words carefully: "When you took his dabs: who else was there?"

"How can I remember – it was fifty years ago, for Christ's sake."

"Let me try and help you", said Barney. "That day there was a man charged with murder at Savile Row. A topping job."

Summerscales looked at Iannou. He blinked, his blue eyes seeming to be part of a mechanism flailing through mountains of long dormant and unwanted brain material. Moments passed and then: "That stupid cadet, the religious kid! He nicked some nutter for chopping up a tom – is that it?"

"Go on." Iannou sensed an adrenalin surge but knew not to expect too much.

"The cadet and the nutter were all up in the CID office when we got there with our flasher to take his dabs. There was me and Bernie and our flasher and the cadet and the DI or a chief inspector I think with the topping job. He was all covered in bandages – hadn't he been burnt or something….?" He broke off, thinking, and then: "Andy Sellick was there taking his dabs at the other desk."

"There was more than one set of equipment for taking dabs, then?"

"At least two, maybe more. It was always busy up there, never a part of the day without some prisoner or another being processed – fingerprints, antecedents, CRO forms - you know."

"Were they close to each other, the two sets of fingerprint-taking equipment?"

"Right together. One on one desk and the other on the one next door. A couple of feet apart."

Iannou nodded. "You were saying about Andy Sellick?"

"I've got it now" said Summerscales: "There was a bloody fight – well, not a fight but a bit of a set-to. Andy Sellick was taking the topping job's dabs and I was doing our chap's –"

"At the same time?"

"More or less I suppose. Anyway, I'd just finished when our flasher's off across the office heading for a window. After, we reckoned he'd spotted an open window and we were only on the first floor. Anyway, I'm off after him – I can't remember if Bernie was there or not – but all hell's let loose. There a desk turned over, papers and all manners of crap flying all over the place, everyone's shouting and screaming and there's bloody chaos. I remember it was the cadet who stopped the flasher – sort of body-charged him and knocked him over and then everyone's on top of him." He shook his head and smiled, relishing the memory.

"And what about Michael Folmer – that was name of the topping job?"

"Well he couldn't go anywhere, could he? He was handcuffed to the desk or a typewriter or something."

"Where was Sellick while all this was going on?"

"Well he was there, I know that because he'd been taking chummy's dabs but what he did when all that happened I can't say."

"And this was after the dabs had been taken – the flasher's and the topping job's?"

"Right about that time."

"After?"

Summerscales stood up and indicated for Iannou to finish his beer. At that instant he realised that a very great deal seemed to hinge on the precise details of what had taken place in the CID office that afternoon and years of evidence-giving in one witness box or another had taught him the folly of being too sure.

"Right about that time."

Iannou walked to the bar and joined Summerscales. "During all that fuss, would it have been possible for the topping job to have swapped his dabs with your flasher's?"

"What – by reaching over and swapping the forms over?"

"Yes."

Summerscales thought, a smile flickering across his mouth as the enormity of the outcome of such an action successfully achieved sank in.

"Nothing to stop him, I suppose. So long as he could reach."

"Which you said he could."

The old man nodded: "Oh, yeah. He could've reached, I'm sure of that."

Before they left Iannou and Jackie promised to keep Summerscales informed and up to date with developments. In the pub car park, slightly unsteady on his feet and with an afternoon of liquid relaxation still in front of him, he said: "That cadet left the job. After they topped his pal for cutting up that old tom he went a bit funny in the head: as far as I remember, he went into a monastery or something."

Whereas Strathearn was cheered by the recent development, Jim Bassett was, uncharacteristically, positively jubilant. Ignoring the glances from the "nosmos" he lit a cigarette and seemed disappointed that no whisky was being offered despite the early hour.

"That's it, then, that's it", he cackled, winking largely at Gregory and nudging Mott in the ribs with his elbow. "The bastard swapped the dabs over – that's how he did it." An inch of cigarette ash fell on to his tie and: "I knew there was an answer, I always did. There had to be – more reliable than all that DNA fingerprints are: never have been two sets alike and never will be."

The Old Man was less sanguine. "Well, it's certainly a possibility I have to agree –"

"Guvnor! How can you say that?" said Bassett. His cigarette had burned down to the point which his fingers were burning and he was frantically searching for the non-existent ashtray. "There's no other explanation, is there? That's what he did – and this other bastard knew it."

He squeezed the hot end of the cigarette between his finger and thumb and wincing at the pain and dropping hot ash on his trousers he put the remains in his jacket pocket. "All those years ago it wasn't like now, you know. There was a wooden block with a brass plate on it and this had to be covered with this sticky ink by a roller. Then chummy's fingers were rolled on to the plate, covered in ink and then put on the paper."

There were procedures, he said, specifically designed to counter prints being attributed to a wrong person. First – and before anything else - the name of the subject given at the time of his arrest was written at the top of the form; the prints off the fingers and thumb of the right hand followed by those of the left were then taken and transposed into the spaces provided on the form, each of these being marked Right Thumb, Right Fore, Right Index etc. On the reverse of the form a space was allotted for the palm of each hand and another for the two thumbs, these latter being applied to the form simultaneously, the two thumbs resting on the form at the same time. At that point the subject was required to sign the form and after his signature a further imprint of his right index finger was applied in a designated space above the signature and in this manner there was no room for error and confusion of identities was obviated.

Bassett sniffed. He had contemplated and reluctantly discounted the possibility of another cigarette. "In practice it was – and probably still is – a different matter and in those days it was all down to the bloody ink and the mess. Invariably the form would be affixed to the bench and all of the prints would be taken – five fingers right, five fingers left, turn the form over, right palm, left palm, two thumb prints and the one right index. Then, when it was all done, they'd get the prisoner to sign the form, his name would be written on the front and that was that – and the security check had been beaten because the single index finger print hadn't been added *after* the signature. Like I said, it was all down to annoyance factor: if they did it the right way - the prints were taken and chummy'd wipe his fingers with a rag soaked in petrol or thinners in order that the signature could be placed in a clean manner on the form. This done, the index print needed to be added – and this followed by another cleaning with the rag. It was less bother to do it the quick way - the straight run-through of the fingerprints followed by the signature at the end."

Gregory said nothing. He was thinking of a cottage in Devon and what an old lady had told him. What was it she'd said? *"He was such a practical joker - anonymous telegrams to people - stealing garden gnomes and having post cards sent by them from all around the world to their owners."*

And anagrams.

If Bassett was right – and Gregory was sure he was – then during the confusion caused by Short's escape effort Johnnie Marriott had been able to swap his fingerprints with the flasher's. Then, when the fuss was over and with no one suspecting what had taken place, he signed the fingerprint form in front of him, just as Short, or whatever his real name was, had signed the one in front of him. The forms had then been filled in by the officer taking them – Summerscales for Short and Sellick in the case of Marriott – and they would have been sent to the Yard overnight. Neither man had previous convictions (those taken at the time of Marriott's Berlin problem having been destroyed) and thus the fingerprint identities of the two men had been exchanged, effectively for all time.

Later, Mott said: "That must be what happened. I always knew that something associated with the damn fingerprints had gone wrong at a time when both Folmer and this Creepy were together and this fuss in the nick was the ideal time."

"I'm sure it was", Gregory agreed. "It only needed the smallest window of opportunity and the right circumstances and it was done." He thought and went on: "And according to his sister, that Johnnie Marriott was up to every trick in the book: I can just see him doing that, can't you?"

Mott agreed he could and: "Short or whatever he's called would have to have known though."

"It wouldn't have been hard for Marriott to let him know one way or another, would it?"

Mott nodded agreement and then: "The one thing I can't get over, though, is what happened when they took Marriott's dabs in prison. They take them after sentencing, don't they? So what went wrong there?"

"In a word, Dave, nothing. I thought of that and spoke to the governor at Bellmarsh. The dabs they take in the nick stay there: they're not sent to the Yard and so there's no comparison made with the dabs on file on the fingerprint department. The ones they take in the nick are purely for their use."

***

Martin Calder Sturge had slept late. Throughout the night a series of nightmares had wakened him, seemingly every few minutes, and no matter what he did each time he slipped back into sleep the rats were back, crawling, eating, breeding and gnawing their lithe grey bodies into places where they were not welcome. Twice he had left his bed and moved into one of the three single beds, hoping for relief and comfort, but he awoke in the grey morning, cold and exhausted, in the double bed. The pillows were damp, he was not sure with tears or sweat, and throwing them on the floor he lay, his head on the bolster and his thumb in his mouth, half sleeping in an exhausted and semi-comatose state. He rose at noon and bathed, dozing in the warm water but jerking awake every few seconds, fearful that the rats would return but grateful that the night had passed. He had seen rats as they darted across his allotment, their long tails like thick, tapering lengths of greasy cord and their filthy, evil mouths and teeth infected with God-knew-what and he had heard them as they went about their business in the space below his shed floorboards. They were beasts he loathed above all others.

Dressed, he boiled and egg and sat at the kitchen table with bread and butter and weak tea.

Thinking.

It was less than a month now and still he had made no decision. He felt tired, exhausted, due to both his sleepless night and the stress of the enterprise which he had undertaken. His entire being was weary, even beyond its years, and he feared that death would come before the complete breakdown of his reason which he knew to be imminent. He felt neither remorse nor sadness for what he had done in recent weeks and felt driven to carry on, although he did not understand by what force. He did not fear the insanity he knew was growing in his mind like some wild, unreasoned and often screaming cancer but he longed for the care and company of his mother

227

and sisters, although in his heart of hearts he knew that this could never be possible.

***

That evening in The Gun, Gregory felt less on edge. The issue of the Folmer/Marriott fingerprints seemed to have been resolved – if only from an official view point - and although he was aware of the inevitability of press queries and coverage at a later stage he felt that a great burden had been lifted.

He bought drinks for Mott and Iannou and crisps for Jackie Daniel, jokingly refusing to buy diet coke. Then, quietly to Mott: "This bastard's been a medical student or a mortuary keeper, something like that, Dave. Both the quacks said that: the one who did poor old "Toothpick" and Findlater with the Mitre Square girl."

He sipped his beer and almost in a whisper: "This Short or whatever his name is didn't want to get nicked, did he? All that being chased across London and then trying to get out of a window in the nick – he'd got a lot to lose, Dave."

"That's what I said, but not too many people like being nicked for flashing, Guv."

"No, I know they don't, but I've got this feeling." He looked around the crowded bar at the Friday night crowd and wondered briefly what it must be like to lead a normal life. Then, turning back to Mott: "I know it may be a problem or even impossible but –"

"Medical students kicked out shortly after the day he was nicked. I knew you were coming to that –"

"And don't forget mortuary staff."

"Guv, I don't think the students is going to be even remotely possible after almost fifty years let alone the damn mortuary people –"

"But you'll have a go?"

Mott bought more beer. He studied Iannou and Jackie Daniel for moment, watching as they talked and laughed together and catching an infinitesimal flash of eye contact between them he suddenly knew for certain what he had been suspecting for some time. Grinning, he turned to Gregory: "Guv, I've got a feeling that Barney and the plonk are an item –"

But Gregory was gone.

Moments before, with his back to the bar, he had known beyond any doubt that Creepy was there. Watching. The horror-cold had started at the top of his back between his shoulders, and as it rose to his neck causing his hair to prickle and a shudder to make his body visibly quiver, he turned, white-faced, and scanned the crowd, at the same time fearing for the security of his bladder. Suddenly there was a raincoat, blue eyes, grey hair and a half smile by the open door and then – nothing. He pushed through the crowd and into the street.

Seconds later Mott was by his side. "Guv! Are you –"

"He was here, Dave. The bastard was here looking at us." His voice was hoarse and as Mott looked at him a colossal shudder crossed his entire body. "I'm telling you, Dave – that Creepy bastard was in the pub – watching us."

"Are you sure?" Mott looked along the empty rain-soaked street. He saw no one, but he could not help recalling that they were standing, literally, on the same ground the 1888 Ripper had trod, the same Ripper who had a knack of disappearing.

"It was him" said Gregory. "Don't ask me how I know, but it was him."

Mott knew he must not misjudge the situation. To scoff would cause alienation, probably irreconcilable, and he knew that Gregory was not a man given to either exaggeration or flights of fancy. He walked with him quickly along Brushfield Street and into Commercial Street and then, the rain blowing in, they ran back to the Gun.

At the bar with two large whiskies, Mott said: "Are you sure?"

"Yes, I'm sure. The day after "Toothpick" I was in the Chairmen at the back of the Yard and I'm sure the bastard was there." He knew he dare not tell Mott about Rosie; Strathearn knowing of their relationship was one thing – Mott quite another. "He's having a game with us, Dave: and he's winning hands down."

**

About an hour later, PC George Massingbird-Munday stood in a shop doorway at the Turnpike Lane end of Wood Green High Road. He shivered slightly as he watched the torrential rain stair-rodding across the deserted street, the puddles reflecting the garish amber of the street lighting and the full gutters swirling down to the sewers. Squinting, he looked towards the dark, night sky and saw only a blackness which seemed to start some feet above the tops of the street lamps and at the same point as the rain seemed to start. He lit a small cigar, cupping the match in his gloved hand, and looked at his watch.

Known to his colleagues as "Mockingbird-Tuesday" or "'Arrer George", he was in every sense of the word a career policeman. Since his earliest memories he had wanted only to be a London policeman. Not a sergeant nor an inspector, not a detective or in the mounted branch, the under-water search unit or in the women police. Just a London copper: on a beat. And he had achieved that aim. From a wealthy and respected Essex family, he had attended Harrow School (hence 'Arrer George) but having left with results of interest to neither Sandhurst nor even the most lack-lustre polytechnic-type university, and after two years spent in a stuffy and rather Victorian Solicitors' practice of which his uncle was the senior partner, his parents gave their blessing and he joined London's police force. "Duck to water" and "shit to a blanket" were expressions which had been applied by varying strata of society, but whichever it was there was no doubt that George had found his true place in life – and that can be said of few men.

Turning up the collar of his raincoat, he left the doorway and walked slowly towards the Turnpike Lane underground station. George did not mind night duty, no matter the weather, and unlike most of his colleagues he could always be found on the street as opposed to being confined to the station and bogged down with paper work. Paper work was something which did not bother George: paperwork resulted from arresting people or issuing summonses and George had done neither of these for years.

George was not remotely politically correct and the truth was that he did not fit into the modern police force. The hierarchy had no time for him, they didn't want him any more but saw no point in confrontation by way of disciplinary action as his thirty years were almost done and in less than a year he would be gone. He had spent most of his service at Winchmore Hill, between Wood Green and Enfield, where he had been a leading light in the Neighbourhood Watch scheme, given talks to schools and the Women's Institute and had been well known and looked upon with a great deal of affectionate regard. Married with two children, now both at university, he lived in a quiet road backing onto Broomfield Park; he knew everyone and everyone knew George. He had been moved to Wood Green in recent months, not so much due to an anonymous letter to his superintendent alleging that he was involved in an amorous relationship with the matron of a local residential home for the aged, but more to his reference to one of the women police as being "the station bike", an unkind although accurate statement which, unfortunately for George, was made in the hearing of the women in question. Still, he didn't mind Wood Green and it had its compensations.

He stood in a doorway on the corner of the High Road and Westbury Avenue and smoked his cigar, at the same watching the driving rain and the comings and goings at the pub opposite. He looked at his watch again: a minute past eleven. He threw the cigar end into the gutter and, hands behind his back and at the regulation speed, he strolled along Westbury Avenue.

Five minutes later, and in a narrow street off the main road, had anyone been watching they would have seen an aging and somewhat over-weight policeman remove his helmet and, having looked carefully about him, enter the front garden of a small terraced property and go into the house through the front door which he had been fortunate enough to find open.

George had met Charlotte Leyton three days after his arrival at Wood Green. Having found a purse in the High Road she handed it to him as he patrolled his beat and she experienced a guilty thrill as she breathlessly gave him her name and address. A quick reference to the lost property register revealed that the purse was claimed later the same day – and who could criticise George for making a call on the finder to notify her of the result of her honesty? She was married to a maintenance worker on the London underground: there were no children, she told George and giggled as she added: "Probably because he's on permanent nights." By the end of the week he had found that she was a first-class cook and that her after-dinner preferences involved him wearing his policeman's helmet and little else.

Closing the front door behind him, George made his way through the dark hall and into the open plan kitchen/breakfast room, the smell of a good dinner and the prospect of an hour or so of needful exercise making his heart, which was not altogether inexperienced in such matters, increase its beat by half. She kissed him on the cheek: a wifely kiss which, he had come to learn, was part of the two hour game she liked to play. She was not forty, he reckoned; slim with dark hair and enormous brown eyes, she was attractive in a common way, the sort of girl who had gone to the local comprehensive and had been ever-popular behind the bike sheds.

"Steak and kidney, George", she said, rattling saucepans and seeing to a basin, cloth-covered and secured with string, from which the most delicious odours were emanating. "You're just in time – there's nothing worse than kate and sidney when it's overdone."

There were two pint bottles of strong beer on the table and after treacle tart and custard a half bottle of whisky appeared beside his coffee. Charlie (she insisted he call her Charlie) was not long on small talk; she watched him eat his dinner, listening patiently while he grumbled about the modern police force and where it would all end. Then, with the plates washed up and put away, she muttered: "I'm tired, George: I think I'll have an early night", and she was gone.

He poured some whisky into the glass she had left him and sat in the dark kitchen. Ten minutes passed and he got up, put his helmet on and with his glass in his hand and the bottle stuffed in his trouser pocket, he climbed the narrow stairs. Outside one of the bedrooms he stopped and drew breath and then, knocking briskly on the door and in an urgent tone he said: "Mrs. Leyton! Mrs. Leyton! Are you there?"

"Who is it – what do you want?"

He adjusted his helmet, and barely able to suppress a giggle: "It's the police Mrs. Leyton. I need to see you on a matter of great importance."

Twenty minutes later the sound of a car pulling up outside prompted her to grab his arm with the hand which was not handcuffed to the brass bed head. Her fingernails dug into his flesh with such ferocity he nearly cried out. "That's Nigel!" she said, panic in her voice. "I'd know that car engine anywhere." Suddenly she was struggling to get free, at the same time reaching beside the bed to find his trousers, his shirt, anything. "For Christ's sake, George! Do something – bloody Nigel's home!"

The handcuff, luckily, was of the plastic strip type and within seconds she was free. Panic ensued as George gathered up his clothes and was hustled across the landing and into a back bedroom. "Get out of the window", she hissed throwing boots and socks after him, "there's a flat roof on the old outside toilet and you'll be down in the garden – and for Christ's sake be quiet." He could hear the key in the front door lock and knew that Charlie, by then in a dressing gown, was going down to meet Nigel. He dressed hurriedly and from the snatches of conversation he could hear he gathered that Nigel had been unwell during the early part of his shift and that he had taken sick leave. She would make him tea, she said; and best thing he stayed in bed all day tomorrow.

Dressed, George lifted the sash window. As Charlie had said, the roof of the outside toilet was just below him and from there it was a short distance to the ground and the rear garden. As he sized up his situation, he realised that Charlie and Nigel were both in the kitchen/breakfast room which was just below him and that he must, by necessity, drop from the roof of the toilet to a point immediately in front of the window. Sitting on the window sill, he hefted his legs over and turning on to his stomach he lowered himself on to the slate roof, praying that he did not slip on the wet tiles and that the structure would bear his not inconsiderable weight . It was still raining – his mind turned to his raincoat and in a flash of fear he realised that he had left it downstairs.

He crouched on the sloping roof, the rain soaking into his serge tunic and trousers and wondered if death from pneumonia would be preferable to facing the wrath of Nigel, the inevitable dismissal from the force which would follow and, worst of all, the initial fury followed by the sulking months of silence from Mrs. George at home in Palmers Green. A cat, wet and with breath smelling of smoked haddock, joined him and he was about to shove it off the roof when the kitchen door opened and he froze. As he looked, his police raincoat was thrown out into the garden, he heard the key turn in the lock and as the light was extinguished he gathered that they were taking the tea to bed where Nigel, bless him, would be more comfortable.

Minutes later, standing in the lane at the back of the house with his breath heaving both from the exertion and the relief, he straightened his uniform and once sure that all was in order he walked quietly to the end of the alley and found himself in a yard some forty yards square fronting on railway arches and with lock-up garages and industrial units on three sides. He was about to cross this area, making his way towards the street, when he noticed lights on in one of the garages and realised that he was not alone. He looked at his watch: 12.20am. Curious, he moved nearer.

20.

Saturday morning and Gregory and Rosie slept late. The weather was bright and cold and in the early afternoon they drove to Richmond and walked beside the autumn river, arm in arm and sucking toffees. No matter how much he felt he needed to, he knew he must not mention the previous evening's incident in the Gun. Following a great deal of persuasion and cajoling she seemed to have accepted that her worries of being stalked were unfounded but for his part Gregory was seriously and deeply troubled, convinced that Creepy was watching them as part of his bizarre game. They watched the anglers, adroit and skilful with the vast length of their Thames roach poles and they laughed guiltily at the antics of a Cocker Spaniel as it tried to chew a toffee Gregory had fed it behind the back of it's evidently very superior owner. They had tea and cream cakes in Kingston getting home in the early evening and after baths and several glasses of wine they walked to the Broadway for Chinese food.

The following morning Mott arrived at Leman Street before 8.00am only to find that Gregory was there before him.

"What's this, Guv? Sunday morning! Couldn't you sleep?" He instantly regretted his wit, remembering that Gregory had told him that sleeping had become a problem, but if Gregory had noticed the gaffe he ignored it.

"Thought I'd treat you to breakfast, Dave. Get you fit for all that digging you'll be doing next week – all those medical student archives and all those mortuary keepers!"

In the canteen over eggs and bacon Mott said: "You really do believe he was there on Friday night in the Gun, don't you?"

"I know he was there, the same as he was in the Chairmen like I told you. You can think what you like, Dave, but you take it from me – he was there."

"Guv, don't misunderstand me, but we've only got the E Fit thing and you know what they're like – "

"Dave, it's got nothing to do with E Fits or what he looks like or anything else. He was there – I'll stake my life on it."

Mott said nothing. He knew that Gregory was under great strain and although the idea that he was subject to flights of fancy was inconceivable, he felt concerned - and at the same time ashamed that that he should even consider the possibility.

"About tomorrow, Guv – the medical students. I've got Archie McGibbon starting in the morning but to be honest the situation looks pretty black. With the medics, all we can do is to contact the London teaching hospitals and hope that they may have records of the students all those years ago, but to be honest I think it's a dead duck – and the mortuary keeper aspect's even worse."

Gregory nodded. He fetched fresh mugs of tea from the counter and as he sat down Mott could see the effect the stress and worry was having on him. "Yeah, I know, Dave, but there may come a time when I have to illustrate to people who may control my future that I have done everything possible - no stones unturned. Do you know what I mean?"

Mott did know. In the unthinkable event of no one being charged with the murders, a report would be required to show that everything possible had been done, every avenue explored and every possibility examined – and the course of Gregory's career may well be decided by the manner in which the report was received.

Gregory sipped the weak canteen tea. He frowned at the stewed after-taste and: "Yeah, well let McGibbon do it, Dave. Get a couple of the DC's to give him a hand – I need you here to cheer me up."

***

In Churchley Avenue Sturge was engaged in his Sunday cleaning ritual. He had not slept well again, the rats coming in the small hours, this time with blood on their thin, grey lips and spiky whiskers. He had woken, terror-stricken and sweating, but each time he had drifted off to sleep the odious beasts were back, swarming through his sleep-clouded and confused mind and making him pray for the relief of morning. By 10.30am he had finished his cleaning and was sweeping the few leaves which had fallen on to the front garden path into a black dustbin bag. Sturge liked the front garden: it reminded him of winter rose bushes being pruned almost to the ground and it reminded him of warm summer evenings, his mother making strawberry jam in the kitchen and the scent of the stewing berries heavy in the air. The back garden, though, reminded him of other things.

He picked up his bag of leaves and the garden broom and walked to the high, black gate leading to the back of the house – a movement observed by George Massingbird-Munday as he drove by in his aging Jaguar with Mrs. George beside him.

Later, over lunch in a pub in Southgate, she said: "I don't think I ever saw his mother, but everyone said what a peculiar woman she was. She must have been dead for twenty years – I remember people talking about the funeral: no one went, you know. Just him. He wouldn't have anyone there."

Stella Massingbird-Munday was a handsome women. She was not a beauty, nor could she fairly be described as pretty, but handsome she certainly was. In her late forties, her straw-coloured hair had retained its colour and lustre and her eyes were as blue as they had ever been. She favoured only the slightest make-up, and this not to disguise the few skin blemishes her age had brought, but to brighten her otherwise pale complexion. Her lipstick was carefully chosen for colour and a slight suggestion of perfume hinted at both flair and impeccable taste.

Taking care to leave out any details of his late dinner with Charlie, George had told her how he had been quietly patrolling his beat when he had seen Martin Sturge tinkering with a vehicle in a lock-up garage at the Harringay end of Wood Green High Road, almost two miles from where he lived. "I watched him for must be a quarter of an hour and then he locked the garage and cleared off."

"And you're sure it was him?" she asked. "Absolutely sure?"

George stopped trying to count the slices of roast pork on his newly-arrived plate and looked up: "It was Martin Sturge. Christ, I ought to know him: we've lived in the next road all these years and I was the local copper. I knew everyone."

"But what was he *doing*, George? At one o'clock in the morning?"

"Stell, I honestly don't know. There was a light on in the garage and I could see a white van of some sort." He gave up counting meat, poured himself a large glass of the house red and started his lunch. "It was dark, I was about thirty yards away, the light in the garage was not good, the door was at an angle to where I was standing – I did my best."

"But he hasn't got a van, has he?"

Mouth full, he shook his head: "Not that I know of. What the hell would he want with a van, for God's sake? At his age?"

***

Sturge burned his leaves on a small fire at the back of the garden. He added some garden waste and a pile of old newspapers and stood watching as the thick smoke from the damp, smouldering leaves joined that of a million other London Sunday bonfires. Sturge liked bonfires but the back garden made him uneasy. There were no pleasant memories there, just unhappiness and guilt.

He walked across the lawn to the fishpond. He watched as a shoal of magnificently coloured carp, some of which had been fed by his mother, lazily patrolled the shallow water and suddenly and without warning the tears came. He looked from the stone face of the Mannekin Pis to the flagstones surrounding the pond and as the tears coursed down his thin face he became conscious of the swirling, misty jumble of confusion in his mind. It had been there for years, this mental disorientation, but until recent months it had laid in the background, dormant, unnoticeable most of the time, almost like some strange form of tinnitus. Lately, though, there had been changes and he had realised that the condition was worsening and the fog was coming more often and with a greater intensity.

The exertions of house cleaning and clearing the leaves had tired him and this, combined with a lack of sleep, made him feel weak. He walked to the house and locking the kitchen door he made and tea and sardine sandwiches.

***

The letter arrived with Gregory's coffee. Being addressed to "Mr. Gregorie" he immediately knew it's origins and impatiently waited for it to be opened by one of the SOCOs who was then be able to examine it for fingerprints.

Dear Old Boss,
Time passes so slowly when you haven't got much to do, don't you think? But it gives you time to consider things a bit and to do a bit of Reading. I been reading THE GOOD BOOK, like my mother taught me, and look what I found in Chapter 7 Ecclesiastes, verses 26 to 28.
AND I FIND MORE BITTER THAN DEATH THE WOMAN, WHOSE HEART IS SNARES AND NETS AND HER HANDS AS BANDS; WHOSO PLEASETH GOD

SHALL ESCAPE FROM HER BUT THE SINNER SHALL BE TAKEN BY HER.

BEHOLD, THIS HAVE I FOUND COUNTING ONE BY ONE TO FIND OUT THE ACCOUNT: WHICH YET MY SOUL SEEKETH, BUT I FIND NOT: ONE MAN AMONG A THOUSAND HAVE I FOUND, BUT NOT A WOMAN AMONG ALL THOSE HAVE I FOUND.

So it's not only the whores, Old Boss – it's all of them – and they better watch out because I'm razor sharp now – pun intended (!) and I can't see you buckling me. Especially if your looking for a doctor as the papers said you were.

Try again, Dear Old Boss.

From Hell.

Jack.

There were two fingerprints, evidently left intentionally on the inside of the envelope flap, and within twenty minutes he knew that they matched those of Folmer/Marriott. He faxed a copy to Strathearn who phoned him immediately.

"Mike, this bastard's going off the rails, you mark my words. I could never see how he was going to stick to the 1888 schedule and I have to agree he's been bloody clever up to now, especially the Mitre Square job, but I think he's going to change tack."

"In what respect?"

"Who can tell, Mike? With a nutter? And my bet is that whatever this one's got wrong with him, it's getting worse by the day."

"Now he's saying he's not a medic", said Gregory, chewing at the end of his pen.

"Don't take any notice of that: speak to Sean Findlater, Mike – he'll tell you otherwise."

"What do make of the Bible text, Guv?"

"Aye, well I've seen that before. In a nutshell this prophet or whatever he was is saying that as you go through life you'll only meet one man in a thousand you can trust and no bloody women at all. Then he says, your Creepy that is, that it's not only toms he's got a down on but all women – and they all better look out. Like I say, Mike – he's changing tack."

Mott, relieved to be taken off the medical student enquiries, read the letter several times, then found a Bible and checked the text. "This is a clever bastard, Guv. He's clever and he's a nutter and there's nothing more dangerous."

He thought, breathing deeply through his nose and rubbing his chin. "This guy's not going swipe some poor hooker off the street this time, I'm bloody sure he's not. He's going to do something spectacular, it's going to be his finale, the main event, and I don't think he cares if he gets caught or not."

Gregory swallowed nervously and made a decision. Nodding towards the door, he said: "Shut the door, Dave, please."

It took two minutes to tell Mott about his relationship with Rosie Lewis and a split second for him to realise from his face that Mott had known all the time. He was conscious, too, that Mott may not have been entirely convinced that Creepy was watching him and he realised that what he was about to say may go towards straining his credibility even further.

"Dave, I want you to understand that Friday night in the Gun, he was there. Taking the piss if you like, the same as he was in The Chairmen and like I said I'll stake my life on it. Now, Rosie says she's sure that she was being watched by some bastard creeping about on Ealing Common and there was one night when I got back to her place when I was sure there was someone there, watching me."

Mott frowned and looked concerned. "She reckons she's being watched?"

Gregory nodded. "She's come round a bit in the last few days but I know she's still scared to death." He told Mott about the visit by the local police car and that their search of the

242

common had been fruitless and, for good measure, he made sure that Mott knew of The Old Man's apparent acceptance of their relationship.

"See, this concerns me Guv," Mott said quietly. "I don't want to worry you but like I said I reckon this Creepy's going to put on something special for his last outing. To be honest, until you mentioned all this about Rosie Lewis I wasn't too sure that you weren't imagining a few bits here and there, but now...." He broke off, unsure if he should go on or not, and then: "You don't think he'd have a try for one of us do you? Or someone connected with one of us?"

Frowning, Gregory shook his head – an indication not of dismissal of Mott's thoughts but of his own lack of understanding of the situation. "Christ knows," he said in a low voice, "but I hope not, Dave." He shuddered inwardly. "Oh, God, I hope not."

There was silence, each man thinking of the implications but saying nothing, and then: "Whatever he does next, whether it's a hooker or not, I'm sure he'll stay in the East End", said Gregory.

"How can you be so sure?"

"Up to now he's stayed with the general 1888 format, Dave. He got round the non-existent Berners Street and he even went to the length of sending poor Tracey Gallop in a packet to Mitre Square." He walked to the window and stared into the drizzle, tracing a pattern in the condensation on the glass. "No", he said, turning back to Mott, "I agree with Strathearn. The bastard's deteriorating mentally and I think he's running out of ideas as far as hookers are concerned and with keeping in line with the original Ripper, but I'm sure that whatever he does next he'll do it in the East End and he'll do it on the same date as the first bastard did his last one."

Later in the day Gregory telephoned Findlater who was quite adamant: whoever had butchered the pitiful "Toothpick" and Tracey Gallop had some form of medical experience.

Unknown to Gregory, but apparently with the approval and co-operation of Strathearn, second post mortem examinations had been carried out by two independent professors of pathology and all concerned had agreed that the excision of the various body parts from each victim could only have been effected by someone with some experience in that field. "Now, that's not saying your man was a doctor or a pathologist", said Findlater. "It could be that he is or was a mortuary technician or that he worked in some capacity in operating theatres or even path. labs, but whichever way you look at it, to do what he did, that experience and knowledge must be there somewhere."

"What about a medical student?"

"Yes, that's possible", said Findlater. There was a silence and then he sniffed and went on: "Mind you, not a first or second year student – he'd need a bit more practice than that."

As the day progressed the turmoil in Gregory's mind increased and there were times when he felt he was starting to question his own abilities and possibly his reason. Although he felt sure that Creepy had been in the Gun and before that in the Chairmen, in his heart he knew that he had no evidence whatsoever and – and more worrying this – he felt that Mott was not happy with what he probably felt may be coming an obsession on Gregory's part. He was sure that to mention his concerns to Rosie would be fatal: almost certainly she would put the matter before Strathearn and although The Old Man currently appeared willing to turn a blind eye to the relationship with his PA, Gregory was sure that he would see a serious conflict which could reflect on Gregory's handling of the enquiry and that almost certainly he would be taken off the investigation.

***

George Massingbird-Munday's tour of night-duty over, he finished a late shift at 10.00pm and after a few pints of bitter in the pub next to the police station he begged a lift home from the local patrol car. Two cheese and pickle sandwiches and a large glass of scotch later he was snoring beside Mrs. George. Some time after 4.00am he awoke and made his way unsteadily to the bathroom and in the few seconds of bliss he experienced whilst the pressure of the urine on a bladder weakened by both age and abuse was relieved, George suddenly came awake. Someone, somewhere, he recalled, was looking for a white Transit-type van and although for the life of him he could not remember where he had come upon this information, he knew that it had been somewhere in the hundreds of confidential police circulations of which he had vaguely become aware in recent weeks. Back in the bedroom he put on the bedside lamp, but the sight of Mrs. George, hair in curlers and an unpleasant snarling grin on her face which somehow reminded him of Bela Lugosi, made him think again about waking her for a chat and he spent the rest of the night trying to recall who was looking for a white van and for what reason.

***

Shortly before 6.00am and whilst George was tossing and turning and cursing his active and sleep-resistant brain, a few streets away Martin Calder Sturge was up. With his bed made and a place laid at the kitchen table for breakfast on his return, he pushed his bicycle into the lane at the rear of his house and whistling softly to himself he pedalled through the waking suburban streets. At his allotment he opened the shed and having found a torch and taken a moment to listen to North London's thin but pleasant contribution to the dawn chorus, he made his way to a spot between two rows of Brussels sprouts.

***

Very much as had been expected there was no possibility of tracing records of medical students or mortuary technicians of almost half a century earlier. He had done his best, McGibbon told Mott, and he had stressed the urgency and importance of the enquiry, but the fact was that the records had been long destroyed. Although this was exactly what Gregory had anticipated it did nothing to improve his frame of mind and over cheese rolls and pints of bitter in Dirty Dick's in Bishopsgate he vented his feelings to Mott.

"Dave, if we don't catch this bastard he's going to do another one on the eighth of November – he knows it, we know it and the world's press knows it. If The Old Man's right – and I think he is – then it could be any poor woman anywhere in the East End and any time over a twenty-four hour period. Not in the street this time, Dave, in her own house – "

"If he sticks to the 1888 format."

"He will. Be sure of that, Dave, he will. So what chance have we got? He could do it any-bloody-where."

Gregory knew that if Creepy moved the goal posts a fraction their chances of success were reduced a thousand-fold. Even if the impossible was achieved and every hooker in east London was cleared off the streets, if the killer turned his attention to any woman, anywhere, the world became his oyster and the odds on capture lengthened drastically.

That afternoon Mott raised the possibility of getting Manny Marks to make an E Fit of the man who had delivered the package containing the body of Tracy Gallop to Mitre Square. Gregory re-read the old man's statement.

"The description he gives is more or less the same as those people in the Lee Bridge Road pub and the barman in the Canterbury Pilgrim." He thought, hands behind his head and his chair tilted back to its limit. "I hate those bloody E Fit things. People see things differently, we all know that, and what worries me is that old Mannie'll come up with something completely different from the one the pub people did and that makes another possible query on ID at a later stage for some bright barrister to confuse a jury with."

Mott nodded agreement. "Leave it, then. And when we get the bastard he can go on an identification parade and let the old man try and pick him out."

***

Massingbird-Munday got home at seven. His wife made tea and they sat in the kitchen.

"Well?"

"You first", said Stella, almost hugging herself with excitement.

George sipped his tea. He got up and found the tin of biscuits where his diet-conscious wife had hidden them. "Well, it's not a lot really. You know these copy-cat Jack the Ripper murders they've had in the East End, well there was a message saying that a white van like a Transit may have been involved. That's all, really."

She pouted and put the lid on the biscuit tin. "Is that it?"

"Mmnn, I'm afraid so. Any strange white vans to be notified to the incident room at Leman Street."

"And have you? Notified them?"

"No." He thought a moment and went on: "I mean, it's not strange, is it? Just because old Sturge has got a van we didn't know about. I'll get no bloody thanks wasting their time with that."

He poured himself more tea and wrenching the tin from his wife took two more chocolate biscuits. "What about you? What did you get?"

Stella Massingbird-Munday, doyenne of the Palmers Green Women's Institute, Chair of the Lady Conservatives and suprema of the Neighbourhood Watch, grinned. Snatching back a biscuit from her husband, she pushed it unbroken into her mouth and, fluttering her eyebrows at him, full-mouthed she mumbled: "A bloody sight more than you, you can be sure of that!"

First there had been morning coffees with several of the Tory Tarts as George liked to call them. Lunch at the golf club had been followed by tea and cream cakes *chez* Mrs. Harrup, late of the Social Services and currently lady president of innumerable charitable organisations in the area and, said Stella blowing biscuit crumbs over her husband, what the ladies in whose company she had spent the day did not know about Palmers Green and Winchmore Hill, was not worth knowing. George nodded and sat back.

***

It was dark when Martin Calder Sturge arrived at his allotment. He leaned his bicycle against the side of the shed and shivered as the chill evening mist penetrated his thin nylon anorak and turned the sweat on his back to ice water. Behind the silence and false rural surroundings of the few acres of garden plots he could hear the never-ending traffic stream of the North Circular Road and as he looked towards Hornsey and the West End the lights of a million households sitting down to pre-soap opera fish and chips and beans on toast winked at him through the cold night haze of approaching winter. He unlocked the two padlocks securing his shed and once inside and ignoring the alarmed scuffle and metallic rattling emanating from the bench, he lit an oil lamp.

There had been no trouble catching the beast, the cage with its hinged door and steel pressure plate in the floor having been baited with a lump of bread and set between his rows of vegetables but as he looked he wondered if the rat was not as big as he had originally thought and that imprisonment and enforced starvation had reduced its size. By the thin, yellow light of the lamp he gazed at the grey whiskered shape with its hairless and almost skeletal tail and as he realised that, for its part, the rat was watching him he felt horror and revulsion.

He took a paper bag from the pocket of his anorak. Smelling food, the rat rattled against the metal cage causing

Sturge to recoil but regaining his resolve he took a raw chicken leg from the bag and gingerly opening the hatch in the top of the cage he dropped the meat in. Initially the grey horror ignored its supper, gazing up at what it had imagined may have been an escape route and, grey whiskers and pink snout quivering with excitement, it stood on its back legs sniffing at the now closed door to freedom. Then, dropping back to all-fours and with the urge to feed evidently stronger than that to attain its freedom, it turned towards the pink, glistening meat. Sturge, fascinated and at the same time disgusted, watched as the rat dragged the chicken leg to the farthest corner of the cage and turning its back towards him but with one agate-bright eye fixed firmly on its captor, it started to chew, its yellow needle teeth tearing at the meat and sinew, crunching into the bone.

His mind-fog had started as he pedalled up the hill towards The Triangle at Palmers Green. He threw the cycle into the garage, not caring if it scraped the aging Fiesta, and by the time he dropped into an armchair in the quiet drawing room his tormented mind was a tumultuous, fermenting cauldron of confused and unrelated thought. The Mannekin Pis and his father loomed large in his tangled psyche, as did the crab-faced undertaker who had loitered obsequiously at the back of the empty crematorium at his mother's lonely funeral; the sisters came and went, flitting across his consciousness, and, as ever, there was the pleasurable terror of beatings and the stench of cold urine on a flag-stone floor. His open eyes gazed unseeing into Churchley Avenue, his thin hands clutching the arms of his chair, the fingers digging deep into the fabric, and as a million unrelated thoughts strived for attention in the maelstrom of his madness, Sturge's subconscious prayed for death.

***

His wife's revelations, George knew, rendered inactivity on his part out of the question and the knowledge that he must shortly place his trust in some CID officer he had never met terrified him. He was fairly certain that the information he had was of the background type and that no court attendance would be required, thereby denying some over-keen defence barrister the chance to winkle out precisely where he had been and what he had been doing when he had seen Sturge, but the idea of even one other person knowing made him feel cold inside. As much as his wife had – apparently – ignored the suggestions of his affair with the buxom matron of the home for the aged in Hazelwood Lane, he felt that a second, similar suggestion of impropriety on his part may prove to be somewhat excessive, both from the point of view of the job and his marriage, and his mind worked overtime as he envisaged the sack from the force, the forfeiture of his pension after almost thirty years service, divorce and spending the rest of his life penniless and alone in some cheerless bedsit.

Mid-morning he drove to Turnpike Lane and parking his car in the tube station car-park he walked slowly to where he had seen Sturge. Standing where he had been that night, he counted down the run of lock-up garages and noted the colour of the door of the unit in question. The doors were of the up-and-over variety and although there was little difference in one from another, the local graffiti artists had ensured positive identification. Later, after a couple of large whiskies, George made a phone call.

**

"I was hoping that this could be off the record so to speak" said George. He felt uncomfortable in Mott's presence, wary of his notebook and unable to decide if he could trust the man or not.

"How off the record do you want it to be?"

"Well, totally if possible."

Mott closed his book. He'd met a hundred like George: public school idiots who just wanted to be uniform coppers. Scared to go in the army and not bright enough for the church, they saw a career as a London bobby a cop-out on life with a pension at the end of it.

"Do you want to tell me why?"

George had expected this and his response was well rehearsed. "Well, I was night duty, sir, and to be honest I was, well, off my beat. I was, um, I was making a private call when I ran across what I've come to see you about."

You were shagging, you bastard, thought Mott. He said nothing but nodded in what he hoped was an understanding fashion. Perhaps, he thought, this double-barrelled George wasn't too bad after all: he was taking a chance by passing on whatever it was he knew – a total arsehole would have kept his trap shut and seen himself safe.

Mott listened as George described coming on Sturge and the white van.

"Is that it? You see some old chap tinkering about with a white van in the middle of the night and you think it might be connected with these murders because - am I right - because he lives a few miles away from where his garage is and because you never knew he had a van? Is that it?"

He glared at George, suddenly resenting his well cut blazer and cavalry twills. You *are* a prat, he thought, resenting the silk tie and highly-polished brown brogues. You're what I thought you were – a public school prat, with no idea of what the job is really about.

George gazed back at him coolly. "No, Mr. Mott, that is not it."

In a calm and precise voice he described how he and his wife had known of Sturge for years and although, he explained, it would be incorrect to say that he had kept an eye on him as such, he had, well, felt he was "an odd bugger" and that -

"There are lot of odd buggers about", said Mott, "and just because he's got a van you didn't know about doesn't make him suspect for being a serial killer. Does it?"

George was losing patience but aware that a wrong word from Mott to the powers-that-be at Wood Green could cause him a great deal of trouble, he bit his lip and went on.

"No", he said patiently, "it doesn't." He straightened his tie and prepared to play his ace. "Not on its own." He swallowed and looked at Mott who had now replaced his notebook in his pocket and was displaying all the signs of bringing the discussion to an end. "But there are rumours – and I stress that's what they are – that he was medical student of some sort and he got drummed out of the brownies for some sort of sex problem back in the fifties. And that after that he worked at the Prince of Wales Hospital in Tottenham, possibly in the mortuary, for two or three years, although the general opinion is that he hasn't worked for over forty years."

Scarcely daring, he glanced at Mott: the note book was back out. He went on: "There's an old woman, a widow, who's told my wife that her husband went to school with Sturge and that he was a funny sod even then and – " he looked directly at Mott "- the other kids reckoned he slept with his mother."

George stopped and took a deep breath. For a moment he watched Mott writing in his book and then: "Apparently the father cleared off during the war and from what I can make of it no one ever heard of him again. The mother died twenty odd years ago, apparently: he wouldn't have anyone at the funeral – just him."

Mott stopped writing. Suddenly the public school prat had evolved into a well-informed, salt-of the-earth old copper and his dislike of George's choice of attire had changed to envy of his taste and sense of style.

"And you're sure it was him in this garage – with a white van?"

George nodded. "Absolutely." Out of the blue the butterflies had been replaced by a tight, breathless feeling in his chest and stomach and he experienced a thrill of excitement he could only liken to that he felt immediately prior to sex with some hitherto untried conquest. "He's got a car as well", he said. "An old Fiesta – and a bike he uses to go to his allotment."

"Allotment?"

"Mmn, he's got an allotment, vegetables and all that. Somewhere off the North Circular Road. Apparently he spends a lot of time there."

He was a tall man, George said in answer to Mott's enquiry. White hair, thin of both face and form and in his early seventies and although the E Fit he was shown was a vague resemblance it was by no means a good likeness.

Later, in the canteen, Mott said: "Now, I'm not saying your man-with-a-van is the one we're looking for, but just suppose it is and we come up trumps: there's a commendation in it for you." He chuckled, winked at George and: "Might even be a bleeding knighthood."

George fingered the cheese sandwich Mott had bought him and prayed that he had done the right thing.

***

Gregory listened carefully to Mott's account of his meeting with Massingbird-Munday.

"Has anyone been out there? To look at this garage?"

"No, Guv. Not yet. I thought there was no immediate rush and that it'd be better to put you in the picture first."

Gregory nodded and wondered where the butterflies were, the butterflies he had come to expect when things started to fall into place. "Tell Barney and Jackie Daniel to take this chap Sturge to pieces, Dave, and you're to give them a hand if they need it. I want to know the ins and outs and arsehole, everything that makes him tick - and I want it yesterday."

That evening he made a lying excuse to Rosie and went to Fulham.

***

"Martin Calder Sturge, Guv, born 21 June 1933., which makes him 70. There's no trace at CRO" said Iannou, reading from his notebook. "The first record the Inland Revenue have got of him was in 1959., when he was working at the Prince of Wales Hospital in Tottenham. There's no record of what he was doing there but they say that he stopped working in 1962, and there's no record of him working again. What ever it was he did at the hospital couldn't have been much, though, judging by how much the tax people say he was earning."

"Did he drawnbenefits?" asked Gregory, making notes.

"No. He never applied. He gets his old age pension now but before that the DHSS have got no record of any payments or claims and the revenue say he sent in returns every year regular as clockwork. Always not working and apparently living off capital."

Gregory nodded. He did some sums on his blotter and: "He started at the hospital when he was about 26. So he could have been a medical student before that, couldn't he?"

Iannou agreed and went on: "His mother was Margaret Elizabeth Sturge, maiden name Calder. She died aged 79 in 1984 and since then he's lived at Churchley Avenue on his own."

"What about his father?"

Iannou looked at Jackie Daniel. "He was Ernest Terence Sturge, Guv", she said shuffling through a bundle of papers. He was born in 1903 –"

"And according to Mockingbird Whatsit's information" said Mott "he pissed off during the war and no one's ever seen him since – and I can't say I blame him if what everyone says is right."

"Yes" said Jackie, blinking at Mott and not appreciating the interruption. "He cleared off but a bit later than that – in 1946 actually, after the war had ended. The revenue's file says he was employed as a type-setter by the *"Sunday Dispatch"* and had been since he was a boy. He was medically unfit for active service due to TB apparently. Anyway, the paper notified the revenue in December 1946., that he was no longer employed by them –"

"Who says this, the revenue or *The Sunday Dispatch*?" asked Gregory.

"The revenue. The Dispatch is long gone and so are all their records." She sorted through her papers again, and: "Anyway - and this is where it gets odd – there's no record that he ever worked again, no tax, no returns, nothing."

"DHS – benefits, dole?" asked Mott. "What about his old age pension?"

"Well, I was coming to that. Like I said, no employment records and no tax presumably mean no work. He was 43 when he dropped out and so he was well short of his stamps for his pension. Anyway, the DHS wrote to him at Churchley Avenue when he was 65 and after about a year they got a letter back from Margaret Elizabeth saying that she hadn't seen hide nor hair of him since the war and nor did she want to."

"Well, he could have been self-employed" said Gregory. "Dodging about here and there, bit of cash-in-hand work when he felt like it – lot of men fancy that sort of thing, you know." He grinned and winked at Mott: "I know one or two not too far away from here." Then, suddenly serious again: "Mind you, it doesn't make up for not claiming whatever pension he was entitled to: you'd of thought he would have done that."

"Not half so strange as the fact that he's still alive" said Jackie. "Aged 100."

"Alive?" said Mott. "Are you sure?"

"Well, there's no death certificate" said Iannou, smiling. "We know for sure he was alive in 1946 and there's no death certificate at the registry. You can take it as gospel that there is no death certificate for an Ernest Terence Sturge of any age between then and now."

There was a silence and then: "Well, he's not alive, is he?" said Mott. "Not aged 100. I mean, it's possible, but not very bloody likely, is it?"

"No, it isn't" agreed Gregory. He loosened the knot of his silk tie and cleaned his glasses on the broader end. "Mind you, let's say that he cleared off as you say and moved to, well, somewhere in Yorkshire where no one knew him. Say he calls himself Bill Bloggs, lives there for twenty-five years and dies of natural causes –"

"Death certificate in the name of Bill Bloggs" muttered Mott. "And no record of the death of Ernie Sturge. I'd never considered that."

"He wouldn't be the first. One of the anomalies in an otherwise excellent system." said Gregory. Pushing his glasses high on his head he stretched, arms above him, hands clenched together. "Mind you – it's early days."

With Jackie and Iannou gone Mott said: "What do you think?"

"We can't ignore it" said Gregory, "it's more then we dare do." He thought, his back turned towards Mott, staring out of the window at the grey and rain-threatening sky. He knew that if little or nothing was done and Sturge proved to be their man his career would be over but he was also well aware that at that stage of the enquiry it would be rash to waste manpower on surveillance with the little evidence they had.

"This Mockingbird Whatsit – what's he like, Dave?"

"Nearly fifty, public school, more country club and pink gin than pints of bitter and a game of darts, but not a bad bloke. What've you got in mind?"

Gregory nodded but said nothing.

"A fingerprint'd be nice, Guv. Clear it up right away" said Mott.

"The last thing we need to do is to alarm this chap," Gregory said finally. Back in the sixties, he told Mott, there were a number of prostitutes murdered in West London. "The enquiry got nowhere until a chap on the White City Estate topped himself. I don't know if he left a note or not but the forensic people were able to bolt him up tight for all of the crimes by way of paint traces on the bodies matching paint in a car spray place he had, or something like that." There was no doubt that the killer was the suicide, he told Mott, absolutely certain, and with the agreement of the Coroner the cases were all closed and marked as being solved.

"A few years later, though, one of the Sundays says there was doubt it was him, then there were a couple of books, you know the type of crap – the odd suggestion that the forensic was fitted up and –"

"They re-opened it all?"

"No, I don't think so, but the overall effect was that the whole thing was left in doubt and the investigating officers were for ever viewed with suspicion. That A6 bloke – Hanratty: his family screamed blue bloody murder they'd hanged the wrong man; it went on for years and years, enquiry after enquiry and Bob Acott who did the investigation died with it being suggested he'd fitted the bugger up. Then they dig him up, bloody ages after: they check the DNA and find out it was him all along – but can you imagine what it did to Acott and his family?" He turned towards Mott. "This one musn't kill himself, Dave: I don't want him sussing anything at all so no surveillance, no poking about in his garden or any of that. When we're sure we'll go in, but not until then."

Iannou and Jackie Daniel, he told Mott, were to make contact with Massingbird-Munday and very quietly they were to see and interview his contacts and to get as much detail and background on Sturge as they could. They were to go near neither his home, his garage nor his allotment and it was to be stressed to them that an ultra-low profile was to be adopted. "Get in touch with the uniform superintendent at Wood Green and get Massingbird-Munday taken off his normal duties and –"

Mott interjected explaining George's concerns and that he had been off his beat and engaged in extra-constabulary matters when he had seen Sturge. Gregory smiled and shook his head grimly: "Things never change, Dave, do they?"

Mott, wondering if the last comment was relative to his activities in Canning Town of years before and Strathearn's subsequent breakfast visit to his home, grinned and nodded agreement.

"Ring him, Dave, and tell him that Barney and Jackie will be in touch. Tell him to make sure that he gives them all the help he can and that they meet all the right people – or else!"

***

Within minutes of meeting her, Iannou realised that Mrs. Beryl Harrup, late of the Social Services and the Chair of an assortment of local charities, was not a lady to be trifled with. In her sixties with grey/blue hair and sporting a heavy woollen skirt and a great deal of green duffel coat, she occupied what was obviously George's favourite armchair. Smoking cigarettes with inch long tips, which after the first insertion between her lips became caked in bright red lipstick, she glared at Barney, from time to time glanced condescendingly at Jackie and totally ignored George and his wife – who had been good enough to lend their home for such discussions as the two detectives needed to have.

"Through my position within a Government Department" she said imperiously, "I find I am bound by the data protection legislation and, furthermore, the constrictions of the Official Secrets Act and I must make it clear to you that I am therefore unable to disclose to you any knowledge that I may have acquired through my employment."

Barney smiled politely. "I quite understand your position, Mrs. Harrup, and accept that if you feel unhappy about discussing the Sturges with us, we must respect your wishes." He looked at Jackie, wanting to wink but not daring to chance it, and went on: "However, I think that you will find that any data relative to the prevention or detection of crime is outside of the act as such and that as our enquiries come within that area you are perfectly at liberty to tell us anything you wish."

Mrs. Harrup frowned. She looked coldly at Jackie who much to Iannou's admiration smiled benevolently back at her. She was evidently about to take her feelings on the Data Protection Act further when Stella Massingbird-Munday arrived with coffee and biscuits, accompanied by George carrying a second tray bearing a full cut-glass sherry decanter and glasses. The conversation turned to matters of the weather, the state of government and a gentleman Mrs. Harrup had known who occupied a senior position "at the Yard" in the sixties; glasses of sherry were poured and consumed (Barney and Jackie taking only coffee) and, as if by magic, the dragon which had been Theodora Harrup underwent some form of metamorphosis and became a mild-mannered and pleasant old lady ("call me Teddy"), prepared to do anything she could to assist.

She had known Sturge's mother well, she said, and added: "As well as anyone could know her, I suppose." She described her as being a tall, dark-haired woman, dressed winter and summer in a brown cloth coat and matching beret. She doted on the boy, Martin, and recalled that even in his early teens, and much to the amusement of other teenagers, he would be seen to be holding his mother's hand when walking in the street or park. She talked at length about his solitary upbringing and that he was not allowed – or disinclined – to associate with other children and how he seemed to spend his leisure time helping his parents in their garden.

Suddenly out of Bristol Cream, she smiled at George and moved the position of her glass on its silver coaster, pushing it a little closer to the decanter. Refilled, her mood seemed to change and in a low, solemn voice, tinged with a mixture of shock and sadness, she said: "I can tell you, Mr. Iannou, that at some time during the war the school notified the local authority that Martin Sturge was being physically abused, evidently by his parents."

She described how marks of evident beatings had been seen on his back and buttocks and that the school nurse had informed the council. "Nothing ever came of it, though: Martin said he'd fallen out of a tree or some damn nonsense and when his mother went along with the same tale it all died a death."

"What about the father?" asked Iannou.

She gave a snorting, dismissive laugh: "Poor man. I never knew really but my parents said he just upped and went. About the end of the war it would have been. Margaret – Mrs. Sturge – never said anything. Nothing at all. It just leaked out, like things do: he's gone and that was that." She laughed again, the same derisive snigger: "I don't imagine she cared one iota. Nor the boy, for that matter."

"You never heard of him again?" asked Jackie.

"Not a word." Frowning, she shook her head slowly. "Dead now, of course – must be."

Alone in his old Mondeo, Gregory had driven to Palmers Green. Had Mott known of his visit, and had Mott have asked, Gregory would have told him that as Sturge was a suspect, the only suspect, it was right that he should see where he lived. The truth, though, was that Gregory desperately needed to know if, when close to the house occupied by the man who may be Creepy, he would experience the same eerie, cold feelings which he had felt in The Two Chairmen and The Gun.

Sturge's house, he found, was well-kept with immaculate front garden and brightly painted gate but there was nothing unusual – not that he thought that there would be. He drove slowly down the avenue, the driving rain forcing him to set his windscreen wipers at maximum and the demister at its highest fan speed, and although he wondered about the secrets held behind the black-painted front door and the format of the myriad fingerprints he knew would be spread throughout the rooms, he experienced no unusual or peculiar feelings.

From the council he had learned the location and description of the allotment leased by Sturge and as he gazed at the neat lines of vegetables and flowers and the large, white shed he wondered, but felt no stress and no sensation of unease. Had he known, though, of the presence of a hungry rat in a cage-trap on a bench in the shed, a rat which was being weaned on to a diet of strictly rationed raw meat, he may have had cause for some thought.

Mrs. Dorothy Osborne ("call me Dolly") was, Iannou estimated, well over 70 and in better health than many half her age. She had no apparent need for spectacles, her hearing was perfect and, as Jackie said after their meeting, she had a better grasp of reality and what was going on around her than many detective constables. She made them tea and they sat in the kitchen of her small house in a quiet road off Alderman's Hill, Jackie immediately finding that her lap was to be adopted by a large, yellow cat, which showed it's appreciation of this hospitality by means of a vibrating drone, kept up throughout the whole of their ninety minute stay.

With tea the colour of terracotta tiles poured, she asked: "Who are you interested in – Martin or his parents? I've known the whole tribe, oh, since before the war, I suppose."

Iannou smiled and sipped his hot tea. "Start with Martin, eh? We can go on to mum and dad later, perhaps."

Tommy, her late husband, had gone to school with Martin Sturge, she said. She had gone to a private, girls' school and didn't know him in those days – other than by reputation. "The girls at Tommy's school were scared to death of him" she said. "It wasn't that he touched them or chased them, or anything like that, but, well, from what Tommy said it was the way he looked at them and things he said: nothing rude – just things, if you know what I mean."

Jackie, stroking the monster cat, nodded. "There was just something about him?" she asked.

"Mmmn. They all said that."

She paused and fiddled with a ring on her left hand, turning it round and round on her finger as if she was scared, or shy, to go on. Then: "Well, he's gone now and it was all those years ago so I don't suppose it matters, but, well, my Tommy, when he has a lad, he was a bit of a tearaway." She stopped again and wiped her eyes with a small handkerchief.

"Anyway, when he was about 14, one night him and another lad broke into the Sturges' house – stupid, like kids do. Tommy told me, it was late at night and they crept round the place, seeing what they could steal I suppose, and, well, when they got upstairs they went into one of the bedrooms and Sturgey – Martin – he was in bed with his mum."

"How old was he then? Sturgey?" asked Iannou.

"Same age as my Tommy – 14."

"What did he do?"

"Nothing. What could he do? He couldn't tell anyone for fear he'd have his collar felt, could he? He only told me years later."

"What about his dad?" asked Jackie. "Did you know him?"

"Well, I did, but not well. He cleared about then – 1946. You know about that, do you?"

"A bit", said Iannou, "but go on."

"There's not a lot to know, really: he just went, gave up his job in the print and cleared off." She poured more tea, smiling at Jackie and putting her cup and saucer on the low table beside her and the cat. "That's what *she* said, anyway."

Jackie, sipping tea, looked at the old woman over the top of her cup: "What do you mean, Dolly?"

"Well, Margaret said he just walked out on her, for no reason at all, but Tommy and I never thought it sounded right. You wouldn't meet a milder more inoffensive little man than Ernie Sturge; he was a proper little gentleman, truly he was, and I never thought he could have walked out and left her with that weird Martin, no more than what he could've flown to the moon – and my Tommy agreed with me."

"And you never heard he'd died?"

She shook her head and then, laughing: "He's got to be dead after all these years: if he's not he's over a hundred."

As far as work was concerned, she was sure that Martin Sturge had worked at the hospital in Tottenham. "Probably as a porter or something like that" she said, "but he didn't stay long, no more than three or four years, if that."

She remembered her husband saying he'd seen him waiting for the bus early in the mornings and then, later, saying that he'd heard he'd left and that as far as she knew he'd never worked again. "I don't suppose he had to", she said. "There was always plenty of money – from what I heard, Margaret Sturge was left very well after her parents died."

"When he left school" asked Iannou, "did he go to university or anything like that?"

She shook her head: "I never heard that" she said, frowning and gazing at the yellow cat, now asleep but still droning. "There was something though, something he did after he left school, I remember Tommy telling me about it but I'm damned if I know what it was."

"A medical student, perhaps" suggested Iannou. "What about that?"

She shook her head: "It's fifty years ago now – it's all gone I'm afraid."

"Married?" asked Iannou, already knowing the answer. "Girl-friends? Anything like that."

The old lady gave a snorting, disdainful laugh: "Huh! Fat chance of that! There wasn't a girl who'd go near him."

Before eight the next morning Mott found Iannou having his breakfast in the canteen. He bought tea and sat down at the same table.

"Barney, when I was at training school in nineteen-hundred and frozen to death, a fat old sergeant told me that the two quickest and surest routes to misery in the Metropolitan Police are to sod about with prisoners' property or to get involved with women police." He stirred his tea and in a low voice he went on: "And I know you're too straight to mess about with property."

Iannou finished his sausages. Mott thought he detected a blush in the Mediterranean complexion. "It's love, Guv."

Mott sniffed. "Is it." He nodded, pensively. He stirred his tea and watched four uniform PCs playing solo at the adjacent table. Then, as Iannou was getting to his feet to return his plate to the counter: "He was right, then."

"Who, Guv?"

"That fat old Sergeant."

Later, in the main office, Gregory apprised the whole team of the situation. Seated at a table with Mott on one side and Tony Carter on the other, he outlined the situation as to Folmer/Marriott, the fingerprint hoax and Sturge.

"He is the only suspect we've got," he said, "and he's got to be eliminated or nicked, one way or the other, before the eighth of November." He looked at Mott and Carter, the latter who would be expected to contribute both man-power and ideas now that a suspect had come to light, inviting contributions.

"One print'd do it" said Carter, "then we'd know for sure. The trick is to get it without him knowing."

"What about search warrants and steaming straight in?" asked McGibbon.

"And if we're wrong?" said Mott. "We risk him going off to the press and the real bugger'll go even further under ground than what he already is."

"I've been and looked at his drum and his allotment" said Gregory, "and I can tell you that from a surveillance point of view the house is pretty much out of the question unless we could use a property opposite. There's a couple of garages to let opposite the one where his van is which would be ideal and there's no problem watching the allotment and his garden shed, but that's not going to take us anywhere at all, is it?"

It was common ground that as the killer seemed to have used his Transit van on each of his outings that the likelihood was that he would do so again and that if any observations were to be carried out the van should be the focus at the initial stage. Both Gregory and Mott were firmly against full time surveillance at that stage, although Tony Carter was inclined to disagree.

"I'm for going in now" he said. "If we're wrong, we're wrong; we can always apologise all round and start over again." He nodded, seemingly in agreement with his own statement, and then: "Anyway, my bet is we wouldn't have to."

There were considerations, Gregory pointed out, two of these being the time factor and the ever-lurking press. "We're over a fortnight away from when his next outing's likely to be" he said. "I'll go along with surveillance on his garage – if we can rent one next door or something – but I think that to watch the house full time, twenty-four-seven, would be fatal."

Surveillance of this type was not like watching a gang of suspected bank robbers living in rooms and flats in the back streets. This was in a well-to-do suburb and even if some neighbour could be persuaded to co-operate, the chances of total secrecy were remote, especially when the gossip factor was taken into consideration. Turning to the matter of press, he said: "If we're wrong, they'll have a field day, you can be sure of that." He turned to Mott, and went on: "The next thing'd be that Vic Peace'd get in on the act – it doesn't bear thinking about."

By mid-morning it was agreed. Arrangements would be made to find premises from where Sturge's lock-up garage could be observed on a round-the-clock basis; Iannou and Jackie Daniel would persevere with their background enquiries relative to Sturge but no surveillance would be carried out in Churchley Avenue. Gregory was convinced that he was taking the correct course and that time was on their side. He was sure that Creepy – Sturge or otherwise – would not strike again until the day chosen by the 1888 killer and if all further enquiries came to nothing he reasoned that Sturge could be brought in the day before and kept over a couple days, exactly as they had done with Peace. Later in the day, and unbeknown to Mott and the rest of the team he would apply for search warrants for Churchley Avenue as well as Sturge's garage and garden shed.

Gregory left Leman Street at 9.00pm and drove to Ealing determined that he must let Rosie know that she may be in some danger and over beans on toast and a glass of whisky he told her of his feelings. At first fear and panic registered in her eyes but she listened carefully.

"So it's just that one weekend – in a couple of week's time? Is that it?"

Gregory finished his beans and getting up from the table placed the plate in the sink. "That's it. Just a couple of days."

"So what am I going to do, Mike? Go and stay with my mother?"

He laughed. "You can if you want to, Rosie." He poured whisky into his glass and grinned at her. "I'd thought a couple or three nights in a hotel somewhere – with me there to make sure that you were safe."

21.

Saturday 25 October.

Although keen to assist, NHS personnel staff were unable to take the enquiry further. Staff records for over ten years ago had been archived and destroyed three years after that. Over the next few days and pointed in the right directions by Massingbird-Munday and his wife, Iannou and Jackie spoke to a selection of Palmers Green residents all of whom had something to say about Martin Sturge or his parents, even if they had never met them personally. There were stories and rumours, conjecture and gross exaggeration and, both detectives reckoned, a smattering of lies. They heard that Ernie Sturge had been killed fire-watching in the blitz, that he had been arrested for murder and hanged in Cardiff and that he had run off with a woman who used to sing with the Joe Loss band. They were told on reliable authority that the late Mrs. Sturge had been murdered by Martin, that she had been committed to Friern Barnet Mental Hospital and had died there and that she was not dead at all but alive and well (presumably aged over one hundred) and living in Hackney with a man who sold hot dogs from a barrow in Leicester Square. They were told that Martin Sturge (and this was common ground) had worked for a few years in a hospital somewhere in North London, and there were hints and suggestions of all manners of impropriety, mainly of a sexual nature, and ranging from indecent exposure in Broomfield Park to grave robbing and necrophilia.

Shoofie Coots, though, was different, and both Barney and Jackie Daniel were agreed on this. A widower, well over 80 and inclined to doze off, Shoofie lived with his daughter and son-in-law in a pleasant house near Bounds Green tube station. He had been the Sturge's gardener, Massingbird-Munday had told Barney, and it would be worth their while to see him.

His daughter brought them coffee and chocolate biscuits in the large conservatory at the rear of the house and the old man, seated in a wheel chair with a heavy tartan blanket over his legs, seemed pleased and excited to see them.

"It's not that I can tell you anything that I know", he told them, "but it's feelings I had then, when I was working for 'em, and feelings I've had ever since."

He started doing the Sturge garden when Martin was a child and sometime during the war. Ernie Sturge was there in those days: "I got on with him okay," said the old man. "There was always a shilling or two extra at the end of the week and if he was there and she wasn't, there was coffee and a few biscuits."

Ernie Sturge had left just after the end of the war, he remembered. "I just come in one morning and he wasn't there. The boy was at school and the old woman never said a word about Ernie going. Not a word. At the end of the week she give me what was owed and that was that." He dipped a biscuit in his coffee and sucked off the soggy end. "I knew he'd gone, of course: my missus heard and so did all the neighbours. But she never said a word, Mrs. Sturge didn't."

He closed his eyes, rocking slightly in his wheel chair and his daughter winked at Iannou and nodded, indicating that he was still with them, just taking a rest.

"It was when we was making that damn fish pond he left", he said moment later, but with his eyes still closed. "If he ever did."

Iannou looked at the old man's daughter, eyebrows raised, enquiringly. She nodded and shrugged, as if to let Iannou know that all would be made clear.

The grey, red-veined eyes opened again. As if to focus his attention and to keep him from dozing, his daughter handed him his cup and saucer and another biscuit.

"Can you explain?" asked Jackie, smiling at him and, in the way that nurses have with old men, flirting.

"Well, I don't know: it was never something I could have put a finger on and something what I never have talked about, but to me it seemed ever so –"

He paused, evidently lost for a word. "Coincidental?" suggested Jackie.

He smiled. "Coincidental. That's it." He grinned at her and winked. "It was right about the time he went and the pond was, oh, I don't know, about two-thirds dug, I suppose, and one morning she said it hadn't got to go any deeper and I was to put in the lining and get the cement ordered." He closed his eyes again, his head shaking slightly in the manner of those afflicted with some form of Parkinsons.

"What did you think, then, Shoofie?" asked Iannou, faintly embarrassed to be calling the old man by his nickname.

There was silence for a full minute and then the eyes opened: "It doesn't really matter what I thought, does it? At the time I thought a lot of things and it's something I've always wondered about, but it's what you think that matters, ain't it."

A short time after the fish pond was finished she got rid of him, he said, and he never went to the garden again. "Years later I knew they had paving stones come for round the edge, the stone masons told me I think." He sniffed and finished his coffee. "They laid them themselves I was told." He winked at Jackie again, causing her to giggle. "They boy was older then, see. Sixteen or seventeen I shouldn't wonder. I suppose he done the donkey work."

Wednesday 29 October.

Sturge had spent the morning at his allotment. The rat, which by then had learned to associate his arrival with the scraps of uncooked meat on to which it had been weaned, had greeted him with twitching, shivering whiskers and brief, staccato squeaks of anticipation. It was thinner, he noticed, thinner and hungrier and with a look of merciless malevolence in its black, darting eyes.

The weather was bright and cold and Sturge pottered. He tidied and weeded his rows of vegetables and for ten minutes, leaning on his hoe, he chatted to his neighbour about the things which those who have allotments share interest. Just before one o'clock he threw an old sack over the rat's cage, locked his shed and with a large bunch of chrysanthemums and a string bag full of vegetables in a basket hanging from the handlebars of his bicycle, he left for home.

The cold air and the slight mist caused him to become breathless and some distance up the slight incline from the North Circular Road towards the Triangle at Palmers Green, he dismounted and started to push the cycle. Towards the top of the hill he stopped at a pedestrian crossing which would take him to the correct side of Green Lanes for the short ride to Churchley Avenue. Not venturing on to the crossing, he watched the cars as they passed and suddenly, as if in a dream, he saw two faces that he knew; a flitting glimpse of a man and a woman as they drove over the crossing in the direction of Wood Green. He knew the faces well and he knew that he had seen them in recent weeks, but try as he might he could not recall the details.

At home, the memory became forgotten. He arranged his flowers in two vases, one in the large kitchen and one in the drawing room and having consumed a cheese sandwich and a bottle of lager he went into the back garden. Fetching the garden broom from the garden shed, he swept the leaves off the paving stones surrounding the fish pond, taking care that no debris fell into the water. The carp, sensing the onset of winter, had become sluggish and were confining themselves to the deeper parts of the pool, but as he peered into the green water, he saw the sideways wagging of a red and silver tail and a length of burnished flank as one of the larger fish rolled in the muddy depths. He gazed at the statue of the Mannekin Pis and going on hands and knees and using the flat palm of his hands he scraped the slight traces of moss off the flat stones surrounding the pond.

And then, as he knew it would and as it always did when he visited the fish, the fog started to swirl into his head. For a moment he relaxed and laying full length, half on the grass and half on the paving slabs, he allowed his brain to submit to the images of his childhood miseries and to the jumble of countless unconnected and random pictures which his madness forced through his already tortured mind. Eyes wide and staring into the fish pool, he saw his dead mother in her oak coffin, resplendent in her lace-edged shroud, the undertakers' powder and rouge greasy on her white marbled face; crowding into the confused mental jumble, there were parties in the drawing room with his younger sisters and there were days on beaches, swimming in the cold sea, picnics and hide-and-seek.

Ten minutes passed and with his mind still hosting the swirling and tumbling images, he got to his feet and moments later he stumbled into an armchair in the drawing room.

Hours later and with his face prickly with stubble he awoke. The room was cold and he knew it was night. The fog shadows were no longer there but although his mind had cleared he felt exhausted and drained by the mental trauma of the afternoon. The big house was still as he climbed the dark stairs, the one stair on the bend nearing the top creaking as it had since he was a child, and within a few minutes he had found the warmth and comfort of his mother's bed. There were no dreams that night, just the black nothingness of how he imagined death would be, but suddenly, as the first sparrow chinked at the cold dawn, breaking the silence of the night, he woke, eyes wide and fear causing his empty stomach to churn.

The memory had come to him in his waking moments: that evening in The Gun, the girl with her pretty eyes, smiling and joking with Gregory as he bought her crisps and the dark-haired foreign-looking detective watching them over his glass of beer. Suddenly, as the turn of a switch illuminates a darkened room, all was clear and he knew that he was being watched. The fat policemen with the ridiculous name, the local beat copper or whatever he was, who had driven by the house on a Sunday morning, he could accept. But Gregory's assistants? In Palmers Green?

As he made tea he realised that his fear was not relative to his capture. That, he knew, was inevitable and he had accepted it. His worry was arrest before he had finalised what he had set out to do, completion ensuring his place in history. Decisions had to be made and plans formulated.

He left the house at eleven, knowing that he would never return. He had made sure that all of the beds were made, that the furniture was dust-free and that everything was in its place. There would be visitors, he knew, and everything must be in order. He left on his bicycle, going by way of the lane at the rear of the house, and wearing his anorak and cap and with his cycle clips in place he rode slowly through the back roads to Arnos Grove. At the underground station he left the bicycle against a wall by the entrance, supposing, rightly as it turned out, that it would be stolen by lunchtime.

Although he could be forgiven for not having done so, had Gregory arranged for more comprehensive surveillance, shortly after dark those concerned would have seen a small Ford van arrive at the allotment site. Sturge, by then dressed in a newly purchased blue suit, left the vehicle and after a few minutes in his garden shed he returned to the van, placing the rat's cage carefully in the back. Then, having carefully padlocked the shed, he drove down to the North Circular Road and an hour later interested parties would have seen him leave the M25 and join the M3 at Staines and, humming the theme from "The Great Escape", head towards the West Country.

Saturday 1 November.

The arrival of a large bouquet of flowers for Jackie Daniel brought about a series of different reactions. She read the unsigned card, which read: "To Jackie – with admiration" and ignoring the hoots and ribaldry from her male colleagues she borrowed a vase from the canteen and placed the arrangement on her desk. In response to the inevitable enquiries and salacious comments she said that she had no idea as to the sender and could only assume that it was one of the Palmers Green families they had called on over the last few days. Mott, winking at everyone in sight, took Iannou aside and told him that he reckoned Massingbird-Munday was the sender. He then compounded Barney's misery by adding: "A right crumpet man, that 'Arrer George. What do you think he was doing the night he saw Sturge in his lock-up?" He looked round, theatrically conspiratorial, and in a low voice: "Off his beat and shagging, wasn't he?"

During the course of the morning and seeing that Iannou was put out Jackie took him aside. She did not know the sender, she assured him, and even if it was Massingbird-Whatsit it made no difference. She straightened his tie and kissed him on the cheek. "They're from that Shoofie – I'm sure they are." She smiled at him, her dark eyes laughing and: "And even if they're not, you've got nothing to worry about – I promise."

***

Mid-morning on Monday 3 November and disaster struck. Massingbird-Munday had been on the phone, Mott told Gregory: it looked as though Sturge had gone missing. One of his local contacts, a postman, had told Massingbird-Munday that he had been trying to deliver a package to Sturge's house for several days and that he had never been able to get a reply to his ringing. That morning he had looked through the letter box and seen that previously delivered post had not been picked up and was still lying on the floor and one of the neighbours said that Sturge had not been seen for several days.

Tony Carter, whose team had been given the garage surveillance, reported no movement and the Transit had not been moved. McGibbon was dispatched to Palmers Green and reported back within an hour that Sturge's old Fiesta was still in his garage at the back of the house.

A meeting with Strathearn was scheduled for that afternoon and with Mott and Carter waiting in the outer office he saw The Old Man alone.

"You've had no surveillance on the house?"

"No sir. We covered the garage where the white van is, twenty-four hours a day –"

"But not the house?"

"There were reasons for that. From looking at the house and the street I was sure he would have sussed any surveillance, no matter how we did it. The only possible way was to use a house opposite but it meant taking a terrible chance from the point of view of gossip, kids, comings and goings and, well, to be honest, there was the manpower situation as well."

He paused, trying to assess Strathearn's reaction, but The Old Man, back to him and looking out over Victoria Street, said nothing.

"I accept he was in the frame, Guv – but no more than Vic Peace was. Okay, he's got a white van and he's the right age and all that, but the rest of it – all that sleeping with his mother and working in mortuaries – it's all gossip and rumour."

Strathearn turned and faced him. He nodded and walking to his desk he sat down. "The problem, as I see it Michael, is that if it is this feller Sturge we're looking for, and if he stays adrift long enough to do the last one on the eighth of November or when ever it is, it could be said…."

His voice tapered off but almost immediately he looked at Gregory and smiled: "Let's just hope your luck holds, eh?"

With Mott and Carter in the room it was agreed that the search warrants Gregory was holding would be executed immediately and that teams of SOCOs and forensic technicians were to take the three locations to pieces.

"What about the press?" asked Gregory.

"Yes, I've thought about them" said Strathcarn. "We might be needing them in the next few days but until we know for sure it's this Sturge chap we're after we daren't issue a press release." He thought, drumming his fingers on his desk, and then: "Get your searches going, get the SOCOs in, and when we know what we've got you can have a press conference and let them have what we think will help them and us."

Tuesday 4 November

The entry and searches of the three premises commenced at first light the next morning. Carter and three of his surveillance team levered the padlocks of the lockup garage and whilst McGibbon and two others entered the garden shed on Sturge's allotment Gregory, Mott, Iannou and Jackie Daniel watched while the front door of the house in Churchley Avenue was forced. Each team was accompanied by SOCOs and forensic specialists and the greatest care was taken not to alert neighbours and the public.

As Carter had surmised, the Transit van occupied only a small part of the large lock-up and within half an hour of their arrival it was loaded on to a transporter and covered in tarpaulin sheeting it was removed to the police garage for examination.

Towards the back of the premises was a steel table of the sort used in commercial kitchens and immediate chemical testing showed traces of blood invisible to the eye in numerous places on the surface and elsewhere. Carter found wood and bits of plastic sheeting which he was sure would be found to match the materials used to pack the body sent to Mitre

Square. At the far end of the unit they found a stove with a shaky metal flue pipe leading through the asbestos roof and in the ash he found the remains of burnt clothing. He reported to Gregory by phone.

"On the face of it, I would say that what he did to "Toothpick" and the Mitre Square girl he did here."

He had found no knives, he said, but they were still looking and the interior of the transit had not been touched and was being left to the forensic people. A painstaking fingertip examination of the whole garage was being carried out and taking into account that Sturge appeared to have not been at all concerned with covering his tracks, Carter was sure that he would find evidence of the presence of Tracey Gallop and possibly more.

"There is one thing I thought you like to know: on a shelf by the steel table there's a photo of an old woman in a silver frame. I'll lay odds it his mother and if he did use the table for cutting those girls up, it's like he's got her there watching him."

In "Southwold" everything was as Sturge had left it. The two vases of chrysanthemums were drooping but although the house was cold due to lack of heating, it smelled of polish and care and attention. As Gregory had expected, there were fingerprints everywhere one would expect them to be and within twenty minutes he was able to telephone Strathearn and tell him that they matched those on the "Ripper letters." There were sixteen books relative to the 1888 Ripper, a computer and printer and in the bedside cupboard of what he took to be Sturge's bedroom, he found a shoe box full of letters all addressed to Martin Sturge.

Gregory was fascinated by the tidiness of the house and the evident fastidiousness of its occupier. It was as his mother was wont to say: a place for everything and everything in its place. Although by mid-morning the SOCOs were testing for blood, taking fibre samples from everything and hundreds of possible exhibits were being placed in bags and labelled, the overall impression remained that the property was occupied by substantial and reliable elderly people who still valued and adhered to the principals and traditions of an earlier generation.

With the organised chaos of the white-overalled forensic officers going on around him, Gregory sat in an armchair in the drawing room, leafing through the Ripper books and the box of letters. Earlier, he had gone into the back garden with Jackie Daniel and been shown the fish pond and statue to which Shoofie Coots had referred. He had admired the great gold fish as, goggle-eyed, they rose to the surface as if they were interested in all the activity, and taking a stick he had poked through the ashes of Sturge's bonfire site. Frowning, he watched as a SOCO covered the polished surfaces of the antique furniture with fingerprint powder and then, and as if to remind him that he was a part of what was taking place, his mobile telephone rang. McGibbon from the allotment.

"Guv, I think you ought to get over here." Usually a placid, unexcitable man, McGibbon sounded shaken up and on edge.

"What have you got?"

"There's this work bench in his shed, Guv, and underneath it, right at the back by the shed wall we've found a sort of partition with a space behind it." His voice was shaking and Gregory sensed that whatever he had discovered had brought him close to nausea.

"He's got the bits he cut out of those poor little cows: they're here, pickled in bottles of some sort of chemical liquid stuff."

Tuesday 4 November.

The SOCOs and forensic technicians remained in "Southwold" and the allotment shed and garage for the next two days. The fingerprints found in the house tied Sturge into the Ripper letters and put him with the woman identified as being Kelly Goggin in the Row Barge in Lea Bridge the night of her death and although the full forensic and laboratory reports would not be available for several days Gregory knew there was going to be a wealth of evidence forthcoming. "McGibbon's lunch" as some wag had named the macabre bottled pieces of anatomy he had unearthed, had been identified as being a uterus, a section of vaginal tissue and most of a bladder in one jar and a kidney and part of a womb in a second. Although the DNA matching had not arrived back, Gregory was sure that these related to Kelly Goggin and "Toothpick", but it was the discovery of a third container, much older than the other two, and containing a single womb which caused him to wonder. Findlater, the pathologist, was of the opinion that this was at least forty years old and as such could have no bearing on the current matters. It could be some ancient medical specimen, he suggested, some exhibit stolen by a medical student from a laboratory or from any one of a dozen sources but he was adamant about the age and although it went for DNA testing with the other material, Gregory came to the conclusion that it was of little importance.

Mid-afternoon and he called Jackie into his office. "I want you and Barney to go and see the sisters, Jackie. I'm afraid we've only got first names but from the letters they've written to him I think they're both unmarried so presumably they're still called Sturge. One of them lives in Amersham and the other one's in Hertfordshire somewhere – the addresses are on the letters."

"Sisters, sir? What sisters?"

He pushed the shoe box on his desk towards her. "He's got two sisters – Susan and Pamela or Pammie as she signs herself. They write to him more or less every week."

"This is the first I've heard of any sisters, Guvnor. None of the Palmers Green people who know him have ever mentioned any sisters and as far as I'm aware he was an only child."

"Well, someone's writing to him, Jack, I can promise you that, and they both sign themselves off as his sisters." He opened the shoe box and took out a handful of envelopes, some blue, some pink, some white, and went on: "I've not read any of it really, just glanced through but you have a good read and see what turns up. I think we need to see them – and anyway, he might be staying with one of them."

She picked up the box and leafed through the letters. "Okay, fine", she said, hesitantly. "It's just that I can't understand why no one's mentioned them before."

Friday 7 November.

Gregory had arranged for a press release for the afternoon. In addition to those discovered at the house, a large number of his fingerprints had been discovered in the garage, the allotment shed and in the van and substantial traces of blood had been detected on a plastic-covered mattress in the van. Following discussions it had been agreed that Sturge would be described as being "sought in connection with the on-going enquiry" and that his full details and the E Fit would be released.

Jackie Daniel, who had been fully occupied with the letters found in "Southwold", was of the opinion that they were not genuine. "I rechecked with all the Palmers Green Pensioners" she told Gregory "and they are all adamant that there were no sisters." She smiled at him. "Shoofie Coots' missus worked in the local doctors' surgery from the time she left school in the thirties until she retired in the mid-sixties and he says there were no sisters and if there had been he would have known about it."

"But the letters?"

"Well, for a start both addresses are false. The one in Stevenage doesn't exist and there's no one called Sturge living at the other one and there never has been. There's no National

Insurance record of anyone called either Susan or Pamela Sturge born between 1933 when Martin Sturge was born and 1960 when his mother would have been too old to have kids."

Gregory took off his glasses. He gazed at the pretty girl and wished he was younger.

"You have been busy, haven't you."

She smiled again, blushing.

"Have you read them, Guv? Properly I mean?" Before he could answer she spilled the contents of the shoe-box on his desk. The letters were now in order, she explained: two packets, each secured by an elastic band, one relative to Susan Sturge and the other to Pamela and all in date order.

"If you look at the postmarks, Guv, you'll see that none of them were posted in Hertfordshire or Buckinghamshire, in fact they've all been posted somewhere in North London and a lot of them in Palmers Green, Wood Green or Winchmore Hill. Whoever wrote them has tried to make two sets of handwriting, one for Pam and another for Sue, but sometimes the writer's got confused and you find bits of Pam's scribble in Sue's letters and vice-versa."

She opened several of the letters and placed them in front of Gregory, indicating the passages to which she referred and the questionable handwriting. "And you haven't read them?"

"Not really."

"Well, there's a lot of reminiscing about childhood, mum and dad and all that sort of thing but there's something strange as well, corrupt – I can't explain it, sir, but like they've both been in some sort of incestuous relationship with Martin Sturge and that they miss it and would like to start it all up again."

She selected a letter which she had tagged with a yellow post-it slip. "This is from Pam: blah-blah-blah-de-blah and then 'darling Martin, how I miss you and I know that Susie does too. Could we come home? Would we be welcome? All together again in Mummy's big bed – just the three of us alone and together for ever....' Is that sort of letter a sister would write to her brother, Guv?"

He took the letter and read it. "Is there much of this?"

"Quite a lot. But they also talk about the fish pond a lot, happy memories of the fish and playing by the water. You remember I told you what that Shoofie chap said –"

"About him not being told to finish it the day after the old man went on the trot? Yes, I remember."

He leafed through the letters, careful not to upset her orderly categorization.

"What do you think?"

She frowned, unhappy at being asked to make what she felt may be an important assessment but, at the same time, pleased that he had that confidence in her. "Well, for a start I don't think there are any sisters." She thought carefully, unwilling to be thought imaginative or naïve. Then: "I think he's a total nutter, Guv. I think he's invented two sisters, God above only knows why or for what purpose, and I think he's writing the letters to himself. He's fantasising, like some little boy with a miserable childhood."

Gregory nodded and smiled at her. He swivelled his chair and, facing away from her and towards the wall, he said: "Maybe he wanted sisters and never had them?" He stared at the blank wall for a moment and, swinging his chair back and facing her: "But whatever the reason is, I think you're right."

After the press conference at the Yard Gregory went with Strathearn to his office, leaving Mott to make his own way back to Leman Street. He winked at Rosie as he passed her in the outer office and smiled as she nodded towards her week-end bag, ready for their West End hotel.

Later, as he drove back to Leman Street, he was concerned and angry to see Mott deep in conversation with "Wonkeye" Jerrry outside of a public house in Northumberland Avenue.

22.

Saturday 8 November.

The owner of the Elmlea Residential Home for the elderly in Ashburton, Devon was sorry to say goodbye to Bill Black but she quite understood his position and that a move from London to the West Country may be too great an upheaval for him. She liked the old man and his quiet, rather eccentric ways, and she had enjoyed caring for him but when he had arrived he made it clear that his stay was merely a trial and that he could make no decision as to permanent residency until he was quite, quite sure that he would be happy. She knew only too well that bereavement prompted people to make rash decisions and as much as she would have liked Bill to stay, she knew that the wrong move so soon after the death of his wife could be a disaster for all concerned.

The taxi came shortly before 6.00am., and dropped Bill forty minutes later in front of St. David's railway station in Exeter. He watched the cab drive away and then, from time to time changing his heavy suitcase from hand to hand, he walked the short distance into a side street opposite the station where the staff and residents back at Elmlea would have been surprised to see him open the doors of a small blue van and throw his suitcase into the back. He took off his raincoat and threw it in beside the suitcase and having found the keys in his trouser pocket, he started the van and, ignoring the rat, rattling and squeaking in its cage, he drove up the hill into the city, looking for signs for London.

He should have known they may have been getting near when he saw that fat copper with the ludicrous name driving along Churchley Avenue that Sunday morning. He remembered that he had felt a slight frisson of apprehension but over-confidence and the ever-increasing and worsening bouts of foggy confusion had resulted in complacency. Still, seeing Gregory's pretty little policewoman and her pal in Palmers Green – and remembering them from The Gun – had prompted action, and he had enjoyed his brief stay in Devon, despite the problem of the rat. Having telephoned in advance, he had driven the van (a cash purchase from a newspaper advertisement) to Exeter and having parked it he took a taxi to Elmlea. His wife had recently died, he had told them, and he was anxious to get away from London and old memories. He had agreed that he would stay for a short time on a trial basis and had paid in cash.

Where better to hide an old fool than amongst a crowd of others, he had reasoned?

Every day, after breakfast and an hour of newspapers and gossip in the comfortable lounge, he would leave Elmlea and take the bus to Exeter where he fed the rat on scraps of raw meat he bought in butchers in either Ashburton or Exeter. Every two or three days he emptied the cage of the creature's droppings and once he moved the position of the van, ensuring that it was parked in what he took to be a working class area. He loathed the rat and was frightened of its foul, infected teeth and its long, ever-twitching whiskers and inquisitive eyes, but it was an essential part of the game plan and nothing was going to deter him from that.

At first he had been concerned that his daily absences from Elmlea would be queried but to his surprise the only comment was to the effect that he was missing a lunch which he was paying for. He cheerfully excused his absences by stories of long walks on Dartmoor and – in case anyone spotted him in Exeter – walks by the canal and visits to the maritime museum. Strangely, although the nightmares persisted, the debilitating bouts of mental fog lessened – a phenomena he put down to his absence from "Southwold."

He hummed to himself as he drove towards London, tunes from Gilbert and Sullivan and the old hymns he had known since school assemblies, but as Devon turned to Somerset and Wiltshire he felt his mood getting heavier and he fell silent. At the turn-off towards Andover he left the A303. He had several cups of strong tea and two cheese rolls in a café on the edge of an industrial estate and finding an ironmongers shop in the main street he purchased two large rolls of adhesive tape of the type used for packing and sealing large cardboard packages and cartons, a metal colander and the stoutest pair of industrial gloves that was in stock.

At about this time the matron of the Elmlea Residential Home for the elderly was enjoying a cup of coffee and a chocolate Hobnob when the door of the staffroom burst open and she was confronted by two very excited old ladies, one of whom was holding a copy of the Daily Telegraph.

Back on the road he made good time through the light Saturday traffic and by the time he joined the North Circular Road his depression had abated and light opera had turned to full-throated rendering of "Jerusalem", the rat cowering in a corner of it's cage, evidently terrified by the noise.

Turning off at Brent Cross, he made his way through Golders Green and to the Whitestone Pond. He drove the van twice round the car park adjacent to Jack Straw's Castle. "H-h-h-ello, T-t-t-Toothpick," he muttered, and then on through Hampstead and into Camden Town. Turning of Tottenham Court Road, he drove into Berners Street and asked the young policeman who had been deputed to stand outside The Knights of Erotica the way to Mitre Square. In Kings Cross he was disappointed to see that both the Canterbury Pilgrim and the coffee stall were closed and in an act of breathtaking bravado he called in at Leman Street police station and asked directions to Venture Street, Stepney.

***

The little house had been left to her by her grandmother and she loved it. During the three years since she had moved in she had spent all of her available time and money on renovation and although still far from what she wanted, it was starting to take shape. The tiny kitchen her grandmother called "the scullery" had been knocked through into the outside lavatory forming a good-sized kitchen/breakfast room; the extension had continued to the floor above and a bathroom, complete with walk-in shower and "his-and-hers" wash basins had been constructed and overall, apart from the dust and builders' tools and paraphernalia, things were relatively comfortable.

She opened the boot of the Picasso and taking out her three Tesco carrier bags of groceries she set them on the ground as she slammed the boot-lid and operated the remote central locking. She walked the few steps to the front door of the small terraced house and placing one of the bags on the step she slipped the key into the lock and suddenly, coming as if from nowhere, he was behind her. In a flash, a micro-second, she experienced both confusion and terror: she saw grey hair and blue eyes; she heard the vile obscenities forced through tight-clenched, gritted teeth and before the merciful darkness of unconsciousness her racing mind noted and queried the presence of a grey, metal colander.

***

Mott, never a devotee of the Constabularies, had to admit that the Devon and Cornwall had done him proud. A detective inspector and a sergeant arrived at Elmlea less than half an hour after the call from the matron and within two hours over a dozen fingerprints they had found in "Bill Black's" room arrived on Gregory's desk. Thankfully, pressure of work had prevented the Elmlea staff from cleaning the room ready for a new occupant which made their job easier, but nonetheless both Gregory and Mott were impressed.

Minutes after the arrival of the prints it was established that Bill Black and Sturge were one and the same, but he was long gone from Ashburton and with little hope of finding him. Neither the matron and staff nor the residents at Elmlea could assist overmuch: he was a pleasant enough man who kept himself to himself. It seemed that he spent most of the day out, walking it was thought. He spoke to very few people and was very polite when he did, and no-one recalled anything unusual about him. As far as anyone knew he had arrived in Devon by train and taxi having booked his short trial stay by telephone. It later developed that the contact address in London which he had given was false and it soon became clear that on leaving Elmlea he had disappeared.

Gregory, though, knew that he would be in London that day.

***

After what seemed like hours later she drifted towards consciousness. She winced as she registered the sharp throbbing of headache, and from the tight and painful sensation on the left of her upper face and the impaired sight she realised she had sustained a blow to the head with the ensuing swelling round her left eye. She felt cold, cold of the sort experienced due to lack of bedclothes on a winter's night and as her level of awareness increased she knew that she was naked. She blinked at the grey ceiling, peeling in places and as yet unvisited by the decorators and as she understood the enormity of what had happened and of what may be to come, she realised that she could not move. Collecting her thoughts, she remembered that she had returned from her shopping shortly before 1.00pm and that judging from the thin light that was left in the room she sensed it was late afternoon.

Stretched above her head, she realised that her arms were secured to the brass bed head of what she realised was the single bed in her spare bedroom. Bands of what she took to be some form of adhesive tape were wound around her head, covering her mouth, and extending beneath the bed and in such a manner that lifting her head or movement side to side was not possible. Her legs, parted, were similarly secured at the ankles, knees and thighs and with more tape bound round her upper body, wound round her in the manner of an Egyptian mummy, she was cocooned, helpless and unable to move or to call out.

Every second it seemed as though the daylight diminished and as the light in the room became greyer and her vision became less clear, so the temperature fell.

For a moment she lay still, ceasing the straining of arms and legs and the futile attempts to arch her torso, and she listened, desperate to know if she was alone.

Nothing. The little house was silent. Outside, she could hear the sounds of traffic and the kids, home from West Ham and Millwall, playing football in the street. She could hear the pigeons skittering on the roof and gutters of her house as they started to make arrangements for their roosting and, far away, the hee-hawing of some busy police car or fire engine as it hurried through the East London streets. Forcing her eyes to the extremities of left and right and taking the deepest possible breaths through her nose, she sought frantically for something, anything, which may aid her to escape and as tears of frustration and fear formed, she relaxed her muscles and ceased the ineffectual struggle against her bonds.

She could not sob any more than she could cry out and as she lay in the half-light, alone and unable either to escape or to call for help, she started to wonder the purpose of her assailant and whether her nakedness and humiliation had been the total of his warped endeavours, or if he would return. Suddenly, anger and violent frustration replaced fear and gritting her teeth behind the sticky gag and clenching her eyes tight shut, she arched her back and strained her muscles in an effort to break or even to stretch the strapping which restrained her so tightly. Then, as she forced her midriff a few inches off the bed, through her tears and the tapes wound round her face, through the space he had left her between the bridge of her nose and the middle of her forehead, she glimpsed grey metal and forcing her head a few further centimetres above the horizontal, she realised that the colander had been attached in some manner to her bare abdomen.

Clenching her teeth once more and forcing head upwards against the restraining layers of tape which crossed her forehead, passing beneath the single bed and crossing and recrossing again and again, she peered downwards, across the gag. The colander, she saw, had been taped to her stomach in an upside-down position; strips of the adhesive material were wound around the handles and over the base and having been passed under the small of her back, the utensil was firmly fixed to her. Holding her breath and straining the muscles of her eyes, she saw that the join between the metal of the colander and her skin had likewise been sealed by more adhesive tape, and as she tried to squirm, suddenly she felt movement on the skin of her stomach and she understood that the reversed colander, securely affixed as it was to her bare and unprotected abdomen, contained some living creature.

Instinctively she froze, allowing her torso to relax on the mattress. She listened carefully. At first there was nothing, just the hum of traffic and the Cockney shouts of kids going home for burgers and Match of the Day, but as she lay motionless, barely daring to breathe, she heard the scratch of tiny claws as they pried at the holes in the colander and as she felt the pressure of tiny feet and a warm body on her skin, with tears of terror running over the tape on her face, she voided her bladder.

Two hours later and the offices at Leman Street were quiet. Gregory had left for the evening and was on his way to the hotel in Russell Square where he and Rosie were to spend the weekend. Mott, his feet up on the desk in Gregory's office, was going through the forensic reports and evidence while Iannou tinkered with the HOLMES system, inserting the various data obtained from what had become known as the "Palmers Green Pensioners." Jackie had the day off (they had yet to arrange to have simultaneous rest days) and McGibbon and two others of the team were reading and checking statements.

The phone in Gregory's office rang. Startled, Mott's feet hit the floor with a crash. "There's a chap at the front counter, sir. Asking for Mr. Gregory. Says his name's Martin Sturge."

Mott suddenly felt very cold. He felt the muscles in his stomach contract with anticipation and he realised that the hand which was holding the telephone was shaking.

"I'll be down" he said. And then in a low voice: "For Christ's sake - don't let him go."

By the time Gregory got back to Leman Street, Sturge had been relieved of his clothes. In a white, cotton protective suit and slippers he was seated in an interview room with Mott and McGibbon and had been given a plastic mug of strong tea.

Gregory introduced himself. Sturge smiled, his blue eyes somehow at the same time both friendly and iceberg cold.

"I want no lawyers, Mr. Gregory, and I will not speak to any recording device which you may place in front of me. I do not propose to discuss what I have done other than to tell you that I intend to admit everything when the time comes. I am sure that I have left you plenty of – " he stopped, as if searching for a word and smiled at Gregory "- *clues*, if that's the right word, and we all know that I shall never see the light of day again – and that when everyone is agreed that I am as mad as a hatter, I shall spend what time I have left in the comfort of Broadmoor or some such place."

Gregory stared at him, trying to assess the depth of his insanity and at the same time desperate to know the answer to the yet unasked question. He watched as Sturge sipped tea from his plastic beaker and for a moment he studied the thin hands which he knew had done the unspeakable.

"But there's one more, isn't there, Martin? The last one."

Sturge nodded: "Yes. The last one", he said thoughtfully. His eyes narrowed and Gregory sensed that some awful pleasure, some sweet but shocking memory, had been recalled.

There was silence broken only by the hum of traffic and the wind rattling the ancient sash windows. Then: "Are you going to tell us about it? The last one?"

"As I told you, Mr. Gregory: I will not discuss what I have done: It is all there for you to discover and all will come clear." He paused and gazed at the window, smiling. Then, and almost a murmur: "In time, of course."

"People are going to be asking you why, you know."

"I imagine they will, yes." He smiled again, the same vague grin, cold and disinterested. "And they can ask away."

Gregory nodded and looked at Mott. Outside, he said: "He's done one, the bastard. He's done another one: he's just waiting till it turns up."

Mott agreed: "I'm sure he has: that's why the bastard's given himself up."

Later, in the interview room, Gregory said: "Do you want to tell us about Michael Folmer, Martin? You had us really worried for a while, all those fingerprints turning up all over the place."

Sturge closed his eyes tight shut and smiled, rocking in his chair, his arms crossed and wrapped round his thin frame as far as they would go.

"We know you were in Savile Row at the same time as Folmer and we know about you trying to jump out of the window –"

"And we know that Johnnie Marriott – that was Folmer's real name – swapped the fingerprint forms over" interjected Mott.

"Then you know it all, don't you?"

"We don't know about the one you've done today, though, do we?" Mott's tone was threatening. He was angry, incensed by the man's arrogance and his total detachment from the horror he had brought about and the misery he had reeked.

His eyes shut tight again and rocking in his chair, Sturge said: "My mother always said that if you can't talk nicely, don't talk at all. And you're not talking at all nicely, Mr. Gregory's assistant."

At 11.00pm they gave up. They both knew that they had not interrogated Sturge and what had taken place had been more in the way of a friendly chat. Gregory knew there was a fine line and that if the man and his madness were not handled correctly and with judgement he was likely to clam up for ever. He had been happy to talk about Folmer and had told them he had learned about the swapped fingerprint forms in the prison van on the way to court the following morning and how they had both thought what a joke it would be if Sturge's prints were to surface (as Folmer's) years later. He was willing to talk about Elmlea and his short time in Devon but as soon as they tried to move on to the four murders or his activities of that day the eyes closed and the child-like rocking in his chair was back.

With Sturge safe in a cell for the night and with a PC posted outside the door, Gregory told Mott to arrange for some form of covert recording device to be in the interview room for the following day. Sturge's refusal to have his conversations recorded worried him and he was not prepared to take any chances. There was no doubt in his mind that Sturge was quite insane and that his mental state would obviate a full airing at the Old Bailey, but in the event of any internal enquiries or suggestions that he may have acted without judgement he would be better placed with recordings than without them.

It was past midnight as he drove back to Russell Square. Try as he might, he could not detach his mind from the thought that somewhere in east London some poor woman lay alone and mutilated and that had he acted differently and applied closer scrutiny to Sturge, her life may have been saved. Finding the hotel bar closed, he woke Rosie and rifled the contents of the room's mini-bar.

***

The room had been dark for hours, the small amount of light coming from distant street lamps and a watery moon as it showed occasionally from behind blowing clouds. She was cold, colder than she had ever been in her life, and the cramp in her arms and legs had become one constant and unremitting pain but she dare not move for fear of disturbing whatever it was that felt warm as it slept on her stomach. By way of experiment and trial and error she had come to realise that movement on her part caused the creature to become active and to move in circles within the confined space of the colander, at the same time prying with tiny needle-claws at the holes in the metal as it sought a means of escape.

In her heart she knew that the beast was a rat, although her mind refused to accept it. More recently she had noticed a smell, a sour, foetid stink which she imagined was the creature's urine and faeces gathering beneath its metal prison and although the thought of her skin being in contact with such ordure appalled and disgusted her, she had other, far more serious thoughts clamouring in her aching head. With her eyes tightly shut and scarcely daring to breathe, she wondered what was going to happen when the beast became hungry or when it realised that escape lay through the soft, warm floor of its tiny cell.

Just after four and when Gregory had been in his comfortable Russell Square bed for two hours and coinciding with Sturges third visit to his cell lavatory to relieve his weak bladder, her worst fears were confirmed. From the movements and slight pressures on her skin she knew that the creature was awake but as she lay, her eyes tight shut and trying to breathe with as little body movement as possible, she knew that there was an urgency and purpose about its shuffling and turning, a resolve which she had not sensed before.

They started at seven o'clock. Mott had obtained a briefcase with a built-in microphone and recorder and Sturge paid no attention as he placed it beside the table. Tea and coffee in plastic beakers was provided and Sturge was given two bacon sandwiches. From the outset he made the running and at first Gregory and Mott were happy to let him do so. He referred to the "Ripper Letters", laughing at the concern they must have had when the fingerprints were seen to match those of Johnnie Marriott and confirming that he and Marriott had spoken both in the prison van and at Bow Street.

He toyed with his sandwiches, leaving the crusts uneaten, and then: "They framed me for that flashing, you know. That's what started it all off really."

Gregory, sensing a breakthrough, scarcely dared to breath. "Go on."

"I liked to watch her, the fat old tart in Walker Court. She was such an ugly, horrible thing and I liked to watch the men she got to go up and see her more than anything. One of the coppers told me that she'd complained about me watching her and so they came down and framed me – said I flashed at her."

Gregory was not about to argue. He nodded understandingly: "You gave them a run for their money, though."

Sturge smiled and rocked in his chair. "Mother would have killed me if she knew I had been watching a prostitute…." His voice tailed off and he closed his eyes, apparently in thought. Then, apparently a decision made, he opened his eyes. "I was at the London, Mr. Gregory; the London Hospital and in my third year –"

"Medical training?" asked Gregory.

"Mmnn. That's why I pleaded guilty you see." If the hospital authority had come to know of his arrest it would have meant instant dismissal, he said. The arresting officers told him they knew he had given a false name and address and that if he denied the charge he would be kept in custody for a week at least. "They told me if I admitted it, it would be a fine and straight home – and they were right."

The problem was that he was seen at court. "One of the doctors from the London was in the public gallery, Mr. Gregory. I think his brother or someone had been arrested for some sort of drink driving thing. Anyway, he recognised me and that was that. I was gone in a week."

He was distraught, he said. His mother had sacrificed so much for him to have a medical career and it was months before he had the courage to tell her. "I was living at home, you see, and I just kept going out every morning and letting her think I was going to the hospital."

He started to rock again, eyes closed and his arms around himself, as if he was cuddling his thin frame. "She knew in the end of course," he said softly, "like she knew everything."

"And then what, Martin? The Hospital in Tottenham?"

"My! Haven't you been doing your homework, Mr. Gregory?" He paused and toyed with the crusts of his sandwiches. "Yes. In the path lab. Till they got sick of me and that was that from the work point of view."

"You stayed at home?"

"With Mummy."

Gregory looked at his watch. Just before eight and still no report of some poor women being found hacked to pieces. He knew that mentioning the murders may result in silence and he sensed that, like himself and Mott, Sturge was waiting, the difference being that Sturge was savouring what to him was a joke.

"Tell me about your father, Martin."

He pouted, like a child and the rocking started once more. He glanced at Gregory, a sideways, sly look and Gregory sensed that whatever he said next would be a lie. "He left when I was at school. Mummy said he didn't love us any more and he just went."

"And Pammie and Sue?"

The eyes closed and he turned away from them, twisting in his chair so he was facing the wall. "They left me, too," he said softly. There was silence, and then: "I don't think I want to talk any more. Not now, anyway."

In his office Gregory said: "Jackie Daniel's right: there are no bloody sisters, they're just fantasies." He looked at Mott, trying to forget the renewed misgivings festering inside him relative to "Wonkeye Jerry", knowing that at that stage of the investigation he did not need to be sidetracked. Not for the first time, he wished he had not given up smoking.

Mott nodded. "He didn't want to talk about them, that's for sure."

Moments later they were joined by Iannou who had just come on duty. Keen to know what had taken place he listened intently as Mott played the recording of the interview. "Does he know that we know he was in Devon for a week?" he asked.

Gregory was about to reply when his phone rang. He spoke briefly and then: "That was the station officer. They've moved him into a cell so he can use the toilet." He thought for a moment and then: "Funniest thing: that sergeant says he came in the nick Saturday dinner time and asked the way to some street. He says he's a hundred percent sure it was him, no doubt at all."

Mott looked at him, a half-grin on his face. "Sturge? Came in here Saturday morning?"

"So he says. Asked the way to Venture Street in Stepney."

"Where?" asked Iannou, suddenly pale and with fear in his dark eyes. "What street?"

"Venture Street, Stepney. Wh- "

"Jesus Christ" said Iannou. "That's where Jackie lives. And she's not come in yet!"

Sated with skin, blood and subcutaneous fat, the rat woke as the front door came off its hinges and crashed to the uncarpeted hall floor. It blinked at the sunlight filtering through the holes in its prison and instinctively felt fear.

On the blood-soaked bed Jackie Daniel did not move.

The sight caused Gregory, Mott and Iannou to freeze momentarily as they burst into the small bedroom. Jackie was unconscious and the trauma and loss of bodily fluids had had made her so pale that at first they thought she was dead. Blood had seeped from beneath the colander and running down either side of her naked body had soaked into the mattress. Her efforts to free herself had caused the packing tape to cut into her flesh and her wrists and ankles were caked in the semi-congealed ooze. The area of her abdomen surrounding the colander was purple and black and the slight movement of her shallow breathing caused fresh blood to ooze from beneath the sticking tape.

Trying not to panic, Iannou found the kitchen and returned with two knives and a pair of scissors. Carefully, he prised the edge of the tape from her skin and inserting the point of one of the scissor blades he started to cut into the sticky material. Gregory and Mott, a knife each, were cutting through the restraining materials at her wrists and ankles, all the time talking to her and trying to bring her back to consciousness.

And suddenly, as a section of the edge of the colander came free from tape, the rat emerged. Squeezing between the rim of its metal prison and the yielding emptiness of the girl's stomach, it emerged, blinking and seemingly semi-comatose, into daylight. Horrified and fleetingly uncomprehending, Iannou stared as it cleaned its eyes and face, thick with congealed blood and flecks of flesh, its claw-feet scraping, sifting and combing through the matted grey fur and over the ever-twitching nose and whickers. Then, self-control regained but loathing what he knew he must do, he swiped at the creature hitting it with the flat of his hand, causing it to fall to the floor. For a moment it lay, stunned and at the same time sluggish due to the hours of restricted movement and over feeding, but Mott, taking a short step, crashed its head with one stamp of his brown brogue.

The colander removed, they saw a gaping wound approximately the size of the rim of a teacup. It was impossible to know the depth of the injury, awash as it was with half congealed blood and filaments of what appeared to be shredded skin, tissue and pale yellow fat. The three men all felt surges of panic as they realised there was little they could do to help Jackie and that, in all probability, her lack of consciousness was a blessing. Mercifully, an ambulance, summoned by Gregory as soon as he had seen Jackie, arrived within minutes.

He was to accompany Jackie to hospital, Gregory told Iannou, and under no circumstances was he to leave her. Knowing of the detective constable's closeness to Jackie and fearful of his anger, at that time Gregory was unwilling to allow him into Leman Street and near to Sturge and as the ambulance was leaving he telephoned his office instructing another officer to make his way to the hospital and to keep a watchful eye on Barney.

He found Mott in the half-plastered kitchen washing his shoe in the sink. At first he said nothing, watching as the rat's blood and brain tissue ran into the drain. Then, as Mott was replacing the brogue on his foot: "What a bastard, eh?"

Mott nodded and Gregory saw what he knew were dried tears on the man's face. "Is she going to be okay, do you think?"

"Who knows, Dave. But she's in the best place and they'll do all they can, I know that." He watched as Mott washed his hands in the sink using Jackie's washing-up liquid for the purpose and then: "Sturge, Dave: there's no possibility that you - ?"

"Guv, you've got no worries with me on that account I can promise you that." He was neither offended nor was surprised by Gregory's concern as to his ability to refrain from violence when once more in the presence of Sturge. He wiped his hands on a tea towel and: "He's a nutter, Guv, and as far as I'm concerned the best thing is to get this whole mess sorted out, get him out of the nick and try to move on."

Twenty minutes later and the forensic term took over. At Leman Street Gregory phoned the hospital and was told by Iannou that although it was early days the indications were that Jackie would survive. It seemed that in an effort both to feed and escape, the rat had gnawed into the girl's body consuming both skin and flesh but that it had not bored to a depth sufficient to breach the lining of the stomach and intestines or to damage other organs. The blood loss was crucial, as was the risk of infection, but she had regained consciousness and early indications were positive.

Before resuming the Sturge interview they agreed that they would make no mention of the horror at Venture Street, this with a view to seeing how Sturge would react and in an effort possibly to ascertain the extent of his insanity. Sturge, it was to turn out, had different ideas.

For ten minutes they skated around the family set-up at "Southwold", unsuccessfully trying to draw him out regarding his mother and his sisters. There were periods of silence, rocking and hugging himself, and overall a total disinclination on his part to discuss anything appertaining to what he had done. Coffee came and having drunk half the contents of his plastic beaker and without warning, he said: "Don't you want to know how I found out where Miss Daniel lived?"

There was a silence. Mott glanced at Gregory but before either could reply, Sturge went on: "You have found her – I know you have, so why are you teasing me?"

Gregory swallowed. Shocked at Sturge's complacency and seeming disregard for what he had done, he felt he was on the verge of extreme violence but knowing that control was essential and trying to hide his anger, he said: "I was hoping you'd tell us, Martin."

"You sent her flowers," said Mott quietly, "and I imagine that had something to do with it."

Sturge crumpled his coffee beaker. "Very good, Mr. Gregory's assistant. Very good indeed." It had only taken a phone call to Leman Street, he explained: "I said I wanted to send flowers to the pretty detective on Mr. Gregory's squad who had been making enquiries in Palmers Green and someone gave me the name is easily as that." He smiled at Mott who, like Gregory, was finding it hard to control his feelings.

"And her address? How did you get that?"

"She's not dead, is she?" His voice was toneless and with neither expression or emotion. He started to rock, his face pinched and contorted and his mouth drawn to one side as though he had suffered a stroke. "Like a ravening beast had attacked her, they said about Mary Kelly, like some wolverine or terrible, ripping vulture bird had got inside her."

His voice tailed off and as his eyes seemed to glaze, the lids fluttering, a string of silver beaded saliva started to fall from his chin on to his white protective overall.

Sturge was charged with four murders and attempting to kill Jackie Daniel. He did not ask for legal representation and did not object to being remanded back to Leman Street in order that he could be interrogated further. Watching him as he stood in the dock of the magistrate's court, Gregory realised that that his mental state was fast deteriorating and whatever questions they needed to ask they were likely to have little time to get the answers.

A bed was set up in the largest of the interview rooms and with a table and several chairs Sturge was installed but, very much as they had expected, Mott and Gregory found the going hard. The recording tapes from the briefcase were mounting but as one of the office staff mentioned to a colleague after one morning of listening and typing, most of it was of no account whatsoever. Sturge was happy to talk about the fingerprints and Folmer/Marriott and he rambled sometimes incoherently about a vast selection of topics, but he closed down the instant that anything that he did not like was mentioned. These silences could last for hours and often longer and Gregory was desperate to avoid them at all costs.

On the morning of the second day there was a minor breakthrough. They had barely sat down at the table when Sturge, still in underwear and a dressing gown, said: "You asked me how I found Miss Daniel's address, Mr. Gregory."

Gregory, who was shuffling through the numerous files and mountains of paper, hoped that Mott's briefcase was switched on and functioning and nodded.

"I did."

"Well, I told you how I got her name, didn't I? Once I had that it wasn't very hard, really. Just a question of money."

He had telephoned a private investigation firm who told him that knowing her name and Jackie's occupation they could get her home address in a day. "I sent them two hundred pounds in an envelope and when I phoned them the next day they gave it to me over the phone. As easy as that."

He couldn't recall details of the company other than that it was in London and they didn't press it. As Mott said later, although it was almost certain that the investigation firm had obtained the data illegally, at the time they could not have known who Sturge was or his reasons for wanting the address and little was to be gained in wasting time chasing them.

Late in the afternoon Gregory edged the conversation round to Sturge's sisters and, as he had expected, there was a silence with the usual rocking in his chair. Gregory had noticed that this behaviour was becoming more common and he felt that a total breakdown of Sturge's mental balance was becoming imminent. Preferring to coax him rather than press him, he gathered his papers together and giving tacit indication that the interview was at an end he pushed back his chair. Sturge watched him: not the sly sideways look they had come to know but an open-faced and confused, almost worried, stare.

He got up from his chair and shuffled in his canvas slippers to the cot bed and lay down, his back to them and his knees raised in foetal position. Gregory and Mott watched as he crushed his forearms to his chest and, with his knees now almost under his chin, he rocked. For two or three minutes they watched him and then he spoke. Later, both Mott and Gregory would swear that they felt the temperature in the interview room fall to such a degree that goose-bumps formed and the sweat caused by the time they had spent in the centrally-heated environment turned to ice-water.

"I gave them presents on their birthdays." The voice was soft but at the same time in some way excited. Higher and clearer than normal, it was the voice of a boy in his youth: "Teaspoons I gave them, silver ones, and Mummy was really, really cross when she found out."

Gregory felt a shiver on his cold back and at the same time he experienced a sensation of fear combined with shock. It was not fear of the man or of what Gregory knew he was capable, but fear of something that he did not understand.

"Ninth of June nineteen forty-nine Pammie and first of August nineteen fifty-one Susie." The boy's voice petered out and for a moment the silence of the interview room was broken only by his deep breathing. Then, turning towards them on the creaking cot, he whispered: "Apostle spoons, they were. Silver with the little figure on the top of the handle."

Gregory looked across the table at Mott who was white and unblinking. They said nothing, understanding that Sturge was in a world of his own and that whatever they said he would ignore, even if he heard it. For a moment, the seventy year old man was gone and they were in the presence of a being some sixty years younger.

"They never came and saw me after that. They said they'd come but Mummy said they never would and she was right. Like she always was."

He was weeping now, the tears rolling down his face and the dribble of saliva starting to form in the corner of his mouth. Then, looking straight at Gregory who later recalled the look on his face as being both evil and, in a way he could not explain, pathetic, he whispered:

"There is more than you can ever know."

Later that evening Sturge was sectioned under the Mental Health Act and removed to a secure unit. As Gregory watched him climb into the back of the large van he knew that the man had gone forever and that the rest of his life would be seen through eyes and a mind half a century younger.

Reports had come in from the laboratories and very much as had been expected Sturge had sought to hide nothing and there was a wealth of evidence to associate him with all of the murders. Fibres from Kelly Goggin's clothes had been found in both Sturge's Transit and his lockup, DNA from traces of urine found in the van matched that of "Toothpick" and the wood and packing material found in the garage was an exact match for that used to parcel up Tracey Gallop. Hairs from "Toothpick"'s dog were found in the van and traces of blood found in the steel table in the garage were relative to "Toothpick", Kelly Goggin and Tracey Gallop.

The extensive press coverage since the press conference with the added thrust since Sturge's arrest and court appearance had varying results. McGibbon and a detective constable travelled to Luton to meet an 88 year old gentleman who had worked in the pathology department at the Prince of Wales Hospital in Tottenham and recalled Sturge clearly. "Strangest bugger you ever met", he said. "He spent all his time in the damn mortuary – you just couldn't get him out of it." In a detailed statement he said that Sturge had an obsession with watching the post mortem examinations and that in the end the hospital was obliged to get rid of him for neglecting his work in the laboratory. "At least, that's what they said, but a story went round that there was more to it than that and they hushed it up."

Pressed by McGibbon, and on the understanding that it was not included in the statement, he said: "Well, the rumour was that he got a bit too friendly with one of the bodies and that he was caught alone in the mortuary one night after it had closed – but it was a rumour and that was all."

McGibbon nodded wisely as if revelation of this nature were a daily occurrence: "Male or a female was it?"

There were countless telephone calls from an assortment of persons who knew Sturge or thought they knew him, all offering information of varying significance. Vic Peace phoned Mott offering congratulations and giving assurances that all was forgotten and forgiven and that no civil actions were pending and Gregory received a text message from Rosie to the effect that she felt it would better if he had his breakfasts in Fulham from then on.

With Sturge no longer in the station Gregory's reservations about Iannou disappeared and he returned to active duty at Leman Street. Jackie was on the mend but it would be a long haul, from the points of view of both physical and mental recuperation, he said. The damage to her abdomen would be repaired by way of plastic surgery once all risk of infection from the rat was known to have been negated and, overall, he told the team, she was on the road to recovery. Privately he told Gregory that he doubted if she would ever return to duty again.

The DNA reports arrived towards the end of the week and with Mott Gregory went to see Strathearn at the Yard. Of the three containers that had been found in Sturge's allotment shed, one was found to contain the uterus and other material from the pathetic "Toothpick" and the second a kidney and part of the womb that had been hacked out of the body of Tracey Gallop. The third jar, the scientists were agreed, was much older, at least fifty years. It contained the womb of an unknown woman estimated to be in her late twenties and who had borne at least one child. The manner of the removal of the organ was amateur and unlikely to have been made by surgical practice which seemed to exclude the possibility that it was some sort of medical exhibit, as did the manner in which it had been preserved and the liquid in which it was contained.

"Of course, we mustn't lose sight of the fact that he worked in a path lab and would have had access to all that sort of gubbins", said Mott. "The old chap McGibbon saw in Luton said he was a weird sod, always hanging about in the mortuary – anything was possible."

Strathearn agreed. "Anyway, it's fifty years old, at least and there's nothing to suggest he was cutting women to pieces when he was in his twenties, is there?"

Gregory nodded. He was reluctant but he had to agree that there was no point in commencing lengthy and costly investigations into what was almost certainly a red herring and if The Old Man was happy that it was of little or no consequence that is where the matter would rest.

The garden at Southwold, though, was a different matter and on this point Strathearn was adamant. "I understand that it's only this old gardener – Stupid Whathisname –"

"Shoofie Coots", muttered Mott, smiling.

"Yes, him. Well, it's only what he said but it's got to be done. I can just see it ten years down the line when the house is sold to some yuppie pair and they decide to enlarge the fishpond or something and find an extension of Kensal Green cemetery down there." He laughed, sardonically: "We'd never live it down, none of us, so get the bloody spades out."

***

The work at "Southwold" commenced shortly after 7.00am and with frost thick on the ground. Mott, who had had the presence of mind to bring milk, made tea and with Gregory he stood in the kitchen watching as tarpaulin screening was erected around the fish pond and, supervised by Iannou, uniform policeman in Wellington boots armed with nets and buckets trapped the numerous Koy carp and removed them to another location. By 8.00am a small and noisy pump was active and within half an hour the water had been extracted and the bottom of the pond, almost a foot of black mud, was revealed. The largest of the water plants were removed and laid to one side and the Mannekin Pis was carefully lifted from its concrete plinth and placed at the far end of the lawn. With the mud removed and the concrete bottom revealed, Mott left the kitchen and joined the perspiring work force.

With a pickaxe one of the policemen started to prise up the flagstones which surrounded the pool and bordering on to the lawn and as each stone was lifted it was placed on edge leaning against a tree. The concrete bottom of the pond was proving to be thicker than anyone had imagined and despite the efforts of several large and muscular policemen, sledge hammers and pickaxes were having little effect. The ever-resourceful Mott suggested a pneumatic drill and with the assistance of Sturge's Yellow Pages and the mention that "Scotland Yard" needed the equipment urgently, delivery was promised within the half hour.

An hour passed without the drill and the trail of mud across what had been Sturge's spotless kitchen floor had increased. Leaving Mott and Barney in the cold, Gregory moved silently from room to room in the still house wondering about the occupants and what may have gone on there. His mind was constantly going back to Sturge, his lined face, evil and at the same time desperate for understanding, and his last words to him: "There is more than you can ever know." Gregory was looking for something, answers, which he knew were there in "Southwold", but how could he expect to find the answers, he reasoned, when he was not entirely sure of the questions.

Still no drill but suddenly there was Mott, breathless and flushed with excitement. Gregory was in the dining room, seated at the mahogany table as he burst in, mud now having reached the Axminster carpet.

"What were they called, the sisters?"

Gregory looked up from what he was doing. "Susie born first of August nineteen fifty-one and Pammie born ninth of

June nineteen forty-nine", he said, parrot-fashion and as Sturge had told them.

"You better come and look at this, Guv", said Mott, "and prepare yourself for a shock."

He did not notice the dark blue morocco leather case on the table in front of Gregory and he did not see four large sterling silver Apostle teaspoons nestling in the expensively crafted green satin lining - beside the empty spaces where the two missing spoons had once been.

The cause of Mott's elation was two of the flagstones which had been prised from the border of the pool. Iannou, it developed, had been examining these and had noticed that there appeared to be writing scratched on the underside of two of the stones. Brushing away a half-century of earth and worm and woodlice tracery, they read on one: "Susan Sturge – 1/8/51" and on the second: "Pamela Sturge – 9/6/49."

The bodies were found that afternoon. Two small oil-cloth parcels, each barely a foot in length, each secured with lengths of what appeared to be electric flex. Neither was more than two feet beneath the stone slab which had marked their presence, known only to Martin Sturge since the death of his mother. Late in the evening, by the light of arc-lamps and with the breath of a dozen and a half policemen and forensic technicians and Sean Findlater misting in the bitter air, they found eleven further parcels beneath the base of the pond. As Mott was to remark later, Ernie Sturge had gone to pieces.

The examination of the remains took place the following morning in the mortuary of North Middlesex Hospital in Edmonton. The two small parcels contained the decomposed and virtually skeletal remains of two female babies both of which, Findlater was sure, had reached full term of gestation and had had a separate existence from the mother, albeit of short duration. Around the neck of each corpse was a remnant of a bandage strip and although decomposition and decay rendered any definitive opinion impossible, there seemed little doubt that each child had died as a result of strangulation by a ligature. The little bodies were unclothed but in each package was an Apostle teaspoon, apparently placed in the tiny hand following death. On the back of the bowl of one spoon the word "Pammie" had been scratched with a pointed implement, a nail or similar, and the other bore the word "Susie."

The eleven parcels discovered beneath the base of the pool were also formed from oil-cloth, each package having been carefully wrapped and secured with strong cord. Unwrapping and photographing took in excess of three hours but by late morning, the greater part of an adult male cadaver was arranged on one of the steel tables. Much of the softer tissue, the viscera and smaller organs had decomposed and broken down into a muddy glue, but the limbs, the torso and the skeletal structure had remained. Adipocere, a fatty wax-like substance caused by the body being moist or damp and with lack of air and an absence of bacteria, was present on the back, buttocks, chest and stomach and also on one side of the head which was barely little more than a fleshless and skinless skull. There was a massive cranial fracture to the left of the skull, which left Findlater in little doubt that the cause of death had been a severe blow to the head with some solid and heavy implement. The body had been cut into sections by what appeared to be have been a knife or knives and a saw and it was quite certain that no knowledge of anatomy had figured in the dissection.

On one thing, Findlater was adamant: "To dismember a man of that size, dealing with the massive blood loss, viscera, cutting and sawing through bone and sinew, making up eleven packets and then disposing of them in the partially excavated fish-pond, you're talking about a day at least."

"Could a woman on her own have done it?" asked Gregory.

"Superwoman, perhaps. But not one I've ever met."

***

Two days later Gregory walked to the London Hospital to see Jackie Daniel.

He found her in a private room off one of the main wards. Surrounded by more flowers and fruit than he had ever seen before, she looked tired and ill but, he had been assured by the consultant, she was well on the way to recovery.

"Hello, Guv" she smiled. "Good of you to come."

"Sorry not to have been before, Jack", he said. "I don't have to tell you what it's been like."

They talked for twenty minutes, mainly about Sturge and his sisters. Then, shifting uncomfortably in her bed, she said: "But why the rat, Guv?"

"There no accounting for insanity, Jack, you know that, and the further he progressed along the line followed by the 1888 chap, the more his mental state deteriorated and the more irrational he became. One or two of the books about the original Ripper refer to Mary Kelly – the last one he did – as looking like she had been attacked by an animal, a wolverine or something like that, and that her body looked as though some beast had got inside her and torn her to bits from within. That's all we can think of."

"And you think that's what he intended for me?"

"I don't think there's any doubt."

Coffee came with biscuits and then: "Archie McGibbon told me about the bits he found in the shed." She giggled, and then: "He says one of them's about fifty years old – is that right?"

"Yes" said Gregory, trying to resist his third custard cream. "The Old Man doesn't think it's connected. He reckons it's probably some sort of medical exhibit or specimen or something. So that's that."

She shifted again, wincing with pain and Gregory realised it was time to go. "Not connected?" she said, wide-eyed. "Of course it's connected. If not to Creepy then to the other sod, Marriott or Folmer whatever he was called." She closed her eyes and muttered, more to herself than to Gregory: "Bet your life it's connected."

That afternoon Mott and Iannou came back from Palmers Green, having spent two days watching the SOCOs and ensuring that the correct photographs were taken and that the house was given a microscopic examination.

"They reckon Ernie was killed in the bathroom, Guv, maybe even when he was in the bath. They've turned up a mass of blood traces on the floor. There's been new lino several times over the years by the look of things but the tests are positive on the skirting boards and also where the floor meets the wall."

Gregory nodded and leaned back in his chair, glasses in characteristic place on his forehead. The spoons found with the bodies of the two babies matched the four in the Morocco leather case and there was no doubt in his mind that Sturge had been a party to their deaths. Gregory knew that his mental condition rendered it academic to a large degree, but he needed to tie loose ends to bring closure.

The next day, with Mott, he saw Shoofie Coots. The old man was distraught about what had happened to Jackie Daniel and on hearing from his daughter that Gregory was coming the following day he had arranged for an enormous bouquet of flowers, which he handed to Gregory with strict instructions that it be given to Jackie with his best wishes.

Pleased that his assumptions had been correct, the old man was happy to go through his story again. The pool was half dug, he said, about two-and-a-half feet deep, probably. He came in one morning and Mrs. Sturge told him that she didn't want it any deeper and that the waterproof concrete was to be laid.

"She said the mixer and the sand and cement would be there the next day and sure enough they was. I was on me own and it took three days to knock it out and that was that.

When I'd done at the end of the week she paid me off and I never went back."

"And when did Ernie Sturge go missing?" asked Gregory.

"I never see him after that morning, the day she told me to stop digging. That would have been about the Tuesday, I expect, and it was the weekend that everyone knew that he'd gone."

Gregory, making notes, thought a moment and then: "I want you to think carefully, Shoofie: where was Martin Sturge about that time?"

Thinking, the old man looked at Gregory. "He was there, wasn't he? Where else would he be?"

"You're sure?"

"Quite sure – and I'll tell you how I know, shall I ?" A look or triumph on his face, he went on: "He was about thirteen, I suppose, thirteen or fourteen, and he'd been helping me dig out the fish pond. I always used to meet him in the mornings when I was getting to the house and he was leaving for school, and I remember – it was that day, the day she told me to knock it on the head or the day after – that I see him at the gate and he said he was going to miss the exercise."

"You're sure?"

"Sure."

"And that was right when Ernie Sturge went missing?"

"Right then."

That evening Gregory phoned Rosie. She understood that the activity and associated stress surrounding Sturge's arrest had kept him occupied, she said, and she apologised for "dumping" him (a word Gregory associated with the school playground and bike sheds) by way of a text message – again, a mode of communication he neither understood nor liked. It was going nowhere, she explained, and although she had enjoyed his company and friendship, she felt that enough was enough. Gregory had mixed feelings: like Rosie, he knew that their relationship was of the ships in the night variety – but he dreaded the loneliness of his rooms in Fulham.

In the days that followed they learned from the scientists that the DNA from the body of Ernie Sturge matched that found in the traces of blood found on the floor of the "Southwold" bathroom. If Shoofie Coots was to be believed, Martin Sturge was certainly around at the precise time his father disappeared and, Findlater's opinions considered, there seemed to be no doubt that at best he had assisted his mother in disposing of the body and in the worst, and most likely scenario, he had been a party to his murder.

The DNA samples taken from the tiny corpses of the two babies matched neither that taken from Martin Sturge at the time of his arrest nor that of Ernie Sturge, proving that neither of the Sturge men was the father. This eventuality completely threw Gregory who had been convinced that an incestuous relationship had existed between Martin Sturge and his mother and that this liaison had resulted in the birth of Pamela and Susan.

***

Smoked salmon and beigels in the Beigel Bakery in Hounsditch. Mott had lemon tea, sour with no sugar and Gregory drank a black coffee.

Mott stirred his tea, squeezing the slice of lemon against the glass with his spoon. "Well, if Ernie Sturge wasn't the father of the damn sisters and Martin wasn't either, God knows where we stand."

"Someone was," said Gregory. "That's a certainty." He finished his beigel and wiped his mouth with the green paper serviette. "When I saw Jackie in hospital she said something: she said she reckoned there was no doubt that the fifty year old part of McGibbon's lunch was connected. I told her that Strathearn said it was probably some sort of medical exhibit or something and she said that was nonsense. It was connected, she said, she was sure. If not to Creepy then to Marriott or Folmer whatever he was called."

They were silent as the waiter brought plates of salt beef and potato *latkes* to the next table, and then: "Get a DNA sample from that woman in Devon, Dave - Marriott's sister. Get the chap who got the fingerprints from that old peoples' home in Ashburton to do it." It would be better if the Devon and Cornwall people liaised with the vicar in Nether Sampford. Mott would find all the details in the file, he said. He wanted it done nicely but as quickly as possible.

With the blue and white crime scene tapes gone and no young policeman at the gate it looked like any other house, with no hint of the horrors the large rooms had witnessed in the past. Sturge would have been appalled at the state of the front garden, Gregory mused, but somehow the uncut lawns, the dead leaves and the general neglect over recent weeks seemed to suit the place. Inside the front door he collected the mass of circulars and other mail strewn across the hall floor and placed it in a pile on the dusty hall table. The house was cold and seemed to retain an atmosphere of melancholy and gloom of the sort he associated with crypts beneath the ancient churches he had trudged around as a boy on holiday in France. There was a great silence, barely broken by the hum of Palmers Green business, and the odd shaft of thin wintry sunshine held the dust, visible and floating like tiny organisms suspended in the clearest of water. Walking from room to room he switched on all the lights, upstairs as well as down, and finding a small radio in the kitchen and after some fiddling with buttons and dials, he was joined by The Temperance Seven who were Home in Pasadena.

He did not know what he was looking for but he knew that somewhere in "Southwold" there was something, although God only knew what, which would cut a path through the secrecy and tangle of wickedness which had dogged him for months. He opened all the cupboards and display cases and taking out each ornament and each piece of china or glass he examined it carefully; he leafed through a hundred books and he looked behind pictures and pulled furniture away from the walls. In the kitchen he took crockery from the shelves and on the landing at the head of the stairs he removed the piles of sheets and pillow cases from the airing cupboard. Two hours and he had found nothing; The Temperance Seven had been replaced by a short story and he wished he had eaten breakfast in the Leman Street canteen.

Standing at the window in one of the small, back bedrooms he watched a team of squabbling sparrows as they fought and argued over the rights to the freshly excavated earth surrounding what had been the fish pond. He sat on the single bed and then, lying full length with his head on the pillow, he gazed the ceiling. Had this been Martin Sturge's boyhood bedroom, he wondered? But where were the old books? The old Beano and Dandy annuals and the worn copy of Treasure Island with many of its thumbed leaves free of the raggedy binding? Where had he played, the adololescent Martin Sturge? Where were the old school books, the odd photo? The stuff of boyhood, often the lifeblood of the perennial bachelor, was missing, and Gregory found this strange.

His mind drifted off, thinking and wondering about the world the boy would have known in the years shortly after the war. Years of rationing, austerity and, what were those things called? Anderson Shelters….

Shoofie Coots was having his lunch. In his wheel chair in the conservatory he watched the television, cheese and pickle sandwich and a glass of Guinness.

Anderson shelter? Well, they'd had one, he knew, because like so many they never used it and he had stored plants and all manner of stuff in it. It was at the back of the garden, he said, right in front of the garage.

"Not now, it's not" said Gregory. He had hoped for the offer of a sandwich but Shoofie's daughter had been on her way out to the hairdressers when he got there and the old man was dabbing up crumbs with a damp finger.

"No, I don't expect it is", said the old man. "The council was supposed to come and take them away but they never did and a few years after the war most people filled the damn things in, covered them over with dirt and grew marrers on 'em, something like that."

It was there when he left, he said, he was sure of that and if Gregory couldn't find it now, that's what had happened.

In the event, it was not hard to find and the digging took barely two hours. As Shoofie had said, there was a slight bulge in the ground in front of the garage and with the lawn turf removed they rapidly came on the corrugated, curving roof of the shelter. For maximum protection against air-raids, an area of ground had been excavated and once constructed the earth had been piled back on the sides and roof of the shelter. A few crumbling brick steps lead down to the entrance, a large hole in the steel front, which had been had boarded over. The floor was inches deep in water, thick cobwebs and thicker dust were everywhere and there was strong smell of decay and musty air.

Whatever it was that Gregory had hoped to find was not there. By torch-light, they saw piles of newspapers and magazines, old tools and a broken bicycle; there were several rotting blankets on a structure that seemed to have been a bunk bed and there were numerous tins of unidentifiable food, the labels long since rotted and crumbled away.

Sorting through the piles of sodden newsprint Mott said: "There's papers here dated as late as 1959, Guv, so they must have shut it up after that."

At the far end of the shelter, which in fact was barely eight feet away, Gregory grunted. His shoes were full of muddy water, the battery in his torch was failing and he had a trail of cobweb hanging from his hair. "They probably used it as some sort of garden shed", he muttered. "That Shoofie character said something about marrows."

The lack of headroom caused him to stoop and his back ached. He was disappointed with the negative outcome and felt guilty that he had been responsible for a wasted day and several very dirty and irritable policemen. He turned to face Mott and in doing so his mind registered something incongruous, something that did not fit. He focused his weakening torch beam, scanning the wall and ceiling and straining his eyes through the dust and thin, yellow ray of light. At first nothing, rusty metal and the grime-encrusted junk of a past age and then, jammed between the partially collapsed planks of a home-made shelving unit, he saw the inconsistency. At first he thought it was plastic or waterproof sheeting of some sort, but later it was identified as a stain and moisture-proof cloth of the sort used to cover kitchen tables. Tied with string, the package was about a foot long by six inches wide and weighed, Gregory supposed, about two pounds.

They opened the parcel in Sturge's kitchen, Mott cutting through the string with scissors and carefully folding back the waterproof packaging. First, they saw a buff envelope, unsealed and with the single word "Folmer" printed in heavy blue pencil on the front. Inside, a sheaf of newspaper cuttings, yellow with age and all relating to Marriott's trial and subsequent hanging. Then, a number of red-covered note books and the remains of two rotted and frayed elastic bands which had secured them.

The lights burned late on the top floor at Leman Street that night. In Gregory's office the notebooks were laid out on a desk and photographed from various angles. An initial examination showed that they consisted of a form of diary, evidently complied by Martin Sturge and starting in 1946., when he was thirteen years old and finishing on the day of Folmer's execution in 1958. Over the years, the writing changed, as did the style of prose; there were drawings and there were doodles when the writer seemed to have been lost for something to say and had allowed his pen to wander on the page, but overall the eleven notebooks contained a detailed description of what had taken place in "Southwold" during that twelve year period. Reading them for the second time, and later reading the typed transcripts, both Gregory and Mott came to understand the onset of the mental illness of the writer and how, over the years, this condition worsened.

In a rounded, schoolboy hand, the first book described how Sturge came home from school one afternoon to find his mother naked in the bathroom and in the process of dismembering his father. She had killed him, she said, because of his inability to satisfy her sexual needs.

"She said that if the police knew what had happened, she would be hanged and I would be put in a home. She told me I would never see her again and that I would not go to school but be in a Doctor Barnardo's or something like that."

He described how she made tea and they talked in the kitchen. She said that during the course of an argument she had hit him and he had fallen and smashed his head against the bath: *"She said that was sorry but that she had hated him for years and that if we kept our heads everything would be OK and it was probably for the best."*

He was frightened to leave her, terrified of being alone or in some home and later they both undressed and, naked, resumed their terrible task in the bathroom. It took all night and the next day, but in time the job was done and the grisly parcels were spread in Shoofie's partially constructed fish pond and covered with soil.

"I was tired and frightened and that night Mummy made me stay with her in her bed. What we did in bed was wrong, I know it, but she said we were alone in the world and that all women other than a boy's mother were wicked and dirty. We had a secret and no one must know, so we must stay at Southwold and guard it."

They took turns in reading aloud from the books, Gregory reading while Mott made notes and vice versa. Halfway through the second book, Gregory reading, his voice faltered.

"12 December 1947. Mummy's friend came to tea. He was funny and always joking. I must call him Uncle Johnnie, she says, and he will look after both of us. He said he was a soldier in the war and had killed Germans. Later, in bed, Mummy told me that he will never take my place but he will come and see her sometimes. She says no one must know and it is another secret."

"Oh, Christ", said Mott. "Marriott! She knew Marriott!"

Gregory felt a chill in his spine and the hair on his neck prickled. Reading, he said: "He says Marriott stayed over Christmas but slept in a spare room but he knew that Sturge was sleeping with his mother…."

"It is Marriott, isn't it?" asked Mott.

Gregory went on: *"Uncle Johnnie comes from Devon and he says we'll all go there in the summer and see his mum and dad. He is 24 now and younger than Mummy but she says it doesn't matter…."*

"It must be him."

"How the hell did she meet him, I wonder?" said Mott.

Gregory shook his head. "It can't have been long after his court martial in Berlin. His sister said no-one knew what he did between then and when he got nicked in the West End and that the father was sending cash to the solicitors for him."

They stopped reading at 4.00am and with the notebooks locked in Gregory's safe he found an empty cell and slept two hours under an itchy blanket which smelt faintly of vomit. Back in the station at 8.00am Mott found him in his office, surrounded by the notebooks, the remains of bacon sandwiches and cold tea on his desk.

"Well, it was Johnnie Marriott", he said, "and by the end of 1948 he knew all about Ernie being in the fish pond."

"She must have told him," said Mott.

"She did. And in the December she also told him she was pregnant –"

"Pammie, that'd be."

" – and, listen to this: *"Johnnie says that if anyone knows about what me and mummy do we'll both go to prison. He says that when the baby comes we must help it to die and no one will ever know."* They told the boy he was the father, Dave."

"But the DNA says he wasn't."

"And they did the same a couple of years later when she was pregnant with Susie."

There was silence, both men seemingly coming to terms with what they were learning. "We know who the father is now, though, and the DNA from Marriott's sister will leave no doubt."

Mott nodded agreement, and then: "But how the hell did a woman like that out in Palmers bloody Green meet a bastard like Johnnie Marriott?"

Gregory got up from his desk and put his dirty plate and cup on a side table. "I don't think we're ever going to know the answer to that, Dave." He sat down again, and sorting through the notebooks, he said: "Anyway. Listen to this."

""*9 June 1949. Baby Pammie was born in the night. Uncle Johnnie was there and he made me pass her away and said it was for the best."* Then he says he took one of the spoons and put it in her hand and Marriott dug the hole and they buried her."

He passed the book to Mott who read the passage. "And the other baby?"

"The same. More or less exactly."

Mott thought a moment and then: "The second one, Susie, was in August 1951 and Creepy was how old – eighteen by then?"

Gregory rubbed the stubble on his chin. "He goes on a bit about National Service coming and how he was medically unfit and then by 1954 he started as a medical student at the London."

"Was Marriott still around?"

From the notebooks it seemed that Marriott had discontinued his association with Sturge's mother, probably

318

in 1953. The narrative gave no reasons, saying only that "Uncle Johnnie" did not come to "Southwold " any more and that his mother never mentioned him. At about this time there were long, rambling passages relative to his efforts to be accepted at the London Hospital and, later, how he found difficulties fitting in with other students and the high cost of the tuition. From time to time he made references to "Pammie and Susie" but never his father; he spoke of his mother in adoring terms and even the most naïve and well-disposed reader would have suspected that their relationship was far from normal.

"How did he meet Marriott again?" asked Mott. "Does he say?"

Gregory sorted through the books until he found the one he wanted. *"I was arrested yesterday"*, he read, *"and I was in Court this AM. They said I exposed myself to a dirty old woman in the West End but the police told lies. I watched her and that was all, but I pleaded guilty at court, just to get it out of the way."* He looked at Mott, and turning a page went on: *"Uncle Johnnie was in the police station, too. It was a surprise to see him after three or four years but I was not surprised to know he had murdered a woman. Not the first, from what he had told me....."*

Gregory paused, and looked up: "He says it was a coincidence, them both being charged on the same day at the same nick, and to be honest, I think if there was any more to it he would have said so."

The riveting factor, though, was that Sturge obviously knew about Marriott's Berlin activities. Both Gregory and Mott were agreed that for Marriott to disclose this to the boy Sturge, their relationship must have been of an extremely special and unusual nature and one that was cemented by the knowledge of murder that each had about the other.

Following the exchange of the fingerprint forms, Sturge wrote, they had talked at Bow Street court the following morning. *"Johnnie knew it was all up this time and that he was for the big prize but he didn't seem to mind one bit. Mummy had always said that he was mad and I think now that she was right. How he laughed when I said that he could come back to life - and how I laughed when he told me about the Folmer name he had given being an anagram."*

As well as the news cuttings about the trials and the hanging, Sturge had written extensively in the notebooks of his feelings at that time. His thoughts seemed to range from one extreme to another. On the one hand, he expressed ecstatic joy that Marriott would shortly be gone from their lives and pages later he seemed on the verge of mental trauma due to the forthcoming loss of "his friend." He had scrawled illegible notes in pencil across some of the press cuttings and in his book there were childish drawings of gibbets with match-stick men, but the narrative stopped on the day of the execution, as if closure had been brought to a part of his life.

23.

The German police officer, Horst Lippmann, was most helpful and Gregory was grateful that his command of English was so good, something he had come to expect from many foreign policemen but not, sadly, from even the most senior in England. He was pleased and honoured to receive the kind telephone call from so senior and important a police officer at the famous New Scotland Yard. During an hour-long telephone conversation, he listened with keen interest to the history of the crimes from Marriott and Folmer through to the gruesome discoveries at "Southwold" and Gregory was sure he was making notes. He asked intelligent and pointed questions about how Marriott and Sturge had swapped fingerprints, commenting: "Yes, I can see how that could happen – but only if the system is not complied with and the name is written on the form and the signing is allowed to happen after all is finished."

He said he was very pleased to have been able to assist, if only in a small way, and he was happy to know that the information he had been able to find in the Berlin police archives had been helpful. Gregory, slowly coming to the point of the telephone call and marginally ashamed at his duplicity, offered to send a copy of his complete report, an offer which was gratefully and enthusiastically accepted. A translation would be prepared, said Lippmann, and it would be made available to trainee officers in the criminal investigation branch as a classic and fascinating example of the investigation of a complicated and extraordinary series of murders. There was a small point, said Gregory, which would enable him to finish the report: could Lippmann ascertain if Helga Eva Schwimmer's son, referred to in the Military Police files regarding the case, was still alive? "Oh, and to dot all the i's and cross the t's as we say in England, if he is, where he is now."

A tap on his office door and Gregory peered over his glasses at Mott.

"Happy birthday Guv", he said, grinning, and handed a large envelope to Gregory.

"How did you know it was my birthday?" And then, answering his own question: "There's nothing you don't bloody know, is there."

Suddenly, framed in the doorway were Iannou and McGibbon and others of the team behind them. "Christ! What's this? Some sort of deputation?"

"Open the card, then", said Mott moving further into the office, the others crowding behind him.

The picture was hand done by some cartoonist, of which the force boasted several. It showed the dome of the Old Bailey, complete with the statute of Justice and, in unmistakeable caricature, Gregory with tie, hair and glasses blown and battered by the elements, endeavouring to place a weight in one of the scale pans. Signed by every member of the team, the words on the inside were:

One cannot buy nor hope to twist
Thank God, the British journalist.
But seeing what the man will do
Unbribed, there's no occasion to!

"There's a present to go with it", said Mott. "It's a bit on the large side and we couldn't bring it upstairs."

Still holding his card, Gregory went with Mott and with the rest of the team following they made their way down the stairs and into the charge room. At first Gregory saw Tony Carter standing by the desk, a broad grin on his face, but as he moved aside he saw Wonkeye Jerry and the blonde "actress" who had set him up in Brighton. He turned to Mott, a searching look on his face but before he could speak Mott said: "This is Jeremiah Peach, Guv: I think you know him."

He winked at Gregory and looking towards the woman, he went on: "And this is Anna-Marie Maureen Slater – who I think you've met."

Gregory continued to stare at Mott, eyebrows raised and a half smile on his face. He was about to speak but Mott, adopting the tone of an archetypal policeman giving evidence, went on: "Enquiries and observations have revealed that these two persons live together as man and wife, sir. At oh-six hundred hours today in company with Detective Chief Inspector Carter and other officers I saw them both at their address – 108, Galbraith Terrace, Camden Town, London North West where, on being confronted with such evidence as I have, they both admitted the following offences: wasting police time, obtaining a payment of eleven thousand pounds from the Sunday People by deception and, last but by no means least, conspiring to defraud."

Later, in Gregory's office with the scotch bottle open and his birthday card in pride of place on his desk, he said: "How did you get on to them, Dave?"

"I got wind of it at that press conference – the last one. A contact put me right before the meeting, said that Wonk-eye was living with the tart and they set you up to get a few quid out of one of the Sundays. Anyway, the rest was easy: I just cracked all matey with Wonk-eye, said I'd give him a bit of inside stuff on Sturge if I got it and he agreed to meet me after the conference. I gave him a load of crap and he gave me his home 'phone number and when we knew where he lived we just sat on it."

Gregory remembered Northumberland Avenue. He felt guilty and poured more whisky.

The middle of the following week he received a call from the ever-efficient Lippmann. He had traced Helga Schwimmer's son, he said. "His correct name is Schwimmer forename Oscar and he was born 27 November 1922. He now lives in a hospital for old persons in Frankfurt and there they tell me that he is very ill and near to dying."

Gregory wrote the address on his pad. "Is there a family?"

"No, I think not. They tell me that he does not have callers for many years and that they think there is no one close to him."

***

That night, at home in Fulham with pizza and cheap red wine, Gregory thought long and hard. He knew that by the time he got clearance from the German authorities Oscar Schwimmer would almost certainly be dead. He also knew that in the highly unlikely event of Sturge appearing in any court what he intended would be at most peripheral and, more likely, irrelevant to any proceedings against Sturge. He was sure that an application to Strathearn would at first be met with the delay he knew could be fatal. He was sure that The Old Man would never authorise something which may bounce back and bite him at a later stage, but he was equally certain that in the event of all going to plan and without adverse comment or criticism, Strathearn would expect his large share of the recognition.

From the airport he took a taxi to the suburb of Bergen Enkheim to the east of Frankfurt. It was snowing when the driver dropped him outside Clinic Hoffmann.

"Herr Oscar has little time", the elderly nun told him. "Maybe go tonight, maybe tomorrow – but soon." No one had visited, she said, and it was assumed that he had no family. She did not ask Gregory his relationship to Schwimmer but, seemingly pleased that someone – even a foreigner – cared about the imminent death of her patient, she showed him to a small room on the first floor.

Then old man was either deeply asleep or in a coma. With one eye partially open and his toothless mouth agape, his shallow, laboured breathing heralded death. He wore a blue, short-sleeved hospital gown and his arms, both evidencing faded tattoos, rested on either side of the thin and wasted body. Gregory saw that he held a rosary in his right hand, the beads wound round the thin, blue-veined wrist. A catheter leaked cloudy urine into a glass container beneath the bed.

Embarrassed and feeling faintly guilty, Gregory sat beside the dying man. Ten minutes passed and then, hoping that a passing nun or nurse would think he was embracing the old man, Gregory leant over him. From his inside jacket pocket he took a rubber-corked glass tube containing a cotton swab on a wooden spill and deftly wiping it around the interior of the old man's sagging cheek, he obtained the DNA sample he needed.

Waiting for his plane and warm in the airport restaurant, he ordered coffee and a steak sandwich. Constantly feeling the test-tube in the breast pocket of his jacket and aware of the two sets of customs awaiting him, he felt the fluttering of large-winged butterflies as they irritated his diaphragm but he knew that scotch was not a good idea. After his meal, in one of the lavatory cubicles he removed the wooden spill from the tube. He broke off the cotton swab and having wrapped it loosely in his handkerchief and thrown the tube and what remained of the spill into the waste bin, he moved towards the departure lounge and his flight.

Within minutes of landing at Heathrow he made a telephone call.

***

Jackie Daniel came into Leman Street the next day. In a wheel chair pushed by Barney Iannou she made her way to Gregory's office and said that she should be back to work, albeit restricted to "light duties", by the end of January. Laughing, she said she hoped that this would not just mean making tea for Gregory.

"No, I'm afraid not, Jack", he said. "I'm all done here and back to the Yard after Christmas." His report had been concluded, he said, and that was that: "No more East End eels and beigels, I'm afraid – back to the fourth floor and whatever misery 2004's got lined up for me."

She nodded. "We will miss you."

"Well, if you feel the need to see me, I'm only over in Victoria Street." For a moment, and not for the first time, he wished he was twenty years younger but then, and momentarily ashamed, he winked at Iannou and said: "Anyway, I thought you were packing it all in and going off to live in Milton Keynes and have a tribe of kids."

Leaning over his desk she kissed his cheek. "No, not yet, Guv." She smiled at him: "I haven't found the right man yet."

The morning of the 23 December the much-awaited forensic report arrived on Gregory's desk. Very much as expected, the DNA which had been taken from Marriott's sister, Suzanne, showed conclusively that Johnnie Marriott was the father of the dead infants which had been found in the garden at "Southwold." To his annoyance, there was no reference of the sample from Oscar Schwimmer and the request which Gregory had made. Later, in the Magpie and Stump, opposite the Old Bailey, all became clear.

The ancient pub was crowded with the various strands of society with business in the Central Criminal Court, wigless barristers, solicitors, policemen and those awaiting the dispensation justice, all taking lunchtime refreshment in the same oak-lined bar. Gregory bought two pints of bass, ordered plates of ham and turkey salad and moved to a table in the corner of the room where having exchanged seasonal greetings with his guest, he was handed a sealed brown envelope.

***

That evening he was expected to be present for festive drinks in Strathearn's office. The idea of spending time with The Old Man and a group of other Yard brass in various stages of intoxication appalled him only marginally less than being obliged to make polite conversation with Rosie who would certainly be there. Through the Yard grapevine, he knew that their relationship had become common knowledge and although he was not concerned by what people may have thought, he felt that to be seen at a Scotland Yard social gathering with her, "dumped" or otherwise, may have been unwise. In the event, though, his worries were needless.

Mott had gone on leave. It seemed that "Big Shirl" had lost an aunt and gained a legacy and although she had fostered hopes of a conservatory, Mott had felt that a Christmas and New Year cruise was a far better idea. They had argued for weeks but the idea of new clothes and escape from Christmas cooking finally won her over and that morning they had left for Miami and several islands in the Caribbean.

The rain threatened sleet and the windows of his office were misted over. The several thick files relative to the enquiry were on a side table and his desk was clear.

The phone rang at 4.30pm.

When he got to the Coopersale Unit on the outskirts of Epping, Gregory found that they had not moved Sturge from where he had been found and that he was still hanging from the cistern pipe in one of the lavatories, a pool of urine on the floor beneath him. He had used strips of towelling, tied into a length and knotted about his neck. By securing the other end to the pipe and then taking the weight from his legs he had strangled himself. The coroner had been notified, a somewhat disinterested and indifferent male nurse told him, and there would be an internal enquiry.

As he looked at the thin, twisted body and the tongue, thrust between the blue, blood-flecked lips, he felt a twinge of pity for the man he had pursued and who without any doubt had done the unspeakable with neither feeling nor remorse. Martin Sturge had not been born wicked, he thought: he had been corrupted and perverted by those older and more used to the ways of the world, and, he hoped, God would find a place for him.

Christmas Eve and Gregory ate eggs and bacon in the Yard canteen. The news of Sturge's suicide had been leaked and most of the papers gave the story a deal of coverage. Borrowing a paper from a uniform PC at an adjacent table he read through the report and was embarrassed to see himself described as the Yard's "foremost crime buster" and, to his mind a sickening soubriquet, "Gregory of the Yard." At the bottom of the page, and in such a position that only the knowledgeable would understand the relevance to the Sturge matter, he read that freelance journalist Jeremiah Peach had been sentenced to nine months imprisonment for wasting police time and fraud and that Ann-Marie Maureen Slater, unemployed, had been fined two thousand pounds for similar offences.

Strathearn arrived on the stroke of nine.

The Old Man, bright of eye and with a hint of expensive toilet water about him, showed no hint of the previous evening's excesses. He listened as Gregory described Sturge's suicide and then: "I hear you went to Germany."

Gregory was not surprised. He had known that it was unlikely that he could pass through British customs and passport controls without Strathearn coming to hear of it and he was fairly confident that Mott, who had known what was taking place, would have had a hard job keeping it to himself.

"Yes", he said. "It was off the record and it's not in the report", nodding towards the neatly bound files he had placed on The Old Man's side table ready for his attention. "I traced the son of the woman Marriott chopped up in Berlin after the war. He was dying in a clinic and Frankfurt and I managed to get a DNA swab off him." He hesitated, not wanting to embarrass Strathearn, but then: "I called in a favour from a friend in the lab and got them to do a match for me under the table."

Strathearn nodded. "And?"

"It matched that DNA on that womb, sir; the fifty year old one we found in the allotment shed." And then, unable to stop himself: "The one you said was probably some sort of medical exhibit."

There was a silence and he wondered if he had gone too far. Strathearn stood as he had seen him a hundred times, his back to the office and gazing out of his high window over London. Then, turning, and with half a smile: "Aye, well." He sniffed, a slight cough and: "We all make mistakes sometimes, Michael."

His report, Gregory explained, described the womb as being "unidentified" and referred to "possibilities" and "likelihoods." There was no mention of Germany or his visit to Oscar Schwimmer but he had left an anonymous note, typed on plain paper for Strathearn's personal attention. "We can only imagine that Marriott got it back to England somehow and probably gave it to Martin Sturge as some sort of souvenir or curiosity."

And so there was closure. Outside of the Yard he watched the buses, packed with shoppers and their excited kids, as they queued to pass the Abbey on their way to Oxford Street and credit card heaven. It was cold, and thin drizzle seemed to hang in the air before getting to the ground, the sort of weather that breeds the flu', his mother would say. He looked at his watch: not yet 10.00am but the Sally Ann trombones and trumpets were blasting goodwill and Royal David's City from outside St. James's Park tube station.

Christmas Eve and he had no plans. He knew that his wife was going to stay with her parents and that Emma was off somewhere in Europe with a tribe of giggling girls, hell-bent on breaking hearts and drinking too much cheap alcohol. Bugger Mott, he thought, going away at Christmas. He wiped the rain off his glasses and found his car.

Within half an hour he was in Fulham and an hour after that he was on the M3, the ancient Mondeo rattling protest but meeting the challenge. He had changed into a casual shirt and khakis and with a change of clothes in a bag, he headed west.

He arrived in Nether Sampford just after six. There had been no rush; by Wincanton and with the rain behind him he had stopped for sandwiches and a pint of bitter and in Exeter he had taken an hour to wander round the shops, something he had not done for years.

When he had phoned Savage and asked him to book a room for him at the Nether Samford pub, the vicar had insisted that Gregory spend the Christmas with him at the vicarage. Without him he would be alone and, in an attempt at humour: "Even a copper's company's better than none at all!"

They had dinner in the vicarage. Savage, a widower, employed a cook- housekeeper who he rightly described as something of a wizard in the kitchen. Large gin and tonics were followed by smoked salmon – "from the Exe – none of that Scottish farmed rubbish" and the rib of beef was the best that Gregory could remember. Savage fussed with the wine – Pomerol with the beef and a Medoc with the Stilton – and suddenly they were alone with only port and Armagnac for company.

Suzanne was away for the holidays, said Savage, which would give him time to think about what to tell her. "It's a hard thing, Michael, to have to tell an old lady her brother was an even bigger monster than she had reckoned." He lit a small cigar and gazed at the fireplace through unseeing eyes. "He was, wasn't he? A monster?"

Gregory sipped his brandy and nodded. "I'm afraid he was."

Savage nodded. "You think he did two in Berlin? The one he was tried for – and acquitted, of course – and an earlier one?"

"It's hard to say, Charlie. Certainly a street woman had her throat cut in 1946 in Berlin on the same day as the first of the

330

1888 Ripper crimes, and Marriott was in Berlin at the time. It's not a lot but –"

"It's enough, in view of later events." Savage was silent for a few minutes, thinking, and then: "Do you think he corrupted Sturge, Mike?"

"Who corrupted who, Charlie? Neither of them were born wicked I'm quite sure of that, no more than Sturge's mother was, and you could say that she was the evil influence on Martin. Let's not lose sight of the fact that he was involved in chopping up his dad long before Johnnie Marriott came on the scene."

Both men sat, almost dozing, glasses in hand and staring into the dying log fire. Ten minutes passed before Savage got to his feet. "Come on then, Michael Gregory."

Startled, Gregory looked up from his armchair. "Are we going out?"

"Midnight Mass, Michael. I've got to do what they pay me for."

They walked through the still night, the cold air nipping at their ears and making eyes water. The three pubs, the Sampford Crest, the Tiverton and the Ring of Bells were discharging their Christmas Eve patrons and Gregory realised that a large percentage of these were making their way towards the church. The night was moonless but a million stars a billion miles distant were visible and as they walked Gregory wondered if the pathetic "Toothpick" with her spiky hair, her innocent grin and her heart-rending stutter knew they were there. He wondered about the other three sad and pitiful victims of Sturge's lust-fuelled evil and he wondered what had turned his mother into the husband and infant slaying monster she became.

Few senior policeman have much in the way of religious conviction. They become both cynics and pragmatists but, for the greater part, they come to understand and accept human failings. During the course of the short service, Gregory watched the good people of Nether Samford. He joined in with their carol singing and he muttered their prayers, but his mind wandered to the photograph of the fair-haired, grinning lad on Suzanne Marriott's piano. "That was Johnnie", she had said, "before he went mad." That boy had come to this church, he thought; he had been christened here and had things been different he would probably have been married here as well. He thought of the awful, unspeakable crimes of both men and he wondered what had made them the way they were. He thought of the scaffold-beam in a dark corner of Pentonville and he wondered if there truly was someone or something that may or may not forgive. Or did it all go black and become like it had been before birth?

Outside, he waited while Charlie Savage embraced and shook hands with his parishioners. It had got colder, causing him to stamp his feet and rub his hands together. He moved towards the lee of the church porch, hoping for shelter from the wind, and as he did so he caught sight of the great white marble slab which was the Marriott family memorial. There were no flowers, just white stone, pale in the starlight and the dim glow from the church windows.

He knew there were only ashes left and that Johnnie Marriott had gone for ever, but as he stared at the grave he felt the hair at the back of his neck start to prickle and he shuddered.

About the Author

John Rigbey is an ex-detective officer of the Metropolitan Police. Leaving the force in 1972, he formed what is now one of the leading private investigation company in the south-west of England. He has almost half a century of experience of the criminal justice system and is regarded as being an authority on London's underworld of the sixties and seventies.

He has been a regular contributor to an assortment of legal and similar publications over many years.

He lives in Devon, England.

Printed in the United Kingdom
by Lightning Source UK Ltd.
124806UK00001B/1/A